SCANDALOUS REUNION

"Do you remember our first kiss, Annie?"

"Giles, this is a most inappropriate conversation."

He grasped her arms and turned her to face him, pulling her into the shelter of the trees that ringed the garden. "You haven't forgotten any of it, have you?"

"No," she whispered, caught—and held—by his gaze. Had anyone before ever looked at her so, with such tenderness, such yearning?

"Nor have I. I think it began something like this." Cupping her face, he brushed his thumbs along her cheekbones, and her eyes fluttered shut. "Then I put my arm around you, like so." He drew her, unprotesting, toward him. "You put your arms around my neck."

Standing on tiptoe, she followed his direction. He stroked her cheek with the backs of his fingers, his eyes never leaving hers. For one endless, eternal moment they gazed at each other and then, at last, at long last, he lowered his head and his mouth touched hers . . .

A Memorable Collection of Regency Romances

BY ANTHEA MALCOLM AND VALERIE KING

THE COUNTERFEIT HEART   (3425, $3.95/$4.95)
by Anthea Malcolm
Nicola Crawford was hardly surprised when her cousin's betrothed disappeared on some mysterious quest. Anyone engaged to such an unromantic, but handsome man was bound to run off sooner or later. Nicola could never entrust her heart to such a conventional, but so deucedly handsome man. . . .

THE COURTING OF PHILIPPA   (2714, $3.95/$4.95)
by Anthea Malcolm
Miss Philippa was a very successful author of romantic novels. Thus she was chagrined to be snubbed by the handsome writer Henry Ashton whose own books she admired. And when she learned he considered love stories completely beneath his notice, she vowed to teach him a thing or two about the subject of love. . . .

THE WIDOW'S GAMBIT   (2357, $3.50/$4.50)
by Anthea Malcolm
The eldest of the orphaned Neville sisters needed a chaperone for a London season. So the ever-resourceful Livia added several years to her age, invented a deceased husband, and became the respectable Widow Royce. She was certain she'd never regret abandoning her girlhood until she met dashing Nicholas Warwick. . . .

A DARING WAGER   (2558, $3.95/$4.95)
by Valerie King
Ellie Dearborne's penchant for gaming had finally led her to ruin. It seemed like such a lark, wagering her devious cousin George that she would obtain the snuffboxes of three of society's most dashing peers in one month's time. She could easily succeed, too, were it not for that exasperating Lord Ravenworth. . . .

THE WILLFUL WIDOW   (3323, $3.95/$4.95)
by Valerie King
The lovely young widow, Mrs. Henrietta Harte, was not all inclined to pursue the sort of romantic folly the persistent King Brandish had in mind. She had to concentrate on marrying off her penniless sisters and managing her spendthrift mama. Surely Mr. Brandish could fit in with her plans somehow . . .

Available wherever paperbacks are sold, or order direct from the Publisher. Send cover price plus 50¢ per copy for mailing and handling to Zebra Books, Dept. 3808, 475 Park Avenue South, New York, N.Y. 10016. Residents of New York and Tennessee must include sales tax. DO NOT SEND CASH. For a free Zebra/ Pinnacle catalog please write to the above address.

A Summer Folly
Mary Kingsley

ZEBRA BOOKS
KENSINGTON PUBLISHING CORP.

To Carin Cohen Ritter, who has been such a great help to me and has helped make publishing a positive experience;
And to Meredith Bernstein and Elizabeth Cavanaugh. Your advice, support and encouragement have kept me going, and make me feel I have someone on my side.
I'm honored to call you friends.

ZEBRA BOOKS

are published by

Kensington Publishing Corp.
475 Park Avenue South
New York, NY 10016

First printing: July, 1992

Printed in the United States of America

Chapter 1

The mists lifted, and suddenly, there it was. Land. At this distance, England was only a cloud on the horizon, but land, all the same. Standing in the bulwark of the ship, Anne Templeton felt a lump come to her throat. Home, after all these years. Her family. Dancing and assemblies and the best of society. Sophisticated clothes in colors she could wear, now that she was a widow past the first blush of youth. Home. Facing down the scandal she'd left behind years ago. Facing Giles again.

"Mama!" A small boy careened across the deck, nearly knocking down a sailor. "Diah says we can see England!"

"So we can, pet." Anne lifted her son, whirled him around, and then settled him on her hip. Jamie, one of the few good things that had happened to her these past years. He favored her; his reddish gold curls gleamed in the sun, and his skin had acquired the same golden hue that life in Jamaica had given her. He looked like a little heathen, she thought affectionately. God only knew what the proper people of English society, particularly his father's family, would make of him. Or her.

"It's only a cloud," Jamie said, and wriggled in her arms.

"You're too heavy for that, lovey," Anne said, and

5

set him down. "We'll be there soon enough. You'll see."

"Will I like England?" he asked, for the thousandth time.

"Mm, I think so. The grass is very green and you'll have your own pony. And we're going to live in a castle with the duke."

"With a moat and a drawbridge?"

"Yes, but no knights in armor, I'm afraid."

"I'm going to be a knight when I grow up. Diah!" He dashed back across the deck, and the tall man walking barefoot toward them with a peculiar grace, lifted him, his head, completely bald, glistening mahogany in the sun. "Diah, does that look like land?"

Obadiah shaded his eyes with his hand. "I see signs in the clouds," he intoned, in a sepulchral voice that sent shivers down Anne's spine. "I see hauntings, a dragon, and a fair knight."

"Really?" Jamie said. "Are there ghosts in the castle, Mama?"

"No, Jamie, Tremont Castle is not haunted. You are a complete hand, Obadiah," Anne chided, but she was smiling. She had caught the glint in his eyes that told her that this prophecy, at least, was made in jest.

Obadiah inclined his head. "Thank you, lady."

"Though the Tremonts do tend to live in the past. I fear the next weeks won't be easy, Obadiah."

"How long will we be staying, lady?" he asked, in cultured tones that would not have been out of place in a Mayfair drawing room.

"I don't know. Jamie, lovey, why don't you see how Nurse is?"

"I don't want to," Jamie said.

"But she'll want to know we're near land. Hm, maybe I'll go tell her—"

"No, I'll go!" Jamie wriggled free of Obadiah's grasp and ran off. Anne smiled as she watched him go, but her eyes were worried.

"I don't know," she said again. "It depends on the

duke. And if I know him . . ."

"A hard man, lady?" Obadiah said, when she didn't go on.

"No. Oh, no. A good man, and fair. Or he was. It's been a long time." She fell silent again, and this time, Obadiah stayed equally silent, while the crew stepped around them, eyeing them with wary respect. Obadiah was in her employ, but he was far more than a servant. He was confidant, advisor, and, above all, friend. When Freddie had died last year, leaving her with a plantation poorly run and saddled with debt, Obadiah had helped her straighten matters out. He was the best overseer Hampshire Hall had ever had; he was respected by servants and house folk alike, and he had consulted with her on a program that had the plantation running well again. Until the duke had meddled, sending an overseer of his own to replace Obadiah, undoing all the changes they had made, and ordering her back to England. That he was now guardian of her son and had the right to do what he had made no difference to Anne's resentment. Thus she had asked Obadiah to accompany her, ostensibly to get his position back. She wondered what the Tremonts would make of him.

"When I left he wasn't the duke," Anne said abruptly. "His father was still alive and he didn't have the responsibilities he has now. He and Frederick were cousins. We all grew up together. It was natural for Frederick to name him Jamie's guardian, and I suppose we would have had to return to England sometime." She grimaced. "I don't know what the duke has in mind, but I have the awful feeling he'll want us to stay. Jamie should be educated. The Templetons go to Eton, and then Oxford. Family tradition."

"Not a bad one, lady."

"No, perhaps not. But no one's even thought of changing it. If things were done a certain way one hundred years ago, all the more reason it should be

7

done that way now. Tremont Castle isn't haunted, Diah. The Tremonts are too dull for it."

Again Obadiah smiled. "You're not dull, lady."

"No." Anne smiled back. "Scatterbrained and flighty, perhaps, at least Frederick said so, but never, never dull."

"Mrs. Templeton." Captain Warwick, short and portly, came up, touching the brim of his cap. "We'll be making landfall in Portsmouth soon. When we're docked I'll find an inn for you."

"Thank you." Anne smiled at him. It wasn't his fault, after all, that he'd been given the task of bringing her back to England. Like her, he'd had no choice. When the Duke of Tremont ordered something done, it was done.

Soon they were passing through the Solent, the narrow passage between the mainland and the Isle of Wight, and their destination was in view. Jamie pointed with excitement at the men of war in Portsmouth harbor, and all of them looked with awe at *Victory,* Admiral Nelson's flagship. They dropped anchor, and, after the ship had been visited by a customs official and the quarantine doctor, a lighter was put over the side for the Templeton party. The odors of salt and tar, fish and horse assailed Anne's nostrils as the boat was rowed to the quay, and another scent, elusive, but familiar. A fresh scent, a scent that reminded her irresistibly of spring, a scent she had never found in Jamaica's lush tropical gardens. The scent of England. A feeling of rightness settled in her, and the lump rose in her throat again. She was home.

Captain Warwick gave her his arm as they walked up the stone stairs at Portsmouth Point, she and Jamie giggling at the way the land seemed to shift under their feet, so used were they to walking a constantly moving deck. He had found rooms for them at the George, the captain said, casting a look back at Obadiah, with a place in the stables for her servant. Obadiah, hefting a trunk on his shoulder, said nothing, but Anne's lips tightened. She was about to demand better lodgings when she caught sight of a man at the end of the quay, and all other concerns flew from her head.

In contrast to the bustle around him, crew loading and unloading ships, people embarking or streaming toward the coaching offices, the man stood very still, his hands, in pearl-gray gloves, resting atop the silver knob of an ebony walking stick. His coat and pantaloons were black, his shirt white, his waistcoat the same pearl gray. He was hatless; the only sign of life, of color, in him, was his hair, still the color of ripe corn, ruffled by the breeze. It couldn't be—.

"Hello, Anne," he said, and she stopped still, the lump in her throat lodging in her stomach. The Duke of Tremont. Giles, whom she had once thought she'd marry.

Chapter 2

He had changed. That was Anne's first thought, and she didn't know why it surprised her so. After all, it had been seven years. She had changed in that time. She had grown up. It was suddenly very important that he realize that she was no longer the girl she had been. That girl had been thoughtless, silly. That girl had left him, with barely a second thought.

Except for speaking Giles hadn't moved, and yet Anne had the sense of tremendous power held in check. Perhaps it was the way he stood, leaning forward ever so slightly, his hands clenched on his walking stick. Perhaps it was the way his eyes, those penetrating, clear gray eyes, were studying her, sizing her up, as he might an opponent. Outwardly he wasn't so very different. Older, of course; it showed in his eyes, which no longer held the light she had remembered. He seemed taller, somehow, and his leanness had a whipcord strength to it that was new. He was, undoubtedly, a man. A man used to power. She could tell by the way he waited for them to come to him. He would be a formidable opponent, she thought, shivering.

The duke smiled. "Welcome home," he said, and Anne realized she had forgotten nothing about him, not his voice or his smile or his face. Nothing.

He came toward her, his hand outstretched, and she

10

panicked. She wasn't ready for this. There was only one thing she could do. To the surprise and amusement of the fishmongers, the sailors, the passersby, she dropped into a deep curtsy. "Your Grace," she said, and rose, her eyes sparkling, to see him regarding her, his face blank, except for the faint color on his cheeks. Good heavens, was he embarrassed? "May I tell you how sorry I am about your father?"

Giles's eyes flickered briefly. "Thank you. And who is this?"

Anne looked down. Jamie, usually not at all shy, was clinging to her, hiding behind the skirt of her traveling dress and peeping at Giles with one eye. "This is my son, Your Grace. James. This is the duke, Jamie. Make your bow to him." For answer, Jamie clutched harder at her. She stared at Giles, silently challenging him to comment on Jamie's lack of behavior. Instead, looking not the least bit discomposed, he inclined his head.

"James. A pleasure to meet you." His eyes went past her, and though not by a flicker of a muscle did he show surprise, something in his very stillness gave him away.

She hurried into speech, not certain why. "And this is Obadiah Freebody," she said, almost defiantly.

"Ah, yes. I recall the name."

"I thought you would."

"Come." He reached out and grasped her elbow, so quickly and smoothly that she couldn't pull away without causing offense. "I've a carriage waiting."

"Captain Warwick found rooms for us at an inn."

"That is no longer necessary. Come," he said again, and this time Anne went along, across the cobbled street to the carriage he indicated. It was a large traveling carriage, painted in the Tremont colors of maroon and gold, with the ducal crest on the door. In spite of herself, Anne was impressed. Giles, her childhood friend, was really a duke.

"Mama? Where's his crown?" Jamie piped up.

"Hush, lovey. What crown?"

11

"You said a duke was like a prince, but there's no crown."

Giles's fingers tightened on her elbow. "We'll stop on the way to Tremont, of course," he said, handing Anne into the carriage. "We'll be there by tomorrow evening. Up you go." This to James, whom he swung in effortlessly. "He looks like his father."

"Mama says I don't."

Giles glanced up. "A trifle pert, is he not?"

Anne, settling herself in the carriage, glared at him. "He's high-spirited."

"Ah. Of course." Giles stepped back from the carriage. "Enjoy the ride. We've a long journey ahead," he said, and turned away.

Her lips tightening, Anne leaned back against the squabs as the carriage drove away, ignoring Jamie's excitement at the carriage and at meeting the duke, and Nurse's exclamations over what a fine gentleman the duke was. She was used to being in charge of her own destiny. Since when had she allowed a man to take over her life so efficiently, and with nary a protest from her? That would change. It would have to.

Hours later, after Nurse had stopped exclaiming with excitement, after Jamie's bouncing had turned to whining, and after even Anne herself was starting to feel cramped, the carriage drew to a stop. Before her in the twilight stood an inn, the Fox and Hounds. Long and low and rambling, of the flint and brick architecture so common to this part of the country, it was so familiar and dear that Anne felt that lump in her throat again. Home. Though it was far cooler than she was accustomed to, and though the sun had hid behind clouds all day, she was home, and she was happy. Grinning, she spread her arms wide and twirled around.

Giles dismounted from his horse, a chestnut stallion, in time to see her. "Anne," he said, frowning.

"Yes?" She looked up at him, her eyes bright.

"You are behaving in a most unseemly manner."

"Heavens!" She burst out laughing. "You sounded like your father then."

"Anne." He shifted onto his other foot. "People are staring at us."

"Just the stable boys. Are you embarrassed? Oh, really!" She laughed again, and he quickly came to take her arm.

"Come. You're causing a scene."

"You *are* embarrassed," she chattered. "You never used to be when I did something funny."

"Some people grow up, Anne."

Anne's head came up at that. She was about to retort when a series of thuds, followed by a wail, made her spin around. Jamie lay sprawled with his face down in the inn yard, just beyond the carriage stairs. "Oh, dear!" Anne pulled away from Giles. "What happened?"

"I couldn't stop him, ma'am," Nurse said, looking apologetic and scared all at once. "He wanted to go, and before I knew it, he had."

"I know how fast he is, Nurse." Uncaring of her lilac traveling gown, Anne knelt on the ground, taking her son by the arms and hoisting him to his feet. Tears mingled with the dirt on his face to present a most pitiful sight. "Now, let's see what you've done, lovey."

"I fell down, Mommy."

"I know, pet. Hm. No scrapes. Maybe a bump on your forehead." She rose. "You're all right. Just tired."

"No, I'm not! I'm not tired, Mommy!"

"Hush, pet," Anne waved Nurse away and picked Jamie up. "I think we'll have some milk and bread, and then to bed, pet."

"But I'm not tired!"

"I know you're not."

"I want to go home." He knuckled his eyes. "I want to go back to Jamaica."

"I know, lovey." Casting an apologetic look at Giles,

13

she walked past him into the inn. "I think we'd best just go to our rooms, Your Grace. If you don't mind."

Giles followed her in. "We have much to discuss, Anne."

"Tonight?"

"Tonight. I'll have dinner served in the private parlor."

"But," she began, and stopped. Giles had turned his back to her and was talking to the innkeeper. He was ignoring her! He'd never done that in the past; she didn't like his doing it now. "Very well, Your Grace. I'd curtsy, Your Grace, but I think I'd fall over."

Giles turned, and their eyes clashed. "Will half an hour be sufficient, Anne?"

"Oh, doubtless," she said, and climbed the stairs toward her room, her son heavy in her arms.

It was closer to an hour before she came downstairs. Jamie, all protests to the contrary, had quickly fallen asleep. It was she who had needed the extra time. Ignore her, would he? Treat her like someone he could order about? Well, they would see about that. And so she pulled out her most fashionable gown, of coral pink muslin, and sent it out with the maid to be pressed. She managed to bind her unruly curls into a reasonably neat knot, and she even took out her secret pot of rouge, applying a very little bit to her cheeks and lips. There, she thought, turning so that she could see herself in the tiny dresser mirror. Let him ignore her now.

A maid opened the door of the private parlor for her and she swept in, her gown whispering about her. Giles, pouring wine into goblets, glanced up, his face impassive. He, too, had changed for dinner. Though he still wore black, his waistcoat now was of white satin, embroidered in white, and his coat was of the finest superfine. Against the dark color, his hair shone almost a silver blond. He looked most elegant, she thought, unhappily aware that her most fashionable gown was also two years old. Neither had there been

14

the slightest flicker of admiration in his eyes.

"Good evening, Your Grace," she said, and swept into another curtsy.

Giles corked the bottle and set it down, the wine a rich ruby against his waistcoat. "Do you plan to curtsy to me every time you see me, Anne?"

"But isn't that what I should do?" She smiled at him as he seated her. "I haven't been near a duke in a very long time, you know. Perhaps I've forgotten how to behave."

"I think you know," he muttered, sitting across from her, and Anne hid a smile. Ah, a hit. Apparently he didn't like having his consequence pierced. Did no one tease him anymore?

"Jamie went off to sleep as soon as I put him to bed," she said, as the maids came in with the fish course, poached turbot in lobster sauce. "He was worn out, poor lamb."

Giles sipped at his wine, and then looked at the glass with surprise. "A tolerable vintage. He seems a trifle spoiled."

"Spoiled?" Anne stared at him. "Jamie's not spoiled. He's very bright for his age."

"He is pert. He talks to his elders when he hasn't been spoken to first. And he whines."

"Whines—Giles, he's only five years old!"

"Do you know, that is the first time you've used my name?"

"I don't spoil him, Your Grace." She bit the words off. "He is a normal, lively child, thank heavens. I never could abide those quiet, well-behaved children who sneak around and misbehave when you're not looking. Jamie's not like that. Nor am I. People noticed me." She paused. "They still do."

"Mm-hm. Jamie will have to behave himself at Tremont."

"He will. Oh, he's so excited about going to a real castle. He's disappointed there won't be any knights."

15

She smiled. "Do you remember, we used to play Robin Hood? You'd be Robin, and Freddie always loved playing the Sheriff, I never did know why. And I'd be Maid Marion."

"We were children, Anne."

"And then you and Freddie would have those ferocious battles with toy soldiers. You always won the colonies back from the Americans, I remember. Do you still have those? Jamie would love them."

"They're put away. They're quite valuable, you know."

"Is that the true worth of something, Your Grace?"

"They are no longer appropriate as toys." Giles sipped at his wine again. "I notice you're not wearing black."

"Freddie has been dead for over a year."

"Why not half mourning, then?"

"Giles, wearing dark clothes in a place like Jamaica makes no sense. It's too hot."

"But you're not in Jamaica anymore."

Anne opened her mouth, and then shut it again. "Well," she said, staring fixedly at her soup. "Have you any other criticisms of me?"

"I'm not criticizing you," he protested.

"No?"

"No. At least, I didn't mean to." He sat back as their dishes were removed and a succulent roast was served, along with new potatoes and minted peas. "You've been away from England a long time. You may have forgotten how to go on."

"And you plan to teach me? Oh, Tremont!"

He looked surprised by her laughter. "What?"

"When you used to be as active as I, you were the one who led Freddie and me into mischief, as I recall."

"I've grown up, Anne."

"So have I." Serious now, she laid down her fork. "I've had to. I'm not the same as I was seven years ago."

16

Giles shifted in his seat. "A lot has happened since then."

"Yes, of course." She hadn't meant to talk about the past. She hadn't meant to bring up what had once been between them, at least, not yet. Maybe not ever. "You needn't worry I'll disgrace you, Your Grace. I do know how to behave."

The look Giles gave her was doubtful. Anne stared steadily back at him, daring him to answer. At last, with a little shrug, he picked up his fork again. "Then we can at least converse like civilized people. Did you have a pleasant journey?"

"Tolerable." There, let him see that she could be as civilized as he.

"And are you glad to be home?"

"Yes." Anne's smile softened. "Yes, I am. I didn't expect to be, you know. I love Jamaica. But when we made port—well, I didn't realize I'd missed it so much." She glanced up, her gaze encompassing the huge hearth, the plaster walls, the oak beams darkened by the years. "It's so—so English. I'd forgotten how green the grass is, and that houses look like this and," as the sound of raindrops hitting the diamond-paned windows reached them, "that it rains so much. Obadiah will have trouble accustoming himself to that."

"I think we'll leave off discussing him until we reach Tremont Castle."

Anne started to speak, and then smiled. "Very well. I suppose it wouldn't do for us to quarrel my first night home."

"We aren't going to quarrel."

"Oh, I think we are, Your Grace. Without a doubt."

Giles leaned back, studying her with a little frown. "You have changed. You never used to be so contrary, Anne. Flighty, yes, but not contentious."

"How kind of you to pay me such nice compliments. I could add that you never used to be pompous or arrogant, but we did just promise not to quarrel, did we not?"

17

"So we did." He held up his wineglass in a mock salute, but his smile didn't reach his eyes.

He had changed, Anne thought. Once he had laughed at jokes, even against himself. Now he seemed so filled with his own importance that all traces of humor were gone. A shame, that. Whatever else one said about Freddie, there was no denying he'd had a sense of humor. It had sometimes been his only saving grace. "Tell me about your life now, Your Grace."

He shrugged. "Not much to tell. I didn't go off to the West Indies."

The bitterness in his voice startled her. "But you're the duke now. You must have responsibilities you didn't have before. Have you sat in Parliament?"

"Yes. I do so every spring."

"Oh! So you're in London for the season. How exciting."

He shook his head. "No. I rarely go out, or entertain."

"Oh."

"I've found there's more to life than parties and socializing."

"That sounds very like something your mother would say."

"She'd be right," he said imperturbably. "I knew ever since my brother died I would be duke, and that I'd have duties. I'm the head of the family now, and I have estates to run. I'm also the magistrate for the neighborhood."

"How interesting."

Giles slanted her a suspicious look. "I think so."

"And your mother and sister? Are they well?"

"Yes. Mother has some rheumatism, but I suppose that's to be expected for her age."

"Mm-hm. Beth never married?"

"No. She believes her place is at home."

Anne laid down her fork. "And you countenance that?"

18

"Of course I do."

"But she's so pretty and sweet. For her not to marry is a waste."

"You know nothing about it," he said sharply, and after a moment, she shrugged.

"No, I don't, do I?" She applied herself to her food. Even the rich roast beef, something she had missed in Jamaica, couldn't distract her from her thoughts. Poor Beth, not allowed to marry, by the sound of it; poor Giles, thinking that was natural. He had never married. She wondered why. *And poor me.* The prospect of living at Tremont Castle was even less appealing than it had been. Thank heavens it was only for the summer. No matter what Giles might think, she and Jamie would soon be on their way home.

They finished the meal in silence. When the sweet had been served, Anne rose. "I've had a long day, Your Grace. If you'll excuse me, I'll go to my room now."

Giles inclined his head. "Good night, Anne."

"Good night."

In her room, Anne undressed quickly and fell into the deep feather bed. Deliciously warm and cozy though it was, she couldn't sleep. Her mind was too filled with all that she'd seen and done that day. It was too filled with thoughts of Giles. The weeks ahead were not going to be easy. Of course she hadn't expected them to be, but she had thought she would find some common ground with him. Like it or not, he did have the final say on Jamie's destiny, and hers, as well. It was unfair that he should have such control over their fortunes when she had shown herself to be a good estate manager, but that was the law. Bemoaning it would do her little good. As far as Giles was concerned, he was far more qualified to run her life, simply because he was a man.

Oh, the arrogance of him! Anne sat up, punched her pillow, and then flopped down again. He'd never been like that before. Serious, yes, solemn, even, at times,

19

but then, in his circumstances, who wouldn't be? The responsibilities awaiting him had always been impressed upon him, so that he had never seemed as carefree as other children she'd known, even allowing for the age difference. Yet he'd had his moments. When he had come to visit his relatives, neighbors to Anne's family, he'd led Freddie and her into mischief more than once. And then, there had been that season. That one, magical season, seven years ago. . . .

No. She wouldn't think about that. It was over, past, done with. The man she had known then was gone. If he had changed, though, she had, too, and that was something she didn't think he yet appreciated. He would learn. If he thought she would tamely submit to his edicts, he would soon learn differently. She had no intention of letting the Duke of Tremont dictate to her.

With that thought in mind, Anne turned over yet again, pulled the pillow over her head, and at last fell asleep.

The carriages behind him, traveling at a slower pace, were visible only by the clouds of dust they stirred up. Bent low over his horse's neck, Giles galloped recklessly, the only release he allowed himself anymore. He had responsibilities, duties he'd never had as a young man. He couldn't behave as he had then, even had he wanted to. No, he was perfectly content with his life. So why was he feeling so restless?

It had seemed a simple enough thing to do, to meet his cousin's widow upon her return to England and take charge of her son. He was, after all, head of the family. Simple, yes. Easy, no. He should have realized that, where Anne was concerned, nothing would be easy. He'd got over her long ago. He had. He just hadn't been prepared for the reality of seeing her again.

God! He dug his knees in harder, and Wildfire, his mount, lengthened his stride even more. She was more

20

beautiful than ever. How could that be? She was older, and he'd always understood that life in the tropics was hard on a woman. Yet there she had stood, her skin unfashionably brown, true, but glowing; her outfit undoubtedly not in the first stare of fashion, but flattering to a figure that was curvier, more lush, than he'd remembered. She was not the girl he had known. She was a woman, adventurous, outgoing, vivacious, everything he was not, everything he didn't want to be. And she'd not been happy to see him again.

Flecks of foam were appearing on Wildfire's neck, and he eased up, patting the horse and straightening in the saddle. They had a long road ahead of them, and it wasn't fair to take his frustrations out on his horse. But then, Anne had always had that effect on him. He didn't like that. He liked being cool, calm, in control. In the space of just a few hours Anne had nearly made him lose that control. He didn't think she knew it, but when she had curtsied to him last night, showing an immodest, but very attractive amount of bosom—

He shifted in the saddle. Very well, she was beautiful. He'd been with beautiful women before and remained unscathed. He'd manage now. What bothered him more was her lack of deference to him. Him, the head of the family, and a man. Good God, she had warned him that they would quarrel. Why hadn't he left well enough alone and left them in Jamaica?

But, there it was. He had a duty to Freddie's son, to see that he was properly educated and that his property was well managed. The changes Anne had made in the management of Hampshire Hall, installing a former slave as overseer, finding new markets for the plantation's produce, planting new crops, made him profoundly uneasy, even if they had worked. Things were best done as they always had been, the time-honored way. Whether Anne liked it or not, he would run things as he saw fit.

Turning in the saddle, he saw that the carriage had

drawn nearer. The impulse to ride back and check on his guests' comfort was almost irresistible, but he managed to stifle it. What good would it do him? Anne would likely say or do something outrageous, and Jamie would be pert. And he would be left with a picture of bouncing strawberry blond curls and cornflower blue eyes. He wasn't attracted to her. He couldn't be. He had his life well in order, and there was no place in it for a woman so lively, so outspoken, as Anne. When they had matters settled to his satisfaction, he would allow her to live as she pleased, whether here or in Jamaica. Then he'd be done with her. Until then, however, it was going to be a very long summer. God help him.

By the time they had traversed most of Hampshire and were nearing Tremont Castle, the skies had clouded over, making the day gloomy and damp. The coachman kept casting uneasy glances up at the sky, but it wasn't until they were actually on the drive to the castle that the storm broke. Thunder clashed, and bolts of lightning made the foliage of rhododendron and azalea flash theatrically bright. Giles bolted for shelter, and, inside the carriage, Anne tried to hold onto what remained of her sanity, while Nurse muttered prayers and Jamie imitated thunderclaps. It needed only this. Anything more different from Hampshire Hall, she couldn't imagine.

Shouted on by the coachman, the team rocketed down the drive. The carriage rocked for a moment as it went over the drawbridge, darkened momentarily under the shadows of the portcullis, and at last came to a stop under a more modern portico. They had arrived at Tremont Castle.

Jamie was bouncing up and down in his seat. "Mommy, where's the moat?"

"Outside the wall, pet, where it belongs. Now, Jamie,

I want you to mind your manners. You're going to be meeting a very grand lady."

The carriage door opened, and Giles was there, holding out his hand to help her down. They were under shelter, but the gusty wind drove in sheets of rain that quickly penetrated the thin muslin of Anne's gown. Giles held a coat over her as she scurried inside, stopping at last in the hall. All was as she remembered, she thought, looking around. The small door to the castle gave no clue to the magnificence inside, so that most visitors were dazzled. Though Tremont Castle was centuries old, this was no medieval hall. Rather, it was a splendid space, tiled in marble, with a graceful staircase branching up to the main floor of the house, where the State rooms were located. On a summer day this was one of the more welcoming rooms in the castle, with sun streaming through the oriel windows set high up in the wall, but today it was dark and gloomy. Anne shivered with more than just the cold as she turned to smile at the servants, lined up to greet them. Goodness, there was old Benson, who'd been butler here when she was a child. He was smaller than she remembered, and wiry, but he held himself so proudly he seemed tall. He also looked as starched-up as ever. And Mrs. Mac-Pherson, the cook, who looked round and jolly but who had rapped Anne on the back of her hand with a wooden spoon for stealing cookies. The impulse to curtsy struck her, but this time she resisted it. Like Giles, they would neither understand, nor appreciate, the gesture.

She smiled instead, stepping forward. "Benson, how nice," she began, and stopped. For all the attention the staff was paying her, she might have been invisible. Instead, they were looking past her, the expressions on their faces ranging from consternation to mild shock. Anne turned to see what they were looking at, and saw only Obadiah, carrying in a trunk on his shoulder. What in the world?

At that moment, thunder crashed overhead, making her jump. She turned, and in the following flash of lightning, a squat, brooding figure was briefly brightly illuminated on the grand staircase. "So. You've come back," the figure said, and the lightning flashed once again.

Chapter 3

For a moment the group in the hall stood transfixed, even Obadiah standing with that special stillness that was his alone. Then Giles moved, crossing the hall. "Good evening, Mother. I trust your headache is better?"

"Tolerably, tolerably." Julia, Duchess of Tremont, waddled down the remaining stairs, short but substantial in black bombazine. Behind her flitted a slender figure in gray. Good heavens, this woman had nearly been her mother-in-law, Anne thought. What a lucky escape she had had.

"Your Grace," she said, and swept into a curtsy that, this time, held nothing of mockery. "Thank you for inviting me to visit."

"Hmph." Julia stopped before Anne, looking up at her. She was a little dumpling of a woman with a face that had once been pretty, and even now should be congenial. Instead it looked discontented, the mouth narrow and bracketed by lines, the eyes suspicious. She had never liked Anne even though she was the daughter of Robert Warren, the Viscount Pendleton, and that, apparently, hadn't changed. Anne hadn't expected it to. "Giles told me what he was going to do, and so it was his decision. He is head of the family now."

"Yes, ma'am."

"Mama!" Jamie called from across the hall, where a suit of armor stood, somewhat incongruously among the marble and gilt, at the bottom of the stairs. Some illustrious Templeton ancestor had doubtless worn it in battle. "There are knights here!" He turned his shining gaze up at Giles, whose face was impassive. "Do you wear this?"

Anne laughed. "Oh, Giles, do you remember the time when you did put it on? When we were playing knights and ladies—I unseated Freddie, as I recall—and then we couldn't get you out of it."

"Giles never did anything so foolish." Julia sailed majestically past Anne. "We'll have tea in the small drawing room. You'll want to wash the dust of the road off you."

"Yes, ma'am." Anne watched the duchess go, suddenly recognizing the woman who followed in her train. Giles's sister. "Beth! How lovely to see you again."

Beth turned and gave her a shy smile, but the duchess cut off anything she might have said. "Come, Elizabeth. I need you." Beth's face turned crimson and her smile looked forced as she hurried on behind her mother. Good lord, what was wrong with this household?

"I was right, lady," Obadiah said, his voice low. "There is a dragon in this house, and we've just met her."

"Oh, hush, Diah!" She stepped away from him, before she betrayed herself by laughing. The entire incident reminded her of nothing so much as a gothicky novel. *Let's see, what one? Oh, yes.* The Dark Castle. *Heavens!*

"Mama." Jamie hurtled himself at her. "Can I go sploring?"

"No, Jamie, no exploring yet. Remember what I told you," she went on, as Jamie opened his mouth to protest.

"Yes, Mama," he said, docile now. "I'll be good."

"Good." She bent down, fondling his silky curls. "Later on, you and I will go sploring together. All right?"

Jamie's face lit up in a beautiful smile. "Yes, Mama."

"Come." Putting her hands on his shoulders, she turned him toward the stairs. "Let's go get cleaned up."

"Benson will show you to your rooms," Giles said, and Anne turned to smile at him. The words she had been about to say died in her throat. Giles. Oh, Giles. All the pain, all the intensity of the youthful infatuation she had once had for him came flooding back. He had been the first person really to pay attention to her, the first one to understand her, the first man who had ever kissed her. With Giles, she had always felt complete, somehow. And he was handsome. Lord, was he handsome. Time had only added to his attractiveness, broadening his shoulders, adding maturity to his face. It had tested him, honed him. It had changed him. Once she had been able to tell what he was thinking, even if to others he seemed inscrutable. Once his eyes had been alight with life. Now they were closed to her, too. It hurt to see him so. In that moment, she wished she had never returned to England.

She became aware that Giles was staring at her, a quizzical look on his face. "Thank you," she stammered, and turned, almost racing up the stairs, to Jamie's audible delight. It was past. It was over. She had her own life now, and that was what mattered. She would discuss the plantation, and Jamie's future, with Giles; visit her family; enjoy the delights of England for the summer. Then she would go home.

Jamie protested at having to take a nap, but fell asleep almost as soon as he was tucked into bed in the old night nursery. Anne smiled down at him and then looked around the room, shuddering. Ghastly place, with huge, dark furniture and embroidered mottoes on the wall. No light, no color, no laughter. It was no place for a child.

Her own room wasn't quite so gloomy, but here the weight of the Templeton history was apparent. The huge tester bed was of time-darkened oak and was so high that a stair was needed to reach it. The small, diamond-paned windows let in little light, and tapestries hung on the wall to keep out the damp. Fortunately the counterpane was a cheerful red, and the carpet, though old and worn in places, was bright with color. Everything was clean and tidy, her housewifely eye noted, just old, as if all life had been suspended for the past several hundred years. Not her life. She was alive, and she intended to celebrate that fact.

Her coral pink muslin frock was pressed into duty again. Anne gazed at her reflection in the dressing-table mirror as the maid who had been assigned to her brushed her curls and caught them up with a cherry-colored ribbon. Color, at last. She might be a guest of the Templetons, but she wasn't about to let them change her. She had worked too hard, come too far, to turn back now.

A footman jumped to open the door of the small drawing room for Anne, and she smiled at him. Like many other country homes Anne had visited, Tremont Castle had the family apartments on the ground floor, with the State rooms above. The small drawing room wasn't really small, except in comparison with the State Drawing Room. She was about to walk through the door, when voices came out to her. "Really, Giles!" Julia's voice. "Why you had to invite her here."

Anne jumped back. "I have an obligation, Mother." Giles's voice, sounding surprisingly mild.

"Far be it from me to discourage you from your duty."

"Yes, Mother."

"But even I think this is a bit much. Yes, I agree her son needs discipline. Imagine letting a child run loose the way she does! But to bring that—that servant—"

"Mr. Freebody was overseer of Hampshire Hall."

"And you replaced him. Now don't try to convince me you're happy to see her, because it won't fadge. Not after what she did to you. She's as flighty and willful as ever."

"I'm glad to see her again." That was Beth, soft and tentative, and Anne's heart went out to her in gratitude. No word of support from Giles, the cad! Anne could feel her face flaming at the things Julia had said, and she was aware that the footman beside her was listening as avidly as she. It would be all over the servants' quarters in a few minutes. Some people would say that was what she deserved for eavesdropping. Well, why not really give them something to discuss?

Rolling her eyes at the footman, which made him snigger, she swept into the room, a ravishing smile upon her face. The three people seated near the fireplace looked up at her with varying degrees of surprise. "Your Grace! I really must thank you again for letting me stay."

The footman sniggered again. Julia's eyes went past Anne to him, and then returned. "You are late. Pray, be seated. Beth, tea for Mrs. Templeton."

A worthy opponent, Anne thought, choosing the gold satin-striped sofa instead of the old and rather lumpy-looking brocade chair Julia had indicated. "Thank you so much. But, please, must we be so formal? After all, we are family."

"I prefer formality." Julia raised a quizzing glass—a quizzing glass, for heaven's sake!—and studied Anne through it. From anyone else, it would have been considered an insolent gesture. "What is it that you are wearing?"

Anne looked down. "A frock."

"A frock, indeed." Julia let the quizzing glass drop. "You are a widow. You should be in mourning."

"Frederick has been dead for over a year, Mother," Giles said, before Anne could reply, making her look at him in surprise. Was he actually defending her?

"Hmph." Julia's eyes were cold. "You always were a frivolous young miss."

"Yes, Your Grace."

"I thought marriage might settle you down, but apparently it hasn't."

"I think your frock is lovely, Anne," Beth said softly, and Anne flashed her a smile of mingled sympathy and complicity. Poor Beth, dressed in governess-y gray. With her light brown hair and her pale complexion, the color made her look like a timid little mouse.

"Thank you. Everything looks the same." Indeed, it was all so much the same that, for a moment, Anne felt she'd stepped back in time, to when she had been a child and had visited here. The furniture that had once seen long and honorable use in the State rooms, which had been remodeled when Giles's grandfather had made his fortune investing in the East India Company, had been consigned to the family's private living areas. As a result, their drawing room was furnished with an oddment of items. The sofa on which she sat, of fairly recent vintage, sat cheek by jowl with a magnificent carved oak chair cushioned in red velvet, which Julia always claimed as her own. The carpet was worn, Persian, and probably priceless, and the curtains at the long narrow windows were of simple muslin. As in her room, tapestries again hung on the walls, and over the mantel were the inevitable hauberk and lance, reminding one and all that the Templetons had always fought for king and country. Theirs was a long and distinguished history, and the castle was steeped in it. It was to Julia's credit, Anne thought, somewhat grudgingly, that she'd been able to make any part of it a home. The only complaint Anne had at the moment was the damp chill, which she'd forgotten. She wished she had a shawl, an item she hadn't needed in Jamaica.

As if he read her mind, Giles spoke. "You look cold. Shall we send someone for a shawl?"

She smiled at him, absurdly grateful for this minor thoughtfulness. "Thank you, but I fear I no longer own any such thing."

"Oh, you may borrow one of mine," Beth said, and Anne smilingly shook her head. She would rather freeze than wear anything so dull as Beth likely possessed. If she weren't careful, she would become as gray as the castle, and everyone in it. What had happened to turn Giles that way?

"I must visit a dressmaker while I am here," she chattered. "I am so sadly lacking in clothes. Is there a good one in the village?"

Beth, to whom she had addressed this question, looked blank. It was Giles who answered. "There's one in Basingstoke, I believe."

"Oh, wonderful! You'll come with me, won't you, Beth? You must know far more about the current styles than I."

"You want me to come?" Beth said. "Really?"

"I am not certain I can spare you, Elizabeth," Julia said, frowning heavily. Anne was about to speak, when, at that moment, there was a great crash of metal in the hall.

Giles jumped up. "What in the world—"

"Jamie," Anne said at the same time, and ran out into the hall. She could not say how she knew that Jamie was responsible for the noise, except that all her motherly instincts were clamoring. If there was mischief, Jamie was certain to be in the middle of it.

In the hall, Benson and the footman who had admitted Anne to the drawing room were staring in consternation, and more servants were appearing, from all over the castle. The suit of armor at the bottom of the stairs had toppled over and was in pieces. Leg pieces and arm pieces were scattered helter-skelter across the tiled floor; the hauberk had somehow landed right side up, and the helmet lay on the stairs. Protruding from the helmet, looking pitifully small, was the body of a small boy. Anne briefly closed her eyes. *Oh, Jamie, and on our first day! Couldn't you wait to get into mischief?*

"Jamie!" she said, her voice sharp, and the small arms and legs began to thrash about.

"Mommy!" The wail echoed hollowly, making a few of the maids step back. "Mommy!"

"Oh, good heavens." Anne sat on a stair and reached for her son's flailing arms. "I'm here, Jamie. Let's get you up and out of this thing."

"Mrs. Templeton. Do you know how old that armor is?" Julia demanded.

"Ancient, I imagine. Now, hold still, pet, and let's get this helmet off."

"It won't come off, Mommy. I tried."

"The child is a brat," Julia said in ringing tones, and Anne looked up at Giles. It was at times like these that she most missed the presence of a father's guiding hand for Jamie. She had not been a docile child, but she sometimes had trouble dealing with a young boy's antics.

"Come, James." Giles went down on one knee before them, putting a hand on Jamie's quivering arm. "Men don't cry about things like this."

Jamie hiccupped. "I'm sc-scared."

"Quite. You should be. I was when I got caught in the armor."

Anne looked up at him in surprise. "Were you?"

"Now, stop crying, my lad. We're going to get you out."

Whether it was the masculine voice of authority that reached him, or the fact that Giles was a stranger, Jamie stilled. Only a few pitiful sniffles issued from under the helmet. "I'm sorry, Uncle Giles."

"And well you should be," Julia said.

"Hold still, James." Giles put his hands on either side of the helmet, and pulled. Anne, her hands on Jamie's shoulders, could feel him quivering, but he didn't cry.

Remarkable. If it had been only she dealing with this, he would have been in hysterics by now. Never mind that her own nerves weren't quite too steady. It wasn't fair that a stranger controlled her child better than she did. "There, James, it's coming loose. Watch your nose—here it comes, over the ears—there!"

With a pop, the helmet came free. Jamie looked up at Giles with his huge blue eyes and then fell into Anne's arms. "Mommy."

"There, pet." Anne hugged him, rolling her eyes at Giles. To her surprise, he grinned. "You're all right."

"Is the helmet dented?" Julia said loudly.

Anne gave her a look. "Come, pet." She rose awkwardly, Jamie a heavy burden in her arms. "You and I are going to go upstairs and we're going to have a talk."

"He deserves a sound thrashing, if you ask me."

Anne's lips thinned. "No one asked you, Your Grace. If you'll excuse me?"

"Well!" Julia exclaimed, but Anne was already on her way up to the nursery.

It took time to get Jamie settled after his adventure, time to impress on him why he should never do such a thing again, time to find out why he had done it. Anne returned to the drawing room to find the tea tray removed and all signs of nourishment gone. And she had just bitten into a cream cake, she thought wistfully.

"Is James all right?" Beth asked, and Anne smiled at her.

"Yes, thank heavens. How little boys survive childhood, I don't know. I wonder my hair hasn't all turned gray by now."

"Hmph. None of my sons misbehaved like this," Julia said. "If you would give him the spanking he deserves—"

"I do not beat my child." Anne's voice was suddenly hard, making the others look at her in some surprise.

"Jamie knows how to behave. He is simply an active little boy."

"Hmph! My boys never got into such scrapes."

"Actually, Giles." Anne turned toward him, smiling. "Can you guess why he did it?"

Giles looked surprised. "No, why should I?"

"Because he heard me say that you'd done it, and if Uncle Giles did it it must be all right."

Giles's face actually colored, to Anne's amusement. "Did you tell him my father gave me a sound thrashing afterward?"

"No. I told him we all three were punished. Which, as I recall, we were."

"And which we deserved." Giles's tone was dry as he rose. "We'll discuss that later. We keep country hours for dinner."

"Of course." Anne would never have expected such a modern innovation as the late town dinner hour. "I shall just see how Jamie's doing and then I'll take a rest. Oh, and Beth. Perhaps if the rain lets up tomorrow we might go to Basingstoke."

Beth's face lit up. "Oh, I'd like that."

"I will need you tomorrow, Elizabeth," Julia said sternly. Anne turned to her and would have spoken, but was forestalled by Giles.

"You and I have matters to discuss, Anne. Perhaps you could put off your trip for another day."

"Of course." Anne smiled graciously at them all as she rose. She knew when she was defeated. "I'll see you at dinner, then," she said, and, after curtsying, glided out of the room. Behind her she could hear Julia's voice. She didn't want to think what the old besom was saying. Imagine suggesting that she spank Jamie! Anne trembled with indignation at the thought. She had never laid a hand on her son in his life, and as for Freddie—well, that was past, and men had a different view of these things. Raising Jamie was her responsibility now, even if Giles thought he had a say in it.

34

Raising her chin, Anne walked up the stairs toward her room. They were not going to change her. No matter what else the Templetons did this summer, they would not change her.

Giles looked once again at the letter the morning post had brought, and then sat back, tapping it thoughtfully on his desk. This was an unlooked-for complication in a life already fraught with complications. Never let it be said that he would neglect his duty; however, what did one do when duty dictated two conflicting choices? He would have to do some serious thinking on this.

In the meantime, he had quite enough problems at home. The presence of Anne and her son, not to mention her servant, in his household was already causing upheaval. Obadiah had, so he understood, scared most of the female staff into silence, though he'd said and done nothing out of the ordinary. James—well, clearly a man's hand was needed in his upbringing. Giles had some thoughts about that. Finally, there was Anne. His house had been peaceful before she came. Now his mother was visibly ruffled—strange, she had never liked Anne—and Beth was pouting because his business with Anne today prevented their going to the shops in Basingstoke. Beth, of all people. If Anne were having such an effect on her, perhaps it would be as well to cut her visit short.

And yet—and yet, he had liked seeing her in his drawing room last evening. He agreed with his mother about the value of old and treasured furnishings and traditions, but sometimes the effect was dull. He felt like a traitor just thinking that, but there it was. Too many old and faded tapestries, too much dark wood, too little light. Anne in her coral pink had been a welcome flash of color, something he hadn't even realized he missed. She was energetic, alive, vivid. She was also dangerous, reminding him all too well of a time that was gone. The pain and humiliation of that moment when he'd learned that she'd married someone else were surprisingly sharp and clear, though until yesterday he'd managed to forget them. His life was proceeding well, along well-charted paths. Yesterday he would have been content. Today, he was restless.

There was a knock on the door and Anne came in, before he could even call for her to enter. That was the way she always had been, active, impatient, moving, and so pretty she sometimes took his breath away. Her morning gown of jonquil muslin, with its long sleeves and high neck, brightened the room as nothing else could do. With her hair bound back by a matching ribbon she looked like a jonquil herself, he thought, and then berated himself for such fancies.

"Good morning," he said, rising, his face a mask that gave away none of his thoughts.

"Good morning. What a glorious day." Anne sat in one of the leather armchairs that faced the fireplace and, after a moment, he joined her. "Isn't it amazing how much brighter it is even in here with the sun?" She glanced around, taking in the warm colors of the Axminster carpet, the rich red leather chairs, the burnished mahogany desk. "I gather your mother had nothing to do with this room."

"Why do you say that?"

"I don't see anything old. Did you actually spend money on new furniture in here?"

"Yes."

"Oh, don't poker up so! I think it's wonderful." She regarded him curiously. "What has happened to you, Tremont? You never used to mind teasing."

He cleared his throat. "We have some things to discuss."

"Ah, yes. Your summons to me this morning. Well, discuss away, Your Grace."

"Are you always so flippant about things?"

36

"Oh, always."

Giles frowned; this did not bode well. "We have some serious matters to discuss, Anne."

"I don't see what. Restore Obadiah as overseer, let me manage Hampshire Hall, and agree with me that Jamie is much too young to be sent to school."

"You do intend to be flippant about this, then."

"Oh, no." Anne looked straight at him. "I'm quite serious."

"Anne." He made his voice patient. "I realize it's been hard for you since Freddie died, but you no longer have to manage alone. A woman shouldn't have to worry her pretty head about such things—"

"Don't you talk to me about a woman's frailties, Giles Templeton! As I recall I used to beat you in races, even if I was younger."

"Maybe I let you win."

"Ooh!" Anne jumped up and strode across to the window, and her arms crossed on her chest. "No. I promised myself I would not get angry about this. I said I would deal with it sensibly, no matter how odiously high-handed you behaved, summoning me back to England as if I'm some chattel."

"Good. If you're not angry perhaps we can discuss this rationally."

Anne gazed at him for a moment and then sat down again, her spine very straight. "Very well. If you wish to be rational. Obadiah!" she called, and Obadiah came in, carrying several large, leather-bound books. "These are the ledgers from Hampshire Hall. Note the top one carefully, Your Grace." She smiled. "Thank you, Obadiah."

Obadiah flicked a glance from her to Giles, and then bowed. "Lady."

"As I thought," Giles murmured, turning over the pages. "I'm sorry, Anne, but this tells its own tale. Entries missing, columns totaled wrong—I know you're intelligent for a female, but this bears out what I was saying. Managing a plantation is too much for a woman."

Anne's smile was just a little malicious. "Pray note the date of the ledger, Your Grace."

Giles looked down and drew in his breath. "This can't be."

"Oh, but it can. Freddie was still alive and in charge."

Giles stared at her a moment, and then abruptly pushed the ledger away. The one below told the same story, of missed payments, crop failure, poor investments. The next one, though, kept in a different hand, showed some changes. Servants' wages had risen, but so, apparently, had productivity. The tobacco and sugar crops showed a sharp rise in yield, and in export. Every column totaled correctly, and if the estate still showed a loss, it was smaller than it had been. The next ledger, the final one, for the year just past, showed nearly every aspect of the plantation running at a profit.

Giles closed the book, his brow wrinkled in a frown. Good God. Anne had shown herself more astute at management than ever Freddie had. "I agree about freeing the slaves," he said abruptly. "It costs the plantation more money, but—"

"But," she agreed. "Freddie and I both hated it. So did they. What it costs for wages and housing is more than made up by the extra work the servants put in, now that they have their freedom. Oh, I'll admit we lost some, but the rest seem happy. And Obadiah is an excellent overseer."

"A former slave, Anne."

"What has that to say to anything?"

"It's all very well when he deals with local people, but when he has to deal with merchants and ship's captains—"

"I've taken care of that part."

Giles closed his eyes. "Dear God."

"And done well, too. You see, like you they think I'm

38

helpless and innocent."

"I assume they've learned," he said grimly.

"Oh, yes, and quite fast, too." She smiled at him. "So you see, Giles, it really would be foolish for you to replace me."

He shook his head. "No. You've done a decent job for a woman, Anne, but my decision stands. Mister Tyler will remain as manager of Hampshire Hall."

"'For a woman,'" she mimicked. "'For a female!' Were you always this patronizing? Or is it just since you've become duke that you've got like your father?"

"My father has nothing to do with this."

"No, I suppose not." The look she gave him was infinitely sad, and beyond his comprehension. "Tremont, we were doing very well in Jamaica. I don't see why I can't return."

"You'll be needed here, Anne."

"Here? Why?"

"Because Jamie needs to be educated."

Anne went very still. Here it was, the main battle of the war between them. "I plan to hire a tutor for him, one who would like to live in Jamaica."

Giles shook his head. "I was thinking about Eton."

"He's too young!"

"In another few years he won't be."

Anne gripped the arms of her chair. "No. No. Freddie told me about Eton, about the beatings he received and the cruelty of the older boys. I will not expose my son to that."

"You may not have a choice," he said quietly. "I am his guardian, Anne."

"And I am his mother. And don't tell me you received a good education at Eton, or that Freddie did, either! I'll wager I learned more from my governess. No." She rose and stalked to the door. "This discussion is ended, Your Grace. While I have any say in the matter, my son will not attend Eton."

"You have no say in the matter."

"He's my son. Not yours."

"As James's trustee, I could cut you off without a penny, you know—"

"Go ahead."

"—and I could have James raised here. Without you."

Chapter 4

Anne stopped at the study door. "You wouldn't," she said, turning.

He wouldn't, of course. "If I have to, Anne—"

"No! He's all I have. Oh, Giles, must you use him to get your revenge on me?"

"On you?" he said, surprised.

"Jamie is innocent. Don't make him suffer for the past."

"Make him suffer—Anne, I'm trying to do what's best for him. He needs an education. He needs the proper training to take his place in life."

"I realize that! Why do you think I've done what I have? For myself? Jamie knows the plantation as well as I do, and he knows the people. He's been over every inch of it, he has friends there—don't you see, he could never get that at Eton. Giles." She stepped away from the door, her face holding an unaccustomed expression of pleading. "Please. I'm only trying to do the best for him, too. As your mother did for you."

"I realize that, Anne. I don't mean to make this difficult for you, but I have my duty."

"Your duty. Oh, yes, I've heard about that." Her eyes narrowed. "You never married."

He looked at her in surprise. "Anne, for God's sake, what has that to say to anything?"

"I used to wonder why. Now I know. What woman would want to live with you, you pigheaded, arrogant—man!"

"Anne!" he exclaimed, and crossed the room as she whirled out the door. "Anne, for God's sake—"

In the hall, Anne was already pounding up the stairs. Giles looked after her and then closed the door softly, returning to his desk. What had happened to his peaceful, ordered life?

Running his hand through his hair, Giles sat back. Life had suddenly become devilishly complicated. Being the head of the family, managing his estates, and sitting in the House of Lords, all involved a great deal of work, but it was manageable. This new obligation was different. Anne wasn't like his tenants or his family. Anne had a mind of her own, and no qualms about using it. When had that happened? The girl he had once known had been bright, amusing, willful, but never so stubborn or independent. No matter what he decided, she would fight him. He wasn't used to having his authority questioned, nor the peace of his house disrupted by the antics of an undisciplined child. What disturbed him most, though, was the little flip his heart gave whenever Anne walked into a room.

His eyes fell on the letter. Another obligation, but one that seemed less onerous than it had. If nothing else, it would mean his leaving Tremont Castle for a time, and that suddenly was something greatly to be desired. His head came up in the posture he unconsciously assumed whenever he had made a difficult decision. He would answer this obligation, and the rest of his duties be hanged.

A high piping sound reached Giles's ears as he stepped from his study into the hall, and for a moment, he paused. A child's voice, singing. "Tom, Tom, the piper's son, stole a pig and away he run." Briefly, very briefly, he smiled. James, of course. Who else? The boy was as undisciplined as his mother. That was something

42

else that would have to change.

Jamie was holding onto the wrought-iron railing of the staircase and swinging back and forth, each time coming perilously close to the suit of armor. At the sight of Giles, his eyes widened and he broke off swinging. "Uncle Giles!" Heedless of the slippery marble floor, he dashed across the hall and threw his arms around Giles's legs. "Mama says you have some toy soldiers for me," he said, looking at Giles with eyes that were so much like his mother's that Giles was stunned into silence. Never had he been greeted like this. It was strange. It was also rather nice.

"James, I am certain your mother also told you how to greet me," he said, sounding repressive even to his own ears. Jamie stared at him blankly, and then stepped back, making a perfunctory bow that reminded Giles of Anne's mocking curtsies. In spite of himself, he smiled, though by the time Jamie looked at him again his face was stern. "What are you doing here alone?"

"Nurse's asleep. Uncle Giles?"

"James, I am not your uncle."

"Mama said I could call you that."

"I am the duke, James. You must address me as 'Your Grace.'"

Jamie giggled. "That's silly. Grace is a girl's name."

Again Giles's lips twitched in a smile. "That has nothing to say to it, James. Now go along to the nursery before I tell your mother you're here."

"All right." To Giles's surprise, Jamie slipped his hand trustingly into his and let himself be led to the stairs, swinging from side to side. "Uncle Your Grace?"

Giles couldn't help it; he let out a laugh. "Yes?"

"What happened when you put on the armor?"

"My father punished me, James, as I deserved. The armor is very old and very valuable."

Jamie's eyes were unblinking. "My father used to punish me, too."

"Did he?"

43

"Mm-hm. Until Mama made him stop. I didn't like it," he added confidingly.

"Discipline is a part of life, James." No wonder the boy ran wild. He would definitely have to do something about this. "Run along to your nurse now, lad," he said.

"Yes, Uncle Your Grace." Again Jamie bowed, and Giles couldn't resist. For a moment he laid his hand on the boy's head. When had he last touched a child? Jamie was trusting, vulnerable, innocent. Perhaps Anne was right. Perhaps Eton wasn't the place for him. Lord knew Giles himself had been unhappy there, until he had toughened up. Jamie was a Templeton, though, and if there were one thing that Giles had known since childhood, it was that Templetons followed tradition. Not yet, though. Giles's fingers lightly feathered through Jamie's hair. Not yet.

Jamie shook away Giles's hand in a gesture that was definitely masculine. " 'Bye," he said, and dashed for the stairs, stopping for a moment to bow to the armor. Then, giving Giles a look that held more deviltry than innocence, he ran up the stairs, the sound of his feet echoing in the hall.

Undisciplined and wild, Giles thought, but there was a smile on his face as he turned away and headed toward the breakfast room. Jamie would be all right, with the proper guidance. At bottom, there was good stuff in him. Something else for Giles to see to before he left.

The gong summoning the family to luncheon had just rung, and Giles entered the breakfast room to find the ladies of his family assembled there before him. Unerringly his eyes went straight to Anne, who answered his look with one of her own. It was on the tip of his tongue to mention James to her, but he refrained. What had happened in the hall was between him and the boy.

"I have news," he said, after they were seated and the

44

meal was served. "I had a letter this morning from Brighton."

"Ah," Julia said, sounding satisfied. "I wondered if you were going to tell us about that."

Giles cast her a look, momentarily annoyed, though he wasn't certain why. Of course his mother would know what was going on in her house, even if it were Giles's business. "Yes, well, it is, as you probably guessed, from the Prince of Wales. Or, rather, Colonel McMahon, writing on his behalf."

Anne, seated to his right, choked on her soup. "Prinny? You are funning us, aren't you?"

"No. Why?"

"Oh, don't poker up so! You must admit, there's no one more unlike you than Prinny—"

"Giles did him a great service in the spring," Beth said softly.

Anne stared at him. "Really? What?"

"Nothing of consequence." Giles spoke crisply, annoyed again. "The Templetons have always done their duty to the Crown."

"Of course."

"Is he going to recognize what you did?" Julia asked, sipping at her water glass. "It's high time."

"Apparently." He paused, suddenly less certain of his decision than he had been a few moments ago. "He's invited me to stay with him in Brighton."

Julia nodded approvingly. "It is no less than you deserve. It is no laughing matter, Anne."

"I'm—sorry, ma'am." Anne wiped futilely at her eyes. Giles's pronouncement had sent her into gales of laughter. "But even in Jamaica we've heard of Prinny's Marine Pavilion, and the thought of Giles staying there—"

"I will be staying at the Old Ship," Giles said, considerably annoyed by her laughter.

"When will we be leaving?" Beth said softly, and silence descended on the room.

45

Giles could feel Anne looking at him, though he didn't know why. "I shall be leaving within a sennight. I'm sorry, Beth. The invitation was for me, only."

"Oh."

"To the Pavilion, you mean," Anne said. "There's no reason you couldn't bring your family to Brighton."

"'Tis prodigious expensive," Julia said.

"That is not to the point," Giles said. "I do not plan to be there long. I'm sorry."

"You don't sound it," Anne muttered, earning a glare from Julia. "My parents are to be at Brighton this summer."

"Are they? I shall be certain to give them your regards."

"Do that. In the meantime, would you excuse me? I find I have no appetite." With that she rose, curtsied briefly, and went out, leaving silence behind her.

"Well!" Julia touched at her lips with her napkin. "She is as spoiled and willful as ever. It was a lucky day for you, Giles, when she married Freddie."

"That's past." Giles's voice was curt. His mother was right. Anne was willful, and so was her son. Or so he had thought, before Jamie had slipped his small hand into his. So he would have thought, had he not seen an emotion in Anne's eyes that troubled him. Disapproval. Now what had he done to earn that?

In the rose garden, Anne sank down upon a stone bench, reaching out to pluck a rose, a deep peach in hue. The rain had finally ceased, and Tremont Castle looked as it had in her childhood, not a fairy-tale castle, but a place of history and romance. The sun somehow found a golden glow deep within the stone walls, and the moat, though now little more than a ditch, shone with the reflections of the irises and day lilies that lined its banks. It was beautiful. A beautiful prison. At that moment, Anne wanted nothing so much as to go home.

"Anne?" a soft voice said, and she looked up. "Are you well?"

"Beth. Of course I am." She smiled. "Come sit next to me. I am sorry I behaved so. I fear I sometimes let my temper get the better of me." Would she never learn? Now she not only had to mend fences with Giles, but she was hungry. She strongly regretted the stuffed hen she had left on her plate. But Beth wanted to go to Brighton. Anne had seen it in her eyes, and Giles's refusal was what had triggered her temper.

"I know. 'Twas a disappointment, but then, Giles knows best."

"Don't you ever get angry with him?"

"Oh, no. I know he's doing what's best for everyone."

"Really. I find it very high-handed of him."

"Oh, but you don't know him as I do. He has such responsibilities. He told us just now he doesn't want to leave the farming at this time of year, but he feels he has no choice."

"He must have an estate agent."

"Oh, of course, but he takes his duties very seriously, you know. And I must admit, you are right. Giles seems an unlikely person to be a favorite of the Prince. But how lucky he is." Her voice took on a wistful note. "Imagine the people he'll meet, and the entertainments he'll be invited to."

"Beth, did you ever have a season?"

"No."

"Good heavens, how awful! No wonder you want to go to Brighton."

"Oh, it's no one's fault," Beth said quickly. "Papa died just before I was to go to London, and so that was that. Since then, Mama's needed me."

"I see." Selfish old woman. She herself would never be such a possessive mother. "Don't you wish to be married?"

"Oh, no, not anymore. I used to have such foolish, romantic dreams, but that was a long time ago. I'm quite on the shelf now."

"Lady Elizabeth Templeton, sister of the Duke of Tremont? There must be plenty of young men who would want you."

"Yes, but not for myself. I'm not like you, Anne. I'm quite plain."

Anne pulled back and studied her. "If you would dress in brighter colors and leave off wearing caps—"

"I would still be plain." Beth gave her a shy smile. "It's all right, Anne. I've quite come to terms with it."

"Mm." Anne looked down at the rose in her hands without seeing it; its petals, scattered across her skirt, were in delicate contrast to the blue muslin. "Well. I must go in. I've some apologies to make."

"Anne." Beth placed her hand on Anne's as they rose. "You won't make Giles angry again, will you? Please?"

Anne hesitated. "Very well," she said, finally, and was glad that Beth could not see her fingers, firmly crossed behind her back. This matter was not settled. It was high time someone argued with the duke.

Anne met Giles in the hall as she came back into the house. He paused, his hand on his study door. "Are you over your temper?" he asked.

"Yes, you insufferable prig," she muttered.

"Excuse me?"

"When do you leave for Brighton?"

"Next Wednesday. I've some business to see to first." He stepped toward her. "I suppose you want to go."

"No, not particularly."

Giles looked at her in surprise. "No?"

"No. Think, Giles. If we're seen in company together, after what happened seven years ago, what do you suppose people will say?"

Giles looked taken aback. "Nothing. I am the Duke of Tremont, after all, and you're my cousin's widow."

"Don't be naive. You know very well people have

long memories. They'll be glad enough to talk about us."

"I never thought you were a coward, Anne."

"I'm not. This is a battle that doesn't seem worth fighting. Still." Her smile was wistful. "I would like to see the Marine Pavilion."

Giles made a gesture with his hand. "It's hideous, in monumentally bad taste—"

"Does that mean that all the furnishings are new?"

"Excuse me?"

Anne's smile was sweet. "Nothing."

The look Giles gave her was suspicious. "I dislike Brighton. If I didn't have to go there, I wouldn't."

"You might have fun."

"Fun? I doubt it. I will make my appearance as the Prince expects me to, and then come home. And that is all."

"How dull. Beth will not be missing so very much, after all."

"Beth doesn't want to go, now that I've explained matters to her."

"Of course she doesn't. She worships you. Everything you do, she thinks is fine."

"I'm thinking of Beth's best interests, I'll have you know. She wouldn't enjoy Brighton."

"But she never had a season."

"She seems not to miss it."

"Oh, Giles!" Anne's voice was exasperated. "For heaven's sake, do you really believe that? She's young, and yet she has no life of her own."

"Of course she does. She seems happy enough."

"I don't believe she knows differently. But if you were to ask her, Giles, I think you'd find that she does want more. She deserves to marry and have her own family."

Giles frowned. "Did she ask you to speak with me?"

"No. In fact, she asked me not to. I'm meddling, as usual. And to no effect, I can see."

"I want Beth to be happy. I don't believe that her happiness lies in such a superficial place as Brighton."

Anne gazed up at him, startled. He sounded bitter, and she couldn't for the life of her understand why. After all, she was the one who had been wronged seven years ago. "Beth has the right to choose."

"Beth doesn't know better." He opened the door. "I've made my decision on this, Anne. Pray don't meddle any further." With a curt bow, he walked away, and went into his study.

Well! Anne went up the stairs, as annoyed with him as he must be with her. The direct approach hadn't worked; she hadn't expected it would. It was time, then, to try something else. Giles didn't know it yet, but battle had just been joined between them.

Tea had been served, and the inhabitants of Tremont Castle were at ease, Giles with one elbow propped on the mantel, Julia and Beth engaged in their embroidery, and Anne, who detested needlework, twisted around to look out the window. She had forgotten how deadly dull life could be in England. In Jamaica she had never been bored, but here there was little for her to do. She wasn't even expected to spend much time with her son.

"I am pleased you are going to Brighton, Giles," Julia pronounced, taking a stitch in her crewel.

Giles looked up. "Are you, Mother?"

"Yes. It can, after all, only add to your consequence."

"And, who knows. I might even have fun."

Anne twisted back to look at him. Had she managed to reach him yesterday? But, no, his face was impassive, his eyes were cool. He was the most confusing man.

"Fun is not why you are going," Julia said. "Remember your duty, Giles."

"I always remember my duty, Mother. In fact, it occurs to me there's one I've overlooked."

"What is that?"

"I should have seen to it that Beth had a season."

Beth looked up, her needle poised in midair. "Oh, but I don't want—"

"Elizabeth is perfectly happy here with me." Julia sent her daughter a stern glance. "What need has she of a season?"

"She may wish to marry, Mother."

"If she does, I'll find someone suitable for her."

"Why is it Giles never found anyone suitable?" Anne asked, prompted by some inner demon. "Isn't marriage one of his duties, too?"

"That is none of your concern, ma'am. What is all this about, Giles? The season is past."

"In London, yes, but everyone is going to Brighton this year. What better place for Beth to make her debut?"

"Nonsense." Julia stabbed at the cloth. "I need her here. Besides, she would need to be chaperoned, and if you think I'll leave that to . . ." Her voice trailed off, but the look she gave Anne left no doubt as to whom she blamed for this.

"Of course she would need a chaperone," Giles said patiently. "That is why you would come along. Now, hear me out, Mother." He held up his hand. "We can well afford to take a house in the town for a few weeks, and we should present Beth to society. Even if she doesn't find a suitor, it will be good for her. And you haven't left Tremont since Father died."

"And think of seeing your son honored by the Prince of Wales," Anne put in.

"There is that." Julia looked thoughtful; apparently she was taking Anne's jest seriously. "It would be a feather in your cap, wouldn't it, ma'am?"

"Mine?" Anne's eyes were innocent. "I have nothing to do with this."

"Oh, really. Am I to believe this was all Giles's idea?"

"Of course it was." Giles sounded irritated. "Anne

51

has already told me she has no desire to go to Brighton."

"Oh," Beth said, and everyone turned to look at her, at the dismay in her voice. "Then we won't be able to go, either. Unless it's all right for Anne to stay here unchaperoned."

"Of course it is not all right." Julia glared at Anne. "I wouldn't leave her alone here in any event."

"Don't you trust me, ma'am?" Anne said.

Julia glared at her again. "It would be most improper. No, Giles. As much as I would like Beth to have a season, it won't do. We will not go to Brighton."

"Do you know, I think I would like to go," Anne said. "I really wouldn't want to stay here alone, and it would be nice for Giles to have someone in his family see him receive his decoration."

Giles bowed slightly. "I agree. Well, Mother?"

Julia looked from one to the other, and then rose, tossing her embroidery down on the sofa. "You are the head of the family, Giles. If you say we are going, how can I argue? You'll have your time at Brighton," she said, looking at Anne, and stomped out of the room.

"Oh, dear." Beth rose. "She's upset. I must go to her."

"She's angry." Anne sounded amused. "When was the last time she didn't get her own way?"

"Oh, Anne, that's unfair! She wants only what is right for us."

"Mm-hm."

"I believe she does," Giles said. "It is true, though, she hasn't left Tremont in years, and perhaps she's forgotten what life outside is like. This will do her good." He smiled at Anne. "Thanks to you, though I don't know how you did it."

Anne grimaced. "Hoist with my own petard."

"Anne! Do you mean you really don't want to go to Brighton?" Beth said.

"Not particularly, no." She looked up to see Giles

watching her, a thoughtful expression in his eyes. "It won't be easy."

"No," he said slowly, "but it may well be time."

Anne didn't answer right away. "Perhaps it is."

"For what?" Beth asked.

Anne shook her head. "Nothing."

"Giles." Beth's voice was hesitant. "Do I really have to go?"

"It won't be so bad, Bethie. In fact, I think you'll enjoy it."

"If you say so." Beth rose. "I think I'd best go to Mama. She seemed terribly upset."

"I think that's a good idea, Beth." She turned. "I'm willing to wager you'll be the hit of Brighton this year."

Beth's face lit up in her rare, sweet smile. "Thank you, Giles," she said, and went out.

Giles smiled after her, and then went back to stand at the mantel again, quite as if he'd forgotten he wasn't alone. "You humbug," Anne said, sounding amused.

Giles looked up. "I beg your pardon?"

"All that talk about your duty. It's all a facade, isn't it? You asked Beth to go because you want her to be happy."

"That is part of my duty, ma'am."

"Mm-hm."

"And if we're speaking of humbugs, when did you change your mind about Brighton?"

"Oh, I think it will be great fun," she said airily. "If you'll excuse me, I think I'll check on Jamie. I promised to see him at teatime."

"Anne." He laid his hand on her arm, and she stopped. "I know why you decided to go, and I'm grateful to you. But if things get too difficult for you in Brighton, we won't stay."

"Thank you, Giles." The warmth of his hand on her was doing strange things, spreading, expanding, so that she seemed to feel it in her entire body. She didn't understand it. She cared nothing for him anymore, nothing. Besides, she was well beyond the point of being so affected by a simple touch. It must be his unaccustomed sympathy, and his utter sincerity. For all she teased him about his duty, she could lean on him if she had to, could rely on him. He would be solid and strong, like a rock. If she had to lean on him. She intended never to be so helpless again. "I do think you're a humbug," she said, and swished out of the room.

Behind her Giles smiled again, wondering if she were aware of the sway of her hips when she walked, or if it were a natural, unconscious movement. A humbug, was he? Perhaps. Brighton would not be the escape for him he had planned, and that he was sorry for; somehow, Anne had made him do things he'd never intended, without even seeming to try. It had felt good, though, to see Beth smile as she had, for the first time in what seemed like years. Maybe it wouldn't be so bad as he feared in Brighton. Maybe.

Chapter 5

When the Duke of Tremont wanted something done, it was done. An agent in Brighton found a house for them, on the Steyne, near the Marine Pavilion, a most fashionable address. The furniture was put in holland covers, trunks were packed, and the family was bundled into carriages. Tremont Castle was left behind; Brighton was ahead.

Anne looked out the carriage window, her feelings decidedly mixed. Her life had changed so, and would change even more once they reached Brighton. Though she was a widow, with more freedom than she had ever had as a debutante, she well remembered what life in society was like, and how hemmed in by rules one could be. It had never bothered her before, but then, she wasn't used to being told what to do by an arrogant, overbearing male. She was used to being in control of her life. That was the problem, of course. In returning to England, she had let that control slip away, had put it into someone else's hands, and she didn't like it one bit. Never again did she want to be subservient to any man.

The cavalcade of carriages and horses stopped at a toll house, and she shifted position. Jamie was heavy on her lap, and, after nearly two days on the road, everyone was tired. She was relieved when the carriage

55

started again, cresting a hill and then starting down again. The light had a peculiar lucidity she remembered well, and the air smelled of salt. The sea must be near. From somewhere, a bell began to peal, as if heralding their arrival, and the occupants of the carriages perked up. They had reached Brighton.

"Look, Mama!" Jamie piped up. "Look at that funny-looking man!"

"Good heavens!" Anne craned her head to see as their carriage passed a gig painted entirely in shades of green. That wasn't what was so odd about it, however. Driving the phaeton was a man who also was entirely green: green clothing, green shoes, even green hair and whiskers. Even his dog, riding beside him, had not been spared; its fur was also tinged green. "I've never seen anything like it."

"I've read of him." Beth leaned forward, her shyness forgotten in the excitement of the moment. "They call him the Green Man. They say he always dresses only in green and eats only green food."

"How odd." Anne leaned back, one arm around Jamie as he continued to stare out the window. "I begin to think Brighton might be tolerably amusing, after all."

"I do not approve of the Prince of Wales's set, even if he is our sovereign's son," Julia declared. "They are, by and large, loose people. I fear, Elizabeth, that we may not find our usual moral standard here. I do hope, however, that you will not allow yourself to be led into bad company."

"But, Mama, a green man!" Beth said, forgetting her usual awe of her mother. "Think of what people at home will say."

"They'll be green with envy," Anne said, and Beth giggled, earning them both censorious looks from the duchess.

"I, for one, do not intend to countenance loose behavior," she said.

56

"What's loose behavior, Mama?" Jamie asked, turning.

"Misbehaving, pet."

"Oh." His eyes were wide and innocent. "Like the time when I was little and ran out after my bath to greet Papa, and he said I was misbehaving because I didn't have clothes on?"

"The child is pert," Julia said, while Anne pressed her lips together to stifle her laughter.

"Yes, lovey," she said, her voice strangled, and Jamie, knowing he'd said something of interest, but not exactly sure what it was, looked from one to the other. "Something like that."

"I won't do that again, Mommy. I promise."

Anne pulled him close and planted a kiss on his head. "I know you won't, lovey."

"Lovey's a girl's word," he said, squirming away.

"Hmph." Julia's face was cold. For most of the trip, Jamie had traveled in a separate carriage with Nurse, but, at the last posting stop, Anne had decided to bring him in with her. Julia had made her thoughts on traveling with a child quite clear. "I should hope not. The boy is ill-behaved."

"Oh, for heaven's sake, ma'am, he's only a child."

"The very reason why he requires discipline. I shall speak to Giles about this."

"Oh, heavens," Anne muttered.

"Am I in trouble, Mommy?"

"No, lovey." *But I am.* Life in Brighton would apparently be as restrictive as at Tremont if the duchess had her way.

It was a relief to everyone when the carriage finally came to a halt on a wide, bustling street, with buildings set closely together and wooden railings setting off the brick sidewalk from the street. Anne eyed their house with approval. Columns of stone, very white against the brick of the building, and bow windows gave it a graceful air, and the wrought-iron railings were

57

delicately turned. Smiling, she turned back to the carriage to assist Jamie, and then stopped, her breath catching in her throat. There it was, the sea, beyond the road and just past a stretch of grass that appeared to be at the top of a cliff. It wasn't aquamarine, as in Jamaica, but blue-gray, reflecting the sullen sky above. As she watched, though, a ray of the sun broke through the clouds that had hovered all day, sparkling on the waves with an almost unbearable beauty. Anne's spirits lifted. Her home was not here. Her home was across that sea, thank heavens, away from the duchess. Away from Giles.

"Giles might have taken a house farther from the shore," Julia grumbled, distracting Anne from the odd little spurt of pain her thoughts had caused her. "One only dreads to think what one's rheumatism will be like! But then, one mustn't complain." Glancing at the sea, Julia shuddered and turned away. "Come, Elizabeth. Assist me inside."

Jamie, taking advantage of the adults' distraction, had wandered away, and Anne went in pursuit of him. She had just given him back into Nurse's care and was about to go into the house herself, when Obadiah approached her. "Lady," he said.

"Yes, Diah? Isn't it grand, to near the sea again?"

"I don't like this house, lady."

Anne began to reply, and then stopped at the look on his face. He was serious. "Goodness, whyever not?"

"Remember my prophecy, lady."

"What prophecy?" Anne wrinkled her brow. "Oh, on the ship. But that was in jest." She smiled. "We've had the dragon, as you pointed out. What is here, Diah? Knights or ghosts?"

"It is not wise to laugh at haunts, lady."

"Obadiah," she chided, lightly touching his arm. "This is a new house. If the castle isn't haunted, why should this be?"

"I don't like it, lady," he repeated.

"I don't know what we can do about it now, Diah, but if it turns out you are right, we will call upon you to exorcise the ghost."

Obadiah's look was reproachful. "Don't laugh at the spirits, lady. Never know what they might do."

"I think in this instance we'll be fine. This is England, Obadiah, after all."

"Yes, lady." His expression still troubled, Obadiah inclined his head and then turned away, to assist in carrying the luggage into the house.

At that moment Giles came around the corner of the house, presumably from the stables. Anne glanced at him and caught her breath, struck by his appearance in spite of her preoccupation. His hair, without his hat, was tousled; his riding coat of forest-green superfine, cut for comfort rather than style, nevertheless fitted perfectly across his broad shoulders; and the buckskin riding breeches molded themselves to his legs. Swallowing hard, she looked away. This was not the aloof, arrogant Duke of Tremont; this was, instead, Giles, the man she had once known. He was far more approachable in his riding clothes than in more formal wear, and as devastatingly attractive. That he was older mattered not. Older, more reliable, more steady. Qualities most women would want in a man. She wished, though, that his eyes would light up, as once they had.

Giles stopped beside her and touched his finger between her eyes, making her draw back in surprise. "What?" she said.

"You're frowning." He smiled a bit as he took her arm. "Is there something wrong?"

"No. Oh, no. I suppose I am a trifle fatigued after the journey."

"You? Are you turning into a proper lady then, Anne?"

She laughed. "Of course not. But there is something, Giles, we haven't discussed," she said, as he escorted her up the stairs and into the house. "Oh. Isn't this lovely."

59

Giles glanced perfunctorily at the wide hall, tiled in black and white marble. A gracefully curved staircase floated upward, while a small, but exquisite crystal chandelier sparkled in the sunlight, scattering rainbows on the cream plaster walls and the molded ceiling. "Yes. What is troubling you?"

"What? Oh. Have you had a chance to speak with Obadiah?"

"With all that's been happening? Hardly. Thank you." The last to Benson, who took Giles's hat. "My life has been rather topsy-turvy recently."

Anne gathered her skirts as she prepared to ascend to the next floor, and the drawing room. "For which you blame me, I gather."

"You and Prinny."

That surprised a laugh from her, and she turned on the stairs to answer. Her eyes caught his, and the words died, unsaid. Giles returned her gaze, his lips slightly parted. Something crackled between them, something almost tangible, and then Benson stepped forward.

"Ahem. Your Grace," he said, breaking the spell. Anne drew in what felt like her first full breath in hours, so stunned was she by what had happened. But what had happened? Preoccupied, frowning a bit, she turned and made her way upstairs, hardly aware of Giles or Benson. A moment of shared humor, and a glance. Nothing more. That, and an attraction so potent she could still feel it as a palpable thing, making her skin tingle with awareness. Never before had she felt like this. Never.

"Your Grace," Benson said again, and this time, Giles turned. Good God, what had just happened? Anne was lovely, surely, and he was no more immune than any other man to a beautiful woman, but this was something beyond his experience. It was an attraction such as he had never felt. His nerve endings still sizzled with the fire of it, so that nothing else mattered. Never before had he felt like this. Never.

Without a word to Benson, Giles turned on his heel and stalked off to the book-room, which he had already decided would be his study. No. He wasn't going to let it happen again. He had been hurt once, and he had learned his lesson. This time in Brighton was an interlude, a break from the realities of life. When summer was over and James's future had been settled, Anne would return to Jamaica. That was beyond doubt. In the meantime, Giles had no intention of letting himself fall into a romance with her. It would only be a summer folly.

By evening it had begun to rain, exacerbating nerves already strained by two long days of traveling. Anne, sitting in the drawing room after dinner, looked at the morose faces of her companions and rose. She had had quite enough of the Tremonts for one day. Doubtless things would look better in the morning.

Carrying her candle, she went upstairs. Because this house was much smaller than Tremont Castle, there was no nursery suite. At Anne's insistence Jamie had been placed in the room next to hers, something which Julia no doubt disapproved, but which Anne found comforting. She had hated having Jamie so far away from her at Tremont.

Quietly she eased open the door of Jamie's room and tiptoed in, instinctively listening for the sound of his breathing. She needn't have been so quiet; he was sitting up in bed, his hair tousled and his eyes wide and solemn. Anne's heart sank. She didn't have the energy to deal with a fractious child tonight.

"Can't you sleep, Jamie?" she whispered, crossing the room to him.

"There's a monster under my bed, Mommy."

"Oh, there is, is there?" Anne set down her candle and knelt down, peering under the bed. "All I see are dust kittens. The maids aren't very thorough." She rose, dusting her hands together. "Do you remember the charm Obadiah taught you? 'Monster, monster, go away, I'll play with you another day?'"

"I don't think it works on English monsters, Mommy. When I said it, he laughed."

Anne paused in the act of tucking him into bed. "I don't think I've ever heard of a monster laughing before."

"He did, Mommy. Then he sang, and he left."

A chill briefly skittered down Anne's spine. Jamie's monster was acting out of character but, with all the changes in Jamie's life lately, perhaps that wasn't surprising. "Try to go to sleep, lovey," she said, stroking his curls. "If he comes back, I'm right next door. All you have to do is call."

Jamie yawned. "And you'll come?"

"I'll come. Word of a Templeton." She smiled down at him as his eyelids drooped closed. Thank heavens, he was going to sleep at last. She'd feared that the long day might have overtired him, making him restless, but the resilience of youth had won out. Kissing him lightly on the forehead, she rose. After what had happened today between her and Giles, likely she'd be the one tossing and turning all night.

By morning the storm had blown itself out, and the family awoke to a glorious summer day. Anne sang as she dressed, irrationally happy. That there was an attraction between her and Giles was probably only to be expected; probably it would always be there. Acting on it was another matter altogether. This morning there seemed no reason why she couldn't enjoy the attentions of a handsome man, especially since there would never be more between them. When summer ended, she and Jamie would go home.

"This is the most amazing house," she said, sitting down to breakfast with the others. "Jamie was up early and he and I went exploring. Did you know it has a heating system, with a furnace in the cellar? That's why there are grates in the floor."

Giles, crumbling a piece of toast, smiled. "Yes, I did, and I'm glad it's summer so we don't have to use it. I don't trust it."

"You don't trust anything new." For answer Giles only smiled, and she went on. "The kitchen is marvelous, with a new stove, and there's even running water."

"Hmph." Julia set down her teacup. "Why should we care about such things? Let the servants deal with them."

"Well, they make our lives more pleasant, too. And have you noticed the furniture? The piano in the music room is inlay work, and the tables in the drawing room are solid mahogany. It's all lovely."

"Must you burble on so early in the morning?" Julia grumbled.

"My apologies, ma'am," Anne said, her voice suspiciously meek. Even for her, the duchess was grumpy today. "I was wondering, though, why we were able to lease such a marvelous house so late in the year. I would think someone else would have had it."

"Someone did." Giles touched his lips with a napkin. "The family who had it left because of illness, and so it became available at just the right time."

Anne cast an approving eye around the breakfast room, flooded with sun. "We were lucky."

"Indeed we were."

"Your Grace." Benson appeared in the doorway. "There are visitors, sir."

"So early in the morning? Who the devil is it, Benson?"

"Lord and Lady Whitehead, sir, and Miss Whitehead."

"Felicity!" Beth exclaimed. "Oh, 'twill be so nice to see her again!"

Giles nodded. "Show them into the drawing room, Benson."

"I already have, Your Grace," Benson said, and, bowing, left the room.

"Benson is getting pert," Anne murmured.

"You'll like the Whiteheads," Giles said, ignoring Anne's levity as he rose. "Whitehead is rather dull, but Felicity makes up for it."

"And it's nice to know someone here," Beth chatted, more animated than Anne had ever seen her, as they left the breakfast room. "Oh, I'm so glad we came."

Anne smiled, politely. She vaguely remembered Lord Whitehead, though she hadn't the slightest idea who his wife could be. For the first time, she was about to meet someone who might remember her from the past. Was she also about to be snubbed?

"Felicity. This is a surprise," Giles said, smiling, as they walked into the drawing room. "Isn't this early in the morning for you?"

"Giles, my dear boy." Felicity held out her hand and raised her cheek for his kiss. "But this is the fashionable time in Brighton, or did you not know? At least you decided to come." She gave Anne a quick smile, and Anne's fears melted, at least for the moment.

"It was in the nature of a royal command." Giles sat across from her, smiling, and looked at the girl sitting next to her on the sofa. "Never tell me this is little Susan."

"She made her come-out this past spring, Giles. As you would know if you'd come to any of my parties. She took quite well." Susan, conventionally pretty and as sweet and placid as her mother, preened at this. "We've had several offers for her, but Whitehead declined them. None to your liking, were they, puss?" She smiled at her daughter. "We'll not force her to marry someone uncongenial."

"You'd want to arrange a suitable match, of course," Julia said. "It is exactly what I would do for my children."

"Are you here for the summer, Felicity?" Giles asked.

"Yes, we've taken a house on the Marine Parade. I must say, I was surprised when I heard you'd leased this one."

"We were glad it came available when it did. Felicity, Whitehead, I trust you remember Mrs. Templeton."

Felicity smiled warmly at Anne. "Of course. You are Viscount Pendleton's daughter, are you not? What an exciting life you've led, traveling so far away. I don't know if I could bear to leave home."

"It is a pleasure to see you again, ma'am." Anne smiled. She did remember Lady Whitehead, who was older than she and had belonged to a different set when Anne had made her come-out. A set, Anne thought ruefully, that she had disdained as being hopelessly slow and dull. It was disconcerting now to meet the other woman's kind smile and unexpectedly shrewd eyes.

"I imagine you miss your home," Felicity went on, causing Anne to look at her in some surprise. "Does society seem strange to you? I know it did to me when I returned to London. I stayed away for a few years, you know, to raise my children."

"No, did you?" A slow smile spread across Anne's face. Try though she might to find other motives, she could see only friendliness in the other woman's words. "I haven't gone out in society yet, but I do remember what it is like."

"I daresay you do. Of course, there is all that business that happened between you and Giles, and you do know how people adore a scandal. But I am persuaded that once you get past that, you will be all right."

For a moment, there was blank silence. "Felicity believes in plain speaking," Giles said after a moment, making Anne smile at the understatement.

"Why, yes, I do believe it is the only way to go on. Now do you not worry about gossip." Felicity reached over and laid her hand on Anne's. "There'll be something else soon enough for the scandalmongers to talk about. Prinny himself causes enough talk for everybody. When you see the Pavilion—Giles, you've been there, haven't you?"

Giles, one arm propped up on the mantel, smiled. "I've never had that honor, Felicity."

"Said so nicely in that ironic voice. Anyone less like Prinny I cannot imagine."

"That is what I said, too," Anne said. "I've a hard time imagining them together. Is the Pavilion really so bad?"

"Oh, no, but it is different. Quite exotic, and of course so warm. Prinny keeps the fires going all the time. I fear he does feel the cold, poor man, and Brighton's air is so bracing. But people like him here, which is more than you can say for Londoners. Of course Mrs. Fitzherbert is no longer here."

"I'd heard she was out of favor," Anne said, striving for a detachment she did not really feel. The Prince of Wales's marriage to Mrs. Fitzherbert had long been a topic of discussion and argument; he had married her when he was young, in a ceremony sanctioned by the Catholic church, but not by the king or government. His second, legal marriage to Caroline of Brunswick had stirred a great deal of sympathy for Mrs. Fitzherbert. "Is she still received?"

"My dear, of course. She decided to break with him, you know, and not the other way around, and she's left Brighton, I hope not for long. She is well-liked here. They call her the Queen of Brighton. That is why I think this was a wise choice for you to make your return into society."

Anne's smile was wry. "It wasn't exactly my choice, ma'am."

"Oh, I know. I've heard about Giles's service to Prinny." The look she sent him was decidedly impish and made her look like a young girl. "Currying favor, Giles?"

"No such thing," he protested.

"The Templetons have always served their country," Julia said, and for a moment there was silence.

"Of course, Your Grace," Felicity said, finally, her tone sober, but the look she sent Anne and Giles was brimming with mirth and complicity. Anne had to look away, lest she burst into giggles. "I do hope your rheumatism is well."

"Tolerable, tolerable. It was a long journey here. But I shan't complain."

"No, of course not," Anne murmured.

"And I must admit that this house is quite tolerable. Not at all like Tremont, of course, but it's well enough."

"I think it is an attractive house, and quite new, you know. That is what makes the rumors so puzzling."

"Excuse me?" Giles said.

"I don't believe them, of course, but it does make you wonder. I don't know why the Fergusons would give up such a delightful location, with five daughters to marry off."

"I understand there was illness in the family."

"So they said, but—" Felicity looked around the room. "You really don't know?"

"What?"

"Why, that the house is said to be haunted, of course."

Chapter 6

Anne broke the startled silence by laughing. "Oh, surely not, ma'am! How could such an attractive house be haunted?"

"I don't know if I credit the rumors myself," Felicity confided. "But there must be some reason why the Fergusons left so quickly. Yes, I know they claimed illness, but I have it on the very best authority that the only thing wrong with Mrs. Ferguson is that her daughters are irredeemably plain."

Giles and Anne exchanged a quick glance of shared amusement. "I know you enjoy a good story, Felicity, but this is a bit much, don't you think?" Giles said.

"'Tis no story. Oh, I know you're thinking me the most awful gossip, but one does hear things, you know. Not that anything very wrong has happened. Except for some strange moaning sounds that supposedly sound like singing."

A chill shivered down Anne's spine. "Oh."

Giles looked at her. "What?"

"Nothing. Except Jamie—my son—is at the age where he imagines there are monsters under his bed, and last night he said his monster sang."

There was a brief silence. "Nonsense," Julia proclaimed. "You cosset the boy too much. It does not do to cater to such fancies."

Giles smiled. "Then what about Charlie, Mother?"

"Oh, nonsense."

"Who is Charlie?" Anne asked, intrigued both by Giles's smile and Julia's rare discomfiture.

"Charlie was a friend I pretended I had when I was Jamie's age," Giles said. "We'd all have tea in the nursery, wouldn't we, Mother?"

"Oh, and there was Nancy," Beth chimed in. "I haven't thought of her for years. Remember, Mama, you made her a rag doll?"

"I never did such a thing," Julia fumed. "Felicity, you were never a light-minded miss. I am shocked to hear you spreading such tales."

"My apologies, ma'am." Felicity's head was lowered, but her eyes gleamed. "I think, though, that it does you great credit as a mother."

"Jamie's imaginary playmate stayed in Jamaica," Anne said, moved by some unfathomable impulse to draw attention away from Julia. Poor woman, she looked so uncomfortable that Anne actually felt pity for her. "That still surprises me."

"But he said the monster sang?" Felicity said.

"I wouldn't refine on that overmuch. Jamie has an excellent imagination."

"Still . . ."

"The house is not haunted," Giles said. "We were merely fortunate that it came available when it did."

"Of course." Felicity rose. "We really must be going. Will you be at the ball at the Old Ship on Wednesday?"

Giles rose, too. "I doubt it. We haven't settled in."

"Oh, you should, Giles. You'll be vastly popular. You're a great prize, you know."

"I? A prize?" Giles said, startled.

"Of course. Did you not know? Young, unmarried, titled, and rich. And no one knows anything about you, because you keep to yourself. Of course you're a prize. I suspect you'll be besieged by ladies when you do appear." She twinkled at Anne. "Hold onto him, my dear."

Giles and Anne spoke at once. "I'm not—"

"We're not—"

"We will not be going Wednesday," Julia said firmly. "We haven't the appropriate clothes."

"That's easily remedied," Felicity said. "Come shopping with us."

"Oh, yes," Susan spoke up. "Please do come."

"I'd like that," Anne said. "I need so much. If you don't mind, Lady Whitehead, I think I will come along."

"Of course I don't mind. And do call me Felicity. Beth, you'll come, won't you?"

Beth glanced quickly at Julia, and nodded. "Yes, if Mama doesn't need me."

"I'll be here," Giles said, surprising all of them. "Why do I not have our carriage brought round, and the ladies can all go together?"

"A splendid idea," Felicity approved. "Whitehead is going to his club, and so he can use our carriage."

"Good. Then it is settled." Anne smiled. "If you'll excuse me, I'll just get my wrap."

"Oh, and I, too." Beth followed Anne up the stairs. "I do like Felicity," she said. "I would so have liked to have her for a sister."

Anne turned from the landing, to see, in some surprise, that Giles was behind them. "Why? Were she and Giles sweethearts at one time?"

"Oh, no. She was close to our brother Edward, though, when they were young."

"I didn't know," Anne said, her eyes going to Giles's. His shoulders had stiffened in the way they usually did when his long-dead brother was mentioned.

"Oh, yes, and it was hard on her, wasn't it, Giles?" Beth went on, heedless. "But she does seem happy with Whitehead."

"Lord knows why," Giles said. There was no trace of

distress in his face. "He's one of the dullest people I know."

"Opposites attract, perhaps," Anne said. "She seems very nice."

"She is. But don't be fooled by her. She's as sharp as they come. She'll be a good ally for you."

"I suspect I'll need one. Is there something you require, Tremont?"

"I wish you'd use my name," he said irritably. "Yes, I'd like you to make certain that Beth has everything she needs."

"Giles," Beth protested.

"Of course I will." Anne's eyes sparkled. "Will you be visiting your tailor, too? After all, you are a catch."

"Oh, stubble it," he muttered.

"Giles," Anne reproved. "Such language."

"You'll hear worse if you continue in this way."

"Then I think we had best go, don't you, Beth?"

"Oh, yes." Beth looked from one to the other, her eyes shining. "But it is so good to hear you teasing each other again."

Giles and Anne avoided looking at each other. "I have work to do," he said stiffly, and turned back down the stairs.

Jamie ran into the front hall as Anne, pulling on her gloves, reached the bottom of the stairs. "May I come, Mommy?"

Anne smiled. "No, Jamie. I'm going shopping, and you'd hate it."

"I don't care. I want to go."

"But you can't." Anne's voice was firm. "Stay here with Nurse, and this afternoon you and I will go out. All right?"

"No! I want to go now!"

"James Robert Templeton, you will not use that tone of voice to me."

Jamie looked up at her, his lower lip thrust out mutinously, and then lowered his head. "No, Mama."

71

"What do you say?"

"I'm sorry, Mama."

"I know you are." She reached out and rumpled his curls, and he pulled away, making her sigh. Her little boy was growing up. "Find something to do, Jamie, and the time will pass. I promise."

"Yes, Mama. Mama!" He launched himself at her as she turned away, throwing his arms around her knees.

Anne swayed a moment, and then regained her balance. "Jamie."

"Don't go, Mama," he said, his voice trembling, and she went down on her knees, uncaring of her gown. "Don't go."

"It's all right, lovey." She rocked him back and forth as he clutched her about the neck. "I'm just going to get new clothes."

"Will you come back?"

"Oh, Jamie. Of course I will." She pulled back, smiling. "I'd never leave you. You're my little man."

"Mama, I don't like it here."

"I know, lovey, but this is how things are right now. We'll be all right. Everything will be fine."

"Word of a Templeton?"

"Word of a Templeton." Anne got to her feet. "Be a good boy, Jamie," she said, and turned away, before she disgraced herself before him by breaking down.

Felicity smiled at Anne as she climbed into the carriage. "Your son is a handsome boy," she said diplomatically. "How old is he?"

"Five." Anne sniffled. "Do excuse me. I'm usually not such a watering pot."

"Oh, but surely he knows you're coming back," Beth said.

"I don't know. He never used to cling so. It's only since Freddie died. My husband," she explained to Felicity. "You see, he was just going into Kingston on business. He planned to be back that evening. Instead, he met with an accident on the way home."

72

"I am sorry," Felicity said.

"How did it happen?" Beth asked. "Mama never did tell me."

"He was dead drunk, of course," Anne said, matter-of-factly, not looking at them. "He was a good rider, but that stretch of road is tricky at night. We found him the next morning at the bottom of the ravine, and his horse with him."

"Oh, Anne." Felicity reached over to lay her hand on Anne's.

"I'm all right. It's been hard on Jamie, though. He's never quite understood why his father never came back with the present he'd promised." She paused. "Jamie always did believe Freddie when he said he'd bring a present."

"How nice of a father to think of his son like that."

"Mm." Anne avoided Felicity's sharp glance. Certainly it would have been nice if Freddie had remembered his promises once in a while. She had grown quite adept at comforting a disappointed little boy; the little boy had come to expect broken promises. "I'm all he has, now."

"Oh, and I think you're a very good mother, no matter what Mama says."

For some reason that tickled Anne's sense of the absurd. "I think I do quite well. Now. It does no good to refine on it overmuch. Jamie has probably forgotten about us already. Let us discuss what we'll purchase for gowns."

Beth drew back into the corner of the carriage. "None, I think."

"None? Whyever not?"

"I don't plan to go into society."

"Of course you will, Beth," Felicity said, smiling. "You'll quite enjoy it, too."

Anne reached over to lay her hand on Beth's. "I know society can be frightening, but I think you'll enjoy it."

"I'm not brave like you, Anne."

"Brave! I'm not brave."

"You stayed in a strange country with no husband."

"Jamaica is my home."

"You must miss it," Felicity said.

"Oh, I do, terribly, and I think Jamie does, too. I'll be glad to go back."

"But Giles said you were staying," Beth said.

"Did he? Then he's wrong."

"Anne! You cannot mean it."

"Yes." She gave Beth a quizzical look. "Does no one ever disagree with Giles?"

"No. Only Mama."

"A shame, isn't it?" Felicity said.

"Heavens, yes. He's grown insufferably high in the instep."

"Anne!" Beth looked shocked, but a little laugh betrayed her. "He's my brother."

"He's a man." Anne managed to make it sound like an epithet. "At the best of times, men can be obtuse."

"I wouldn't know," Beth murmured, looking down at her hands, and Anne sent her another glance. Had Beth never had any suitors, then? "I thought you almost married Giles."

Anne's breath caught in her throat. "Good heavens, that was long ago."

"Yes, but—"

"'Tis past, Beth."

"People will still remember, Anne," Felicity said quietly, and Anne looked at her. There was only friendliness in her eyes. No censure, no condemnation.

"I'll worry about that when I face it. Is this the shop?" she asked as the carriage came to a stop.

Felicity glanced out the window. "Yes, this is Celanie's. You'll like her," she said to Anne as they stepped out. "She's quite as expensive as the best London modistes."

Anne smiled, looking at the small, bow-fronted shop

with approval. The street was narrow, and old. Nearby were other shops, an apothecary, a linen draper's, a grocer's. "Then she must be good. I haven't been in a shop like this since my season."

"I never have," Beth confided softly.

"Then it's high time." Anne stepped back, studying her. Beth was actually quite pretty, or she would be, if she were dressed properly. Thank heavens the style was still for simplicity, which would flatter Beth's petite figure. The proper coiffure would work wonders, too, instead of those dreary caps Beth insisted on wearing upon her soft brown curls. This was going to be fun. "Shall we go in?"

Inside Madame Celanie came out to greet them, with many bows and protestations at the honor done her. After chatting a moment, they settled down to the serious business of studying fashion illustrations, having their measurements taken, and choosing gowns. Anne threw caution to the wind. No widow's mourning for her, or debutante's pastels, either. The simple styles would suit her admirably, flattering her height, while the slightly fuller skirts would mimimize the roundness of her figure. She could afford more ornament, though, than she had as a young girl. Heavens, a lady of fashion needed so much: morning gowns, afternoon gowns, riding habits, and evening gowns. She chose widely, but well. A walking dress in primrose, with ruffles at the sleeves and throat. An afternoon dress in a burnt orange muslin that made her curls shine like burnished gold. Evening gowns, one with a bodice in her favorite dark pink in crepe, with a skirt of white satin; another of turquoise silk shot through with strands of green and gold which would shimmer when she moved. Even Beth, hesitant at first, grew bolder. She chose morning gowns of muslin in white or the palest pastels; afternoon frocks, one in a deeper shade of blue with a ruched neckline, and the other of a lilac muslin that made her eyes look larger and bluer; evening gowns, in delicate apricot silk and jonquil muslin. Of course Susan couldn't resist purchasing a new frock, either. By the time they left the shop, armed with swatches of fabric to match with shoes, gloves, reticules, and whatever else they might need, they were all giddy with excitement.

"Oh, my!" Beth fell back onto the seat of the carriage, fanning herself with her gloves. "I feel so wicked. I cannot believe I bought so much."

"I know." Anne smiled. "Thank heavens Freddie isn't about to scold me for my extravagance."

"Anne!"

"Well, 'tis true."

"Oh, dear. I don't dare imagine what Mama will say."

"Beth, are you happy with what you bought?"

"Oh, yes, but—"

"Then what else is there to say to the matter?"

"Oh, but you don't know what it's like when someone criticizes everything you do."

"Beth." Anne smiled. "It's your life, not hers. You need to stop listening to the criticism. I did."

Beth's gaze was quizzical. "But who criticized you?"

"Oh, here we are at the milliner's." Anne rose before the carriage had even come to a stop. "What a lovely bonnet in the window. I feel certain we'll do well here. Shall we be extravagant again?"

Beth looked at her for a moment before replying. "Oh, yes," she said, and followed Anne out of the carriage.

By the time they were done in late afternoon, they had visited not only the milliner, but the mantua maker and the glover and the shoemaker. Finally, satisfyingly tired, they decided they had bought enough for one day and turned toward home, Anne clutching at the paper-wrapped parcel that held her favorite purchase of the day. It was a parasol, the exact shade of primrose as her walking dress, so frilly and lacy it made her feel deliciously feminine. It had been a long time since she had worn something that made her feel pretty.

As they came out of the last shop, a landau carrying two fashionably dressed women, one of indeterminate age, the other closer to Anne's age, drew near. Parasols raised to ward off the sun, they glanced at Anne and her companions. "My heavens!" Anne said. "Is that Letitia Starling in that landau, with her mother? Why, I haven't seen her in years!"

"She is Lady Buckram now," Felicity said. "Anne—"

"So she finally brought the earl up to scratch? I'd love to speak with her. Letitia was one of my dearest friends when I made my come-out."

"Anne, I'm not sure that's wise—"

"Why not?" Anne raised her hand and smiled. Inside the landau Mrs. Starling made a gesture. The bewigged coachman slowed, ever so slightly, and the two women smiled and nodded at Felicity. Then, facing forward, they drove away, leaving Anne to stare after them in shock. Good heavens! They had snubbed her.

"Well!" Felicity said, in ringing tones that broke Anne out of her shock. "I never did like Beatrice Starling, but this is the outside of enough!"

"Felicity." Anne smiled a little and touched her arm. "It doesn't matter."

"Matter? No, of course not, rude, ill-bred people like that don't matter a jot."

"Felicity!" Anne said, scandalized and delighted at once. "They'll hear you."

"I should hope so. Of all the nerve."

"I should have expected it." Anne stepped into the carriage. "I've been warned. Still." Her voice was wistful. "Letitia and I were once friends."

"Well, you have new friends now," Felicity said.

"Thank you, Felicity." Anne flashed her a smile. "That means much to me." It was a difficult world she'd returned to, she reflected, as the carriage drove off. If even people she'd once counted as friends cut her, what would those who hadn't liked her be like? It didn't bear thinking about.

They stopped at the Whiteheads' house, to leave Felicity and Susan off, and then headed toward home. Anne's spirits picked up. There was what really mattered to her, her son. The misgivings she had felt intermittently throughout the day, about leaving Jamie while she shopped, at last faded. Most likely he hadn't missed her as much as she had missed him. She only hoped he hadn't got himself into mischief.

Benson bowed as he opened the door for them. "His Grace would like to see you, ma'am," he said.

"Me?" Beth said in a quaking voice.

"I believe he means me, Beth," Anne said smiling resolutely. It needed only this. "Has Jamie been up to some mischief. Benson?"

"That's not for me to say, ma'am. Although I do believe the punishment His Grace administered was fair."

Anne stared at him and then bolted down the hall. The nerve of him! No one had the right to discipline her son but herself. No one had the right to lay a hand on him. No one.

"How dare you!" she exclaimed, flinging the door of the book-room open.

Giles, sitting at his desk, rose with alacrity. "Anne?"

"How dare you lay a hand on my son!"

"Sit down," Giles said, so firmly, that, to her own surprise, she did just that. "Now what is this all about?"

"You punished my son." Her hands clutched at the arms of the chair, her knuckles white. "What right had you—"

"Every right. Do you know what he did?"

"I know my son. He's a good boy and he does what I tell him."

"Oh, yes." Giles's tone was ironic. "You told him to find something to do."

"Yes." Anne eyed him. "What did he do?"

78

"He went exploring, up into the attics. He decided to see what was in the trunks, and got closed up in one of them."

"Dear God." Anne's hand flew to her mouth. "I should have been here. Is he all right?"

"He is fine. Fortunately for James there was a maid nearby, and she heard him. She thought he was our ghost."

"But he's not hurt?"

"No, other than a sore bottom."

Anne jumped to her feet. "You hit him!"

"I spanked him, yes," he said calmly. "I think even you would agree it was called for."

"I do not hit my son."

"Perhaps that's why he screamed so. He doesn't take his punishment like a man."

"Because he is only a little boy," she said through gritted teeth.

"It is high time he started growing up. I faced worse punishments as a boy."

"And that makes it right?"

"Anne, James is not hurt. Afterward he said he was sorry, and we had a talk. If you don't believe me, go and see for yourself."

"Oh, I shall. But you and I will have a talk about this. You had no right to do what you did."

"May I remind you, I am his guardian."

"It still doesn't give you the right to beat him."

"I do not beat children! Oh, for God's sake." He rose. "Go see to him. You'll see he's fine."

"He had better be." Anne stopped at the door, staring at him coldly. "Because if he is not, we are going home, no matter what you say." With that, she swept out, slamming the door behind her.

"Oh, Mrs. Templeton." Nurse jumped to her feet as Anne came into Jamie's room. "I'm that sorry about what happened."

"Is Jamie all right?"

"Yes, ma'am. More scared than anything, I'd say. He's asleep, poor lamb."

"Nurse, I do not want that man coming near Jamie again. He had no right to do what he did."

"Well, ma'am, Jamie did do wrong. And it was only one spank. His Grace stopped as soon as he saw how frightened Jamie was."

"He did?"

"Yes, ma'am. And then he talked with Jamie. Really, he was very good, ma'am. He's good with children."

"Thank you, Nurse." Anne took her elbow and guided her to the door. "Why don't you go to your room for a rest? I'll see to Jamie."

Jamie was sprawled on his stomach on his bed, fast asleep, his mouth slightly open and his curls tousled. Nowhere on his flushed cheeks could she see even a trace of tears. Just one spank? That wasn't so bad as she'd feared, and perhaps, as much as she hated physical punishment, Jamie had deserved it. He was an active, mischievous boy. "How is it you look like such an angel now?" she whispered, straightening the tangled covers about him, and then laid her hand on his hair, feeling chilled. "Jamie, you didn't tell him anything about Papa, did you?" Jamie muttered something in his sleep, making her smile. "Never mind, lovey. I'll deal with it."

Smoothing his curls once more, she turned away and began to cross the room to close the drapes. She hadn't got halfway across when she stumbled. What in the world? She looked down, and stifled a laugh. Scattered across the floor were toy soldiers, battalions of them, some in formation, some apparently felled by the enemy. They were finely crafted and detailed, and obviously old. Giles's toy soldiers, the ones he had said were too valuable to be used as toys, telling their own tale of the afternoon's events.

"A firm hand, indeed," she murmured, smiling, and tiptoed out of the room.

*   *   *

"Good morning." Anne sat on the chair the footman held out for her in the breakfast room, and smiled with some surprise across the table at the duchess. Beth wasn't there, nor was Giles. Likely there would be some discussion about Jamie's misbehavior. After some hard thinking and a good night's sleep, Anne had come to the conclusion that Giles was both right, and wrong. Jamie did require more discipline. However, she was perfectly capable of supplying it, no matter what Giles or his mother might think.

Julia set down her teacup. "Good morning." Her greeting was curt. "I wish to speak with you about yesterday."

"I've spoken with Jamie, ma'am." Anne's voice was cool. "I have his promise he'll behave, and I know he'll keep to it as far as he's able. He is still a little boy."

"I was not speaking of your son."

Anne looked up from her plate. "Oh?"

"You may leave us," Julia said to the footman, who bowed and then withdrew, leaving the two women quite alone.

So. This was to be a serious talk. Anne squared her shoulders. "Is there a problem, ma'am?"

"You may say so. I do not like your influence on my son and daughter." She raised an imperious hand. "Now pray do not bother to deny that coming to Brighton was your idea, because it won't fadge. I remember you well, missy, and your tricks."

"Speaking of which," Anne interrupted, "why did Giles never marry the paragon of the girl you chose for him?"

"He decided they didn't suit. But that is not to the point. I will not have you disrupting our lives again, or upsetting Giles. He's been through quite enough with you, eloping with his own cousin."

"What!"

81

"And now you're trying your wiles on Beth. Do you know that last night you were all she talked about? I finally got it out of her what you made her buy."

"She needs clothes," Anne said absently. She was still reeling from what the duchess had said. How had the events of seven years ago suddenly become her fault?

"Beth is not forward like you, missy. She doesn't know how to go on in company. I will not see her hurt."

"What are you saying?" She had forgotten this, the petty squabbling among women in society. In Jamaica she had dealt mostly with men, on estate matters. They were much easier.

"Very well. You wish plain speaking? Then it is this. Leave my daughter alone. And don't think you'll have a second chance at marrying Giles, because I will not allow it!"

Chapter 7

Anne stared at her a moment, and then let out a short choked laugh. "You think I'm angling after Giles? Good God!"

"I know you are. And pray don't use such language in my house, because I won't allow that, either."

"There's a lot you won't allow, isn't there? You won't allow Beth to leave you, you won't allow Giles to marry—"

"I do what is best for my children. If that means fighting you, then I shall. I trust I make myself clear?"

"Quite." Anne's eyes met Julia's cold gray ones squarely. "If, ma'am, and I say if, Giles should decide he wishes to marry me, I will decide on the basis of what is right for my son and myself, and no other. I trust I make myself clear?"

"You defy me then?" The duchess silently returned Anne's stare. "Very well." She rose. "I warn you, however, that I have never lost a battle where my children are concerned, and I've no intention of losing this one."

Anne rose, also. "You bested me once before, ma'am, when I was young. You may have a surprise if you try again."

"I doubt it. You're not up to my weight." And with that, Julia turned and swept out of the breakfast room, leaving Anne trembling with impotent rage. She didn't know what made her angrier, Julia's belief that Anne would lose in any battle between them, or that she still might want Giles. She had more pride, and more intelligence, than to make a dead set for a man who clearly didn't want her. If he had, he would have married her all those years ago, instead of courting someone else. And the duchess implied he'd been hurt by *her* desertion! That made her angry all over again. Julia must indeed think her a fool.

Well, she would learn. Anne sat down. The girl she had been seven years ago hadn't been able to fight the duchess, but Anne had grown since then. She had learned a great deal about dealing with people, and about getting what she wanted. If she decided she wanted Giles, she would find a way to have him. But she didn't want him, she told herself again firmly, setting her teacup down with a soft clink of porcelain against porcelain. The man she had once fancied she loved was gone, replaced by the stodgy, proper Duke of Tremont. If she thought the old Giles was still there, underneath—

Bah. She rose, tossing her napkin on the table. It did no good to think of this. Of course she had regrets about what had happened in the past; she probably always would. That did not mean, however, that she wanted to recreate that past, even if the duchess believed so. Likely nothing would change Julia's low opinion of her.

A slow smile spread across Anne's face. Who was she, after all, to deny the duchess what she wanted? If it were a fight she desired, it was a fight she would get. She would soon learn that her opponent was worthy, indeed. In the meantime, if Anne had to stay in England, she was going to enjoy herself as much as she could.

"Oh, there you are," Giles said, as Anne began to

climb the stairs to her room.

She turned to look at him. "Did you want me for something, Giles?"

"No. I was just thinking of taking a walk to see the town, and I was wondering if you would join me."

Dangerous. "You're certain you want me to?"

"Of course." Giles sounded surprised, and glanced out the sidelights of the door. "We're here. We might as well enjoy what we can."

Anne laughed. "You make it sound a most daunting prospect. Very well, let me change into something more suitable, and I'll be happy to walk with you."

She was ready in just a few minutes, feeling as giddy and excited as a young girl. With remarkable foresight Madame Celanie had sent, just that morning, the primrose walking dress Anne had ordered. With buttons and braiding down the front, and a ruffle at the throat, it was quite the most fashionable frock she had owned in a long time. A bonnet of chip straw trimmed with ribbons and silk flowers, kid gloves, and the matching parasol completed the ensemble. There, she was suitably dressed for Brighton.

Giles looked up as she descended the stairs. Really, she felt like a girl making her debut, all breathless and excited. How foolish of her. For a moment she thought she saw admiration gleam in his eyes, but, if she had, it was quickly masked. It was perhaps just as well. Had she not already decided that an involvement with Giles would only complicate her life?

Giles offered her his arm, and they stepped out. "Oh!" Anne paused at the top of the stairs, staring at the view. The sky was azure, the sea lapiz, and the air seemed to shimmer with light. "Oh, this is lovely. I do love the sea."

Giles slanted her a look as they set off down the brick sidewalk toward the sea. "Is that why you wish to return to Jamaica?"

85

"I like Jamaica for many reasons. Come, I refuse to wrangle on such a glorious day. This is a lovely area. What is it called?"

"The Steyne. A fashionable address, I'll have you know. The Marine Pavilion is farther down, closer to the shore."

"Yes, I saw it last evening when Jamie and I went for a walk." She looked up at him and twirled her parasol. "I never did learn just what the famous service you performed for the Prince was."

Giles looked uncomfortable. "Nothing so very much. Prinny is inclined to be grateful for all manner of things."

"Mm-hm. And how many people does he invite to the Pavilion?"

"More than you might think. My dear girl, I am a duke, you know."

"Oh, pardon me. I forgot I was mixing in such exalted company."

For a moment Giles seemed to forget himself, grinning at her with such carefree abandon that the years melted away. She was a young girl again, hopelessly and helplessly in love. "Why do you never take my consequence seriously?"

"Because you take it so seriously. Now, confess. What was the service you performed for Prinny?"

"Well, if you must know—"

"I must."

"Very well. I was at a levee at Carlton House when Princess Caroline came in, quite uninvited. You do know that she and Prinny haven't been on the best of terms?" Anne nodded; the dissension between the Prince and his wife was well known. "It was obvious she was going to cause a scene. I—well, I was nearest to her, and so—I asked her to dance."

Anne stared at him for a moment and then let out a delighted peal of laughter. "No, really? And for that he's invited you here?"

"It distracted her. She left soon after." He shifted from foot to foot. "Anne, people are staring at us. Must we discuss this?"

"No one is staring at us. Though there are quite a few people out, aren't there?" She smiled brilliantly at Giles. "And I imagine everyone of them knows what you did."

"Anne—"

"Oh, very well, Giles, I won't tease you about it. Though I wonder."

"What?" he asked, with obvious trepidation.

"Have you become one of Princess Caroline's favorites?"

"I begin to think that asking you back to England was a mistake."

That hurt. It shouldn't have, but it did. Anne glanced away from him, concentrating on other things. As they drew nearer to the shore, there were more people, walking, mounted upon fine horses, or riding in bright, shiny carriages. "Is this the fashionable time to promenade in Brighton?"

"Apparently."

"And it's only morning. In London this would be considered the middle of the night." She stopped as they drew level with a plain iron fence. Past a narrow strip of lawn stood a handsome, rather plain building. Palladian in design, it had a central rotunda, oval-shaped wings, and green, shell-like canopies shading the windows. Because of the lawn, in a town where most houses fronted directly on the street, she had guessed what it was. "So this is the Marine Pavilion. Do you know, Giles, I'm almost disappointed? It's not nearly as bad as I'd expected."

"No?" He grinned, and pointed. "What of the dome?"

"Well, yes, that is a little odd." The only thing exotic

87

about the Pavilion was the huge dome, vaguely Oriental in appearance, floating high in the sky behind it. What its purpose was, she could hardly guess. "What is it?"

"That, my dear, is the stables."

Anne looked up at him quickly. Was she really his dear? "The stables? Heavens!"

"They say it cost seventy thousand pounds to build."

"Heavens!"

"Quite. It's a very interesting building, I'm told. Prinny lives in a villa, but at least his horses live in a palace."

"Giles."

"He'd would have all of it look like that, if he could." He grinned at her. "Of course, you haven't seen the inside yet. I understand that that is where Prinny allowed himself free rein."

"Why? What is it like?"

"You'll see."

"I will? Oh, Giles. Am I to be invited, too?"

"If we can arrange it, yes."

"Oh, heavens. I certainly didn't expect anything like that when I left Jamaica."

A wave of homesickness suddenly swept over her, in spite of the exciting events ahead. Brighton wasn't at all like Jamaica, or even London. Instead, it was a small, compact, but bustling place; last evening, during her walk with Jamie, Anne had found that nearly everything of interest was only a few paces away. Most of it was centered on the Steyne, the main thoroughfare, which took its name from the grassy valley where once fishermen had dried their nets and was open on the east to the sea, affording a splendid view. On the other side it was quite built up. Near the Pavilion was Mrs. Fitzherbert's house, now closed up, with its balcony where once the Prince had sat with her and watched the passersby. It was popularly supposed to be connected with the Pavilion by an underground tunnel. The Duke of Marlborough had his house nearby; so did Lord Berkeley, in a mansion appropriately called the Yellow House. Castle Square, where the Castle Inn was located and where most of the stagecoaches stopped, was near to the seafront, while farther inland could be found Donaldson's Circulating Library and Raggett's, a club for gentlemen. Brighton Theatre was located on the New Road, a short street just behind the Pavilion. Beyond that, the sights grew more humble, the streets narrow and twisty, the buildings and cottages made of flint. Even here, though, the fashionable world had encroached, with shops and such, which Jamie had pronounced boring.

He had, however, enjoyed talking with Phoebe Hessell, an old lady they encountered where the Steyne met the Marine Parade. They had bought gingerbread from her basket and listened to her tales of her youth, when she had disguised herself as a man and had gone to war, to be near her sweetheart. Jamie had been less impressed by the sea, and by Brighton's famous bathing machines, wagonlike structures painted red and blue, from which it was fashionable to dip into the swells of the English Channel. Used to diving into the turquoise Caribbean, both Anne and Jamie had scorned such a timid method of bathing, and decided that England was strange indeed.

Anne let out a laugh. "What?" Giles asked.

"Last evening when Jamie and I walked to the shore, he was terribly disappointed he didn't see any whales."

Giles's glance was quizzical. "Whales? Not in the English Channel, surely?"

"But why not? After all, the Prince of Wales lives here."

"The Prince of—" Giles broke off, laughing. "Is that really what he thought?"

"Yes. Children are funny." She shook her head. "We

89

expect them to know things that of course they cannot. When I explained to Jamie that Wales was a country, he was very disappointed."

"He's not far off." Giles sounded thoughtful. "Prinny's grown as fat as a flawn. I suppose we could call him the Prince of Whales. Not the country."

"Giles!" Anne looked up at him, scandalized and delighted. "What a thing to say about your prince! The one for whom you performed such a great service."

"Er, yes. Speaking of whom, Anne, there he is."

"Heavens." Anne stared as a party of people on horseback paraded toward them. Most of the people were familiar to her; she recognized Colonel McMahon, the Prince's private secretary, and Beau Brummell, who had become an arbiter of male fashion. In the middle of the group, well dressed but otherwise undistinguished, rode the Prince of Wales.

"My dear Tremont." The Prince's voice was deep and unexpectedly melodious. Anne had seen him before, of course, but never so close. No longer was he the handsome prince of his youth; he was indeed heavy, with graying hair and the unmistakable protuberant blue eyes of the Hanovers. There was, however, something about the way he held himself, something almost majestic, that made Anne realize that he was no ordinary man. "We had heard you were here. Welcome to my humble home."

Giles bowed. "Thank you, Your Highness. May I present my cousin to you, sir? Mrs. Frederick Templeton."

Anne rose from her curtsy to see the Prince regarding her with twinkling eyes. "You are Pendleton's daughter, are you not?" he asked.

"Yes, Your Highness," Anne murmured. "It is an honor to meet you, sir."

"The pleasure is mine, believe me, ma'am. You must bring her along to the Pavilion, Tremont."

90

Giles bowed again. "Thank you, sir."

"Yes, thank you," Anne echoed. "I would be most honored, sir."

"Good." The Prince's eyes twinkled again. "Brummell reminds me we must not keep our horses standing. Enjoy your walk, Tremont. Ma'am."

"Thank you, sir." Giles bowed again and Anne curtsied, as the party rode away, kicking up a cloud of dust. "That went well, I think."

"Yes." Anne took his arm as they began to walk again, toward the sea. "He's very charming, isn't he? Not at all what I expected."

"No, he's a lot less starched-up than many in society. Some of whom," he added as a landau approached them, "I fear we're going to meet right now."

"Oh, dear." A quick glance at the landau was enough for Anne to recognize the matronly ladies riding inside, Lady Wilton and Mrs. Hammond-Smythe, both arbiters of society, both avid gossips. She remembered them well from her season; doubtless they hadn't forgotten her. Remembering the incident of the previous day, when she had been snubbed, she wanted nothing so much as to turn and flee. Only Giles's hand, tightening unexpectedly on her elbow, prevented her.

"Courage," he said, his voice low. "Good morning, Lady Wilton, Mrs. Hammond-Smythe."

Lady Wilton signaled to her coachman to stop. "Tremont. A pleasure to see you again," she said, with great condescension.

"And you, ma'am. I trust you remember my cousin, Mrs. Templeton."

This time Lady Wilton's look was decidedly frostier. "Of course. How do you do, ma'am? I was just discussing with my daughter, Tremont, as to whether you would be here. One does hear rumors."

"Of course, everyone is here this summer," Mrs. Hammond-Smythe put in. Though untitled, she was

91

even more starched-up than Lady Wilton, who was a countess. "A surprise to see you back in England, ma'am."

"Is it, ma'am?" Anne said.

"Yes. One had thought you were settled in the Indies."

"One was wrong," Anne said, smiling pleasantly.

"We mustn't keep you ladies," Giles said, stepping back and doffing his hat. "Come, Anne. I see Lord Petersham ahead. Shall we go speak to him?"

"By all means. Ladies." Anne smiled coolly. "Old cats," she added, as they turned away.

"Hush. They'll hear you," Giles said.

"I don't care. They're still old cats."

"At least they didn't cut you, Anne."

Anne stopped. "Beth told you."

"Yes." Giles gazed down at her. She didn't like what she saw in his eyes. She could not stand Giles, of all people, pitying her.

Shaking off his hand, Anne strode along. "It was because of what happened in the past, wasn't it?" she said, stopping and turning so abruptly that Giles, hurrying behind her, had to pull himself up short. "Wasn't it?"

"I'm afraid so. Anne—"

"Then why don't they snub you, too? As I recall, you were also involved."

"Who jilted whom, Anne?" he asked, his voice cool.

Anne stared up at him. There. It had been said, what had laid between them since her return. "You know quite well."

"Quite. And it isn't something I wish to go into here."

"Oh, no, of course not. People are watching, so we mustn't cause a scene." This time, when Giles took her arm, she didn't pull away. "It's been seven years, for heaven's sake," she said, more calmly. "I would think people would have forgotten by now."

92

"People don't. Have you really forgotten what society is like?"

They had reached the edge of the cliff. The tide was out, and below them the shingly beach glistened in the sun. Anne took a deep breath, letting the peacefulness of the view seep into her. "No. Oh, I suppose I had forgotten how vicious it can be, but I do remember that people hold onto scandals." She paused. "And we did cause a scandal, didn't we?"

"You did," he agreed gravely.

"What do I do, Giles? I've never had to face anything like this."

"You wish my advice?"

"I thought you were going to tell me how to go on."

That made him smile briefly. "What would you like to do?"

"What I would like to do is extremely unladylike and would only cause another scandal!" She looked up at him. "I suppose I'll just have to face it out, won't I?"

"I can't see anything else to do." He looked away. "Of course, I'll be beside you."

"You will?"

"Of course. Anne." His voice was chiding. "Do you really think I'd make you face it alone?"

"I wouldn't blame you," she said candidly.

"I wouldn't do such a thing. It would be shirking my responsibility."

"Oh. I see. Your responsibility."

"You are, after all, part of my family. I would not see you hurt."

"Mm-hm." This grew worse. She didn't want to renew their past relationship, surely she didn't, but to have Giles acting almost as a kindly uncle was infinitely worse. "Giles, don't you sometimes just want to tell them all to go to hell?"

"Anne!" he said, laughing.

"Don't you?"

"You do need me beside you, I fear." He turned, and again they began walking, on the Marine Parade, the road which ran along the cliff. "If you're alone, God knows what sort of disasters you'll cause."

"It would be fun, though. Admit it."

"Perhaps." For the first time he allowed himself to think of what had once been between them. For the first time in a long time, he let himself wonder why, after all they had meant to each other, she had suddenly married his cousin.

They walked for a few moments in silence. "You were lucky," he said abruptly.

"Why?"

"You escaped."

Anne stopped and looked up at him. "I didn't think of it that way at the time."

"Nevertheless. Do you know how I envied you and Freddie, living as you did? You had the chance to live your own lives."

"Yes, well, it wasn't always easy, and if a mere letter from you can bring me back to England, my life's not really my own, is it?"

"More than you know. You're not hemmed in by duty and responsibility."

"Never mind your duty and responsibility. You have freedoms, too, that most people don't have. Why, Giles, you could do whatever you wanted to. I know." She grasped his arm suddenly. "You must come visit us in Jamaica. I remember that you always wanted to travel. And, if you're worried about your responsibilities, you could see for yourself how the plantation is being run. Oh, the more I think of it, the better it seems! A sea voyage is just what you need."

Very gently, Giles disengaged himself from her. "I think not, Anne."

"Oh." Anne looked up at him. "Oh, Giles, I am sorry. That was tactless of me, wasn't it?"

"Yes." He drew in a deep breath. "But you meant no harm. At my age, I still shouldn't dislike the sea."

There was such vulnerability in his face that she wanted to comfort him, but she didn't dare. The Giles she had once known would have understood. This man might very well reject her. "Then we are both stuck here, aren't we?"

"Is that so bad?"

"No. It could be worse."

"So it could." He smiled down at her. "Shall we brazen it out together?"

"The scandal? Yes." Anne's eyes sparkled. "In fact, can you imagine what everyone will say when they realize we're together? We'll be the talk of the town."

"God save us," Giles groaned, but he was smiling. "Come, let us return home."

"Yes, Giles." Impulsively she laid her hand on his arm. "Thank you for standing by me."

"Why shouldn't I, Anne? After all, you're family."

"Oh, yes." Family. She mustn't forget that, she admonished herself as she fell into step beside him, the glory of the day just slightly tarnished. She was the widow of his late cousin, and that made her his responsibility, nothing more. Surely she didn't wish for more.

Quiet now, they finished their walk, occasionally receiving greetings from passing riders or carriages. In almost every case the reaction to Anne was cool. Foolish though it seemed, it appeared she was going to be punished for something she'd done long ago. Something for which she thought she'd already been punished quite enough.

"Anne." Giles spoke just as Anne was about to go up to check on Jamie, making her turn on the stairs. "About what happened, when you married Freddie—"

"It's past, Giles." Anne gripped the banister, glad she was wearing gloves so that he couldn't see how white

95

her knuckles surely were. "I bear you no ill will."

"Thank you very much." Giles sounded surprised. "Nor I, you."

"Was that all you wished to say?" she said, when he continued to look at her without speaking.

"Hm? Oh, yes. That, and that you have my assurances that neither my family nor I will ever snub you, nor prevent you from going out in society as you wish."

"How kind of you. I gather you no longer fear that I don't know how to go on?"

"Dash it, Anne, that wasn't what I meant at all."

"Oh, I know quite well what you meant. If you'll excuse me, Your Grace, I need to see to my son."

"Anne," he said, but she was already walking up the stairs, away from him. He wouldn't chase her. It wouldn't be dignified, and it would, in some subtle way, give her an advantage in the struggle between them. An undeclared struggle, true, but real, nonetheless. One day it would explode into more than just cryptic, but meaningful, statements.

Frowning, Giles turned and went to the book-room, muttering a curse to himself as the toe of his hessian boot caught in the metal grille set in the floor. Foolish contraption, this heating system, new and therefore not to be trusted. Until this morning, he'd had no other complaint about the house, or about Brighton. Now, though, things had changed. He had since seen the look of deep hurt in Anne's eyes when she'd realized how far-reaching peoples' memories were.

Giles leaned back in the comfortable leather desk chair, closing his eyes. Usually he didn't allow himself to dwell on the past, but today he could not seem to help it. After all these years, there were moments when it hurt as if it had happened just yesterday. He had loved Anne. Calf love, he knew that now, but real and intense, all the same. He never had found out why she had eloped with Freddie. Nor did he understand her simmering hostility on the matter. After all, he had been the one wronged, not her.

And he'd paid for it. Not with ostracism, but with pity, which had been infinitely worse. Society had felt sorry for him, maliciously so. It was the way of the world he lived in. Scorn, disdain, anger—all those, he could have handled, but pity merely made him furious. As had the way people had greeted Anne this morning.

Strange, that. Not that they should be cool; it was Anne's first time back in England, and society had long ago ordained that one who broke the rules must pay. No, nothing so simple. It had been the look in Anne's eyes that had touched him, the wariness at seeing old acquaintances, and then the blankness that had hidden everything. She'd assumed that look quickly, like a mask, as if she had practice at it. It did not accord with the Anne he had known. She had changed.

One thing hadn't, though. When something hurt her, as this morning's events had, it hurt him. Not a comforting thought. What in the world was he going to do?

Anne closed the door of her room behind her, briefly leaning her head against it, her eyes shut. That was over, thank heavens. It had been more of an ordeal than she had expected, and not simply because of society's reactions to her. Being with Giles had been difficult. Yes, he had been unexpectedly supportive during their morning walk, even if what had once been between them was still unresolved. And yesterday, when Felicity had spoken of their "ghost," there had been that moment of shared, silent amusement. It had seemed so easy, so natural. There had been rapport between Giles and her, and she didn't trust it for one minute. If she weren't careful, she would find herself growing attached to him again, and that would never do.

Anne looked at her reflection without pretense, her eyes clear and candid. She had made a mull of her life. She had to admit it. Marrying Freddie had been the biggest mistake of her life, even if Jamie had resulted from the union. Had she married Giles, she would probably have made a mull of that, too. She had been too young, too flighty, to be a proper wife. That she had grown up, changed, matured, didn't matter. The damage had been done long ago, and she could not undo it. All she could do was face the future with as much courage, and sense, as she could.

Nodding her head at her reflection, Anne turned and went out in search of her son.

Chapter 8

The summer season was in full swing. As the cream of the ton flocked to Brighton, more and more entertainments were held. Brighton Theatre announced a varied and interesting schedule of performances, cricket matches were held and horse races run at the racetrack to the east of town, and, of course, nearly everyone began planning their own entertainments. There were routs and soirees and musical evenings, picnics and promenades and Venetian breakfasts, and, most prized of all, dinners at the Marine Pavilion. And, on Wednesdays and Fridays, there were the balls at the Old Ship Inn, which no one wanted to miss. Except, perhaps, Giles.

After much pestering from his mother and sister, Giles had finally agreed to escort them to the ball at the Old Ship. They would, he supposed, have to start attending social events. That he would rather stay home was not to the point. He had a duty to the women of his family. Since they would be in Brighton all summer, it would be foolish to shun the company of others. It was all rather a bother, though. Not for the first time Giles wished he had not let himself be maneuvered into bringing his family with him.

On the night of the ball Anne dressed with special care. Really, she was as nervous as a girl making her come-out, she thought, absently watching her reflection in the dressing table mirror as Jenny, her maid, dressed her hair. It had been so long since she had attended such a tonnish event. Added to that was her fear of being snubbed. She would have friends at the ball, but there would also be people who would delight in cutting her. That she remembered well from her season.

"Thank you, Jenny," she said, and rose, giving her reflection one last critical look. She had chosen to wear the gown of white satin with the coral pink crepe bodice, and to this had added a simple strand of pearls and elbow-length gloves. Her hair was dressed simply, too, pulled back and allowed to fall over one shoulder in a long curl. The gown was far more sophisticated than anything she had worn as a girl, and needed little adornment. She would do, she supposed.

Voices floated up to her as she began to descend the stairs, and she paused, looking down. Oh, dear. The family had already foregathered in the hall. She was late again. The sight before her was so splendid, though, that she stayed still for a moment, taking it in. The golden sunlight of late evening flowed through the sidelights, glinting on the floor like crystal. It touched on Julia, resplendent in a gown of purple satin and a magnificent brocade turban, and on Beth, sweetly pretty in her apricot evening gown. It was Giles, though, who caught, and held, her eye. It was Giles who made her heart stop, as if she were seeing him for the first time. Perhaps, in a way, she was.

He was dressed again in black and white. Stark colors, true, and yet they suited him. His evening coat of black velvet fitted so perfectly across his broad shoulders that she knew it had been crafted by a master tailor, as had the white satin breeches, which displayed legs in no need of padding. Against the rich, dark velvet his hair gleamed brighter, his eyes glinted, and his face looked rugged and lean. He was utterly civilized, of course, and yet, as he prowled the hall in obvious impatience, there was something untamed about him, something totally and unmistakably male. Something that Anne had never before recognized about him, and which set her heart to pounding. He was very much a man who would take whatever he wanted. And if he wanted her?

At that moment Giles looked up, though she had made no sound, and she felt her knees turn to jelly. The light she so missed in his eyes still wasn't present, but she thought she saw something flicker in them briefly. Something to do with her. Stilling the shivers her thoughts had caused, she raised her head and glided down the stairs. She hadn't meant to make quite so dramatic an entrance, but, since she had, she would carry it off in style. They were all watching her, she knew, including Giles. If he wanted her . . .

Reaching the hall, she swept into a curtsy. "Good evening, Your Grace. What a lovely evening," she said, and rose to see Giles shaking his head. "What is wrong?"

Julia had raised her quizzing glass and was studying Anne through it. "That gown is unsuitable," she said.

"Unsuitable? Why?"

"I'll deal with this, Mother." Giles turned back to her. There was something strange in his face. "It won't do, Anne. Not if you're trying to reestablish yourself in society."

"But what is wrong with it?" Anne demanded, all pleasure in the moment gone. Oh, yes, Giles was a man. Just like every man in her life, he was ordering her about. "I understand this is the style."

"It is indecent," Julia said.

"Indecent!" Anne exclaimed, and then started to laugh. "Oh, really—"

"It is much too low, Anne." Giles sounded regretful; she wasn't sure why. "You haven't even a shawl."

"On such a warm evening? Really, Giles!" She stared

101

at him. "When did you become such a prude?"

"I am not being prudish," he said, patently reasonable. "It is my duty to help you mend your reputation, which you'll hardly be able to do by flaunting yourself. Were there time I'd tell you to change—"

"Flaunting myself! For heaven's sake, Giles!" She faced him squarely, her hands at her sides balled into fists, her fan of ivory and delicate netting in danger of snapping. Never had she been quite so angry in her life. "Duty and responsibility! Do you never think of anything else? You've done nothing but order me about since I've returned, and I've had a surfeit of it! I don't care if you are head of the family," she swept on, as he would have spoken, "you have no right to tell me how to behave. And I'm glad to know," she said, her voice bitter, "that you have such a high opinion of me."

"Anne," Giles said wearily. "I don't mean to offend you. If you would only accept my guidance—"

"Not when you've made such a mull of your own life," she retorted.

"Indeed." Giles's voice was icy. "This accomplishes nothing. Come. Our carriage is waiting."

The short ride to the Old Ship Inn was accomplished in tense, strained silence. Giles stared out the window, tightlipped, arms crossed. Were it up to him, he would approve the gown, she looked so damned beautiful in it. But no, he'd had only her welfare in mind, or so he'd told himself. Damn. He'd handled that all wrong. He should have known that the slightest hint of criticism would be enough to get Anne's back up, and he hadn't exactly been tactful. But when he had seen her on the stairs, wearing that gown . . . She had to know the effect it had, how she appeared in it. She had to know she looked appealing and seductive, and very, very beautiful. A woman trying to reestablish herself in society should behave with decorum, not with boldness. The ladies present tonight would be jealous, no question of that, and so all the more censorious. While the men—he knew exactly what the men would say. He was thinking it himself.

He shifted uneasily in his seat, keeping his face turned from her, though she sat across from him. If he moved his legs, just a little, their knees would brush and that would be all he'd need. Doubtless she was enjoying his struggle. She had to know how she appeared. When she had curtsied to him tonight, showing a quite immodest amount of bosom, she had had to know the effect it would have on him, or on any man. As a girl, Anne had been pretty. As a woman, she had an allure that made his pulse pound and his mouth go dry. And it wasn't just the gown. That hair, so artlessly arranged. It made a man's thoughts run wild, made him imagine it, shining gold satin in the candlelight, spread across a white linen pillowcase . . .

Damn. Giles swallowed painfully and crossed his legs, to hide the effect she was having on him. It had been a very long time since he had had so strong a reaction to a woman, if ever. He felt like an eager, untried youth, unable to control his own desires. It wouldn't do. Anne had hurt him once, and he had learned since never to let a woman get too close to him. He had learned not to let this woman get too close. How had she managed to get past his carefully constructed defenses, to find the part of him that still ached for her? It was a part he hadn't even known existed until tonight, and a weakness he despised. Come the end of the summer, she would leave him again. That she had made quite, quite clear.

The carriage came to a stop and Giles rose, anxious to escape as quickly as he could. Damn these breeches, which felt so tight and which concealed nothing. Damn his own lack of control. He had hoped to gain some calm during the drive, but he hadn't counted on the effect her nearness would have on him. The sight of her, the scent of her perfume, the awareness he had, all through him, of her, all conspired against him. This was madness. Thank God the ball was likely to be crowded. He would not have to spend overmuch time with her.

The hall of the Old Ship was already crowded when the Tremont party entered and began to make their way up the stairs, toward the Assembly Rooms. Anne, her head held high, was aware of more than one curious glance in her direction, but not by any overt gesture was she either greeted or shunned. In spite of the crowd of people pressing about her with all their warmth and noise and scent, somehow she was very alone. She was quite cross with Giles. Of course she hadn't had him in mind when she had bought this gown, but it had occurred to her to wonder what he would think of it. Now she knew. Foolish of her to hope that his eyes would rest on her with appreciation; he approved of little she did. That, she should have expected. Why it bothered her was another matter altogether.

Someone passing down the stairs, having apparently already made his appearance and leaving, jostled her. Anne looked up, jolted out of her reverie. "I do beg your pardon," a cultured voice said. "I say—Anne? It is Anne Warren, is it not?"

"Ian," Anne said in unfeigned pleasure, holding out her hand. "Ian Campbell, how wonderful to see you again."

"And you." He smiled down at her, the crooked boyish grin she had once found endearing. It sat less well now on features blurred and thickened a bit by age and hard living, but still it had charm. The light in his eyes as they rested on her was balm to a spirit sorely wounded by Giles's scorn. "I'd heard you were in Brighton, but I'd not thought to see you here."

"Nor I you. I thought such tonnish events bored you."

"Ah, but one must made an appearance. Tremont," he added carelessly.

Giles, standing just above Anne with his hand on his

mother's elbow, nodded frigidly. "Campbell."

"I say, think I'll stay for a while, after all." Ian elbowed his way into the throng and took Anne's arm in fingers that seemed overly warm. "I must say, Anne, you're looking uncommonly well. Life in the colonies must agree with you."

"It does. I am quite happy there."

"I am glad to hear it. After all, you left so quickly."

Anne refused to rise to the bait, but smiled serenely. "Yes. And now I am back."

Ian grinned in acknowledgment of her answer. "Poor old Freddie. So he's gone and left you a widow."

Something in his tone made her uneasy, and she raised her fan, opening it and fanning herself slowly. "Yes. 'Tis warm in here, isn't it? It seems as if all the world is here."

Ian glanced upward. "All the world is. Prinny may put in an appearance, you know, and Brummel is here. Should be an interesting evening." He looked at her. "Most interesting."

Anne fanned herself more vigorously. "And the orchestra is good, I understand."

"Oh, yes." Ian grinned, and Anne forgot for the moment her strange apprehension. "I've heard a rumor that will set the town on its ears. They may play a waltz tonight."

Beth, standing on Anne's other side, gasped. "No! How shocking."

"Good heavens. Even in Jamaica we've heard of the waltz," Anne said. She didn't add that she had been taught it just last year by a visitor to the plantation, or that she had danced it at the last party she had attended before Freddie's death. Her reputation was damaged quite enough as it was.

Giles turned his head slightly. "I hope, Anne, you'll have enough decorum not to dance it."

Anne's fingers tightened on her fan. Of course she had enough decorum, not to mention common sense, but his casual assumption that she didn't was annoying.

"I agree, it is a shocking dance," Ian said, but his eyes, looking at Anne, were inquisitive. Closing her fan, she let it rest for a moment on her right cheek. It had been a very long time since she had used a fan to convey signals to one of her flirts, but she hadn't forgotten how. With that brief gesture, she had just cast discretion to the wind and agreed to waltz with Ian. It would serve Giles right.

Once the Tremont party had entered the Assembly Rooms and had been greeted by Mr. Forth, the master of ceremonies, Giles drew Anne aside. The orchestra was playing, though one had to strain to hear it over the conversation and clatter of people. "I overheard you talking with Campbell," he said, his voice low. "Be careful of him. He is not the same man we once knew."

"I find him charming. Really, Giles, I can take care of myself."

"Remember your reputation, Anne."

Anne twirled her fan in her left hand. "How can I forget it? You are continually reminding me." Again she twirled the fan, and this time saw comprehension dawn in his eyes, as he interpreted the signal she had just given him. *I wish to be rid of you.*

"Very well, madam. If you will not remember your own reputation, I hope at least that you will consider my mother and sister." Giles bowed stiffly and then turned to take Beth's arm, leaving Anne to stare after him, speechless with anger. As if she would do anything to hurt Beth! Did he really think so poorly of her, then? *Pooh to him!* She would enjoy herself tonight.

Giles's own anger was covered by the polite mask he had learned to don at will over the past years. Anne hadn't changed. He was lucky he hadn't married her. She always had been a flirt, and she still apparently was. What had been attractive in a young girl, though, was far less so in a woman. He hadn't missed the interplay between her and Campbell, nor her adroit use of her fan. So, she wished to be rid of him? Well, she was. Never mind that Campbell, too, had changed since Anne had known him, that he was now a wastrel and a gambler, with a very bad reputation. As Anne had reminded him, she was not really his concern. Let her destroy her reputation, if she were so minded. He was far more concerned with his sister, and with making this evening a success for her.

"Tremont seems somewhat discomposed," Ian drawled, taking Anne's arm. She started, and then smiled at him.

"I had forgotten what it is like at a ton party," she said, gesturing toward the ballroom and ignoring his comment. "I am no longer used to such crowds."

"Ah, yes, a sad crush. They are starting the cotillion. Come, let us join the dance."

"I'd like that." Anne let him lead her across the room to where couples were forming sets for the dance, feeling an odd sense of unreality. It had been so long, and yet it seemed like just yesterday that she had been part of society such as this. And yet, so much had changed. There were faces she didn't know, and those that she did looked at her coolly. No one actually snubbed her, for which she was deeply grateful, but no one besides Ian had made an overture of friendliness, either. Instead the eyes that met her own were wary, calculating, distantly polite. Some were people she had once called friend, girls who had made their come-out with her, men who had been her flirts. She no longer had her giddy group of friends to giggle with, nor her reliable male escorts. She no longer had Giles.

The cotillion passed in a blur of music and faces. Ordinarily Anne enjoyed dancing, but tonight she was tense, concerned as she had never before been about making a misstep, and all too aware of people watching her. Not Giles; she wasn't certain where in this crowded room he was, but she doubted he was paying her much attention. And that, more than anything else, sent her spirits crashing down. At least when she and Giles argued there was some connection between them, and a goad for her to behave a certain way; thus she had agreed to waltz with Ian. Indifference, though, was a different matter. It meant he didn't care about her one way or the other.

Ian took her hand. "A trifle warm in here, I'd say," he said, smiling at her, "and no terrace for us to repair to."

Anne tapped him lightly on the arm with her fan. "As if I would go out there with you, sir," she said, smiling. How easy it was to fall into the old flirtatious ways, and to use them as a mask for one's real feelings.

Ian seemed not at all discomposed. "A man can but try. Come, may I offer you some refreshment if we can make it through this crush?"

"I'd like that. And then I really must find the duchess and Lady Elizabeth."

Ian's hand on her back, guiding her toward the refreshment room, was hot and moist. "Why?" He hailed a passing waiter and took two cut crystal glasses of punch. "You're hardly a debutante who needs must stay with her chaperone." He smiled at her over the rim of his cup. "On the contrary, my dear. You are a mature, beautiful woman."

Something in Ian's gaze made Anne profoundly uneasy. It was as if he were looking straight through her gown, and she didn't like it. "Why, thank you, sir. But Tremont is concerned for Lady Elizabeth. This is her first real time in society, you know." She smiled brightly. "I think I would like to see how she is getting on."

For a moment something flashed in Ian's eyes, and then he bowed. "As you wish. Though I'll return to claim my waltz."

"As to that, Ian—"

"Listen!" Ian paused as they reentered the ballroom. "They are playing it already. Excellent."

"Ian, I don't think—"

"Crying off? I would not think you so craven."

"I'm not, but—"

"Come, my dear, you wouldn't want to cause a scene."

No, she was trying to prevent one, apparently in vain. Ian had her arm and was leading her onto the floor. Her second thoughts on the waltz had come too late. If she pulled away from him now, she would only cause the kind of comment she most wanted to avoid. There was nothing else she could do.

Across the room, Giles was in conversation with Lord Ravensworth about the king's health, and the possibility that the Prince of Wales might have to stand in as regent. As absorbing as he usually found this topic, however, tonight Giles's mind was elsewhere. It was Anne who occupied his thoughts. She had done so all evening, especially since she had left the room with Campbell. Campbell, of all people. It should have been him. If he had not antagonized her, it would have been him.

He had been aware of her all evening. How could he not be? She was easily the most beautiful woman here. Not the most stylish, perhaps, or the most daringly dressed, but the only one who drew his eye. She was so alive, so real. No languid posings for Anne, no affectation of the boredom which everyone else considered *de rigueur*. She appeared to be enjoying herself thoroughly, and why shouldn't she? She had what she wanted, a man to hang over her and flatter her. A man to leer at her, damn him. Didn't she see the way Campbell looked at her, with a predatory gleam in his eyes? Didn't she notice the way his eyes drifted down to her bosom, not once, but often? She had been away from society so long she might well have forgotten about loose screws like Campbell, or how to deal with them. The man was a cad, not above taking advantage of the coolness with which everyone else treated her, to get what he wanted. Giles was in no doubt as to what that was. Damn the man, if he hurt Anne, Giles would call him out.

"I say," Ravensworth said, breaking Giles out of his thoughts. "They really are playing a waltz."

"Are they?" Giles said, and looked up in time to see Anne being led out onto the floor by Ian Campbell.

Chapter 9

Giles's first impulse was anger, goading him to cross the room and separate the two. Almost, he did, but the habits of the past years took over automatically. Bad enough Anne was waltzing, and with Campbell, of all people, when the waltz was considered scandalous and anyone who engaged in it, fast. The damage was already done. If Giles went to them, he would only make matters worse by drawing attention to them. Damn, he'd thought Anne had more sense.

None of his thoughts showed on his face as he leaned back against the wall, his arms crossed on his chest. This evening had buffeted him with more emotions than he had felt in the past year, and at the moment he was merely tired. Tired of having all the responsibility, tired of always having to consider other peoples' needs and give little thought to his own. That was life, of course; one grew up and did what one had to. But, as he watched Anne twirling about the sparsely peopled dance floor in another man's embrace, his unruly thoughts took over. She was so beautiful in that dress, and so graceful, that she made waltzing look almost like an art. He wished, suddenly, that he dared to waltz, that he was the one whirling her about the floor, looking down at those cornflower blue eyes that held in them such an expression of—

111

Fear. The thought made him straighten abruptly. For just a moment, as Anne had turned in his direction, he had seen something flicker in her eyes. Consternation, surprisingly; perhaps the waltz hadn't been her idea. Annoyance, and that other elusive emotion he hardly dared believe he'd seen. Fear. But what had she to fear in a civilized ballroom in Brighton?

Casually, so as not to attract attention, Giles began to move along the wall, idly greeting acquaintances but never taking his eyes off the couple on the floor. Anne was a whirl of satin and crepe; her partner, Giles noted disdainfully, resplendent in peacock blue satin. Both seemed now to be enjoying themselves, and Giles applauded Anne mentally. No matter what her real feelings might be, she was carrying this off with style, and her head held high. That was true courage.

He didn't stop to examine his change of opinion from censure to admiration, but instead continued his slow progress through the room. His forethought produced results; when the waltz ended and Campbell took Anne's arm, preparatory to leading her off the floor, Giles was there.

Ian drew himself up short to avoid colliding with Giles, and for a moment an expression almost like a sneer twisted his features. "Evening, Tremont," he said carelessly. "Don't tell me you're planning on making a scene over one dance."

Giles's smile was pleasant, though it didn't reach to his eyes. "Of course not. I am hardly Mrs. Templeton's keeper. She is competent enough to make her own judgments in such matters. However."

"Ah. There is always a 'however.'"

"My mother requires your presence, Anne." He looked at her past the other man as he held out his arm, and saw relief flicker in her eyes. "Shall we?"

"Certainly, Your Grace," Anne murmured, the picture of demure propriety. "Good evening, Mr. Campbell."

"Good evening, Anne. My thanks for the dance. It was—pleasant."

Giles's free hand tightened involuntarily into a fist, but he kept his smile in place. "You'll excuse us, Campbell," he said, and turned, leading Anne away.

Anne glanced up at him curiously as they crossed the room. She doubted very much that Julia wished to see her; this was a pretext on Giles's part to separate her from Ian, and to prevent her from doing anything else unsuitable. She wasn't deceived by his smile or his affable manner. Underneath, he was angry. The Duke of Tremont, usually so cool and unruffled, usually showing little of his feelings, angry? It was a fascinating thought.

"I am surprised you're not scolding me, Your Grace," she said.

Giles didn't look at her. "I think I don't need to. I suspect you're already well aware of what you've done."

"A set-down, indeed." Anne's voice was rueful. "You are right, of course. That was a mistake. I'll surely know better next time."

"Then why did you waltz with him at all?" he demanded.

"Because you so obviously didn't want me to. Good evening, Felicity. How wonderful to see you again."

"And you, Anne." Felicity's smile was wide and genuine. "You waltz so very well. Is it done in Jamaica?"

"It's not supposed to be." Anne returned the smile. "I expect I'll be hearing more about it later."

"Oh, no, you made it look a most attractive dance, and not nearly so scandalous as one would think. Though I hope you won't take it amiss if I tell you that Mr. Campbell isn't quite the thing."

"I'm glad you said that, Felicity, and not I," Giles said. "Anne would cut up at me if I did."

"Perhaps." Anne smiled up at him. "Ian has

113

changed, has he not? He never used to be quite so hard."

"He delights in making mischief, and in destroying reputations," Felicity said. "I wouldn't allow him near my Susan."

"I should hope not. Are you enjoying this evening?" Anne asked Susan Whitehead, whose air of assumed boredom was at odds with the brightness of her eyes.

"It will do, Mrs. Templeton," she replied languidly. "I didn't expect to see such exalted society outside of London."

Anne glanced up at Giles, to see the same mirth sparkling in his eyes that she felt. Had she ever been so young, she wondered, and concluded, ruefully, that she probably had been. And yet, Giles hadn't seemed to mind. He had been young then, too, and more apt to forgive one's lapses. This new Giles, more mature and settled, was a man she didn't know. Aware of his duties, and yet surprisingly tolerant. Perhaps he hadn't changed as much as she had thought.

After a few more moments of conversation, Giles and Anne excused themselves and began to make their way back to where Julia sat. "It would be nice if everyone were as kind as Felicity," Anne said.

"I could remind you that you've brought anything that happens upon yourself," Giles pointed out.

"But, being a gentleman, you won't. How is Beth enjoying the evening?"

"A great deal, I'd say. Of course my mother is watching to make certain she doesn't dance with anyone unsuitable."

"I know I've behaved badly, Giles, but you needn't keep pinching at me so."

"I wasn't," he protested, but was unable to say more. They had reached his mother's side, and he was not about to wrangle with Anne in her presence. Besides, two of Julia's cronies had joined her, Lady Helmsley, and the Dowager Duchess of Bainbridge. Giles didn't relish the idea of facing three such tabbies.

"Good evening," he said, greeting the ladies and making the introductions. They all knew Anne, of course, from years past, but, after tonight's fiasco, their approval of her was more important than ever. After all, he told himself, Beth's reputation might very well be touched.

Conversation was strained and desultory, becoming a bit more lively only when Beth, partnered by the Duke of Bainbridge, the dowager's grandson and a friend of Giles's, came over. Her face was flushed and her eyes shining, and all three of the old ladies smiled at her. "A prettily behaved girl," Lady Helmsley said to Julia. "You must be very proud of her."

"I am proud of both my children," Julia said. "They do know how to go on in society."

By which Julia meant she didn't, Anne thought, catching the speaking look the duchess sent her. Unlike Giles, she was not nearly so sanguine about the old ladies' acceptance of her. She had erred, and erred badly. She was not likely to be forgiven immediately.

It was as quiet in the carriage going home as it had been going out, though the silence had a different quality. Anne, tired, and aware of what she had done, kept her head down, contemplating her fingers, while Julia contented herself with one malicious, triumphant glance. Nothing would be served in talking about the night, Giles thought. It was over, and what was needed now was something to repair the damage. It wasn't fair; what Anne had done was in the past. That she seemed unrepentant, though, was what society would find hard to forgive. And so damned beautiful.

"Anne," he said as they came into the house, and Anne, just starting to ascend the stairs, stopped.

"Yes?"

So damned beautiful. How had he ever let her go?

"Ah, nothing. Good night."

Anne hesitated. "Good night, Giles," she said finally,

115

and made her way upstairs to bed, more than a little thoughtful. Now what had that been about?

In the morning, Anne watched from her bedroom window as Colonel McMahon arrived to talk with Giles. Likely he bore with him invitations to the Pavilion, presenting her with a difficult problem. After the way she had behaved last night, she couldn't possibly go. Sending her regrets would be difficult; how did one refuse the Prince of Wales without offending him? It would be for the best, though. Neither Beth nor Giles would be helped by her presence.

"Enter," Giles called when she knocked on the door of the book-room, and rose as she came in, his expression inquiring. "Is something wrong?"

"No. I simply need to talk with you about something." She settled gracefully into a chair facing him. "I saw Colonel McMahon leave just now."

"Yes. We've been invited to dinner, with a musical evening afterward."

"Heavens. I've heard about Prinny's dinners. Didn't he once decide to show off his prowess at shooting, and make his guests join in?"

Giles's mouth quirked back. "Yes, and from what I understand, both a musician and a footman were hit." He grinned at her, and for a moment any strain that had been between them was gone. "God save us if that man ever becomes king."

"Giles! You, of all people, speaking against your prince?"

"I think even I might be allowed my opinions."

"One would never know. That you feel that way, I mean." She shook her head. "Giles, this is difficult, but I must cry off from attending the dinner party."

"That's a most extraordinary thing to do. Why?"

"My being there won't do you any good."

116

Giles leaned back in his chair, looking at his fingers as they toyed with the papers on his desk. Why had she been scared of Campbell? "It will be difficult to refuse Prinny without causing offense," he said abruptly.

"I know. I thought of that, but I can't see it would be any worse than my being there."

"Crying craven, Anne?"

"No! For heaven's sake, Giles, you know I'm no coward. Usually," she added.

Giles eyed her. "You wouldn't be alone, you know. I'd be there."

"Yes, I know, and I appreciate it. I just don't think it's wise."

"I don't know. You've already caught Prinny's eye."

"God help me!"

Giles grinned. "Well, you have. You're passably attractive, after all."

"Thank you very much."

"And if he does acknowledge you, as I believe he will, it will do a lot toward repairing your reputation."

Anne opened her mouth to speak, and then closed it again. "I hadn't thought of that. Do you think he will acknowledge me?"

"I can't think why else he invited you."

"Unless he thinks me a suitable candidate for an *affaire.*"

"Forgive me, Anne, but you're not old enough for him. No, I don't think crying off will do you any good. Or me, either."

Anne looked away from the sympathy in his eyes. Of all the things Giles could feel for her, the last thing she wanted was sympathy. "I know I made a mistake," she said in a low voice. "I should have known better than to waltz last night. I am sorry if my actions did anything to hurt you or Beth. They weren't meant to. If anyone is to face the consequences, it should be me."

"So it should. And I, too, for goading you into it." Anne turned toward him, startled, and he held up his

117

hand to forestall her protest. "Like it or not, Anne, I do have a responsibility to you, and I shirked it. Had I handled things better, none of this would have happened."

"You take a great deal upon yourself, Giles. Have you forgotten that I am quite capable of making my own decisions?"

"No. Forgive me, I phrased that badly. Of course you can make your own decisions. I merely meant that this was your first time back in society, and you needed the support of your family. Instead, I made you face it alone. I'm sorry."

"It wasn't your fault. I didn't listen to you when you did try to support me."

Giles shook his head. "I tried to tell you what to do. There's a difference. I thought you'd obey me without question, the way Beth does. I should have known better." His mouth quirked back. "The truth is, I was afraid something like the waltz would happen, and when it did, I played a part in it."

"You thought you were doing the right thing—"

"The right thing be damned. I didn't like seeing you with Campbell."

Anne stared at him in frank astonishment. "Giles—"

"The man is a loose screw. If I had supported you as you needed, perhaps you wouldn't have gone with him."

"Perhaps." Anne's voice was absent. She was startled by what he had just said. Heavens, was he jealous? "Perhaps I might have. I liked Ian once, and I didn't know he'd changed. But, Giles. It's my problem, not yours. Or do you plan to tell me again that I'm your responsibility?"

"How do you plan to handle it, Anne? By hiding away and never seeing anyone? You should remember that that does no good. Scandal needs to be outfaced."

Anne glanced away. So it did. It required standing up to people, and behaving as if nothing had happened.

If one showed the slightest sign of fear or apology, people would strike, and strike hard. Her ostracism would be complete. If, however, she went to the Pavilion with Giles, who would dare say anything against her? The only trouble was, she wasn't certain she had the courage for it.

"When I came here I truly thought I didn't need any help," she said softly. "I thought I knew how to handle myself. But I forgot what English society is like. I forgot how much people delight in seeing one make a misstep." She looked up at him, her eyes wide with appeal. "Giles, will you help me?"

"Of course I will," he said easily, giving no sign that he knew how difficult it had been for her to ask that question. "We'll face them all together and tell them to be damned."

Anne laughed, startled. "You sound as if you relish the prospect."

"I do. It's been a long time since I've had a good fight."

"How uncivilized of you," she teased.

Giles grinned at her. "I? The Duke of Tremont? Never think such a thing." He rose, and she did, too, aware that this interview was at an end. "We'll come about, Anne, never fear," he said, laying his hand on her shoulder.

Anne looked up at him, and for a moment all thought fled. His hand was warm on her, so warm, and strong. Comforting, reliable, and large. Too large. A man's hand. Abruptly she pulled away. "Thank you, Giles. If you'll excuse me, Jamie will be needing his lessons," she said, and whisked away, out the door.

Giles stared after her, wondering about her sudden reaction to his touch. What confused him more, though, was his own reaction. Why had he needed, so much, to touch her?

* * *

119

What do we do with a drunken sailor, what do we do with a drunken sailor . . .

Anne stirred drowsily in her bed, a smile curving her lips. She'd had absurd dreams before, but surely this was one of the silliest. Such a song to be dreaming about. What did one do with a drunken sailor, anyway? she wondered, and opened her eyes. It took her a moment to realize that, though she was awake, the singing hadn't stopped. One of the servants must have got into the wine, though the song had a curious disembodied quality that floated through the room. Almost like a ghost—

She sat bolt upright in bed, heart pounding. *Jamie!* Flinging the covers off, she jumped from the bed and sprinted across the room, not stopping for shawl or wrapper or candle. She had to be certain that her son was safe. Though the house was still unfamiliar to her, she found her way with the unerring instinct peculiar to mothers, and opened the door to Jamie's room just as the song trailed off. *Early in the morning . . .*

The silence in the wake of the singing was uncanny. Anne shuddered as she ran across the room, wincing as her bare feet stepped on sharp little pieces of metal. Giles's, and Jamie's, toy soldiers. She'd told him to put them away, but she wouldn't scold him, if only he were all right. "Jamie," she whispered, her voice harsh, and drew a deep breath of relief. Jamie's breathing was deep and even, and her seeking hands found him tangled in the bedclothes, one hand to his face. Gently she pried his thumb away from his mouth and tucked him under the covers, thanking God he was unhurt.

Toora, toora, toora loo, you look like a monkey in a zoo. And if I had a face like you I'd join the British Army.

Startled, Anne jumped up. The singing again, sounding as eerie and as loud as in her own room. Good God, was the house really haunted? A chill skittered down her spine at the thought, even though she knew it was nonsense. The stories about the house and Obadiah's dire warnings aside, she didn't believe in such things. That meant that someone human was behind this.

Anne was suddenly furiously angry. Of all the ridiculous things she had had to endure since returning to England, snubbings, scandal, Julia's superciliousness, and Giles's new arrogance, this was by far the worst. She was going to find out who was doing this, and give him a piece of her mind.

An unearthly glow filled the hall just as she ran out of Jamie's room. Anne pulled herself up short, that chill shaking her again at the sight of a figure floating toward her. Too late. Her momentum carried her into the hall and right up against the figure. Whoever it was grunted in surprise. She realized, with quite unnecessary relief, that it was no ghost, but Giles, carrying a candle. Hard upon that thought, though, came the realization that she was in a different kind of danger. She was in Giles's arms.

Chapter 10

Giles stared down at her, his candle casting a warm intimate glow that surrounded them and bound them together. She was close to him, so close, wearing only a soft nightgown of the finest lawn, so that he could feel her breasts warm against his chest, her thighs pressing against his. Her face, gazing up at him, looked absurdly young; her eyes startled, her lips parted, as if waiting for a kiss. His fingers curled tighter on her arm, and for just a moment he thought he saw compliance, anticipation, in her eyes. Then she moved away.

"Giles," she said, her voice sounding just a bit shaky as she stepped back, running her fingers distractedly through her hair. "When I saw the light I thought— well, never mind."

"I heard singing," he said.

"Yes, so did I." She kept her face averted, so that he wouldn't see the color that was flaming into it, so that she herself wouldn't stare at him. He wore a dressing gown of fine deep blue brocade, and under that his chest was bare, as her fingers had found when she'd collided with him. Bare and hard and warm, and she once again became aware that he was a man, strong, attractive, virile. And somehow far more approachable, with his normally neat hair tousled, and a smile spreading across his face. The Giles she had once known. The Giles she would have married.

Hastily she took another step back, crossing her arms on her bosom. "It's stopped."

"What? Oh. The singing. So it has." He stepped toward her. "Anne—"

"What is all this commotion?" a voice demanded, and Julia stepped out of her room. "What was that singing?"

Anne bit back an almost hysterical giggle. Julia in nightclothes was a sight to see. In contrast to her usual austere manner of dressing, her wrapper was a confection of ruffles and lace and ribbon. Iron gray hair in curling papers peeked out from under a frilly cap, and, most astonishing of all, her face was covered with a thick white cream that glistened in the candlelight. "I'll get my wrapper," Anne choked, and ran into her room.

The family assembled a few minutes later in the drawing room, along with the servants, all in varying states of *dishabille*. Anne had taken the time to pull back her hair with a ribbon and had put on her most fetching wrapper. Now she was curled up in a chair, watching in fascination as Giles paced the room. He had a nightshirt on under his dressing gown. It hadn't been there before, she thought, and ducked her head to hide her blush.

"You say this has happened before?" Giles was saying.

"So I'm told, Your Grace." Benson was looking decidedly ruffled, an unusual state for him, with his thinning gray hair standing up and a smudge on his cheek. "Of course when we came here I heard the stories, but I didn't believe them. No, not for a moment."

Obadiah, leaning against the wall with his arms crossed, stirred. "Somethin' bad about this house," he said, and the other servants stared at him uneasily, one parlor maid making the sign against the evil eye.

"Nonsense." Anne spoke crisply. "I refuse to believe in ghosts. There has to be some explanation for what happened."

"Your man is impertinent," Julia declared. "You should dismiss him."

"Obadiah is his own man and may do as he wishes," Anne replied, though secretly the description of Obadiah as impertinent tickled her. Looking up, she caught Giles's eyes, and saw the same amusement in them. "Mrs. Justice." She smiled at the housekeeper. "Has this been going on for a while?"

"Oh, yes, ma'am, for as long as I've been here. Not all the time, though."

"Full moon tonight, lady," Obadiah said.

"Oh, hush, Diah, you're not helping matters. What does the ghost do, Mrs. Justice?"

"He sings, ma'am." She sounded puzzled. "At least, he makes a kind of moaning that sounds like singing. Never nasty songs, like tonight. And sometimes things will be misplaced."

"But that could happen anyway."

"Yes, ma'am. Still, ma'am, it makes a body wonder."

"I have a hard time taking seriously a ghost that sings bawdy songs," Giles said dryly, and again his eyes met Anne's. There was something different about them, something she couldn't pinpoint. "Has anybody seen anything? Heard anything besides the singing?"

The staff, most of whom worked for the owners of the house and not the Tremonts, looked at each other, shaking their heads. "No, Your Grace," Mrs. Justice said. "Just, as I said. Sometimes things go missing. Of course, there was the hat on the statue," Mrs. Justice said, and one of the maids giggled.

"I beg your pardon?"

"The head of the Prince of Wales, Your Grace, in the hall. The last family that was here, the Fergusons, they weren't like you. Silly girls who'd believe any nonsense,

124

if you ask me! No offense, Your Grace, if you know them."

Giles's lips twitched. He hadn't the faintest idea who the Fergusons were. "None taken. What happened, ma'am?"

"Miss Catherine misplaced a bonnet, and nothing must do but that we look high and low for it. We tore the house apart, and not a sign of it did we see."

"She said I stole it," Maddy, one of the maids, put in. "As if I would. Something ugly, that was. Chip straw with cherries for trim and coquelicot ribbons."

"Goodness," Anne murmured, as some comment seemed to be called for. What had started as a frightening experience was rapidly degenerating into farce. "May I assume you found it?"

"Oh, no, ma'am, but it did show up, the next morning," Mrs. Justice said. "And can you guess where?"

Anne avoided Giles's eyes. "No."

"On the Prince of Wales, of course. The statue, I mean," she added, as Giles shouted with laughter. Anne let the giggles she had been restraining tumble out, and even Julia looked amused. "Well may you laugh, Your Grace, but Miss Catherine was that upset that the entire family left that day."

"How poor-spirited of them," Anne said.

"Me, I always thought Miss Joanna did it, for a trick, like. Miss Catherine's sister," Maddy added.

"Well, ma'am, between you and me they weren't much of a success," Mrs. Justice said. "Encroaching, I'd call them. I think the ghost did us a favor."

"Ahem." Giles cleared his throat. "That's as may be. What we need to know now is if anyone feels they can no longer work here." The staff looked at each other, but no one spoke. "No? Excellent."

"I do not approve of such strange goings-on, Your Grace," Benson said, his mouth pursed. "It is not as it should be."

"Nothing is as it should be anymore," Giles muttered. "Very well. Try to sleep for what remains of the night. We'll figure out what to do in the morning."

"Yes, Your Grace." Mrs. Justice curtsied and then waddled out of the room, gathering the female servants around her like a flock. The menservants trailed behind them, leaving only the family, and Obadiah.

Anne leaned her head back against the chair. Had she really once complained of life being dull? It certainly had been most interesting lately. "A ghost who sings," she remarked. "How can a house as new as this be haunted when Tremont Castle isn't?"

"Old spirits, lady," Obadiah said, and Anne raised her head to look at him. With the servants gone, there was no longer any need to make light of what had happened, for fear of their giving notice.

"You don't really believe that, Diah."

"No, lady." Obadiah crossed the room and sat in a satin-striped chair, causing Julia and Giles to look at him in some surprise. "There's somethin' about this house, though. Don't know what it is, but there's somethin'."

"This is all nonsense," Julia said. "It was one of the servants playing pranks, mark my words."

"How?" Anne said, and Julia subsided.

"What do you think is wrong?" Giles asked, looking directly at Obadiah.

"I don't know, Your Grace." Obadiah's gaze was equally direct. "I don't believe the house is haunted. I would know."

The two men stared at each other measuringly. "Obadiah has the gift," Anne said softly. "Second sight."

"Sometimes." He flashed her a smile. "Not this time. I just know, sir, that there's somethin' goin' on in this house. Someone wants us out. I don't think he'd hurt us, lady," he added quickly, as Anne straightened.

"'He?' You know who is doing this, then?" Giles said.

126

"No, Your Grace. Just a feelin'."

"Well, I think it is all nonsense. Giles, your arm, please." Julia rose stiffly from her chair, with Giles's help. "Old spirits, indeed. I suggest we question the staff thoroughly and find out who is causing this."

"In the morning, Mother."

"Of course, in the morning. Some of us need our sleep. Come, Elizabeth," she said, and swept out of the room, Beth trailing behind her.

Giles turned back to Obadiah. "You'll keep an eye out for whoever's causing this mischief?"

Obadiah nodded. "Yes, Your Grace," he said, and went out, leaving Anne and Giles alone.

Anne rose. "I must go, too," she said in a rush. "We've an important day tomorrow, and I must check on Jamie again—"

"Anne." Giles held out his hand, and she went still. "There are some things I would ask you."

Anne pushed back her hair. "Can it wait?" Now that all the fuss and bother were over, memories of that moment in the hall came crowding back. The sense of safety she'd so briefly felt when she'd realized it was Giles with her; his eyes, looking down at her, inquiringly at first, and then darkening with another emotion, one she didn't want to name; the feel of him, warm and strong against her. That was the most disconcerting memory of all, the one that made her want to flee.

"I suppose it can." Giles's eyes were both wary and puzzled. "But I was wondering about your servant."

"Obadiah is no man's servant," she said swiftly, unease forgotten for the moment. "He is a free man and may go where he wishes. Do you know, he's had an offer to oversee a neighboring plantation, but he decided he wants to stay at Hampshire Hall instead? We're lucky to have him."

"I didn't know that. About his other offers of employment, I mean."

"No, I didn't tell you." She smiled suddenly. "Probably because I was too busy wrangling with you."

"Probably." Giles returned the smile. "This business with the second sight, though."

"Oh, he has it. I've known him to predict the most amazing things."

"Really."

"You don't believe me?"

He smiled. "No, not quite."

"How vexing of you," she answered in the same light tone, and then went still. Of a sudden, she knew what was different about his eyes. The light was back in them.

"Anne?" Giles said, prodding her out of her reverie, and she realized she'd been staring. "Are you well?"

"Oh, yes, quite." She took a deep breath. "As for Obadiah. He warned Freddie not to leave the plantation the night he died."

"Did he, indeed!" Giles stared at her. "Then you think he's right about this house?"

"Yes. There's no one else I'd rather depend on."

"No one?"

"No one," Anne said, and was startled by the disappointment that flashed across Giles's face. " 'Tis late. If I am to be in good form tomorrow evening I must go to bed. It wouldn't do for me to appear before Prinny looking hagged."

"As if you could." Giles walked beside her, his hand on her back. She was acutely, and uncomfortably, aware of its warmth. "Anne—"

"Good night, Giles." Her voice breathless, she spun away from him and dashed for the stairs, not looking back, even though she knew he was watching her. This was an unexpected development, indeed. What did she do now?

By the following evening the incidents of the night

had been, if not forgotten, at least pushed out of mind. Everyone in the household was excited and flustered at the thought of the dinner at the Marine Pavilion. Julia was more cross than usual, Beth more fluttery, Anne more inclined to chatter. Only Giles appeared untouched by all the excitement. "If you ask me, this is a damned nuisance," he growled as they set off in their barouche for the short drive down the Steyne to the Pavilion.

"It is a great honor," Julia said. "I am proud of you, Giles. Though of course it is no more than you deserve."

"Thank you, Mother." Giles's mouth quirked back as he looked across at Anne, unusually silent. Like the rest of them she was in full court dress; her gown of white satin was embroidered with some sort of beading on the bodice, and her hair was pinned up and topped by a ridiculous headdress made of ostrich feathers. A diaphanous shawl draped lightly about her shoulders completed the ensemble, but also tantalized, the sheer material revealing just a hint of white shoulders and bosom. Anne hadn't changed. She was still the consummate flirt in all her satin splendor. He much preferred her appearance of last evening, young and touchingly vulnerable in her nightclothes, with her hair pulled simply back. He'd never seen her quite like that, and it intrigued him. Who was the real Anne? The woman who fought so hard for her independence, the girl who flirted, the ice princess she now appeared? Or the beguiling woman she had been last evening, for so short a time, in his arms?

Anne was trying very hard not to fidget. The satin gown, purchased when she had learned she would be making an appearance at the Pavilion, was one of the most beautiful she had ever owned, and one of the most uncomfortable. The stitching for the intricate beaded embroidery made the bodice stiff and scratchy. Of course she couldn't scratch herself, much as she longed to, and so she was doomed to suffer. Her only consolation was that Giles appeared as uncomfortable as she felt.

He sat across from her, looking out the window, his arms crossed on his chest and his lips set. He hated this, poor man, and yet he was doing as his duty demanded. An admirable trait, particularly as he looked so handsome in his full court dress. Velvet jackets and tight satin breeches would make many another man look like a fop. Not Giles. The years he had spent working at his estates showed now in the breadth of his shoulders, in the strength of his thighs. He was, without a doubt, a man, and a splendid one, very much a duke. Anne, however, far preferred him as he had appeared last night, with his disheveled hair falling across his forehead. Far more approachable, except for that moment in the hall—but, no, she wouldn't think about that. It had been an aberration, born of the surprise of the moment. It would not happen again.

Their carriage drew up at last before the Marine Pavilion, festooned with colored lanterns that gave it a festive appearance. A bewigged footman in the blue and buff livery of the Prince of Wales bowed and admitted the Tremont party into the entrance hall. "Heavens," Anne murmured, startled, as she glanced around. If the exterior of the Pavilion were restrained, the entrance hall was anything but. The walls were painted a brilliant green, and everywhere there was china, dishes, urns, vases, all jumbled together, all so rich in color and detail that one simply couldn't take it all in. She raised dazed eyes to Giles, whose own eyes twinkled, though his face was expressionless.

"'In Xanadu did Kubla Khan, A stately pleasure dome decree,'" he murmured.

"Or some such," Anne answered, and was pleased to see a gleam of amusement appear in his eyes. It was so nice to be in agreement with someone again, so nice to know that one's opinions were shared, without even having to speak a word. Never had she had this kind of intuitive communication with Freddie, or with anyone else, for that matter. Only Giles.

Another footman appeared, bowing, to lead them to a drawing room where they would await the Prince. Everywhere were precious Chinese artifacts of ivory and silk and porcelain; bamboo sofas and lacquer cabinets; vivid colors that assailed one's senses, after the restrained classicism of the past decade. And it was hot, almost stiflingly so. All the fires were lighted, though the evening was warm. For all that, though, Anne found herself rather liking the Prince's folly of a house. It was original and unique. She liked people who had the courage to follow their own tastes.

In the drawing room the Tremonts were introduced to the other guests. As was customary at the Prince's dinner parties few ladies were present. There were only Isabella, the Marchioness of Hertford and the Prince's current companion, and Lady Clermont, to keep her company. Lady Hertford, aging and stout, was dressed in simple white muslin, much too young for her age and her masterful personality, but she was all that was gracious as she greeted them. So was the Prince, accompanied by his bodyguard, Johnny Townsend, formerly a Bow Street Runner, and Lieutenant Colonel Bloomfield, one of his attendents. After shaking hands all around, he gave his arm to Julia to lead her into dinner, since she held the highest rank of the ladies present. For all Julia's censure of the Prince she looked quite pleased, Anne thought with amusement. She was, in fact, smiling.

Dinner was served in a sumptuous dining chamber decorated with more things Chinese. The Prince talked of, among other things, his future plans for the Pavilion; he was, it appeared, not entirely happy unless he was making changes to it. Conversation also centered on the health of the king, who was celebrating his fiftieth year on the throne this year, and on his daughter the Princess Amelia, who had been ill this summer. Anne conversed politely, all the while taking everything in, so that she could tell Jamie about it afterward. The Prince did have some odd friends. There was Sir John Lade who, with his wife, liked to dress up as a coachman and drive, not only his own carriages, but those of his friends; his front teeth had been filed to points so that he could whistle loudly. More sinister was Lord Barrymore, known as "Cripple-gate" because of his lame leg and because his brothers, since deceased, had borne the soubriquets of "Hell-gate" and "Newgate." Next to him Richard Sheridan, the playwright, seemed almost tame, though his antics were as wild now as he neared sixty as they had been in his youth. A rackety group indeed, as Julia had said.

If the Prince's friends were eccentric, the food was splendid and sumptuous. Accustomed though she was to enormous amounts of food being served at dinner parties, Anne was stunned by the profusion of dishes set before them. There were four different soups, and fish dishes including trout and turbot. There were also no fewer than thirty-six entrées: ham, chicken fricaseed in the Italian manner, a timbale of macaroni Neapoli-tan, veal, patés, aspics, and dishes Anne could not even identify. There were potatoes in a hollandaise sauce, green beans au gratin, truffles *a la Italianne,* and orange biscuits. And, just in case someone was still hungry, there were also soufflés of chocolate, apples, or apricots. No wonder the Prince had such an *embonpointe,* Anne thought, glancing covertly at his stout figure. If she ate like this every day, doubtless she, too, would soon be quite heavy.

Various wines accompanied the food, so that by the end of dinner things had got quite merry, and quite loud. It was with a great deal of relief that Anne rose when dinner was finally over, several hours after they had sat down, to follow the Prince to the Music Room. Once again they were surrounded by *chinoiserie,* as they passed through a bewildering procession of anterooms and drawing rooms painted French blue, with more china, Chinese costumes of rich scarlet brocade and gold embroidery, stuffed birds, and models of odd-looking boats, which Giles assured Anne in a low voice really were called junks. Down a corridor in which larger than life figures in Chinese robes held fishing poles from which dangled lanterns. Into a gallery walled with glass, on which were painted birds and insects and fruit and flowers, all in vivid colors, all illuminated from without, so that the effect was rather like walking through a Chinese lantern. When at last they reached the Music Room, a vast oval room that was a model of restraint by comparison, even Giles was looking slightly dazed. Only Julia, who remembered a time when *chinoiserie* had been in vogue, seemed unmoved by the splendor they had passed.

The Prince's wind band was playing, loudly but melodiously, in the Music Room as they entered, and the Argand lamps were lighted, casting a brilliant glow. There appeared to be upward of a hundred people already there, Anne guessed, among them the cream of the ton: Beau Brummell; the Earl of Jersey and his wife; Lords Yarmouth, Petersham, Erskine, and many, many more. All turned expectantly toward the doorway as the Prince's party entered, and Anne's wonder and amazement were abruptly replaced by the urge to flee. These people were likely only to scorn her.

A hand grasped her arm, gently but firmly. "Courage," Giles whispered, and she looked quickly up at him, her fear dissipating. With Giles by her side, she could face anything.

"What do you think of my Pavilion, Mrs. Templeton?" the Prince asked, and Anne, flattered at being singled out, smiled.

"It is most impressive, sir," she said tactfully.

"Indeed. I understand you have a prosperous plan-

133

tation in Jamaica."

"Yes, Your Highness," Anne said, slightly taken aback. "Hampshire Hall. It will be my son's when he's grown."

"I hope we can convince you to remain in England until that time. Eh, Tremont?" And to Anne's astonishment he winked roguishly at Giles, who merely smiled. "Come, Mrs. Templeton. Allow me to show you some of my treasures."

"I would be delighted, sir." Anne took his arm, allowing herself only a very quick look at Giles. This was beyond what she had expected; she hadn't thought she would catch the Prince's eye. Giles had said she was not quite old enough for him. That thought made her relax as they promenaded about the room and the Prince pointed out his various possessions, telling her of their origin and history. He also talked, with surprising knowledge, about Jamaica, drawing Anne out on the subject and making her feel quite at ease. He could be, she knew, petulant and petty and lewd, but tonight he was at his best, urbane, gracious, charming, discoursing knowledgeably on all they saw. By the time they had completed the circuit of the room, Anne was quite thoroughly charmed by him, and quite grateful. If he knew the stories about her, he gave no sign. No matter if she were shunned for the rest of the evening. The Prince of Wales had accepted her, and that was quite enough.

Prince George returned with Anne to the Tremonts, conversing with them for a few more minutes, and then turned to speak with Colonel McMahon, effectively dismissing them. Able to move as they wished for the first time since entering the Music Room, the Tremonts withdrew. "I am proud of you, Giles," Julia pronounced. "You are carrying on the Templeton tradition."

"Yes, Mother." Giles turned to Anne. "You and Prinny seemed to be having an enjoyable conversation."

"Oh, hush. 'Tis disrespectful to call him so in his own

134

home," Anne protested.

Giles's eyes gleamed. "Now you will be able to tell everyone that you once flirted with a prince."

Anne shook her head. "I found him most charming."

"With an eye for beauty. I didn't think to warn you about that."

Anne stared at him for a moment, and then laughed. "I don't know whether to be complimented or insulted, sir."

"Dash it, Anne, I didn't mean—"

"It is a singular honor, to be noticed by the Prince," Julia said. "I wonder he has not paid such attention to Elizabeth."

"Oh, no, Mother, I wouldn't want it," Beth protested. "He quite terrifies me."

Giles smiled at her. "He was taken with Anne, though. I'll wager you'll be the one receiving invitations here in the future, not I."

"Oh, do stop funning me," Anne said, for some reason annoyed with him. He hadn't teased her like this since—since they had both been young, she realized with surprise.

"Anne Warren? Oh, it is you!" a voice said, and Anne turned, to see two women approaching her. Mrs. Starling and her daughter Letitia, Lady Buckram. "I thought it was you," Letitia went on, "but Mama wasn't so sure."

"Hello, Lady Buckram," Anne said, smiling coolly. *Of course you knew it was me. You cut me on the Steyne not a week ago.* "How nice to see you again."

"Oh, and I you," Letitia gushed, reaching for Anne's hand. "It has been so very long, has it not, since we were girls together? I hear you have been happy in Jamaica, and of course, I am a countess now."

"Yes, I know." Which meant, by the rules of protocol, that Anne should curtsy to her, but she had no desire to.

"Did you ever think that one day we would meet

again, and here, of all places?" Letitia waved her hand about. "Such a terrible place, but then, one simply does not refuse an invitation from Prinny! Even if he is bad ton."

"I found him charming," Anne said, in the tone she used when reproving Jamie. "It was an honor to walk with him."

Jealousy flashed in Letitia's eyes, and then was masked. "Of course. They say Prinny does prefer older women."

"Don't hoax me, Letitia!" Anne was laughing. "You forget I know to the day your age! You are, let's see, how much older than I?"

"Oh, la, as if that matters! But it is lovely to see you again, Anne, and I do hope we can get together and have a comfortable coze."

"Of course," Anne said, her smile distant. *Not if my life depended upon it.* What had she ever had in common with this shallow, malicious creature? "I must beg to be excused. I see that the duke requires my presence."

"Oh, of course. Such a handsome man. So interesting to see you two together again, after what happened."

"Yes, isn't it?" Anne kept her smile firmly in place, and gathered up her skirts. "It was nice to see you again, Letitia, Mrs. Starling. I wish you both good day." She turned, her head high. "Witches," she muttered.

"What?" Giles said, materializing suddenly at her side, and she gave him a dazzling smile.

"Which sight do I see first? Though I've seen them all with the Prince already."

Giles gave her a suspicious look. "I realize I do not compare with Prinny—"

"Oh, never."

"—but I will endeavor to do my best."

"Oh, la, I suppose that will have to do," she said, in

a fair imitation of Letitia's flirtatious manner.

Giles glanced from her to Letitia, who, with her mother, was staring at them and talking, and grinned. "Amazing how things change after a simple meeting with a prince."

Anne laughed. "Does this mean I've been accepted again?"

"Probably." Giles smiled down at her. "Does it matter?"

"No, not really. But it should be much more fun now."

"Fun," he chided. "Life isn't fun, Anne."

"I dare you to look at this room and not enjoy yourself."

Giles followed the sweep of her hand, and his mouth quirked. "Very well. You're right, this once."

"Of course." Anne smiled at him, but her opportunity to tease was ended by the approach of more people. Goodness, Lady Jersey, one of the powerful patronesses of Almack's, among others. All spoke to Giles first, greeting him as an old friend, but most also turned quickly to Anne. No shunning here, no snubbing, Anne noted with a mixture of relief and amusement. She had indeed been accepted back into society.

It was a long, but pleasant, evening. The Tremonts conversed with nearly everyone present, and engaged in the applause when the Prince, who genuinely loved music, joined in with the Misses Liddell to sing some country songs. At length, though, the Prince took his leave, and the evening was over. The Tremont party was glad to reach their carriage, riding home in tired, contented silence.

Once home, Anne slipped into Jamie's room to check on him, and was startled to see him sitting on the floor, playing with his toy soldiers by the light of a single candle. "Mama!" he exclaimed, jumping up and running to her.

"Jamie, whatever are you doing up at this time of

night?" she said, picking him up and depositing him on the bed.

"I was waiting for you. You were gone so long, Mommy."

"You should be asleep."

"See what I did, Mama." He scrambled off the bed and knelt on the floor, his eyes shining. "I've set up a battle, just the way Uncle Giles showed me. Play with me."

Anne sighed, going to her knees beside him. As wound up as he was, it would take time to calm him enough to sleep. "Very well, Jamie, but just for a little while."

She was on her hands and knees, searching out a soldier who had been knocked down and had landed under the bed, when there was a footfall at the door. "Thus we have Prinny's current favorite," an amused voice said.

Anne jerked back, banging her head on the bed frame. "Ouch," she said, and looked up at Giles, leaning against the doorjamb. "Unfair. You shouldn't creep up on a lady."

"A lady shouldn't be kneeling on the floor." Giles crouched down beside Jamie, studying the soldiers with a critical eye. "Good tactics, lad, flanking her army like that. Winning, are you?"

Jamie was frowning in concentration as he advanced a soldier toward Anne's line. "Yes. Mama doesn't know how to play. Not like you, Uncle Giles."

"Ladies rarely have a grasp of tactics, Jamie," Giles said gravely.

"Oh, definitely unfair." Anne rose, smiling. She was acutely aware of how she must appear, still in her satin court dress, her headdress askew, and her hair falling about her shoulders. "Jamie should be abed."

"So he should. Why are you keeping him up, Anne?"

Anne gave him a look. "Because—oh, never mind. Come, Jamie. It really is time for you to go to bed."

138

"I don't want to, Mommy."

"Come, James." Giles bent and lifted Jamie, settling him on the bed. "I'll tell you about the Prince, shall I?"

Jamie surprised himself by yawning. "Yes, Uncle Giles."

"Good lad. Under the covers with you, now."

Anne, smiling, went to sit in the chair across the room. Tired as she was, she didn't at all mind letting someone else care for Jamie just now. He had little contact with men, except for Obadiah, and she sometimes worried about the lack of a father in his life. Not that Freddie had been a wonderful parent. Certainly he had never talked with Jamie like this; instead, he'd considered the child a nuisance, and had been inclined to impatience. This was how it should have been with him. This was how it could have been, with her and Giles, had she married him; it was how it still could be, if . . .

Anne sat very still, as Giles's voice lulled Jamie, and her, into dreams. If things hadn't happened as they had. If Giles didn't see her as just a responsibility. If he still loved her. Good heavens, she thought, stunned. She still loved Giles.

Chapter 11

Though Anne had made no sound, Giles looked up at that moment, and their eyes locked. She wanted to look away, she needed to look away, to hide what she was certain was in her eyes, but she couldn't. There was something between them, a bond primal in its intensity, almost tangible, drawing her inexorably to him. For the life of her she could do nothing but return his gaze, molten silver, so fiery she could feel the heat of it across the room. She was melting under it, she was burning up, and she could not stand it. Before she could do anything foolish, such as throwing herself into his arms, she wrenched her gaze away.

Giles looked down, released from the strange force that had held him. "He's asleep," he whispered. What had just happened to him was extraordinary, and he wasn't altogether certain he liked it. Anne. As unselfconscious as a child, playing with her son in her expensive court dress, grasping the essentials of life and not worrying about the details. That touched him. It was as it should be, a woman caring more about the people in her life than for her consequence, yet it was rare in their world. Anne had always been different, lively, full of fun, apt to make up her own mind on matters. He really shouldn't have been surprised when she had returned to England with decided opinions on how her life should be run. He admired that.

And just when had that happened? When had annoyance turned to admiration? When had he become so aware of her, of the way the rich satin clung to curves just a bit too lush for fashion, of spun-gold hair that refused to be tamed, of eyes so blue he could drown in them? He was over her. What she had done to him in the past had hurt, but he'd surmounted it long ago. He didn't understand why memories should be coming back now to haunt him: Anne, in his arms, returning their first kiss with an eagerness and an ardor that had belied her obvious innocence; Anne, an enticing woman in a daring gown of coral and white; Anne, clad only in a cotton nightgown, pressed up against him in a darkened hall. He wanted her. God, he wanted her, and it was madness. When the summer was over, she would go. She had made that quite clear. He would do well to guard himself, and not risk his happiness on a summer folly.

"It's about time," Anne whispered back, and Giles looked up. Once again their gazes locked. "'Tis late. I'll just tuck him in and then go to bed."

"Of course." Giles rose. "Good night, Anne."

"Good night."

In her room, Anne closed her door and then sat on the edge of her bed, hands clasped in her lap, staring ahead unseeingly. She loved Giles. Dear God, she loved him. She, who had sworn she would never let herself fall under a man's power again, had allowed herself to fall in love with a man who assumed power arrogantly and casually, as if it were his right. No, that was wrong. She hadn't fallen in love with him; she simply had never stopped loving him, in spite of what he had done seven years ago, in spite of his treatment of her now. She loved him, and she suspected she always would.

There was no future in it, of course. There couldn't be. They were different; their lives ran along different

141

paths. Though she enjoyed society life, she knew she didn't belong here, following all the rules and regulations and never being herself, never being just Anne. As for Giles, to think of him in Jamaica was ludicrous. She could see him there, though, wearing comfortable breeches and a loose shirt open at the neck, his skin bronzed by the sun and his hair lightened. It was so powerful an image that she swallowed. Master of all he surveyed. Including her.

Her expression hardened. No. Never including her. No man would ever be her master again. She would not put herself, or her son, in such a vulnerable position. Besides, come the end of the summer, she would be gone. It was hard, and it hurt. Oh, how it hurt. It was something she would simply have to live with. She had dealt with much in her life; she could deal with this. Even if part of herself died.

Now that she had been accepted back into society, Anne found that many opportunities were open to her that hadn't been before. Invitations began to pour into the house on the Steyne. People who had ignored her existence before suddenly were on the warmest of terms with her, and those who had at least acknowledged her now appeared to consider themselves her bosom bows. The men who had previously ogled her still eyed her with admiration, but from a respectful distance. She was, in short, quite respectable, and all because the Prince of Wales had smiled at her. The fickleness of public opinion amused her. Giles wasn't prey to it; he made up his own mind. But, there, she wouldn't think about Giles.

One morning she and Beth joined the fashionable promenade along the Steyne, walking on the brick sidewalk and nodding at acquaintances. Beth looked pretty in a walking dress of celestial blue, with ruching at the throat, puffed long sleeves, and braid down the front. Her soft brown hair peeked out from under a chip straw bonnet trimmed with cornflowers and ribbons to match her gown. Complementing her, Anne was again in her primrose walking dress; it was comfortable and cheery, and she knew she looked well in it. With the matching parasol to shelter her from the sun, she felt quite at peace with the world. On such a clear, sunshiny day, receiving greetings from her acquaintances, how could she not? If she wished that it were Giles beside her, not Beth, she kept that desire well hidden. Even from herself.

Eventually they walked into the colonnaded entrance of Donaldson's, the fashionable circulating library, where the ton gathered to exchange books, read the latest London newspapers, and to gossip, much as in London. It was delightful, Anne thought, browsing along the shelves and choosing a book intriguingly entitled *The Mysteries of the Forest,* to have access to the latest books. In Jamaica one had to wait until they were transported across the sea, sometimes with whole volumes missing. That was one advantage to living in England.

"My dear, I was hoping to see you here today," a voice said, and Anne turned to see Felicity. "I particularly wished to speak with you."

Anne smiled warmly. "Felicity. How nice to see you. Have you heard that I am no longer to be snubbed?"

"Ridiculous, isn't it? Oh, not that you're accepted, I think that's marvelous, but that you shouldn't have been in the first place. And all because of what happened in the past. What does it matter today that you jilted Giles?"

Anne's eyes were startled. "I didn't exactly jilt him, ma'am."

"Oh, forgive me, that was a poor choice of words. I meant nothing by it. But then, you must know I believe in plain speaking. That is a lovely frock, by the way."

"Thank you." Anne's smile broadened. She couldn't

take offense at what this woman said; there was no harm meant, and besides, she had never been part of the movement to ostracize Anne. That was the sign of a true friend. "Goodness, who are those handsome men with your daughters? Soldiers, Felicity!"

Felicity turned. "Oh, yes, aren't they marvelous? Well, the barracks of the Tenth Light Dragoons are nearby, you know, the Prince's own regiment, and the officers are delightful young men. Prinny makes certain of that. Why, he chose this very same regiment for Brummell. Quite good family, too," she said, reverting to more current topics. "Mr. Seward, there on Susan's right, is a cornet in the regiment. He is from an old Leicestershire family. Lieutenant Bancroft is a younger son of the Earl of Stratham."

"Heavens. Quite good company for Susan, then."

"Oh, yes. Though, if I miss my guess, Lieutenant Bancroft has been stealing glances at you, Beth."

"Oh, no." Beth was standing at Anne's side, her cheeks pink. "Whyever should he look at me?"

"Because you are a very pretty girl. Come, would you like an introduction?"

"Oh, no," Beth protested, but too late. Felicity was already bustling across the room toward her daughter. "Oh, no, Anne, I shall die of embarrassment, I know I shall."

Anne smiled at her. "I suspect it's very hard to argue with Lady Whitehead once she takes something into her head. Don't worry, Beth, I'll be right beside you, and who knows? He may even become your beau."

"Oh, no. Mother would never allow it."

"But your mother isn't here. Hello, Miss Whitehead. How delightful to see you again."

Susan made a quick curtsy. "Mrs. Templeton."

"And these young men are with the Tenth," Felicity said, making the introductions. She had been right, Anne noted with some amusement. Lieutenant Bancroft, a tall young man with light brown hair and a gentle, but strong, face, did keep looking at Beth, who was blushing quite prettily. Oh, how wonderful it would be if she did find a beau, someone to take her away from Tremont Castle and give her a life of her own. Marriage might not be suitable for herself, but for Beth it could very well signal independence.

"And that is what I wished to talk with you about, Anne," Felicity was saying, breaking Anne out of her reverie. "Life has been so terribly dull lately, I was thinking we should make an excursion to Battle, to see the Abbey."

"I think that's a marvelous idea. I never have been to that part of the world."

"We'll go Tuesday next, if the weather is fine," Felicity went on. "I understand there's a fine inn there for luncheon, and the Abbey is well worth seeing. Not too many people, Anne, just a small party, but I would be delighted if you and Beth would join us. Giles and the duchess, too, of course."

"I can't speak for them, of course, but it does sound enjoyable, does it not, Beth?"

Beth bent her head. "Yes," she whispered, and her eyes peeked up for just a moment at Lieutenant Bancroft, who smiled in return.

"Mama, I would dearly love to have a new frock for the day," Susan said, interrupting in her eagerness. "Do you think—"

"Yes, child, though I don't believe the gentlemen wish to hear a discussion of feminine fripperies." Both men protested at that, adding that they would be happy to provide escort for them. "Very well." Felicity smilingly gave in. "There are some items we need to purchase today. Anne, Beth, won't you please join us?"

Anne smiled and shook her head. "I'd like to, but I give my son his lessons in the morning and I must return home."

"Oh, so must I," Beth said.

"Please, do come, Beth," Susan said. "We hardly

145

ever get a chance to talk. Please allow her, Mrs. Templeton."

"Susan, you are being most forward," Felicity reproved.

Anne smiled. "It isn't my decision to make, but I do think Beth would enjoy it."

"Oh, no, I couldn't," Beth protested.

"Please come, Lady Elizabeth." Lieutenant Bancroft smiled. "We'll watch out for you."

Beth turned. "Anne? Do you mind?"

"Of course not. 'Tis only a short walk home. Do go, Beth, you'll enjoy it."

"Well—very well, yes, I will go." Beth gave an unexpectedly brilliant smile, making Lieutenant Bancroft blink. Anne and Felicity exchanged knowing smiles as they made their farewells. It looked like the beginning of a promising romance. How marvelous, Anne thought, as she finished selecting her books. Perhaps something would turn out well for someone this summer.

Jamie was bored. Nurse had fallen asleep over her crocheting and was snoring, as she did more and more often these days. Mama had gone out, and Uncle Giles was busy with a lot of papers spread over his desk. Sometimes he talked to the ghost, Terence, but even he didn't answer today. Jamie hadn't told anyone about Terence, not even Mama. She wouldn't believe him, just as she didn't really believe there was a monster under his bed. Grown-ups were strange. They did odd, boring things, like tending to business, as Uncle Giles did, or going out shopping, like his mother. He didn't want to be a grown-up; he wanted to stay a little boy forever and ever, and not here. England was a nasty place, cold, noisy, crowded. He missed Hampshire Hall. There he'd been able to come and go as he pleased, and there was always something happening, something to see. Here, he had to stay inside because of all the traffic, and there was nothing to do. Just lessons, and playing soldiers with Uncle Giles, and talking with Terence.

Slowly, never taking his eyes from Nurse, lest she awaken, he slid down in his chair until his feet were touching the floor. Still watching the old woman, he tiptoed with elaborate quiet to the door, which he flung open. Nurse's snore turned into a snort, and then resumed its even cadence. There. He was out. He could finally do some exploring.

It was very quiet in the upstairs hall. Jamie headed for the back stairs, leading to the servants' hall. There he spent an enjoyable time, chatting to the maids and Cook, until old sourpuss Benson came in and frowned at them all. Young though he was, Jamie knew when to beat a retreat. Carrying his bounty, freshly made sugar cookies which Mama would never allow him to have this time of day, he scurried back upstairs, well satisfied with the morning's events. Maybe Nurse would wake up now and read to him. He liked stories. He could even read some words himself. He was getting to be a big boy.

Munching on a cookie and intent on his destination, he trod down the hall to his room. He wasn't aware that anyone else was there until he came up against violet silk skirts that rustled imperiously. *Uh-oh.* Raising his head, he looked up into the stern, forbidding face of the duchess. He was in trouble now.

A little while later, Benson opened the door to admit Anne inside. "'Tis a glorious morning, Benson," she said, smiling at him. "Don't you wish it would stay this way forever?"

"It is not for me to say, ma'am," Benson said.

"Oh. Well, no matter. Where is His Grace?"

"Here." Giles walked toward her from the bookroom. "Good morning, Anne. Do you wish to see me about something?"

147

"Yes, I've something to tell you. Shall we—"

"Ahem. Excuse me, Your Grace, madam." Benson stood ramrod straight, his face long and stern. "There is a problem you should be aware of. With Master James."

"Jamie? Is he all right?"

"What has he done, Benson?" Giles asked with amused resignation.

"What makes you think he has done anything? Jamie is a well-behaved little boy!"

"What is it, Benson? Has Jamie been up to some mischief?"

"I found him in the servants' hall, Your Grace." Benson's eyes were fixed on a point somewhere beyond Giles's shoulder. "Consorting with Cook and some of the maids. Of course, if you'd allowed Mrs. MacPherson to come, instead of hiring a new cook, none of this would have happened. But then, it's not for me to question your actions, sir."

Giles and Anne exchanged looks at this reproof and then hastily glanced away, before they gave into laughter. "Shocking," Giles said mildly. "Was that all he did, Benson?"

"Yes, Your Grace. It is quite enough."

"Quite. I will talk to the boy. Shall we go, Anne?"

"Thank you, Your Grace. I knew you'd be sensible about this."

That last statement, with its implication that Anne would not have been, was too much for her. A strangled laugh escaped her, and she quickly turned it into a cough. "Ahem. Of course we must speak with him, Giles," she said, her voice trembling. "Please, come with me."

"Of course. Thank you, Benson. You old tartar," he muttered under his breath as he and Anne proceeded up the stairs, and Anne choked on another laugh.

"Oh, dear. Benson hasn't changed, has he?" she said.

"Not at all. Sometimes I think he would make a

much better duke than I. He certainly has more consequence."

"I can handle this matter myself, Giles. There's really no need for you to come with me."

"No need! I needed rescuing." He stopped on the stairs and faced her, his face serious and oddly tender. "Anne. We haven't had a chance to speak lately—"

"Come, let's find Jamie and find out exactly what the little rascal did," Anne chattered, turning away. "I'd hate to receive another scolding from Benson."

Giles sighed. "Very well. Let us go."

The hall was as quiet as it had been earlier, except for the low murmur of voices, Jamie's high-pitched, and an older, female one, coming through the door of the nursery. Giles was about to push open the door for Anne to enter, when she caught at his hand. "Look!" she whispered.

Giles looked in over her shoulder and drew himself up in surprise. Through the crack in the door he could just see Nurse, rocking in her chair and nodding her head over her crocheting. That wasn't what was so startling however. Jamie, his back to them, was sitting at the wide nursery table that served as his desk, a huge book set open before him. Beside him, her longer, slightly crooked fingers pointing to a spot on the page, sat Julia, Duchess of Tremont.

"And that was your ancestor, the Earl of Houghton," she said, and leaned back.

"Giles Templeton," Jamie read. "Giles Templeton!" His face shone with excitement. "Just like Uncle Giles!"

"Giles is a Templeton family name. You have inherited a noble tradition, boy."

"What did he do, Auntie Julia?"

"Fought that wicked Oliver Cromwell. Not that it did him any good. He languished in prison until Charles II was restored. Ah, but then he got all his land back, and more, and Charles made him a marquess. The Templetons have always served the Crown."

"That's what I want to do, Auntie Julia. I want to go and fight. Do you think there'll be a war when I grow up?"

"I hope not, boy." Julia's voice was gruff, but the hand she laid on Jamie's head was gentle. Anne and Giles looked at each other in astonishment.

"I hope there is, Auntie Julia! Do you want to see the toy soldiers Uncle Giles gave me?"

"Set them up, lad. On the table, if you please. I'm too old to be sitting on the floor."

"Yes, Auntie!" Jamie scrambled off his chair, and Anne grabbed at Giles's arm, pulling him back. His lips were tightly compressed, his face red, his eyes watering. Anne was not in much better case. With her hand over her mouth and her own eyes dancing, she gestured frantically toward her room. Only when they were inside, with the door safely closed behind them, could they give into their mirth.

"The boy needs a firm hand," Anne gasped, leaning back against the wall. "Oh, Giles."

Giles bent double with the force of his laughter, and then straightened, wiping at his eyes. "Auntie Julia. Never did I think I'd hear anyone address my mother that way."

"What has got into your mother, Giles? I've never seen her like this."

"She likes children. I know, she covers it well. But she really has been a good mother, Anne, though you might not think so now. She never relegated us to nursemaids or governesses, the way most people do."

"How lucky you were," Anne said wistfully. "I hardly ever saw my parents, except for a few moments each day at tea. And of course, when they went to London, I had to stay behind."

"When I went to school for the first time, the other boys laughed at me at first when I talked about

150

Mother. I didn't care. She was splendid when I was young." His eyes were distant. "She was always there for us to talk to when we needed to, and she knew the most extraordinary things. Of course, she's very proud of the Templetons."

"I had noticed."

"Do you know, she was the one who explained different battles to me? She told me about my ancestors, as she's doing with Jamie now, and she would describe what each one did. A much better way to learn history than from a book."

"Then you should understand, Giles, why I treat Jamie as I do. I don't wish to spoil him, no matter what you might think. Life is hard enough. I want Jamie to have a happy childhood."

"Do you know, I never thought of that," he said slowly. "But you do realize, Anne, that you must be careful not to coddle him?"

"In other words, I should send him to school. I'll consider it, Giles." She paused. "What happened to her? What turned your mother into such a cranky old woman?"

He shook his head. "She's always been opinionated. This crankiness, as you call it, only came on recently. I don't know why. I do know it was hard on her when my brother died. And the others, my baby brother and sisters." He paused, too. "Do you know, she never visits the family graveyard anymore?"

"I think I understand that," Anne said softly. "If I lost Jamie—"

"You like children, too. Have you ever considered remarrying?"

"No." Anne turned abruptly away from him, and was as abruptly aware that they were in her bedchamber. Only a few feet away was her bed. Dangerous. "My heavens, it really isn't proper for you to be in here," she said lightly.

"What? Oh." His gaze followed hers, but instead of

151

looking uncomfortable, he grinned. "Why? Do you plan to seduce me, Anne?"

"What—oh, get out! That is low of you, Giles."

"I know." His smile gentled as he gazed at her. "That dress suits you, you know."

"Thank you. Lieutenant Bancroft thought so, too."

"Who the devil is Lieutenant Bancroft?"

"Actually, he appeared far more interested in Beth." Her shoulders held back, awareness of him prickling down her spine. she crossed to the door. "Come, let us go back to the book-room and discuss it."

Giles's eyes narrowed a bit as he followed her out. "Where is Beth? I thought she was with you."

"Oh, we met with Lady Whitehead, and she invited Beth to go shopping with her and her daughter. Along with two very handsome soldiers."

Giles stopped on the stairs. "What!"

"Oh, don't worry, Giles. Felicity assured me they come of quite good families." She smiled up at him from the hall. "Come. Shall we discuss this in private?"

The look Giles gave her was not friendly, which filled her with both relief and regret. There, their relationship was back on its old footing. Just as well. "Very well," he said, and came down the stairs.

Sometime later Anne walked out of the book-room, smiling. In a few moments Giles followed, his face more serious. What Anne had just told him was troublesome, and he wasn't certain how to deal with it. On the one hand, it was good news, but on the other, it could cause considerable trouble. He wasn't so certain that was bad, though. Things had stayed the same for a very long time. Why shouldn't they change?

"Mother." He knocked at the door of Julia's room, and she, sitting in a comfortable chair with the huge family Bible she had been showing Jamie open on her lap, looked up. "Good morning. Have you a moment?"

Julia lowered the spectacles she used for reading. "What is it, Giles? Is there a problem?"

"No." Giles walked into the room and took a chair facing her. "We've had an invitation. I thought you might be interested in accepting."

"What is it?"

"Felicity's getting up an excursion to Battle Abbey next week. We've been invited along."

"An excursion! Really, Giles, you know I don't like to travel. And so near the water, too. You young people are so casual these days."

"Yes, Mother. All the same, it sounds like fun."

"Fun?"

"Fun." He returned her gaze steadily. "Why not enjoy ourselves, if we can?"

"I think not. However, if you and Beth wish to go, I give you my approval."

"Thank you, Mother."

"You are quite welcome. Is that all?"

"Well—"

"Good. Send Beth to me. I require her."

"Beth is not here. She's gone shopping with Felicity." He paused. "And a certain Lieutenant Bancroft."

"Bancroft? What is this, boy, are you hoaxing me?"

"No, ma'am, I wouldn't dare. Felicity and her daughter were being escorted by two officers of the Tenth Light Dragoons, one of whom is a Thomas Bancroft of Surrey."

"Bancroft," she said again. "Of Surrey. Ah. I have it. The Earl of Stratham's third son. Elizabeth could do better for herself."

"Perhaps." Giles leaned forward, his hands clasped between his knees. "Mother, if Beth met someone likely, would you allow her to marry him?"

Julia glared at him. "If he were suitable, yes. I'm not a monster, Giles. I do not keep Beth close to me out of selfishness. At least, not completely," she added. "Beth is sensitive and shy. She'll require someone who will be

153

kind to her, someone who can take care of her."

Giles nodded. "Very well. I'll make inquiries about this Bancroft fellow, and if he's a bounder I'll send him packing."

"Good. Giles, you do know that all I've ever wanted is for my children to be happy?"

"Yes, Mother." He smiled at her as he rose. "Oh, by the by."

"Yes?"

"Did you enjoy your game of toy soldiers?"

To his delight, Julia's face turned crimson. "I was showing the boy the strategy your ancestor used in the Battle of Worcester," she said with great dignity.

"As I recall, it didn't do him much good."

"No, that wicked Cromwell—how do you know about this?"

"I eavesdropped," he confessed. He didn't add that Anne had also been there. Let his mother preserve a little dignity.

"Yes, well, do not refine upon it overmuch. Someone has to teach the boy about his heritage, and Anne is certainly too light-minded to do so."

Giles sat down again. "I think Anne is probably a very good mother," he said slowly. "As you were."

"Pray do not compare her to me! She is flighty and shallow and foolish. And dangerous. She's hurt you once already."

"I doubt she'll do so again."

"No?" Julia's eyes narrowed. "You'd best watch out for her, Giles."

"How so?"

"Because she has decided you will be her next husband."

Chapter 12

Giles sat very still. Anne, as his wife. A strange thought, one he hadn't entertained for a very long time, but pleasant. He needed a wife. He hadn't thought much about it before, but Anne's arrival had made him realize it. He needed someone to be his hostess, to give him heirs. Someone he could talk to, tell his problems and his joys, someone to share his bed. Anne? Remarkable thought, but perhaps not so astonishing as first it had seemed. "That might not be so bad a fate," he said, leaning back, and Julia sat forward, her hands gripping the arms of her chair.

"You will not marry that hussy, Giles! I forbid it."

"You forget yourself, Mother. I am the head of the family. I do not need your permission to do as I wish."

Julia sat back. "Of course not, Giles. I was wrong. Forgive me?"

Giles looked at her a bit askance, wary of this sudden mildness. "Of course, Mother."

"If I spoke harshly, you must remember I am thinking of your good. I will never forgive her for what she did to you."

"It's past, Mother."

"Oh? Don't tell me you've forgotten what happened, and how you felt when you learned she'd gone off with Freddie." The duchess's face softened. "Forgive me for bringing it up again, but what happened was hard on you. I would not see you go through that again."

Giles paced to the window. He remembered well those days after Anne's desertion, the pain, the anger, the bewilderment. Strange, though. Nothing lasted forever, apparently, not even love. What had once been heart-wrenching agony was now only a bittersweet memory. He had loved Anne once. Perhaps it wasn't so surprising that he desired her now. "I need a wife, Mother," he said abruptly.

"Of course you do," she said, so promptly that he turned to stare at her. "You need someone to give you heirs, and I want to see my grandchildren before I die. That Jamie." She smiled, leaning back. "He's an engaging scamp. Undisciplined, of course, but very bright. Children remind you of the essentials of life, and they give you love, Giles. Nothing else seems terribly important when you're holding a child in your lap." Giles was staring at her, his forehead furrowed, and she went on, her head held high. "You should have children, Giles. You have to do your duty and provide yourself with heirs."

"Yes, Mother." Giles sat across from her again, his mouth quirked. The old humbug, he thought affectionately, wanting to reach over and take one of the old gnarled hands in his but knowing that she would, at this moment, reject such sentiment. "I'll start looking around for someone. God knows there are plenty of available females here this summer."

"Pray do not swear in my presence. As to that, I thought Lady Whitehead's daughter was charming."

"Susan? She's only a child."

"All to the good. A healthy young girl who can bear children and who you can mold to your wishes."

"I don't know, Mother." Once he might have agreed with that idea. That, however, had been before his life had been turned topsy-turvy by a golden-haired woman who made him remember desires and dreams

156

best forgotten. The thought of marrying someone young and silly was unutterably depressing. Surely he wouldn't need someone that young, just to have children. Someone older, more mature, a widow, perhaps. . . . "As to that, Mother," he drawled, "Anne has already proven herself to be a good breeder."

Julia bent forward again, and then relaxed. "You think to hoax me. Very well, have your fun. But mark my words, boy. She'll hurt you if you let her. And she'll leave you again."

Giles rose. "It will be time for luncheon soon, and there are matters I still need to see to. If you'll excuse me?"

"Of course." Julia nodded, and then leaned her head back against the chair, closing her eyes. She was so tired, and her joints ached so much. This dratted sea air. But, there, her children's welfare was what mattered, and wasn't it lucky for them she was here? Both might very well make disastrous alliances without her guiding hand, Beth with a younger son, and Giles. Now, there was the real danger. She didn't trust the Warren girl at all. She was flighty, light-minded, and a hussy. Not at all a suitable match for the Duke of Tremont. She thought, though, feeling sleep overtake her, that she had discouraged that prospect. Yes. She had done her work well.

The day set for the excursion to Battle dawned clear and fine. It was a colorful party which set off on horseback along the white, dusty road leading east along the coast, the soldiers in their blue coats and red shakos, the women in fashionable riding habits. Anne's was of soft peach broadcloth, with a matching hat set rakishly atop her head, and Beth looked well in a flattering habit of sky blue. She was, in fact, looking quite remarkably pretty lately. At breakfast this morning her eyes had been bright with anticipation, probably at seeing Lieutenant Bancroft today. Anne remembered well what it was like, that delicious mixture of nervousness and excitement at the thought of being with someone to whom you were attracted. Someone who made you feel more alive, and, at the same time, more feminine. She'd never feel that way again. Being with Giles brought only pain.

It had not been easy living in the same house with Giles this past week. Every time she saw him her heart speeded up, her breath caught, her blood began to thrum. Every time she saw him, she reminded herself that he was not for her, every time, until the conflict within her rivaled the battles that Jamie staged with his soldiers. She wanted him; she didn't want him. She would stay with him; she refused to give up everything she had worked for, for a man who had once chosen someone else over her. For a man who had not, and did not, love her. He wasn't for her. No man would ever be for her again. She'd decided that long ago. It was going to be a very long summer, until she could return to Jamaica.

"A fine morning, isn't it?" Giles said beside her, and she looked up, startled. This was going to be difficult.

"Yes. Heavens, Giles, you're actually smiling. Don't tell me you're enjoying yourself."

Giles's smiled broadened. "Of course. Jamie seems to be, too."

Anne followed his gaze. Jamie was riding his pony alongside Lieutenant Bancroft and was pelting him with questions. "Oh, dear, I hope he won't be a nuisance. I'd like him to see Battle, because who knows when he'll have the chance again, but I fear it will be too much for him."

If Giles noticed the reminder that Anne would someday leave, he didn't show it. "If he tires, I'll take him up with me on the way back," he said easily, making her look at him again. "You look very well, Anne."

"Oh, la, yes, it was thoughtful of you, Giles, to find me a chestnut mare to complement my habit. I declare, I feel most fashionable."

Giles grinned, the twinkle in his eyes telling Anne he knew exactly what she was doing. For some reason that sent a *frisson* of excitement through her. It seemed like an age since she had been young, since she had flirted with a handsome man, since she had simply had fun. The future was distant, and who knew what might happen? For now, she would enjoy the day.

The party rode on, chattering and laughing, eventually coming to the small town of Hastings. Once one of the Cinque ports, its harbor had long since silted up, turning it into a sleepy village. Here the party turned inland, passing the ruins of Hastings Castle and riding along the grassy South Downs, the line of low, rolling chalk hills that were so important a feature in the area's landscape. Eventually, somewhat weary, they reached the picturesque village of Battle.

Everyone agreed that luncheon was the first priority, before setting out to see the Abbey. At the George Inn they engaged a private parlor. Anne, keeping a close watch on Jamie, was relieved to see him wolf down his food with nary a complaint. She was proud of her son. Young though he was, he was behaving like a perfect gentleman, bright and interested, but well mannered. She let him skip ahead of her as, luncheon over, the party proceeded down High Street toward the Abbey. The buildings were a pleasant mixture of styles, from the Old Pharmacy in its half-timbered house at least two hundred years old, to the church of St. Mary, dating from the thirteenth century. Ahead was the gateway to the Abbey, a beautiful old piece of masonry, built when the Abbey had been crenellated, or fortified. Jamie craned his head back, staring at it in awe. "Now this is something like!" he exclaimed, turning his bright shining gaze on Giles. "Are there knights here, Uncle Giles?"

"Not anymore, lad." Giles laid his hand lightly on Jamie's shoulder. "This is where William the Conqueror fought King Harold."

"I know. 1066," Jamie said, with such a smug, knowledgeable air that Anne and Giles exchanged amused looks.

"Precisely. William decreed that an abbey be built here to give thanks for his victory. We'll just pay the gatekeeper and go in."

Jamie scampered ahead, tugging on Anne's hand. "It's all ruins! Come on, Mommy, I want to see!"

"In a moment, Jamie." Anne let him pull her through the gate. "Oh, look, Jamie." Stonework, ancient and yet still precise, was everywhere. What looked like the ruins of a church were to her left, while ahead was a building that appeared to date from more recent times than William's. Elizabethan, perhaps. "Look at that, over there."

"The monks' dormitory," Giles said, joining them and looking at the one building which still stood, ruined but impressive, against the deep blue sky. "Not much left, is there?"

Jamie wriggled free of Anne's grasp. "What happened to it, Uncle Giles?"

"A man named Sir Anthony Browne was given the Abbey when Henry the Eighth dissolved the monasteries, lad. He pulled down most of the buildings and built a home, that building ahead. He paid for it, though. Rather, his family did."

"What happened?"

"Well, the legend is, when he was dining for the first time in the Great Hall, a ghostly monk appeared and told him his family would end in fire and water."

"Like our ghost, Uncle Giles?"

"Not quite, Jamie," Anne said, glaring at Giles. "You shouldn't tell him such stories."

Giles's grin was unrepentant. "Boys like ghost stories. Sir Anthony was one of Queen Elizabeth's guardians when she was young, and he began to build her a house, there." He pointed. "Unfortunately, he died before it was finished."

"By fire, Uncle Giles?"

"Do you see what you've started?" Anne said.

Giles ignored her. "No, that happened later. Actually, only a few years ago." His face turned serious. "His family moved to Midhurst. Do you remember, Anne? Cowdray Park burned down, and then the heir was drowned a week later."

"I remember it well. Jamie probably will, too," she added in a lowered voice. "If he has nightmares tonight, I'll let you cope with him."

"He'll be fine. You coddle him too much, Anne. Come." He took Jamie's hand. "Let's do some exploring."

Grass and flowers had long ago grown up among the ruins, belying the fact that once a great battle had been fought here. Though others were there besides the party from Brighton, the place had a peaceful quality that pervaded Anne's soul, making her relax. For a little while she would forget why she was in England, she thought, listening to Giles deep, patient voice as he answered yet another of Jamie's questions. For just today she would pretend that they all belonged together, she and Jamie and Giles, folly though it was. Reality would return soon enough.

At length she and Giles rejoined the others, who had found a bench under a broad, shady oak. "'Tis warm, is it not?" Felicity said, smiling sympathetically at Anne as she sat beside her.

"Oh, yes, but I'm glad we came. This was worth it."

"And we've yet to see the high altar," Giles said. "We don't want to miss that."

"Oh, dear." Anne looked down at Jamie, whose head was in her lap. His eyelids drooped, and his thumb was tucked securely in his mouth. "I fear Jamie is tired."

"Leave him with me," Felicity suggested, bending to lift the boy onto her lap. He muttered a sleepy protest, and then snuggled his head against her shoulder. "The young people would like to walk some more, I think."

Anne looked over at the others, the two soldiers, and the young girls. Beth was looking up at Lieutenant Bancroft in a starry-eyed way. "We are no longer young, Felicity."

"Of course you are! But in any event, we cannot let the others roam about unchaperoned, can we?"

"I suppose we cannot." Anne exchanged an amused glance with Giles, and then rose. "Very well. It seems we're to be chaperones, Giles."

"Oh? Very well. I suppose it is my responsibility," he said, smiling in such a way that Anne felt her heart twist.

"Quite," she managed to say weakly, hoping her feelings didn't show. Why did she have to love him so?

Lieutenant Bancroft came up to them. "I was just telling Lady Elizabeth about the terrace, sir," he said. "We plan to walk there to see where the battle was actually fought."

"We were just discussing the same thing," Felicity said, sending Anne so knowing a look that Anne was stunned. Did her feelings show so plainly? "Whitehead and I will stay here."

"As you wish, ma'am. Lady Elizabeth?" Thomas Bancroft held out his arm to Beth. She looked a little startled, like a fawn about to take flight, but then, with accomplished grace, she laid her hand on his arm. Anne was so proud of her that she forgot her own role in this matchmaking, until Giles spoke to her.

"If we are to be duennas, Anne, we must go, too," he said, a little twinkle in his eye. "And I would like to see the high altar." Anne forced herself to return his smile and took his arm quite as smoothly as Beth had. There. This was just a simple walk in the Abbey grounds, no different from that taken by other couples. Well, perhaps a little different, since she wasn't on the catch for this man. Nothing, though, was going to happen, and that was just as well, of course. Of course.

They set out together, the three couples, but eventually the differing intensities of conversation and the pace separated them, until Beth and Thomas, far ahead, reached the terrace overlooking the rest of the town. Here they stopped. "Here is where Harold arrayed his men," Thomas said, waving his hand in a broad sweep that encompassed the entire terrace. "William's men came up the hill. Harold nearly won the day, you know. Things would have been a lot different if he had."

Beth, distracted for a moment from what Thomas was saying, glanced back, to see the others far behind. It was frightening; it was exciting. The lieutenant was like no man she'd ever met before, not gentle and philosophical like Reverend Goodfellow at home, or eager and callow like the few boys she had met at local assemblies. The lieutenant had been in the war already, in the disastrous retreat from Corunna. He may have purchased his commission, but he had since earned it. He was tall and walked with a confident stride that managed not to be a swagger, and the arm under her fingers was rock-hard. It was a bit of a relief that Giles was nearby. But not too close. She felt almost giddy with the freedom of it. "Yes." Her voice was a little breathless. She didn't particularly wish to discuss old battles, no matter how important. "I am glad Napoleon never succeeded in his invasion plans."

"Yes, thank God for that."

"What do you plan to do when the war is over?" she asked, surprising herself by her daring in changing the conversation. "If the war ever ends. It seems it's been going on forever."

"It has." Thomas's tone was grim, but he softened it at the anxious look on her face. "As long as anyone can remember, practically. But it will end, Lady Elizabeth.

163

We'll beat Boney. You may be assured of that."

Strangely enough, she did feel reassured. "And then? Do you plan to stay in the army?"

"No. Won't be much need for men like me, then. Actually, ma'am, what I want to do is rather dull," he said, flashing even white teeth at her in a smile.

"Oh, do tell me."

"If you insist. I have a small estate in Kent, a legacy from my grandmother. It's a lovely little place, Lady Elizabeth." He smiled at her again. "I think you'd like it."

Beth made her answering smile noncommittal. "Do you plan to farm? My brother does."

"Yes, and no. It's wonderful land for growing things, but I was thinking of something different. The estate is in a valley. It's sheltered and mild there, and it doesn't seem to rain as much. What I'd like to do is grow grapes."

"Grapes," she said blankly.

"A vineyard. I saw vineyards in Spain, Elizabeth. They're fascinating. And there's a need for it. Do you know, most of our wine and brandy has to be smuggled in? Think of being able to have good English wine, and at a reasonable price. Of course, the vines don't yield for a few years, but I'd say it's worth a go."

"Grapes," she repeated.

"Grapes." He smiled down at her. "I understand what you're thinking. Sometimes I think I must be mad. But, there it is. It's got into my blood. I've read every book I can get my hands on and talked to every vineyard owner I could. I have to try it. Do you think, Elizabeth—"

"Lady Elizabeth."

"—that your brother would approve of a vintner?"

"I think it is much too early to even think of such a thing, Lieutenant," she said, with just the right amount of reproof. She was proud of herself. Even though her heart had leapt at the meaning behind his words, she

164

had managed to sound as calm and composed as the most accomplished flirt. Really, where was this new Beth coming from?

"Of course it is. My pardon, Lady Beth." He grinned at her, so that she didn't have the heart to correct him again. Lady Beth. She liked the sound of that. "He seems rather a starched-up fellow."

"He isn't," she protested. "Really, Lieutenant Bancroft. Do you always speak your mind so?"

"Always," he said solemnly. "I am my mother's despair. I am told that when I was a child she took me to a relative's funeral, and when the casket was carried in I said something rather embarrassing for all the church to hear."

"Oh, dear. What did you say?"

"I believe it was, 'Hey, Ma. What's in the box?'"

Beth burst into startled laughter. "Oh, no! Oh, your poor mother. She must have died with embarrassment."

"She did. Not for the last time. You know, I like the way you laugh."

"You do?" Instantly, she grew serious. "My mother says it is much too loud and unladylike."

"No. It's real. If I hear one more artificial giggle I may commit mayhem. That's why I like you. You're real."

"No, I'm not," she surprised herself by saying. "I'm what my mother wants me to be."

"And maybe your brother, too."

"No. Oh, maybe a little. But then, I think Giles is different, too. I've often wondered, if he'd married Anne as he was supposed to—"

"Mrs. Templeton?" Thomas twisted to look back. Giles and Anne had fallen farther back. "Seems like a mismatch to me. What happened?"

"She married someone else. A cousin, that is why her name is the same as ours. Poor Giles." She sighed. "I think he's had it very hard."

"Tell me about him."

"Why?"

"They teach you in the army to learn about your opponent."

"Giles isn't your opponent."

"He may be, someday." The look he gave her was so meaningful that she looked away. "I'm interested in people, Beth."

"Lady Beth."

"Lady Beth," he agreed. "Tell me about your brother. Tell me why he takes his responsibility so seriously. He does, doesn't he?"

"Oh, yes. Duty is everything to him. I think it always has been. At least, as long as I've been aware. Of course, he knew early on he was going to be duke one day, and our father believed very strongly in tradition and duty. Our mother does, too. Do you know, I wonder if it was hard for him? I never thought about it before."

"He handles it well. But then, being the oldest—"

"Oh, no, he wasn't the oldest. We had a brother, Edward."

"What happened to him?"

Beth was looking out to sea. "He died." When there was no reaction, she turned to see him watching her sympathetically. "It was—it must have been horrible. We used to spend our summers in Cornwall, near where my grandmother had grown up. Edward loved to sail. He was ten years older than Giles. My poor mother, she's lost so many children. In any event, Edward took Giles sailing one day, and a gale came up. Their boat capsized. Edward managed to get Giles up on the hull so he was safe, but he—he drowned." She stopped for a moment, swallowing hard, though she had never known this brother. "He was only fifteen."

"So the duke was only five."

"Yes. He never talks about it, you know. None of us do. But since then, he won't go near the water. I was surprised when he agreed to come to Brighton."

Thomas twisted again to look back. "He seems to be enjoying himself. Now." He turned to face her, and there was so intent a look in his eyes that even Beth couldn't mistake it. "About us—"

"Beth, did you see this rosebush?" Susan called, and Beth and Thomas turned, startled, to see that Susan and Lieutenant Seward were nearly upon them.

"N-no," Beth said. "We should go see it, sir."

"I suppose." Thomas gave her a quick look of regret. "We'll talk more later."

"Oh, yes," Beth said, and wondered at her boldness.

"I feel decidedly old," Giles said, and Anne, who had been looking abstractedly about her, turned toward him. "Am I so much a chaperon that you cannot even talk to me?"

"You are doing your duty," Anne said solemnly, though her eyes sparkled.

"Yes, my damned, cursed duty."

"Giles!"

"Do you remember, Anne, when we were the ones who needed chaperoning? Whoever thought we'd turn out to be so proper?"

"Proper? This conversation is far from proper."

"I suppose it is." He looked down at her, though she kept her head averted. Living in the same house this past week with Anne had not been easy, not since his mother had made that remarkable accusation. Anne, wanting to marry him? Ridiculous. He rather wished it weren't, though. He needed a wife, and she had the advantage of being familiar to him. And he wanted her. Each time he saw her his heart began to pound, he couldn't breathe, and his blood set up a restless rhythm. It bothered him, because he had never been the kind of man to feel, or give into, such lust. He had always kept himself well under control, aware of who he was, and what his duty was. His damned duty, which ordained he must marry a suitable girl, when what he really wanted was to sweep this delectable female into his arms and never let her go. But she didn't want him. He had watched her through all their exchanges in the past days, and he had come to the conclusion that she was either extraordinarily clever and subtle, or that she really didn't wish to marry him. He suspected the latter. She was no more interested in him now than she had been seven years ago.

He was so close. Though Anne's fingers rested lightly on Giles's arm, she was acutely aware of the strength of the muscles underneath his civilized, well-tailored coat. She could feel the warmth of him through the fine fabric; she could sense his eyes on her in a gaze she refused to meet. For, if she did, he would surely see what she tried so hard to keep hidden, that she loved him, she loved him hopelessly and forever, when there was no chance that that love would ever be returned. And, if it were, what would she do?

"Where are the others?" Anne asked, glancing around.

"Somewhere in the grounds, I imagine." Giles held her back. "They'll be fine. This is public, after all."

"I don't know. Giles, do you think Beth can handle Lieutenant Bancroft?"

"There's more to Beth than you might think. And Bancroft seems a decent type."

"You don't mind that he's a younger son?"

"No. So was I, once."

"So you were." Anne kept her voice light. "This garden is lovely. And quiet." For the first time, she realized that she and Giles were the only ones in this part of the Abbey grounds. With the ruins of the church behind them, they were quite isolated. It should have made her uneasy. It didn't.

"Here is where the high altar stood." Giles pointed to a marker in the grass. "They excavated it just recently.

William had it built where Harold fell. The Saxon standards must have flown just about there."

Anne followed his pointing finger, almost able to see it, the chaos of battle, the colorful flags rippling in the breeze. "You know a great deal about it."

Giles grinned. "Mother's doing. Doubtless some Templeton ancestor fought here."

"Thank you for spending time with Jamie. I know answering his questions can be wearing."

"He's a very taking little boy. Very bright." He paused. "And he does need a man's influence."

Anne sighed. "I know. But, please, Giles, let's don't quarrel today."

"I never did want to quarrel with you, Annie."

"Annie? No one's called me that in years." And then only him. The way he was looking at her was strange, disturbing; his eyes were warm, intense, and very much alive with light.

"What happened to us, Annie? We were young once. All of life was before us."

"You know what happened, Giles," she said, her voice smothered. Of all places to discuss this subject! She glanced quickly around, but they were still alone.

"But I never understood why."

"Why?" Her eyes came up, startled. "When you—"

"When I kissed you the way I did, and you kissed me back."

"Giles!"

"Do you remember our first kiss, Annie?"

"Giles, this is a most inappropriate conversation."

"Do you remember it?" He grasped her arms and turned her to face him, pulling her into the shelter of the trees that ringed the garden. "Tell me you remember it."

"Oh, Giles." Something in his eyes, some need, touched her. "Of course I remember. 'Twas in Lady Wilton's garden during a dull musicale. I remember I was terrified we'd be caught."

169

"I remember how much I wanted to kiss you." Giles's voice was low. "I remember how long I'd wanted to—you have very kissable lips, sweetheart, so full and pink—and I remember how scared I was."

"Scared!" she exclaimed, in spite of the odd feelings his words sent spurting through her. Did she have kissable lips? "You didn't seem so."

"I was. You were so young. I was afraid I'd scare you."

Anne chuckled, caught up in the memories in spite of herself. "And there I was, wondering when you were ever going to kiss me."

"Ah, if I'd known that." He smiled. "But I did."

"Yes. You did."

"And you kissed me back."

Anne lowered her head. "I don't remember."

"Yes, you do. Look at me, Annie." His fingers under her chin forced her head up, so that she had to look at him. "You haven't forgotten any of it, have you?"

"No," she whispered, caught, and held, by his gaze. Had anyone before ever looked at her so, with such tenderness, such yearning? Such need?

"Nor have I. I think it began something like this." Cupping her face, he brushed his thumbs along her cheekbones, and her eyes fluttered shut. "Ah, love, your skin is as soft now as it was then. You smelled of violets. Now it's—?"

"Frangipani."

"Ah. I like that. Then I put my arm around you, like this." He slipped his arm around her waist and drew her, unprotesting, toward him. "You put your arms around my neck."

"Not right away."

"No? But soon. And then I lowered my head, like so. And I stopped."

"I didn't know why."

"To give you a chance to pull away."

"I don't want it, Giles." And standing on tiptoe, she

170

looped her arms around his neck, just as he said she had. He stroked her cheek with the backs of his fingers, his eyes never leaving hers. For one endless, eternal moment they gazed at each other, and then at last, at long last, he lowered his head, and his mouth touched hers.

Chapter 13

Instantly Anne pressed up against him, helpless against the firestorm of need raging within her. It was different from that long-ago, tentative kiss. They were different. They had grown, changed, gone through things they had never imagined when young. They had grown apart, and yet, here they were, in the inadequate shelter of a few trees, his hands roaming on her back, her mouth opening to the gentle, insistent probing of his tongue. Much had changed, and yet, nothing had changed. They were still just Anne, just Giles, but with more experience to bring to this particular moment. He was not a laughing young man anymore, nor she an innocent debutante, tasting passion for the first time. Passion, warm and sweet, turning her blood sluggish, her body heavy. Passion, something she hadn't felt in ever so long, something she had never felt with Freddie.

She jerked back abruptly as memory returned, and Giles, caught off guard, let her go. "Anne?" Her eyes were blank and frightened, filled with the fear he'd seen in her when she had waltzed with Campbell. He still didn't understand it. "Annie, what is it?"

"Oh, lord." She passed a shaking hand over her face, effectively hiding it from him. "Oh, lord, Giles, what you must be thinking of me."

"What is it, Anne? Tell me. What's wrong?"

"A headache." She laughed shakily. "I know that sounds dreadfully lame, but I do get the most horrible migraines."

"Annie." He moved toward her, and she stepped back, making him stop. "We were friends once. Can you not tell me what is wrong?"

"Are you adding lying to my other offenses now? Oh, I want to go home." She buried her face in her hands, so forlorn a figure that he wanted more than anything to go to her, to gather her into his arms and hold her, rocking her, promising safety and—what? For the life of him, he didn't know.

"No, Annie," he said gently. "I'm not accusing you of lying."

At that Anne looked up. Giles, so close, and so lost to her. Poor man, he looked so confused; he had probably never had a woman pull away from him in revulsion in his life. She wanted to go to him and touch his face, assure him that it was her fault, not his, promising him—what? She didn't know. All she wanted was to go home, though for the life of her she didn't know whether home was Jamaica, or the place where she had grown up. Or Giles's strong, sheltering arms.

"It must never happen again, Giles," she said, her hands clasped primly before her.

"There are no impediments, Annie. You are widowed, and I'm promised to no one."

Anne gripped her hands tighter. "I'm not Annie anymore. And this must not happen again."

"Why? Just tell me that."

"Because I don't love you." The words rang in the sudden silence, making her safe. "I never did."

To Giles's credit he didn't so much as flinch. "I see. My mistake, Anne. Forgive me."

There was a strange lump in her throat. "Yes, Giles. Of course."

"Come. Let us find the others. A poor job we're

173

doing as chaperones."

"Yes." She came over to him and took the arm he held out to her, standing as far from him as possible. "Giles, we are still friends, are we not?"

"If you ask me that again, I will not be responsible for the consequences," he said through his teeth. Startled, Anne looked up. He looked savage, almost feral, and for the first time she saw a side of him he'd always kept hidden. Oddly enough, it didn't inspire fear in her. Only pity. Like her, he hid himself away from the world.

"Very well." *Oh, Giles. Oh, Giles.* "We'll be cordial, civilized enemies. Agreed?"

"Agreed."

They emerged from the garden to see the other couples returning from their various strolls. Susan looked primly smug; Beth's cheeks were flushed, and her eyes bright. She and Giles hadn't done their jobs as chaperones well at all, Anne thought, but then, who would ever have thought they would be the ones who needed watching?

Though the sun had not yet set, the light had already turned golden. It was a weary, and quiet, group of people who turned their mounts toward home. Jamie had given up the effort of riding long ago and now, fast asleep, was tucked before Giles on his mount. The sight sent a curious pang through Anne. So much that could have been, and would never be. In the space of a few moments, her world had fallen to pieces. She wondered if it would ever be the same again.

The bells at the Castle Inn pealed out several days later, heralding the arrival of important visitors to the town. Soon the news spread as to who they were: the Viscount and Viscountess of Pendleton. Anne's parents.

Anne's hands were cold inside her gloves as she rode

in the Tremont landau toward the house her parents had taken for the summer, on the Marine Parade. She hadn't seen them since her runaway marriage, and she was rather dreading this visit. Through the years she had maintained cordial relations with them through letters, but one image remained unchanged. She still remembered, all too vividly, their reactions to her marriage, the looks on their faces, ranging from her mother's embarrassment and shock to her father's condemnation. It had been wretchedly difficult to face, when all her life she had tried so hard to please them. Perhaps it wouldn't have been so hard if she'd ever felt they truly cared about her.

A butler she didn't recognize admitted her to a house even grander than the one the Tremonts had taken, and led her upstairs to the drawing room. In the brief moment between his announcing her arrival and her mother's rising to greet her, Anne quickly surveyed the room. It was all pink and gilt, with an Axminster carpet in rose and cream and teal on the floor, reminding her irresistibly of a candy box. A perfect setting for the woman coming toward her, her hands outstretched.

"Oh, my dear." Lady Katherine Pendleton pressed a cool, powder-scented cheek against Anne's, and the impulse Anne had had, to throw her arms around her mother, died. "Oh, how wonderful to see you again. Let me look at you. Why, you look quite fashionable. I was so afraid that after years in that nasty place you'd be all brown, like one of the natives. But you look quite well."

Anne kept her smile firmly in place. "Thank you, Mother. So do you."

Katherine preened. There was such a resemblance between mother and daughter that they might have been taken for sisters. Katherine's complexion owed much to rosewater and cream, however, and the rice powder she judiciously applied every day, hoping to disguise the fine lines near her eyes and mouth. Her hair was as golden as Anne's, but it had a brassy tint, hinting that nature had been helped along here, as well. Finally, the most discerning would have realized that underneath her flimsy, fashionable gown Katherine was rigidly corseted. "Why, thank you for saying so, darling," she said. "Come, sit with me. You always were a good girl, except for that one time which we will not mention. How sweet of you to pay us a call, when I know you must be so busy."

"You're my mother."

"Well, yes, of course I am, though I do hope you won't say so so openly in company! I do think we look rather more like sisters, do you not? Though you haven't been rinsing your hair in lemon juice as I taught you, have you? Dear, dear. You know how I dislike red hair, it is so common. Well, never mind. It is so delightful to see you again. Though I did expect you to visit earlier."

Anne's fingers curled in her lap. Nothing she did was ever enough. "I thought you might need time to settle in."

"Oh, la, as to that, you can see we're at sixes and sevens!" she exclaimed, waving a hand around the immaculate drawing room. "But the staff will see to that, of course. You have been in England quite some time now, darling. I'm hurt that you didn't think to visit your parents before this."

Oh, unfair. "I did think you and Papa might come to Tremont Castle. I asked you enough times," she said, the words torn from her. She hadn't intended to say any such thing. She hadn't wanted to show how very much her parents' indifference had hurt her.

"Oh, la, there was so much to do. You understand, of course. But, come, we mustn't squabble! It is enough we're all together in Brighton."

"Of course." Anne smiled and, on impulse, reached over to squeeze her mother's hand. "It is so good to see

176

MORE PASSION AND ADVENTURE AWAIT... YOUR TRIP TO A BIG ADVENTUROUS WORLD BEGINS WHEN YOU ACCEPT YOUR FIRST 4 NOVELS ABSOLUTELY *FREE* (AN $18.00 VALUE)

Accept your Free gift and start to experience more of the passion and adventure you like in a historical romance novel. Each Zebra novel is filled with proud men, spirited women and tempestuous love that you'll remember long after you turn the last page.

Zebra Historical Romances are the finest novels of their kind. They are written by authors who really know how to weave tales of romance and adventure in the historical settings you love. You'll feel like you've actually gone back in time with the thrilling stories that each Zebra novel offers.

GET YOUR FREE GIFT WITH THE START OF YOUR HOME SUBSCRIPTION

Our readers tell us that these books sell out very fast in book stores and often they miss the newest titles. So Zebra has made arrangements for you to receive the four newest novels published each month.

You'll be guaranteed that you'll never miss a title, and home delivery is so convenient. And to show you just how easy it is to get Zebra Historical Romances, we'll send you your first 4 books absolutely FREE! Our gift to you just for trying our home subscription service.

BIG SAVINGS AND FREE HOME DELIVERY

Each month, you'll receive the four newest titles as soon as they are published. You'll probably receive them even before the bookstores do. What's more, you may preview these exciting novels free for 10 days. If you like them as much as we think you will, just pay the low preferred subscriber's price of just $3.75 each. *You'll save $3.00 each month off the publisher's price.* AND, your savings are even greater because there are never any shipping, handling or other hidden charges—FREE Home Delivery. Of course you can return any shipment within 10 days for full credit, no questions asked. There is no minimum number of books you must buy.

4 FREE BOOKS

TO GET YOUR 4 FREE BOOKS WORTH $18.00 — MAIL IN THE FREE BOOK CERTIFICATE T O D A Y

Fill in the Free Book Certificate below, and we'll send your FREE BOOKS to you as soon as we receive it.

If the certificate is missing below, write to: Zebra Home Subscription Service, Inc., P.O. Box 5214, 120 Brighton Road, Clifton, New Jersey 07015-5214.

FREE BOOK CERTIFICATE
4 FREE BOOKS
ZEBRA HOME SUBSCRIPTION SERVICE, INC.

YES! Please start my subscription to Zebra Historical Romances and send me my first 4 books absolutely FREE. I understand that each month I may preview four new Zebra Historical Romances free for 10 days. If I'm not satisfied with them, I may return the four books within 10 days and owe nothing. Otherwise, I will pay the low preferred subscriber's price of just $3.75 each; a total of $15.00, *a savings off the publisher's price of $3.00.* I may return any shipment and I may cancel this subscription at any time. There is no obligation to buy any shipment and there are no shipping, handling or other hidden charges. Regardless of what I decide, the four free books are mine to keep.

NAME _____

ADDRESS _____ APT _____

CITY _____ STATE _____ ZIP _____

TELEPHONE ( ) _____

SIGNATURE _____ (if under 18, parent or guardian must sign)

Terms, offer and prices subject to change without notice. Subscription subject to acceptance by Zebra Books. Zebra Books reserves the right to reject any order or cancel any subscription.

GET
FOUR
FREE
BOOKS
(AN $18.00 VALUE)

ZEBRA HOME SUBSCRIPTION
SERVICE, INC.
P.O. Box 5214
120 BRIGHTON ROAD
CLIFTON, NEW JERSEY 07015-5214

you again. And Papa? Where is he? I thought to see him here."

"You know your father, darling. Nothing must do but that he went to his club. You do know Raggett, the man who has White's in London, has opened a club here? A marvelous idea, and so ideal for someone like your father. He did ask me specially to give you his regards."

"Oh." Seven years. It had been seven years since she had seen her father, and he couldn't even take the trouble to stay home and talk with her for five minutes. Unbidden a memory returned to her. Giles, waiting for her at the quay at Portsmouth. At least he had had the sensitivity to realize she would want a welcome on her return to England.

"Of course he wants to see you, but I imagine we'll run into each other at routs and such. Tell me, what has been happening here? I was sorry we couldn't have come earlier, but there were some matters at Penworth that Pendleton had to see to and I just could not tear him away! But I am certain there is so much more ahead."

"I'm sure," Anne murmured, and sat quietly, letting her mother prattle on about the season just past in London, the pleasures in store in Brighton. Nothing had changed. She didn't know why she had thought things might be different, except that she herself had changed so. She had grown up. She knew now, though, that her parents never would. Their chief concern was, as it always had been, their own pleasure. They had never had much time for the solemn-faced child Anne had been, or the flighty girl she had become; they had little time now for her as a mature woman. Watching her mother's fluttering, birdlike gestures as she talked, Anne felt old, almost as if she were the parent rather than the child. It wouldn't matter that she had been graciously received by the Prince of Wales. Nothing was really important to Katherine unless it pertained directly to her; nothing anyone else did quite mattered. And, Anne thought, with wry amusement, if her mother had dined at the Marine Pavilion, she would now be telling Anne about it. Her parents were the same as they had always been. She had to reconcile herself to that.

"I must be going, Mother," Anne said, when Katherine stopped to draw a breath. "I promised Jamie I'd take tea with him."

"Jamie?" Katherine's brow furrowed, before she remembered and quickly reached up her fingers to smooth away any wrinkles. "Oh, yes. Your son. He is, what? Two, now?"

"Five, Mother."

"Oh, well. I'm sure he won't mind if you're late. Children never notice such things."

Anne smiled as she rose. "Nevertheless. I made him a promise. But we'll see each other again."

"Oh, la, yes." Katherine rose, too. "We'll be going to the ball at the Old Ship tomorrow night, will you?"

"I believe so. We usually do."

"How very nice." Katherine took Anne's arm as they walked to the door of the drawing room, and Anne could almost believe there was a closeness between them. "Do call again, darling, it was delightful to see you again."

"Yes, Mother." Anne pressed her cheek against hers again, and then turned to leave, filled with a mixture of relief and sorrow. It was her own fault, of course, for thinking that her parents would have changed, simply because she had been away for so long. She really should have known better. Perhaps then she wouldn't have been so disappointed.

Giles was just coming out of the book-room when Anne walked into the house. A surge of gladness at seeing him went through her, and she quickly suppressed it. *No expectations, Anne,* she told herself, sternly. *Nothing has changed here, either.* "Giles." She made herself smile. "What is the time?"

Giles looked at her, long, before reaching for his watch. "Half-past three. Good afternoon to you, too."

"Oh! Good afternoon, Giles. Thank heavens, I've time. I promised Jamie I'd be back by four to take tea with him."

"How are your parents?" he asked, and she stopped on the stairs, turning to him.

"My mother is well. Quite the same, actually. I imagine my father is, too. He was at Raggett's."

Giles held out his hand, "Anne– "

"Excuse me, I really would like to change before I go to the nursery," she said, and hurried away up the stairs.

Giles watched her go, and then went back into the book-room. There he stood behind the library table he used as a desk, his fingers resting lightly upon its polished mahogany surface. Papers having to do with his various estates and duties lay in neatly sorted piles on the table, but, though he frowned down at them, Giles didn't see them. Once his responsibilities had mattered most to him. Now something else had taken their place.

He sank down in the chair, his legs outstretched and his hands drumming on the arm. He didn't understand women, not even the ones in his family. Beth seemed more skittish than ever, walking about the house with vague eyes and jumping when anyone spoke to her. His mother, who had always been demanding but caring, now seemed merely fractious. And Anne—Anne was the most confusing of them all.

For perhaps the thousandth time he reviewed what had happened between them at Battle Abbey. He didn't think he'd read her reactions wrong. That she'd been reluctant to discuss the past perhaps was natural; though he still felt it lay between them, he no longer resented it as once he had. They had both been young,

179

and had made mistakes. It didn't seem to matter so much now, with what had occurred between them the other day, the companionship, the closeness, the awareness. Ah, yes, the awareness, of her so close to him, her soft warmth, her gentle scent. And it hadn't been just him, damn it! He pounded the table with his fist. She'd felt it, too. He'd known it from the way she trembled in his arms, from the look in her eyes. For a few moments it had been just as it had seven years ago, that unspoken communication between them, but better, richer, deeper. Would he have kissed her had she been unwilling? Of course not. He was not in the habit of forcing women against their will. No, she had wanted the embrace, the kiss, the closeness as much as he had. Why she had pulled away was something he still didn't understand.

Giles rubbed at his temples, as if to erase his tiredness and confusion. If he didn't understand Anne, his own actions baffled him. He surely knew better than to allow himself to become involved with her. She'd proven herself flighty and unfaithful already, and he had no desire to open himself to that kind of hurt again. Certainly there was an attraction between them; perhaps it was inevitable. It had no future, though. Although Anne appeared to be enjoying herself, he sensed that sometimes she felt as exasperated and imprisoned by society life as he did. He doubted it was a life she would want either for herself or her son, so she would leave. And he, tied by his responsibilities and his duties, wanting to travel but knowing he'd never willingly set foot on a ship, would stay behind. What was between them was a summer folly. It would end when the summer did.

Giles looked at the papers on his desk and then, with a little snarl, pushed them away. To hell with duty. If being with Anne were folly, then so be it. So long as he was forewarned about the future, he would not be hurt by it.

*　　*　　*

"I don't think I'll buy this bonnet after all," Susan Whitehead said, rising from the stool in the milliner's shop. "What do you think, Beth?"

Beth stepped back, looking consideringly at her friend. It was a novelty for someone to actually seek her opinion. She liked it. "The brim is too big," she said.

"I thought so. Oh, well, I don't really need another bonnet." Smiling at the milliner, whose returning smile was somewhat less cordial, they left the shop. "Oh, look." Susan caught Beth's arm. "Look who is coming down the street."

"Who?"

"Lieutenant Bancroft and Mr. Seward."

"Oh, no!"

"What?" Susan looked at her critically. "Now, don't tell me you're shy, because I won't have it," she said, in a fair imitation of her mother's manner. "You look pretty in that frock, Beth. I particularly like the spencer. Blue suits you." Her eyes sparkled. "I dare you."

Beth, who had stepped back against the milliner's bow window in an automatic attempt to hide, looked up. "Dare me to do what?"

"I dare you to speak to Lieutenant Bancroft."

"Of course I'll speak to him," Beth said, falling into step beside her friend as the two men approached. "'Tis only polite."

"Polite!" Susan's eyes shone with suppressed laughter. "Don't hoax me. You don't wish to be merely polite."

"Susan."

"Hush! Here they come. Mr. Seward, Lieutenant Bancroft. How very nice to see you again!"

And so it was that Beth found herself walking on Thomas Bancroft's arm, behind the others, with Susan's maid trailing behind. For the first few

181

moments neither said anything, though Beth was very aware of him, as she had been at Battle. In fact, she could feel his gaze on her almost as a gentle touch, making her at last look at him. His blue, blue eyes had an intent look to them that she had never seen before, but that she somehow recognized. "What?" she said, putting her hand to her cheek, which felt warm. "Have I something on my face?"

"I was thinking how beautiful you are," he said in a husky voice.

Instantly the color in her face deepened, and she twisted around to be certain the maid wasn't following too closely. "You mustn't say such things, sir."

"And why not, when it's true? I told myself it couldn't be, that no one could be such an angel, but now, seeing you again." He paused. "I haven't stopped thinking about you since Tuesday."

Beth glanced away. "Nor I, you." She took a deep breath. "But 'tis much too soon."

"Sometimes it happens that way. It did for my parents."

"My mother doesn't like you," she said abruptly, and hurried on. "Not because of you, yourself, you understand, but she wishes me to choose someone with a title."

"Would she let you go even for a royal duke?"

Beth giggled, though he seemed perfectly serious. "Oh, dear! The thought of one of the Prince's brothers, and me!"

Thomas's eyes gleamed with reluctant amusement. "Well, perhaps not Sailor Billy or the Duke of Cumberland. But you know what I mean, Beth. Would she let you go?"

"Lady Beth."

"That's nonsense. You're Beth. I'm Tom. Would she let you go? Would you let it stop you if she held onto you?"

Beth stopped, looking up at him. "I—don't know.

182

Does it matter so?"

That intent look was back in his eyes. "Yes. It very well might."

"Oh." She continued walking again. "I've never defied her, or my brother, either. They're both good to me."

"Beth, you cannot continue to live your life for other people."

"Except for a husband, you mean."

He looked slightly taken aback. "Yes. No! No, Beth, I don't want you to live your life for anyone, even me. With someone, though. Share your life with someone."

"Who?" she said softly, and his eyes flickered.

"I cannot say. Not here. Beth." His face was serious and tender. No one had ever looked at her like that before. "Would you take a younger son, even if your mother didn't approve?"

"It would depend on the man." She met his gaze directly. "If he were the right man it wouldn't matter to me if he were a younger son or a royal duke or a— a peasant! Yes." Her voice was firm. "Yes, I would do what I had to do, if I thought it was right."

Thomas didn't answer right away. "You are a rare and courageous woman, Lady Elizabeth," he said finally, and, his eyes never leaving hers, raised her hand to his lips. "It is an honor knowing you."

"Th-thank you." The old shyness was back, brought on by the extraordinary compliment, but somehow it didn't matter. She was safe with him. Safe, and at the same time more excited than she ever had been. She felt as if she were on the brink of some marvelous adventure.

Giles was just coming out of the book-room as Beth walked into the house. "You look uncommonly well, Beth," he said, smiling down at her. "Did you enjoy your walk?"

Beth's eyes lowered. "Oh, very much, Giles, thank you." Oh, dear. She couldn't tell Giles about this afternoon. Not yet; perhaps not ever. He wouldn't understand. He would only point out her duty. Beth had always been dutiful and obedient. It was only recently that she had discovered there was something more important in life than being a good daughter. Thomas had shown it to her.

"Come. We'll have tea and you can tell me all about it."

"Oh, I must change first, Giles, or Mama will scold me. Please excuse me," she said, and scurried up the stairs, leaving Giles, for the second time that afternoon, staring after someone in consternation. What was the matter with the women of his family? For the life of him, he would never understand them.

Benson knocked on the door of the book-room the next morning. "Your Grace."

Giles looked up from the letter he had been writing. "Yes, Benson, what is it?"

"There is, ah, a problem in the drawing room, sir."

"Can you not attend to it, Benson?"

"No, Your Grace. I am sorry. It is something you should see for yourself, sir."

"Very well." With a sigh of resignation Giles rose and walked past his butler. What had happened to his neat, orderly life? At Tremont, no one would have dared to disturb him at his work. Life in Brighton was vastly different.

The drawing room looked normal when he walked into it. He didn't know what he had expected to find, his mother ill, perhaps, or some piece of vandalism. But—nothing. "Well, Benson?" He turned to the butler, looking at him from under his brow. "What is so important that I must leave my work?"

"My apologies, Your Grace, but I thought you might want to see—that."

Giles followed Benson's pointing finger and barely

suppressed a laugh. There, in the middle of the floor, were the toy soldiers that had once been his, set up in a most extraordinary way. The green- or blue-painted figures, the enemy, were mostly still standing, some in lines, some hiding behind table legs that in a young boy's mind might symbolize trees. The redcoats, on the other hand, had all been knocked down, still in their neat, precise lines of battle. Giles's lips twitched. "Looks rather as if we've been routed, Benson."

Benson sighed. "Your Grace, I was hoping—"

"Yes, Benson. I'll speak to Jamie and his mother. If you will please tell them I wish to see them."

"Yes, Your Grace. I will summon them now."

A few moments later Anne, a little breathless, came into the drawing room, Jamie in tow. "Yes, Giles, what is it?" she said, brushing a wayward strand of hair away from her face.

"Something I'd like you to see." Giles's lips twitched. "It appears someone has been doing battle in here."

"Excuse me?"

Giles looked at Jamie. "Jamie? Are these not yours?"

"My soldiers!" Jamie broke free of Anne's grasp and ran across the room, falling to his knees. "Mommy, here they are!"

"So this is where they disappeared to. We were wondering," Anne said, smiling.

"Yes." Giles nodded. "And how did they get there?"

Both turned to look at Jamie, now righting the fallen soldiers. "James? How did they get there?" Giles asked.

Jamie looked up. "I don't know."

"Jamie, did you put them there?"

"No, Mommy."

"James—"

"I didn't, Uncle Giles!" Jamie turned to Anne, his smile dissolving. "Mommy, tell Uncle Giles not to be mad."

A slight frown wrinkled Anne's brow as she perched on a footstool near him. "I don't think he is, pet. But, remember what I've always told you about telling me the truth."

"Yes, Mommy, I am. Word of a Templeton."

Anne looked up at Giles. "I believe him, Giles. Jamie does not lie."

"Commendable. Tell me, then, how the soldiers got there?"

"Maybe Terence did it," Jamie said.

The adults turned to look at him. "Who is Terence, lad?" Giles said.

Jamie gave them both that look of impatience that only a child can produce toward adults who seem to live in their own world. "You know, Uncle Giles. Terence. The ghost."

Chapter 14

Anne and Giles stared at each other. "The ghost?" Anne said.

"Terence?" Giles said at the same time.

"What ghost, lovey?" Anne leaned forward. "Jamie, look at me. What ghost?"

Jamie looked up from setting the toy soldiers to rights. "You know, Mommy. He said you heard him singing one night and you ran around looking for him. He said it was funny."

A chill skittered down Anne's spine. "Where did he say this, Jamie?"

"In my room."

Anne looked quickly up at Giles, and reached out to gather Jamie against her, though he wriggled away. "Giles—"

"What do you and Terence talk about, Jamie?" Giles asked, sitting down.

"Things."

"James." Giles's voice was stern. "Leave the soldiers for a moment and answer my questions."

Jamie stood up, his back very straight, his shoulders squared. "Yes, sir."

"Good. What does Terence talk to you about, Jamie?"

"Things. He tells me all about going on a ship, but I

already know about that," Jamie said, with the careless scorn of the young. "He said he'd been to Jamaica, Mommy! And America, too. He told me about a cat with nine tails. I've never seen a cat with nine tails, have you, Uncle Giles?"

"No, Jamie." Commendably, Giles kept his face straight. "What else does he talk about?"

"Well—I told him about Hampshire Hall and Diah and you, Mommy. And you, too, Uncle Giles. He likes you."

"I am honored."

"Mm-hm. He says you're not bad for a bloody aristocrat."

"Jamie!" Anne exclaimed.

"That's what he said, Mommy. And sometimes he sings."

"Dear lord."

Giles sent her a look that held a mixture of intrigue and amusement. "What does Terence look like, Jamie?"

"I don't know."

"Come now, Jamie. You said he comes into your room."

"He doesn't. He just talks to me."

Giles and Anne exchanged another look. "Very well, lad. The next time you talk to Terence, please tell him we would like to meet him."

"Yes, Uncle Giles."

"Run along now, lad. Your mother and I need to discuss something."

Anne rose, her hand on Jamie's shoulder. "I should go with him—"

"He'll be fine, Anne. Sit down."

"Uncle Giles, may I take my soldiers?"

"I'll bring them up to you later. Go along now, lad."

Jamie bowed and, after one wistful glance at his toys, went out. Anne jumped to her feet, crossing the room to the door. Only when she saw Jamie reach the top of the stairs did she turn. "A ghost talking to my son, Giles. Dear God. I cannot have this. I would like to go back to Tremont—"

"Sit down, Anne." Giles was staring at the toy soldiers. "A ghost who apparently doesn't like the British Army."

"Giles."

"Someone who was in the army, by the sound of it. I wonder if any of the staff meets that description."

Anne fell into her seat. "You don't think it's a ghost?"

"Of course not." He looked at her and grinned. "Annie, don't tell me you do?"

Anne blushed. "I don't know what to believe! How does he do it, Giles? How does he talk to Jamie in his room?"

"Yes, that is a puzzle, isn't it? And when he sang, we all heard him. I expect, though, there's some explanation for it. I refuse to believe in ghosts."

"But, Giles, don't you see? This Terence, whoever he is, is bothering my son. I can't let Jamie be hurt."

"Annie." Giles's face was tender. "Do you think I would do anything to put you or your son in danger?"

Anne blushed again. "I'm too old to be called Annie."

"Oh, no. Never too old. Annie, I swear to you I'll do everything in my power to protect you."

Anne searched his face, finding there strength and reassurance. She couldn't imagine how Freddie would have reacted in the same situation. He had not been a coward, but always his first priority had been himself. Giles was different. She could trust him. "I know you will," she said, feeling as if a weight had fallen from her. At last, she could rely on someone. "And I don't really believe it's a ghost, but—"

"But we have to find out who's doing this. We will." He reached over and laid his hand on hers. "We will,

189

Annie. Trust me."

"I do." She returned his gaze for a moment, and then rose. "Well. I doubt Jamie will want to do his lessons, but I must at least try."

"Of course." Giles walked with her to the door. "I'll set inquiries in motion for the staff. We'll find him, Anne." He touched her arm, and she turned to face him. "I promise."

"Thank you," she whispered, and fled.

Giles stood at the door, watching her as she had watched Jamie. He hadn't imagined it. For just a moment there had been that closeness between them again that had been missing since the day at Battle. He still didn't understand what had happened, but, as he headed toward the book-room, he felt lighter, and happier, than he had for a long, long time.

The questioning of the staff began that very same morning. With the exception of a few footmen, most of the servants who were employed in the house were women. The footmen were a mixed group, with several being old enough to have served at one time in the army or navy. None of them had, however, or so they claimed. The coachman and grooms had come from Tremont, as had Benson. Some had seen service, but all denied being the "ghost." Beyond the fact that none of them had been here when the previous tenants had reported hauntings, all seemed unlikely suspects to Giles. And none of the men, whether from Tremont or Brighton, were named Terence.

Giles and Anne met that afternoon in the book-room to discuss the situation. After an anxious morning spent with Jamie, watching him closely, Anne had reached the conclusion that he had come to no harm from his experiences. "Thank heavens children are so resilient," she said, sinking gracefully into a chair across from Giles. "I don't believe he's even scared."

"No, I don't believe he is," Giles said. "You coddle him too much, Anne."

"I do not!"

"The fact remains that we still do not know who is haunting us."

"You are certain it's not staff?"

"As certain as I can be. I'll send to the War Office to learn if any of the footmen did serve, and if we find one of them lied then we have our man. I doubt it will be that easy, though."

"Would he have to have been in the army, Giles? We've based that on very few clues. A song, the toy soldiers, and what he said to Jamie."

"Possibly not. In fact, it could all be part of the hoax. And it is a hoax, Anne."

"Oh, I agree. Obadiah doesn't believe the house is haunted, and I trust him. What worries me, though, is that if it's not one of the staff, then it's someone from outside." She shuddered. "What does he want, Giles?"

"I don't know. He's not a particularly frightening ghost, is he? All I can think of is that there must be something in the house he wants, and that he wants us out."

"I wonder what."

"God knows." Giles leaned back. "Anne, you won't go back to Tremont, will you?"

"I don't know," she said slowly. "Would it mean so much to you if I did?"

"It has nothing to do with me, Anne. I just never thought of you as a quitter."

"Oh. No, of course not."

For just a moment, Giles thought he saw frustration in her eyes. Good. Of course it mattered to him that she stay. It also mattered that she was not, apparently, so indifferent as she pretended. "And I never thought of you as one to run away from things." He looked

191

directly at her over his steepled fingers. "Except for me."

Anne gasped. There. It was out in the open, the subject they had so carefully avoided for the past weeks. Why had he decided to marry another, seven years ago? And why had he then not gone through with that marriage? "Not even from you, Giles," she said with great dignity, rising. "Now, if you'll excuse me—"

"Running again, Annie?"

Anne turned at the door. "You may taunt me all you wish, Giles, but it will not work. I do not wish to discuss the past, and I do not wish to be hurt again. Now, pray excuse me, or I shall be late to go driving with Felicity and Beth."

"Go then, Anne. Run away. But this is not over," he called after her, and then sat back, frustrated. Damn. Just when he had thought he might be making progress, she refused to listen. And here he was, prepared to forgive her for what she had done seven years ago. She claimed she had been hurt? Nonsense. She was the one who had run away. She was the one who had married another.

Searing pain went through him. Annie, his Annie, with another man, in his arms, kissing him, bearing his child. In Freddie's arms. They had betrayed him, both of them, Freddie, his cousin and friend, Anne, the only girl he had ever loved. How had he ever thought he was over it? He wasn't. He wasn't. The pain was as fresh now as it had ever been, and for what? For a woman who had left him, and who would surely leave him again. He could not allow his desire for her to deepen into something more. One day the inevitable would happen. One day Anne would leave, and if he didn't take care, he would be lost, all over again. And then what would he do?

*　　　*　　　*

The Tremont carriage stopped before the Old Ship Inn that evening for the ball being held there. Giles, dressed again in faultless black and white, was a silent, brooding presence as he escorted Anne and Beth inside. What did he want from her? Anne wondered, feeling the tension between them as a palpable thing. He had to know there could be no future between them, and yet he persisted in behaving as if there might be. Oh, how she wished there could be. She had seen another side to him today, a strong, caring side that would protect a wife, rather than hurt her. Something inside her longed to put her burdens before him. Not that she had any desire to sacrifice her independence or her strength, but it would feel good to have someone to share troubles with, someone who would understand and sympathize, who would hold her close in strong, sheltering arms. Someone who understood as well that she needed to make her own decisions. Was she asking for so much? Probably.

"My parents are supposed to be here tonight," she said, as they entered the Assembly Rooms, craning her head to see. "I wonder—oh, look, Giles! There is my father." She frowned. "He looks so old."

"It's been seven years, Anne."

"Must you keep reminding me of that?" she snapped. The past was past, and why Giles wouldn't let it stay that way was a mystery to her. She would not think about it. She would concentrate, instead, on her father, the idol of her childhood. Except— Her brow wrinkled. When had he grown so old? The man she remembered had been lean and vigorous and handsome, and his occasional attentions to his daughter had sent her into transports of joy for weeks. Now he carried a prodigious amount of flesh on his frame, so that he looked shorter than he really was. His face was full, blurring features that had once been finely etched, and dewlaps hung down from his cheeks. His outfit, a modish, but tight, coat of mulberry velvet with an extravagantly embroidered waistcoat, only emphasized his age, though she suspected it was meant to have the opposite effect. He was not at all as she remembered, but still, he was her father.

"Excuse me, Giles." She gave him a polite, meaningless smile as she pulled away. "I must go speak with him."

"Let me escort you." He took her arm again and, before she could protest, began to lead her across the crowded ballroom. "You might be glad of it."

"Giles, I think I can meet my own father with no trouble."

"Not your father, The men with him."

Anne frowned. Of course Viscount Pendleton was standing with a group of men. They had long been his friends, and they looked much like him, from the fleshy faces to the too-tight coats. They had avaricious, amorous eyes. She clutched Giles's arm just a little. She was glad of his presence.

"Father," she said as she reached the group, and one of the men turned.

"Eh? Pendleton, looks like you're being called to account," he said, and the men roared. "Are you sure it's a father you're looking for, girl?"

"Excuse me." Giles's voice was icy. "Perhaps you don't recognize the lady. She is Mrs. Frederick Templeton, Lord Pendleton's daughter."

"Eh? Oh, it's you, Tremont. Didn't see you there. So this is Pendleton's daughter. Don't look like him."

"Lucky for her," someone else said, and the men roared again.

"Damned if it isn't my daughter." Pendleton turned. "Hello, Puss. When did you come back to England?"

Pain seared through her. "Oh, ages ago," she said carelessly. "You haven't changed, Father."

"Oh, no, no." He patted his substantial stomach.

"Must keep my figure, you know. You're looking well, Puss. Come visit us sometime. Your mother would want to see you. We're on the Marine Parade."

"Why, yes, I might. Excuse me, Father. I see someone I must talk to."

"Run along then, Puss," he said, as if she were a child he was sending out to play. "Enjoy yourself."

"Yes, Father." Anne turned, clinging to Giles's arm, staring blindly ahead. Behind her someone let out a guffaw, and then the men laughed again. They had forgotten her already. Her father had forgotten her already.

"Do you want me to take you home?" Giles said in a low voice.

"Yes. No. We can't go, Giles. Beth would have to come with us."

"Beth will understand."

Anne glanced across the room, where Beth was smiling shyly up at Lieutenant Bancroft, resplendent in the silver lace of his dress uniform. "No, I'm all right, Giles. If I leave everyone will know why, and I cannot bear their pity."

Giles squeezed her arm, so quickly that she wondered if she'd imagined it. "Good for you. Why do we not find some refreshment?"

Anne looked up, but the words she had been about to say died at the look in his eyes. Sympathy, again. Was she only someone to be pitied by him? "Oh, listen to the music, Giles. I'd so much rather dance. Mr. Campbell."

The man passing by them, two glasses of champagne in his hands, stopped, looking startled. Then a slow smile spread across his face. "Mrs. Templeton. A pleasure to see you again, ma'am. Tremont."

"Campbell." Giles's voice was clipped.

"You are looking beautiful tonight, Anne, as always. May I offer you champagne?"

195

"Why thank you, Mr. Campbell." Anne took the goblet he handed her and sipped, looking directly at Giles over the rim. Why she was feeling so defiant she neither knew nor cared. She would enjoy herself, forgetting about the past and its pain.

"Oh, a country dance!" she exclaimed as the orchestra started. "It feels like forever since I have danced."

"I would be honored, ma'am," Ian said.

Giles spoke at the same time. "Anne, would you care to—"

"Why, thank you, Mr. Campbell, how kind of you to ask. Giles, you won't mind holding this for me, will you?" Smiling brilliantly at him, she shoved the goblet into his hand and let Ian lead her onto the floor.

"Lover's quarrel, Anne?" Ian asked, his deep voice tinged with amusement.

Anne tossed her head. "I don't know what you mean, sir."

"You and Tremont. The *on-dit* is that you and he are going to make a match of it."

Anne stood stock-still in the middle of the floor, though the sets were forming and people were glancing at her in curiosity. "They say what?"

"Wouldn't be so surprising, would it?" Ian took her hand, leading her into the first steps of the dance. "Everyone still wonders why you threw him over for Freddie seven years ago."

"Because he—" Anne began, and then stopped. Because he had been about to announce his engagement to another girl. Or so she had thought. What if it hadn't been true?

Anne went through the steps of the dance mechanically, all the while thinking, thinking. No one else seemed to know about that other attachment. There had been no talk of it in the family, no gossip among the ton, as surely there should be. She still didn't know what had happened, why the engagement had been called off, but now she needed, badly, to know. Because if no one had heard of it, perhaps it had never existed.

When next she encountered Ian in the dance, she chatted lightly of matters of no importance, the weather, the latest gossip, careful not to reveal what was truly bothering her. The steps of the dance took her away, and then back again. "And it is so nice to see everyone I used to know." she said, quite as if there had been no break in the conversation. She was aware of Ian's sardonic look. He must think her a total featherhead. "Though I don't see others that I knew. Whatever happened to them, I wonder? Peter Whitten, and Michael Phillips, and, oh, what was her name? Jennifer Stafford."

"Jennifer Stafford!" Ian said, just as she had hoped he would. "Why would you care about that mouse of a girl?"

Because Giles left me for her. "Oh, I don't know. She was sweet."

"Dashed dull, if you ask me. You must know--but, of course, you don't, it happened after you left."

"What?"

"The most delicious scandal. She, of all people, eloped."

"No!"

"Yes. With a minister, of all things. They're missionaries now, in some heathen country. God knows where. Only interesting thing she ever did in her life was elope."

With someone else. Not long after Anne's own marriage, her supposed rival had married someone else. She couldn't, then, have been engaged to Giles. Could she?

Ian was bowing to her, and she realized the dance was over. As mechanically as she had danced, she

197

curtsied, and it was only when she rose that she saw Ian regarding her with a warm look that made her extremely uncomfortable. "A pleasant dance," she chattered, as he took her arm. "I do believe I am promised for the next one. I wonder who—"

"Me." He smiled down at her. "You hardly had a chance to have your dance card signed. I've been watching you, you see."

"Oh? And for whom was that champagne really meant?"

"She doesn't matter." He grinned. "The look on Tremont's face when you gave him the glass to hold was a sight to see."

Giles. For the first time, her conscience smote her. She had treated him abominably, and she didn't know why. "Oh, dear, you are right," she said, making a great fuss of looking at her dance card. "But, you know, I am acting as chaperon for Lady Elizabeth tonight, and I must make certain she is all right."

"And here you are, the one who needs chaperoning." Ian's eyes caressed her. "Have you seen the inn's gardens, Anne?"

Alarm bells went off in Anne's head, though she forced herself to smile. "Shame on you, sir, for making such a suggestion!" she said, tapping him lightly on the arm with her fan. "If you would—"

"Which suggestion, Anne?"

"You know quite well, so don't play the innocent with me. Please, I really must return to Lady Elizabeth. She is just over there, with Lady Whitehead. Would you please escort me to her? Or are you so ungallant that I must go alone?"

"Lady, you wound me to the heart. Of course I will escort you. But this isn't the end of it," he said, inclining his head so that his breath stirred her hair. "You are an extremely enticing woman, Anne."

"Goodness, look at the people here!" she chattered,

clutching at his arm and speeding her pace. "There's Lady Cowper, and isn't that Lady Sefton with her?"

"Yes." Ian stopped, and she had no choice but to stop with him, though Felicity, and safety, were tantalizingly close. "May I call on you?"

"Did you enjoy your dance, Anne?" a voice said, and Anne looked up to see Giles, standing behind Beth, watching her, his eyes cold, cold steel. Shock ran through her, settling into a cold lump of dread in her stomach. He was angry. She couldn't bear for him, of all people, to be angry with her, and yet, he had a right to be. She had treated him very badly.

"Good evening, Mr. Campbell," she said, and dropped into a graceful curtsy, covering her emotions with the ease of long practice. Ian didn't matter; Giles did. How she had changed no longer mattered. In spite of everything she loved Giles, and always would. Tonight she had chosen the wrong man.

The ball was over. Giles sat in the book-room, legs outstretched, a glass of brandy by his side. They should never have come to Brighton. It had been a disaster from the beginning, and was only getting worse. He was worried about his mother who, in spite of her apparent sternness, actually enjoyed social events, and yet seemed to be attending fewer and fewer. Beth, shy, quiet Beth, was showing a marked preference for Lieutenant Bancroft. Giles liked the man personally, but, given his circumstances in life, there was trouble ahead. And then there was Anne.

Annie. He leaned back, his hands behind his head. What was happening between him and Anne? More to the point, why was he allowing it to happen? She'd hurt him once, badly, and there was no reason things should be different this time. In fact, quite the opposite. Hadn't she just this evening shown her preference for another man? He'd hated seeing her go off with Campbell, hated to see her flirting with him, so much so that he had wanted to retaliate. Thus, he had been cold to her the rest of the evening, thinking it might wound her. He hoped it had; he devoutly hoped it hadn't.

The door from the hall opened just a crack. "Giles?" an uncertain voice said.

"Come in, Anne." He drained the rest of his brandy and sat back, waiting for her to come to him. Still in her evening gown of coral silk, simply cut but extremely flattering, she came in, closing the door behind her. "Come to gloat?"

"About what?"

"About tonight." He studied his nails dispassionately. "How you showed you can still make any man you desire dance attendance upon you."

"Oh, Giles. No, of course I don't want to gloat." She looked away. "Giles, I—the way I behaved to you tonight was inexcusable. You didn't deserve it. I'm sorry."

"No, I don't think I did deserve it. But then, I don't understand a great deal of what you do, Anne. I never did."

"I don't either, sometimes." She sounded tired as she leaned her head back against the chair. "I try so hard, Giles, really, I do. I always try to be what people want me to be, but it's never enough. My father, tonight." Her voice cracked, and she broke off.

"Annie." He was out of his chair in an instant, kneeling before her, his fingers on her arm stroking, caressing. "Annie, darling, don't cry. Don't. He's not worth it. Your parents are stupid, selfish people."

"Everyone leaves me, Giles. Even Jamie will one day."

"Annie, hush. Come here, now." He gathered her against him, rocking her back and forth, almost as if she were his sister, in need of comfort. Almost, but not quite. "Don't cry, darling."

"Don't be kind to me," she sobbed into his shoulder. "I can't bear it when you're kind to me."

"No? Would you rather I beat you?" he said, and she stiffened. "A jest, Annie. An ill-considered jest. I wouldn't hurt you."

Anne pulled back. "Not that way."

"Very well, Annie. I won't be kind to you." He looked down at her bent head, and an overwhelming tide of tenderness washed over him. "It's not kindness I'm feeling for you, darling," he said, his voice husky as he bent his head. No longer able to resist, he caught her tears with his lips.

Anne went very still. After a moment she pulled back and gazed up at him, her eyes clear and defenseless. "Giles?"

"Not kindness, Annie," he said, and brought his mouth down on hers.

Anne made a little noise in her throat, but her body, treacherous thing, responded, making her arms creep up around his neck, making her press against him. When had comfort turned to passion? When had need become desire? She didn't know. All that mattered was that she was in his arms again. She loved him! She exulted in the knowledge. She loved him. Oh, and it felt so good to express that love, and not hide behind the facade society expected of her. It was glorious to have his strong arms around her, to open her mouth to his probing tongue, to return his caresses with her own touch. No more pretending to be what she was not. With Giles, she could be herself, just Anne, and the wonder of it made her so giddy that she surged up against him.

Giles swayed back; crouched as he was on his heels, his position was unsteady at best. With one arm still holding her tightly against him, he flailed for balance, to no avail. Before he could stop himself he tumbled backward, landing on the soft turkey carpet, with Anne above him.

They lay that way for a few moments, the breath knocked out of them. Anne's hair, coming loose from its pins, fell softly about her, the ends tickling his face. They were close, so close, their bodies pressed together; breast to breast, thigh to thigh. Anne's eyes were wide and startled in the firelight, making her look young and vulnerable. And so pretty. That wave of tenderness flooded through him again as he reached up to tuck an errant curl back behind her ear. Never had he wanted anyone so much. "Marry me, Annie," he said huskily.

Chapter 15

The words jolted through her. To marry Giles. To stay with him forever and ever, to feel for always this blessed sense of security, to be loved. "Do you love me, Giles?" Anne asked, her voice equally husky.

"Love?" Giles sounded startled.

Anne stared down at him for a moment and then scrambled to her feet. "I should have known. What a fool I am, to be gulled by you twice. But this is what you've wanted since I came back, isn't it?"

Giles hastily got to his feet, catching at her shoulder. "Damn it, Anne, no."

Anne went very still. "If you dare to lay a hand on me I will make you regret it, Giles Templeton."

Giles stepped back. "Annie—"

"Don't call me that! I'm not your little girl anymore. I am a woman."

Giles leaned back against his desk, his arms crossed on his chest and a little smile on his mouth. He suspected he knew what had gone wrong. It had all happened too quickly, though it was right. So right. Given time, Anne would see that. "I noticed that, darling."

"I am not your darling!" She backed up a step as he advanced toward her, her hands outstretched, palm out. The look in his eyes, so predatory, so male, frightened her. At least, that was what she thought this strange edginess was, though it was exhilarating, too. She had every reason to fear him, did she not? He was a man. And, different though he was from Freddie, he was still, in some ways, the same. Now that he'd proposed, he expected her to grovel at his feet, to do whatever he wished her to, and she wouldn't. It would put her in his power, and to be in a man's power meant she would be helpless. It meant— "No!" she exclaimed, taking another step back and coming up, hard, against a bookcase. There was no place else for her to go. She was trapped. And there was Giles, slowly prowling toward her, that look in his eyes, so intent, that smile still on his face. He was going to capture her again. He was going to kiss her. So why did she not flee?

Giles stopped just a heartbeat away from her. "No, Annie?" he said, his voice rough and tender.

"No." Something crystallized within Anne, that self-protectiveness she had learned so well. "No," she said again, her voice clear and hard. "I don't want you. I never did."

Something in Giles's face changed. They stayed, staring at each other for a moment, very still, and then Giles stepped back, his expression remote. "My mistake," he said, inclining his head. "I am sorry to have bothered you, Anne."

Anne eyed him warily. He was letting her go. It was what she wanted, wasn't it? "I—yes," she said, and fled the room.

Behind her, Giles pushed his hand into his hair and fell back into his chair. What had he done that was so wrong? More to the point, what did he do now?

"And how is your ghost?" Felicity asked several evenings later. The Whiteheads had taken dinner with the Tremonts and now were drinking coffee in the drawing room, before going onto the theater. "I've heard there have been a few incidents."

For a moment, there was silence. "You heard through the servants, I suppose," Giles said, smiling at her from the mantel where he stood, his elbow propped up.

"Of course. I must say, it is a most unusual thing to happen, Giles. The Duke of Tremont has a ghost. It may even start a fashion."

Giles grinned. "We do not have a ghost. What we do have is someone playing pranks."

"One of the servants, I expect," Julia said. Her hands lay folded in her lap, while beside her her beloved embroidery sat untouched. "Jealous of their betters."

"I doubt that, Mother. No, we don't know who is doing it, yet, but we expect to find out."

"Well! I must say I find it exciting. Don't you, Anne?"

Anne gave a little smile and raised her cup. The question of the house's being haunted seemed of little moment lately, so long as Jamie was all right. This particular ghost was harmless, as Giles had pointed out. It was people who usually caused the problems.

Matters had been strained between her and Giles the last few days, and she saw little hope of their improving. There was too much between them now, old pain, new pain. Giles actually seemed hurt by what had passed between them the other evening, though why that should be, she didn't know. She was the one who had been the fool, but then, she had never bargained on falling in love with Giles again. She had never thought that being in his arms, holding him, kissing him, would be so intoxicating. Most of all, though, she had never expected to feel such searing pain as she had in that moment when she had asked Giles if he loved her, and he hadn't answered. It had been answer enough.

"Well, at least all he seems to be causing is mischief,

whoever he is," Felicity said, and Anne looked up.

"Who?" she asked.

"Whoever is haunting the house. Have you not been attending?"

"Oh, our ghost." Anne managed a smile. "It's rather funny, actually. He sings bawdy songs and appears to dislike the army. What I don't like is that he talks to Jamie."

"But how does he do it?"

"No one knows, but we're looking into it." Giles crossed the room and sat down. In his austere, beautifully cut evening clothes of black superfine and white linen, he look so striking that Anne couldn't keep from staring at him. "I talked with the agent from whom we leased the house the other day."

Anne leaned forward, interested in spite of herself. "What did he say?"

"He was reluctant to talk at first. I'm afraid I was a little, ah, forceful." He smiled at her, and it took all the self-control she possessed not to return the smile. "He at last admitted that he had heard stories, but he denied that he knew anything about it when we took the house."

"I wonder," Anne said, and the others looked at her. "What?"

"Oh, it's silly, but if the agent is dishonest, I wonder if this isn't a scheme to keep leasing the house and gull people out of their money."

"I doubt it. He was terrified I'd take him to court. It's a thought, though." He looked at her, and she lapsed into silence again. "In any event, he finally told me the story of the house. And a lurid one it is."

"Was someone killed here?" Susan Whitehead asked.

"Susan!" her mother reproved.

"Not this house, no." There was a faint smile on Giles's face. "Apparently there used to be a tavern on

206

this site. Rather a reprehensible place, according to the locals, where the riffraff would meet. And pirates."

Susan's eyes were round. "Pirates!"

"Yes. One of them, a certain Terence O'Reilly, owned the place and is said to have hidden his treasure somewhere on the premises. Of course word of this got around, and one night he was set upon by some of his customers. During the fight a candle was knocked over and the place went up in flames. End of tavern, and end of Terence O'Reilly." He grinned at Anne. "And the treasure was never found."

"An entertaining story," Felicity said after a moment, when it became apparent that Anne, staring into the depths of her cup, was not going to answer. "Is Terence O'Reilly your ghost, then?"

"More likely someone impersonating him. You see, when excavations were made to build this house, the builders found some Spanish dubloons."

Exclamations over this bit of news filled the room. Even Anne nearly spoke, if only to accuse Giles of hoaxing them all. It wasn't like him, but there was a gleam in his eye that strongly suggested he was enjoying this. She had no desire to speak to him, however. Not now, not ever.

"How fascinating," Felicity said, when the hubbub had died down. "A fortune, Giles?"

"No, just a few coins. I daresay you'd find some in many a cellar around here. It was enough to keep the old story going, though."

"And so you think that someone believes it enough to want to chase everyone off so he can keep the treasure himself. I wonder—good heavens, what is that?" she broke off, as an eerie voice filled the room, singing.

"Now we're bound to Kingston Town
"Where the rum flows round an' round

207

"So early in the mornin',
"Sailors love the bottle-oh,
"Bottle-oh, bottle-oh."

Anne jumped to her feet and started for the door, her only concern to make certain that Jamie was unharmed. At the same moment, Beth let out a little cry. "The window! Look!"

Anne turned, in time to see a pale shape appear briefly outside a side window, and then drift upward. The singing abruptly stopped, with a laugh that sent chills down everyone's spine. Anne gasped and then dashed upstairs, as Giles started up from his chair and the others exclaimed in shock and consternation at this apparition.

"Your Grace." A badly shaken footman ran into the room, followed by Obadiah. "Did you see—"

Giles pushed past him. "Yes. Where is Benson?"

"In the servant's hall, I imagine, Your Grace. Your Grace, I heard someone running—"

"Find Benson and have him organize the footmen to search the grounds, and hold anyone you find. You, come with me."

"Yes, mon," Obadiah said, sounding startled, but clattering down the stairs after Giles.

Outside, the brick sidewalk was slick with moisture, and Giles skidded, before regaining his balance. It was an eerie night, with fog drifting in from the sea, punctuated in intervals by light streaming out from windows. Off to the left, away from the coast, running footsteps could be heard. "That way!" Giles said, and set off.

"Mon, it might be dangerous," Obadiah said, keeping pace with Giles easily, as they turned from the Steyne into Church Street, earning more than one startled glance from passersby.

"I'll not be chased out of my own home—mon?"

"Man." Obadiah flashed a smile at him. "My

208

apologies, Your Grace," he said, in elegantly rounded tones.

"Good God, you're educated!"

"Yes, mon. We ain't all ignorant slaves."

"My apologies." *Be quiet,* Giles told himself. If he said anything more he would likely only embarrass himself again. The man running beside him had a peculiar dignity and grace, accentuated by his proud bearing and the direct way he looked at people. He had underestimated the man, Giles thought. Perhaps he had also underestimated Anne.

By some trick of the fog, the footsteps ahead of them suddenly sounded very loud. They were now in the older part of town, a warren of narrow streets and lanes. "That's no ghost." Giles put on a burst of speed.

"No, mon. The house isn't haunted."

"Then who's doing this, Obadiah?"

"Don't know, sir, but I've been thinkin' about somethin'."

"Have you—there, he's gone down that alley!"

Still chasing the footsteps, they turned into an alley, skittering on the wet cobblestones, and found—nothing. The alley, running between two shops, ended at a high brick wall which had no outlet. Their quarry had vanished.

"Damn!" Giles's voice echoed in the enclosed space. "Where the hell did he get to—"

Obadiah, more practical, was trying a door set in the side of one of the shops. "Locked, sir."

"Damn, then where did he go? Over the wall?"

Obadiah looked up at the wall. "Likely, sir. Looks like we lost him."

"Damn." Giles pulled out his handkerchief and began mopping at his face. "Let us return home, Obadiah. Perhaps they found something there."

"Yes, sir," Obadiah said, and, at that moment, a light flashed at the opening of the alley.

"Who goes there?" a querulous voice said, and Giles,

209

who had stiffened, relaxed.

"It needed only this," he muttered. "Ah, the watchman," he said, in more normal tones. "Did you see someone come out of this alley?"

"Who be ye?" The watchman, old and gnarled, squinted up at them, apparently not a bit overawed. "And what be ye doing here? Speak in the name of the king, or I'll take ye in."

"I beg your pardon?" Giles drew himself up to his greatest height and spoke in his haughtiest tones. "I am the Duke of Tremont, and this is my servant. We were chasing someone who tried to break into my house. My house! What manner of town is this, when ruffians accost one in one's own home?" Giles advanced upon the startled watchman, who backed up a step. "It is I who should take you in, sir, for allowing the public peace to be so disturbed!"

"I—I'm sorry, Yer Grace, of course, yer right. What—what does this ruffian look like?"

"I've no idea. That is your job to find out, is it not? Now be off with you, before someone else is accosted and I have to report you to your superiors."

"Yes, Your Grace," the watchman stammered, and scurried away, throwing a scared glance at them over his shoulder.

Obadiah's chuckle was rich in the darkness, making Giles send him an inquiring look. "I would venture to say he's never seen such a well-dressed ruffian before, Your Grace."

Startled, Giles glanced down at himself, and let out a laugh. Belatedly he realized how ludicrous he must have looked, chasing a phantom down fog-shrouded streets while wearing evening dress. "Never thought I'd turn into a blood, boxing watchmen for sport," he said, falling into step beside Obadiah and feeling curiously lighthearted. What had started out as high adventure fraught with peril had degenerated into farce. "My life used to be nice and quiet."

210

"Maybe it was time for a change, mon."

Giles stopped, startled, and then started walking again. "Maybe it was, at that." Curiously he glanced up at the man who walked beside him with such serene self-possession. "Where were you educated, Obadiah?"

"My old master taught me. Taught all his slaves. Said we should all know how to read and write and cipher."

"And to speak like a gentleman?"

"Yes." Obadiah's voice was so curt that, for a moment, Giles was at a loss for words. Obadiah intrigued him. A former slave, who apparently still held to the old beliefs and yet not only could manage an estate, but spoke like a gentleman. Not at all the old way of doing things, but interesting.

"How did you come to work at Hampshire Hall, then?" he asked, finally.

"Sold. When my master died."

"Christ." Sold. Just like that. Giles had never before considered what that meant, or what it could do to so proud a man. "But you're free now."

"Sure, mon. Master Templeton freed us all. The fool."

"What?"

"Man had no head for business," Obadiah said contemptuously. "No idea how to manage people. He freed us, sure, but then he expected us to work for him for almost nothing. Most of us, we did. Couldn't get work anywhere else, not when everyone else still had slaves. Glad when Lady Anne took over. Glad to see the end of him."

"Yet Anne misses him," Giles said to himself.

Obadiah shrugged. "If you say so, mon. Wonder what they found at the house."

Giles looked up at him. He'd learn nothing more tonight, curious though he now was. There was something about Freddie, and about Anne's life with him, that he didn't yet know. "Let us go back and see."

211

They returned to a house still in turmoil. The servants were flitting around, talking excitedly. Beth was still in the drawing room with the Whiteheads, though neither Julia nor Anne were anywhere to be seen. A look from Giles from under his brow was enough to scatter the servants back to their posts, though he knew he would not be able to handle Felicity so easily. He had no time to assuage her curiosity just now, though. There were other matters to see to.

"Anything?" he asked Benson, whose thinning hair was standing up and whose cheek was smudged.

"Something odd, Your Grace. It's in the servants' hall."

"Very well." Giles led the way below stairs. "Is anyone missing?"

"No, Your Grace, all are accounted for. Except for those who have the evening off, of course."

"I'll want their names," Giles said as he stepped into the servants' hall, and stopped short. "Good God, what is that?"

On the deal table lay a mass of some grayish stuff, rubbery and flaccid. Attached to it was a long string. What its purpose was, Giles couldn't even guess. "We found that in a tree outside the drawing room window, sir. Rather, one of the footmen did."

"The string was all hanging down, Your Grace," the footman said eagerly. "We pulled at it till it came loose."

Giles looked distastefully at the rubbery mass. "What is it?"

"Ahem. A sheep's bladder, Your Grace," Benson said.

"What? What in the world—"

"Excuse me, sir, but I've heard that people will fill such things with the gas they use in balloons, so—"

"So they'll float, and look like something flying outside a window. I see," Giles said slowly. "Until it got caught in the tree."

"Yes, Your Grace."

"Not the work of a ghost."

"No, Your Grace."

"Did anything else untoward occur while we were gone?"

"No, sir. The duchess decided to retire for the evening, and Mrs. Templeton is in the nursery, I believe."

"Thank you." Giles turned and left the servants' hall. In the passage outside he met Obadiah, who wore a faintly bemused air. "Did you hear that?"

"Yes, sir. Seems to me I've heard of things like that. Easy for him to do, and then be there for us to chase."

"But why? He must know we weren't scared off. And how does he manage so that everyone hears him singing?"

"Well, sir, I've got some thoughts on that. Let me look around and see what I can find."

Giles nodded. "Good enough. Let's hope we catch him soon, Obadiah."

"Yes, sir."

The clock in the hall was chiming just as Giles closed the baize door that separated the kitchens from the rest of the house. Only ten o'clock. It seemed much later, so much had happened in a short span of time. Good lord, what else was going to happen this summer?

The nursery was lighted only by the faint glow of a candle. It gleamed off the pale satin of Anne's gown and the richer gold of her hair as she sat beside her sleeping son. Giles made no sound as he stood watching her, tenderness welling up inside him. "Is he asleep?" he whispered as he walked into the room, and Anne started.

"Yes," she whispered back. "Did you find anything?"

"No." Giles shook his head as he drew over a chair to sit beside her. "Whoever it is led us a merry chase, but we didn't catch him. One of the footmen found something though." Quickly he explained about the

213

sheep's bladder, and saw comprehension dawn in her eyes. "Rather ingenious, wouldn't you say?"

"You sound almost as if you admire him."

"I wouldn't go that far, no. You must admit, though, Anne, that no one's been hurt."

"Jamie believes in ghosts now," she said in a muffled voice.

"All children do, Annie." He reached up to tuck back a stray curl, and she shied away. "Jamie will be fine."

Anne's eyes were huge as they gazed up at him. "He's all I have, Giles."

"Someday he'll grow up and marry, Anne. What then?"

"I'll be happy for him, of course."

"And in the meantime you'll live your life for him?"

"He's all I have," she repeated.

"No, not all." Giles rose, aware of her startled gaze. "We'll be leaving for the theatre soon."

Anne shook her head. "I can't go. I can't leave him."

Giles looked down at her. All the complicated emotions he felt for her rose up within him, the need, the desire, the tenderness. No, Jamie was not all she had.

He reached out to brush her cheek with his knuckles. "Don't stay up too late, then, Annie."

Her eyes held his. "I won't."

"Good. I—good night, Anne."

"Good night, Giles," she said, and he went out, closing the door behind him.

"What an extraordinary adventure that was last evening," Felicity said the following morning as she sipped at her tea. During their morning promenade in the Tremont landau, Anne and Beth had encountered Felicity with her daughter, and had invited them to take tea. They had also met up with Mr. Seward and Lieutenant Bancroft, who somehow had been included in the invitation. "Have you found out yet what happened?"

"No." Giles, leaning against the mantel, shook his head. He had things to see to, estate matters, investments, government business. It was, after all, his duty. But, duty be hanged. It was much too fine a day for him to stay locked in a dark room, working. Surely the sun had never shone so brightly, almost as golden as Anne's hair; surely the sky had never been so deep a blue. Almost as blue as Anne's eyes. Lord, he sounded like a besotted boy, rather than a man who should know better, but he had no regrets. Since the night in the book-room, when he had held her and kissed her, he had been seeing things in a different light. Where it would lead, he didn't know, but that only added spice to the situation. His life had been quiet and dull for far too long. Obadiah had been right. It was high time things changed.

"Giles?" Felicity said, and he realized that she had been speaking to him.

"Excuse me, Felicity. I was thinking."

"Mm-hm." Felicity looked from Anne to him, a gaze he answered with a straight look of his own. "What an ingenious idea, to create something that looks like a ghost." Shuddering, she glanced out the window. "It certainly looked real."

"Not when you see how it was done. I would like to know how he manages the rest of it, but I suspect we shall find out soon. Mr. Freebody is looking into it."

"Mr. Freebody? Oh, Anne's servant."

"Obadiah is nobody's servant," Anne said quietly.

"Of course not," Giles said. "He has agreed to investigate, however, and I'm glad he is."

"Yes. He'll be hard to fool." Anne set down her cup. "He grew up believing in ghosts and spirits. I think he'll be more likely to spot any contrivances than anyone else."

Giles nodded. "He's a good man. Now, what is this I

heard you talking about when I came in?" he asked Beth, who promptly colored. "Some kind of expedition?"

"I've been offered the use of a boat, Your Grace," Mr. Seward said eagerly. "A beauty. There's a crew to do the work, of course, and I thought we could have a luncheon aboard. Lady Whitehead and Miss Whitehead are enthusiastic about it."

"Oh, dear. I fear I suffer so from mal de mer," Anne said, earning a sharp look from Giles.

"Oh, but Anne, we promise not to go very fast," Beth said, leaning forward. "You'll enjoy it, I know you will."

"Felicity, you're going, I suppose?" Giles said. "Very well, then. Beth will be adequately chaperoned. I'll stay ashore and walk on the beach with Anne, to keep her company."

Felicity's eyes sparkled. "But then who will chaperon you?"

"Jamie," Anne said firmly. "He'll enjoy this. And, Your Grace." Anne turned to Julia. "You'll come, too, won't you?"

"Don't be absurd, girl," Julia growled, making everyone turn to look at her. Julia had been so quiet lately that her presence in the room had almost been forgotten. "Most unsuitable, a boat. No, I shall stay here and supervise the search for the rascal who keeps bothering us."

"Very well, Mother." Giles's smile was unexpectedly gentle. "If they catch him, be certain to give him a piece of your mind."

"I intend to." Head held high, Julia walked out.

Giles watched her depart, a little frown on his face, and then turned to the others. "Very well, then. Shall we go?"

Alone in her room Julia brooded, looking, in her

unrelieved black, something like a big, puffy spider. Everything had changed since they had come to Brighton, and it was all that hussy's fault. She had never liked Anne; she was too light-minded, too disrespectful of the past and its traditions. She especially did not like Anne's effect upon Giles. Not that he seemed about to succumb to her lures, even if he did seem to be tempted. He wouldn't make the same mistake twice.

Elizabeth, though. Julia leaned her head back against her chair and closed her eyes. She ached so, in every bone, in every joint, and her daughter was not here to keep her company or to bathe her forehead in lavender water. Elizabeth had changed. She was not her usual, quiet, dutiful self, but instead appeared to enjoy light-minded pursuits almost as much as the Warren hussy did. Julia was glad her daughter had overcome her natural shyness and now enjoyed socializing, but must she neglect her mother in the process? And that man she had taken up with! Giles was taking that matter much too lightly, leaving Julia frustrated, unhappy, and angry. She had lost control of her children, and she didn't know how to get it back.

There, there they all were, she thought, looking out her window, as the others walked toward the shore and their foolish expedition on a boat. Giles, thank heavens, was showing concern for her finer feeling by refusing to go aboard, knowing how she hated boats, but Elizabeth was heedless. It was because of that man, of course. Look at the way she leaned on his arm and smiled up at him. Most unsuitable. No matter that he came of good family and was charming in a roguish way that she herself might have liked when young. He wasn't good enough for her daughter. The fact of his being a younger son aside, he wasn't gentle enough for someone so shy as Elizabeth. She could so easily be hurt. More than anything else, Julia wanted to spare her children pain.

217

Ah, well, it would all be over soon, she thought, and smiled. Matters were proceeding quite well. Summer would be ending, perhaps more quickly than anyone expected. Soon, everything would be all right. Anne would be gone, and the family would be back at Tremont Castle, safe and secure. And life would go on as it should.

Chapter 16

It was a perfect day for a sail upon the English Channel. Fluffy white clouds dotted the sky, and the breeze was brisk. On the beach below the chalk cliffs Anne held tightly to Jamie's hand, while the others stepped carefully into dinghies, to be rowed to the boat anchored offshore. Long and graceful and white, its mahogany and brasswork gleaming in the sun, it looked almost as if it could fly. Anne glanced at it wistfully. She dearly loved sailing, which she had learned in Jamaica. No need to refine on it quite so much, though. Soon enough she would be back there, and she could sail as often as she wished. The thought brought with it a curious pang.

"I suppose I should thank you," Giles, standing by her side, said in a low voice.

Anne looked up. "For what?"

"You've never been seasick a day in your life."

Oh, dear. She had offended his pride. "Giles, you don't think if—?"

"No," he said curtly, closing off that discussion.

"Mommy," Jamie said suddenly, "why can't I go?"

"Another time, pet." Anne squeezed his shoulder.

"But I want to go now."

"James, I do not like it when you whine."

"But, Mommy—"

"Come, James." Giles took the boy's hand and turned away. "Let us see if we can't find some driftwood or shells."

"All right," Jamie said, and though he was clearly reluctant, he let Giles lead him down the beach. Anne stayed behind for a moment. Jamie, and Giles. They were so alike in coloring and features, and they looked so right together that a lump came to Anne's throat. Father and son. As it should have been; as it would never be.

Giles came back to her, looking quizzical. "Is he always like this?" he asked, gesturing toward Jamie, who had climbed atop some rocks and was shouting at the top of his lungs.

"So energetic? Yes. It can be quite wearing at times, but that's what little boys are like." She smiled up at him. "Undisciplined little savages. And from what I've seen, it doesn't get much better as they get older."

"I believe I've just been insulted."

"You? You don't know what it means to be undisciplined."

"Now that is an insult," he said and, catching her hand, began to run.

Off-balance, Anne stumbled, an exclamation tumbling from her lips. Of all the ridiculous things to do! But it felt good to run like this, hand in hand with him, rebelling against all the manners and conventions of their world. Defiantly she untied her bonnet and tossed it away, letting the wind and the salt air wreak havoc with her hair and not caring. She was free, and she was with Giles. All was as it should be.

Jamie joined in the race and, infected by his enthusiasm, they ran on. The beach eventually ended at a point where the cliff above them curved outward, meeting the sea and forming a sheltered corner. Anne dropped down onto a rock, laughing and gasping for breath. "Heavens! I haven't done anything like that in years!"

"Neither have I." Giles's eyes were brimming with amusement as he sat near her, leaning back on his elbows. His neckcloth was askew, his hair tousled, and his hessians had lost their shine to sand and salt. He was much, much more appealing, and handsome, like this. "I suspect we've lost whatever credit we had with society."

"If anyone saw us."

"Depend upon it. Somebody will have."

"Lord knows what they think of me already," Anne said, and smiled. "But your reputation will be ruined beyond repair. Jamie! Don't wander too far, now."

Giles looked down the beach, where Jamie walked, stopping occasionally to pick up a shell or a stone. "Does he swim?"

"Oh, yes. I don't relish the thought of parading a wet little boy down the Steyne, though."

"Nor do I. Do you know, your hair looks pretty like that."

The warmth in his eyes unsettled her. "I must look a sight," she murmured, putting her hand to her hair. Exercise and sea air had probably made it more unruly than usual. "I wonder what happened to my bonnet."

"As your son's guardian I should probably disapprove of your being so profligate," he said lazily. "But not when the effect is so charming."

"Thank you, sir." Anne glanced away. Was it her imagination, or did the sun no longer seem so bright? Or had the lightness simply gone from her own heart? She hadn't forgotten Giles's real relation to Jamie, but neither had she dwelt upon it. She had been content to drift along, sometimes indulging in the fantasy that she and Giles had never been estranged and that Jamie was his son. Such folly. It had to be the product of summer, and sun. The hard fact was that, for all her fine talk about her independence, she was still a woman dependent upon the whims of a man. As she had learned, to her cost, seven years ago. "Giles, why did

221

you never marry?" she said idly, sifting sand through her fingers and avoiding his eyes.

Giles turned to look at her. "That's an odd question for you to ask when you already know the answer."

"But I don't, Giles."

"Damn it." He got up and walked a few paces away, and turned. "Very well. Let me ask you a question myself. Why did you marry Freddie when we had an understanding?"

"Because that was all it ever was, an understanding."

"What the hell is that supposed to mean?"

"Don't play the innocent with me, Giles! What good is an understanding when you are already betrothed to someone else?"

"Betrothed—wait." He thrust out his arm, barring her from going past him.

"Let me go, Giles."

"Not until you explain what you just said."

"I should think it's perfectly clear."

"Not to me. Did I marry someone else, Anne? Did I?"

"No. Did she jilt you, too?"

Giles jerked back, and she slipped by him. "No." He caught at her shoulders, his hands surprisingly gentle. "No, I think we had better talk about this, Anne. It's been between us since you returned."

"It will always be between us," she muttered, her head bent so that she wouldn't have to look at him.

"I was never betrothed to another."

"No?"

"No! Is this some Banbury tale you've concocted to put me in the wrong? You were the one who left. You were the one who married Freddie."

"Because you were going to marry someone else!"

"Who, damn it?" He gave her a little shake. "Who?"

"Jennifer Stafford! Let me go, Giles."

"Who?" Giles said blankly, letting his hands drop.

"Jennifer Stafford. About a year older than me,

222

brown-haired, plump, rather pretty, quite dull and quite sensible. A suitable bride for the Duke of Tremont."

"Not this one. Good God, Anne, if I can't even remember her, why do you think I was going to marry her?"

"Because you were."

"Damn it, I wasn't."

"Oh, don't cozen me so. Do you know what it felt like when I learned that you didn't love me, that you were only toying with me—"

"I wasn't. Annie, is that why you left?"

"Of course it's why I left! I wasn't going to stand tamely by and watch while you married another woman!"

"I wasn't going to marry her! I admit my mother would have liked me to, but— good God." He broke off, staring at her. "My good God."

"What?"

"Anne." Taking her hand, he led her back to the rocks and sat beside her. "Who told you I was betrothed?"

"I don't remember."

"Don't you?" His voice was gentle. "It was my mother, wasn't it?"

"Yes." She stared up at him. "Yes."

"She told me you were only flirting with me, that all you wanted from me was my title and you really preferred Freddie."

"Oh, Giles—"

"It wasn't true, was it?"

"No." She swallowed, hard. "You weren't already betrothed."

"No." They gazed at each other across the wreckage of seven years. "It was you I wanted to marry, Anne. In fact, I—" He broke off. "You wouldn't have married Freddie, would you? You would have stayed here and married me."

"Yes." It hadn't had to happen. Not her heartbreak when she had believed Giles loved another, not her life with Freddie. And not Jamie, the only good thing to come from that life. "It's past, Giles."

"Is it?" He gripped her hand. "Anne, you're here now. We still feel something for each other. You can't deny it."

"It's too late." Gently she withdrew her hand. "We've both changed, Giles. We're not the people we were then, and I have no desire to marry again."

Giles's eyes sharpened suddenly. "Am I to believe that you were so happy with Freddie that you couldn't think of marrying anyone else?"

"No, of course not. But why should I remarry? I have far more freedom now than I ever had."

"And yet, both times I've held you, you've responded to my kiss."

Anne looked away. "I'm attracted to you, Giles. I won't deny it." She rose and walked a few paces away. "But that's all it is. Probably all it ever was. If what we had could be destroyed by one small lie, how strong could it have been?"

"You were young." He rose, too, and she moved farther away. "You made a mistake."

"And I'm not about to make another. I like being independent, Giles. I'm my own person. I don't want to change that."

"Independence can be lonely, Anne."

She turned, and the smile she gave him was sad. "So can marriage. I—"

"Mommy!" Jamie called. "Look what I found!"

"What is it, Jamie?" Anne walked toward him, not certain whether to be annoyed, or relieved, by this interruption.

"A conch shell, Mommy. Listen."

"Why, so it is." Anne took the shell from him, tracing the jagged edges where it had been broken, stroking the satiny pink interior. "This has traveled a long way."

"Do you think Cook will make conch soup, Mommy?"

"Conch soup?" Giles said, coming up behind Anne, who started at the sound of his voice. She was skittish, like an untried colt, and the thought that he made her feel that way was depressing. Not when he felt so much more, when he wanted her to feel so much more. What had been done to them in the past had hurt them, but they could get past it. He knew they could, if she would let them. And there lay the problem, Anne's touchy independence. What had happened in Anne's marriage to leave her that way? "What is conch soup?"

"No, lovey," Anne said, handing Jamie back his treasure and ignoring Giles. "I don't think Cook even knows what it is."

"We could tell her, couldn't we, Mommy? Cook at home knows how to make it."

"I know, lovey."

"When are we going home, Mommy?" Jamie asked, catching at her hand and at Giles's, and walking between them.

"Soon, pet." Anne's eyes met Giles's. "There are some things to settle, but soon, I think."

"Don't you like it here, Jamie?" Giles said.

"It's all right. I like Jamaica better."

"You have family here, Jamie. There are good schools, too."

"School!" Jamie made a noise. "I don't want to go to school."

"Jamie, perhaps there's another conch shell," Anne said. "Do you think you could look?"

"Yes, Mommy. 'Bye!" Releasing their hands, he ran off.

Giles stared after him in amusement. "I would never have spoken to my father in such a way," he said.

"You're not his father." Anne rounded on him, her eyes stormy. "Don't ever try to turn Jamie against me, Giles."

225

"I don't know what you mean—"

"I think you do. You may be his guardian, but I am his mother. I don't care what the law says. He is my son, not yours. I will not allow you to use him against me, and I will not let you take him away from me."

"Anne," Giles protested, as she stalked away. "Annie, I wouldn't—"

"Stay away from me, Giles Templeton!"

"Annie, I'm not Freddie."

That stopped her. Good heavens, what was that supposed to mean? He couldn't possibly know.

She turned to see him watching her, looking confused and contrite and—could it be?—loving, all at once. Damn the man, Anne thought, walking back to him, though a moment before being near him was the last thing she had wanted. Why did he always have this effect on her?

"Thank heavens you're not like him!" Her voice was artificially bright. "At least you can hold your liquor."

"Annie." He sounded mildly reproving. "You do know I want what's best for you and Jamie?"

"I know. 'Tis your duty."

"And what is so wrong with that?"

I don't want to be just duty to you! She shrugged, her smile wistful. "Come, we'll never settle this. Why do we not just go on as we are? As friends?"

Friends! Giles thought. What had he done that was so wrong he deserved that? "Very well. Jamie!" he called, releasing Anne's arm. "Do you know what those are?"

Jamie tossed a scornful look in the direction Giles pointed. "Bathing machines. Boring."

"Boring?" Giles turned to Anne as she came up to them, looking amused. "Is that why you haven't gone bathing this summer, Anne?"

"Among other reasons," she said imperturbably.

"Anyone who has to use a bathing machine is a sissy," Jamie said.

"Jamie!"

"It's true. At home we go right in the water, don't we, Mommy?"

Giles's smile was knowing as he looked at Anne. "Now that is something I would like to see."

A slow flush spread from Anne's throat to her face. "Then take a room on the Marine Parade and use a spyglass to watch ladies bathing, as the young bucks do," she snapped. "Such a civilized country this is."

Giles allowed himself a smile. "Am I to believe, then, that everything is better in Jamaica?"

Anne didn't return the smile. "Just about everything, yes."

"Would it be a waste of my time to try to change your mind?"

"I've no reason to change it, Giles."

"I see." Their eyes caught, and held. "Annie, I—"

"Halloo!" Felicity called from down the beach, and they turned. "You should have come along, it was a glorious sail."

Giles looked down at Anne, and then offered her his arm. "Was it? Yet you came in earlier than I expected."

"The wind came up and it got rough," Mr. Seward said, handing Susan, her face very pale, out of the boat with great care. "Too rough for the ladies."

"Oh, but it was wonderful," Beth exclaimed, looking up at Thomas with sparkling eyes. "We went so fast, it almost felt like flying. I didn't want to come in."

Giles and Anne fell into step with the others as they climbed back up to the Marine Parade, Jamie lagging behind. "Perhaps we should have gone with them," Giles said, his voice low, and Anne glanced away, her heart heavy. More had happened between her and Giles just now than a simple walk. A great deal had been decided, almost without words, and the future was set. Nothing would ever be quite the same again.

* * *

227

Life had changed vastly for Beth since coming to Brighton. It wasn't just that she attended the social events that had once been denied her, or that she could now hold her own in any fashionable gathering. It was that she finally had freedom, to dress as she chose, to go out as she chose, since Mama seemed to prefer her own company these days, and, most important of all, to think as she chose. She had her own opinions on things, and she was rather surprised to find they were strong. She wanted her own life, her own family, and, if her thoughts centered around a certain man who had made her dream of things previously unimagined, that was her concern. Life was quite different from the narrow, sheltered world at Tremont Castle, where once all she had desired was a mild flirtation with the vicar. Now she wanted much, much more.

Accompanied by her maid, she set off toward Donaldson's lending library, glad that the hour of the fashionable promenade was past and she needn't speak to anyone. The weather was not so fine as it had been; clouds were scudding in from the sea, and the wind was brisk. The air was bracing, though, and smelled of salt. Irresistibly she was remined of last week's sailing expedition, and the moment when the boat had heeled and she had lost her balance. Had Thomas not been there to catch her she might have suffered a nasty fall, indeed, but he had been, and for just a moment his strong arms had closed around her. For just that moment she had let herself imagine what it would be like to be held thus forever, to share his dreams and his visions, to have children with him. That last thought, making her blush, had made her straighten, assuring him that she was quite all right, thank you. She hadn't forgotten it, though, that special, magic moment. When she looked in Thomas's eyes, she could see that he still remembered it, too.

Thomas was already waiting for her at Donaldson's when she walked in, though he betrayed his eagerness only by a quick glance at her. Beth's heart beat faster at the sight of him, so handsome in his uniform. Casually, as if she hadn't been waiting all morning for just this moment, she strolled down the aisle toward him, where he stood at a table, idly leafing through a book. "Good morning, Lieutenant Bancroft."

"Good morning, Lady Elizabeth. Beth," he added in a low voice, for her ears, only. "You look lovely today."

Beth blushed. "You shouldn't say such things, sir," she said, though her heart wasn't in the reproof.

"Perhaps not. Not when there are others to hear."

"Is that a good book, sir?"

Thomas glanced down at the book in his hand. "Who the devil knows?" he said, and set it down with a bang.

"Thomas!" she whispered. "Everyone is looking at us."

"No, they're not." He sounded amused. "Everyone else is too busy with their own flirtations."

"I shouldn't have come. If my mother hears of this—"

He sighed. "Beth, I thought we'd settled this."

"Good morning, Mrs. Hammond-Smythe." Beth gave the older woman a bright smile as she passed by, and then returned to her perusal of her book. "I think I will take this, after all."

"Allow me to carry it for you, ma'am."

"Why, thank you, sir." Beth smiled up at him, and was lost. Again it was as it had been in the boat, as if only they two existed. Beth had never felt anything quite like it in her life. It was frightening. It was exhilarating, and she wanted it never to end.

It was Thomas who broke the moment, clearing his throat and stepping back. "Let us pay for this, ma'am. Might I accompany you home?"

"Why, yes, sir." Beth's voice was light. "I'd like that."

"So would I," he muttered under his breath, and a shiver ran down Beth's spine. Never had anyone affected her quite like this. It was enough to make her believe that all her dreams might come true.

Outside, Thomas offered her his arm. She walked alongside him, his height and the strength of his arm making her feel deliciously feminine. She felt as if she were on the edge of something tremendously exciting and wonderful, and she wanted to let herself go, she wanted to soar, secure in the knowledge that Thomas would always be there to catch her.

"I thought we had that particular matter settled," Thomas said, breaking into her thoughts.

Beth looked up. "What matter?"

"Your mother."

"She doesn't approve of you, Thomas, but—"

"Because I am a younger son? Haven't you told her—"

"Please, must we quarrel like this? We so seldom see each other and never alone." She glanced back over her shoulder. Her maid, trailing along behind them, was watching them avidly, but she would be discreet; she had been with Beth for years.

"I begin to think we never will be alone. Good morning." He nodded at an acquaintance passing them on horseback as they strolled along the Marine Parade. To their right was the sea, a dark wine color today under the lowering skies. "When you've seen what life can be like, the freedom from restraint, doing what one wants to do—"

"And yet you're in the army," she pointed out gently.

"Of course." He sounded surprised. "What else could I do? But not forever, dearest. Someday this cursed war will be over and we can be together."

Beth's breath caught in her throat. "Is—that really what you want?"

"Yes." He stopped and looked down at her. "Don't you?"

"Yes, oh yes! But, Thomas." She took his arm and they strolled again, closer together this time. "How long will the war go on? It seems forever."

"I've been thinking on that, Beth. There's no need for us to wait until it's over."

"Thomas."

"Marry me, Beth. Now. We'll be happy, I promise."

"Oh, Thomas." Beth's smile was wistful. Suddenly she, who had led so sheltered a life, felt infinitely older than he. Couldn't he see the problems ahead of them? "Why me, Thomas? Is it because I am the daughter of a duke?"

"Don't say that!" He caught her by the shoulders, making her gasp. "It is an insult to you and to me."

"I'm sorry," she said meekly. "But—"

"Making me sound like a damned fortune hunter."

"Thomas, please slow down. I cannot keep up with you."

He stopped abruptly, and she stumbled against him. "I love you, Elizabeth Templeton. I love your sweetness and your beauty. I love your courage in defying everything you've been taught, and I love the woman inside of you who is a lot bolder and more passionate than you know."

Beth blinked. "What?"

"Ah, sweetheart." The back of his fingers brushed her cheeks. "Did I scare you? I'm sorry, I don't mean to. But when you're in the army you realize how precious life is."

"I'm not beautiful, Thomas. And I'm not bold."

"Bold enough to be seen with me in public," he argued.

Beth glanced quickly around. They had come a fair distance along the cliff edge and had already passed the Royal Crescent, the easternmost houses in the town. Bystanders were few and far between on a day many would consider cold and raw. Beth, though, was no longer aware of the weather. "I can't seem to help it. I want to be with you. Oh, but Thomas!" She grasped his hand, and he brought hers to his mouth to kiss it. "Can you not see the problems? You don't know my mother. I'm sure, given time, she'd come to like you, but she is so concerned with family tradition and honor that she won't approve."

"You're of age, Beth. In any event, isn't it your brother's approval I need?"

"Yes, but—"

"And I've the feeling he likes me."

"He does. But, oh, Thomas, that isn't what worries me! If I defy my mother it will hurt her. I love her, Thomas. I don't want her to be hurt."

"I know that," he said, surprising her, "and I honor you for it. Sometimes, though, Beth, life forces us to make hard choices. Beth." His voice was low. "Will you marry me?"

Chapter 17

Beth closed her eyes. Marrying Thomas would bring with it a great many difficulties. A life without him, though, was not to be borne. "Yes."

"Capital!" He caught her up in his arms, swinging her around, and she squealed with delight. "That's capital, Beth."

"Thomas!"

"You have made me the happiest man on earth." His face grew grave, his eyes studying her, and suddenly she knew what was coming, though it was nothing she'd ever before experienced. Her heart began to pound harder, her fingers tightened on his shoulders, and her face tilted up, like a flower to the sun. Without thought that they were in a public place, not caring who might see and report back to her mother, Beth willingly gave her lips to him, fleetingly thinking of all the romances she had read and this one, climactic moment. And it was all she had ever thought it would be, it was more, his warm lips pressing on hers, her own tingling, returning the kiss, while the blood sang in her veins and her limbs felt weak. She, shy, plain Beth Templeton, was loved. Almost she believed she was the bold, beautiful woman he thought her.

"My God." Thomas pulled away, looking down at her with dazed eyes. "You bewitch me, woman."

"Good," she said, surprising both of them.

He grinned and released her, though he kept his arm around her shoulder as he swung her around, back toward town. "Don't tempt me. Any more of that and we'll be in serious trouble."

"I don't care." She snuggled her arm through his and smiled as they passed her maid, who smirked and dropped a quick curtsy. She had been kissed at last, and at last she felt like a woman.

"I do. I don't wish to have your brother calling me out to protect your honor." He smiled down at her. "I'll talk to him, shall I?"

"Oh, yes," she said, smiling shyly up at him. She felt light and young and free, so free, and all because of the man beside her. All would be well. The future would be theirs.

Benson bowed as Beth came into the house, so preoccupied that she might as well have been floating. "Have you ever seen a more glorious day, Benson?" she said, smiling radiantly at him.

Benson glanced out at the slate-gray sky and shook his head slightly. "Her Grace has been asking for you, my lady," he said, with only the slightest hint of reproof in his voice.

"Has she?" Beth quickly untied her bonnet, handing it to her maid. "I shall go to her directly."

Beth hummed as she bustled up the stairs. Such a day as it was. She wished she could share her good news with someone before she burst with it, but she couldn't. Not yet. Mama would not be pleased. Mama would likely scold anyway, she thought, tapping lightly on the door to Julia's sitting room and going in. Oh, well, let her. It was just her way. Nothing was going to disturb Beth's good mood today.

Inside the room was darkened, to Beth's surprise. "Mama?" she said, and Julia's maid, her face pinched in disapproval, came forward, from the door to Julia's

234

room. "Hannah, whatever is it?"

"Good morning, my lady. She's been asking for you, ma'am."

"Oh, dear." In spite of herself the old, familiar guilt rose within her. She shouldn't have gone out, not when her mother needed her—but why shouldn't she? Mama had seemed perfectly fine this morning when she had stopped in after breakfast, and had said nothing about Beth's staying with her. Of course, she never did. It was simply expected that Beth would. At Tremont, that hadn't bothered Beth very much. Here, in Brighton, it did. Was she never to have a chance for a life of her own? "Where is she, Hannah?"

"Lying down, ma'am."

Beth regarded her in surprise. This was unusual. Mama was not well, but rarely did she take to her bed. "Oh, dear," she said again, and went into the bedroom.

All was dark in this room, too. Beth stood still for a moment, letting her eyes grow accustomed to the dimness. The heavy velvet drapes had been drawn against the day, and no candle burned to alleviate the gloom. "Mama?" she whispered.

"Elizabeth, is that you?" Julia's voice quavered.

"Yes, Mama." Guilt rose in her again as she flew across the room to the massive bed, though she knew she had done nothing so very wrong. She was just able to make out the recumbent form of her mother, reclining against a pile of pillows, a lacy cap atop her head. "What is it, Mama?"

"Give me your hand, child." Julia took her hand in a surprisingly strong grip, and Beth sat on the edge of the bed. "Did you enjoy your trip to the lending library?"

Color rose in Beth's cheeks; she was glad the room was dark. "Yes, Mama. Mama, whatever is it? Are you not well?"

"I have the most dreadful headache—but there, I shall not refine upon it. It does no good to complain

235

about such things."

"No, Mama. I'll just bathe your face with lavender water, shall I?"

"You're a good girl," Julia said, as Beth crossed to the dressing table. "If you would just sit with me, Elizabeth."

"Of course, Mama." Beth sat by her again and softly began to bathe her face.

"A good girl." Julia's hand suddenly reached up to grasp Beth's. "You won't leave me, child?"

Beth paused, and then went on with her task. "No, Mama," she said, her heart heavy. "I won't leave."

"I am sure tonight's entertainment will be an edifying experience," Julia said, as the Tremont landau, its top up against the dampness of the evening, set off down the Steyne. "Lady Tyngsboro is a lady of taste and refinement."

"Dull, you mean," Giles, sitting next to her, muttered.

Julia ignored him. "I am not fond of musical evenings as a rule," she went on, "but I am persuaded that Lady Tyngsboro will not provide shabby entertainment."

"'Tis been so long since I've heard good music," Anne said. "Do you suppose they'll play Mozart tonight, or Beethoven?"

"Beethoven? Bah," Julia said, making the others stare at her. "All noise and thunder. Depend upon it, ma'am, you'll not hear from him in the future."

"At least it would keep us awake," Giles said, his voice gloomy. "Lady Tyngsboro will likely sing hymns again."

"She has a lovely voice. Now I wish to hear no more of this. I have accompanied you to your rackety affairs all summer, have I not?"

"I'd hardly call dining with the Prince of Wales rackety," Anne observed.

"The Prince is above reproach, of course, even if I cannot approve of the people who surround him. Tonight, however, should be worthwhile."

Across the carriage, Anne and Giles exchanged glances of wry amusement. Friends they were, as she had suggested on the beach the other day. Friends who could share a laugh, and who thought remarkably alike on some things. Really, Anne thought, it was the perfect basis for companionship. Why, then, weren't they happy? Friends should be comfortable in each other's company, but they weren't. Once they had talked about everything; now, if by chance they were alone, there seemed to be nothing to discuss. Nothing that was not potentially dangerous. Before, the past had been between them, keeping them apart, but also keeping them safe. Now that was gone. Their discovery of what had actually happened should have cleared the air. Instead, it had generated a new tension between them, something Anne wasn't certain she wished to ease. If only summer would end. Then she could return to Jamaica, and peace.

In the dim light, Giles studied Anne's averted face, noting the purity of its lines, the classic bone structure, the delicately molded features. Friends. Bah. Only a woman would think such a baffle-headed arrangement would work. How could they possibly be merely friends, with all that had happened between them? They had gone long beyond that point, long ago, and there was no going back. The devil of it was, what did they do now? Now that he knew what had driven her to leave him, there should have been no more constraint between them, but there was. She was holding back from him, and the tension between them was growing so thick that he knew other people noticed it. He'd seen that in the glint in his mother's eyes, and in Beth's

237

quick, darting glances. Something would have to be done, and soon, because, damn it! He couldn't take much more of this. He had already waited seven years for Anne. He didn't want to wait much longer.

Lady Tyngsboro's house was ablaze with light, and the line of carriages waiting to discharge their passengers there was long. In spite of her tendency to sing at her musical evenings, Lady Tyngsboro was tolerated, if not liked, by the ton. High-minded though she appeared to be, she also had a great interest in gossip, and a sharp tongue to go along with it. Over the last weeks Anne had learned to present a serene facade to those who showed unseemly curiosity about her or her past, and she was determined to do so now. Lady Tyngsboro had been one of those who had clucked over Anne's high spirits in the past. However, as the Tremont party approached their hostess, Anne was dismayed to see a glint of malice in her eyes. Quickly she looked about for Giles, but he was proceeding far more slowly up the stairs to the drawing room, his arm supporting Julia. Anne would have to face this alone.

"Good evening, ma'am." Anne dropped a curtsy that was of necessity brief, because of the crowded hallway. "Thank you for inviting me tonight. I am sure it will be an entertaining evening."

"Thank you, Mrs. Templeton." Lady Tyngsboro's face was pleasant, in contrast to the sharpness of her eyes. "And Lady Elizabeth. How charming you look."

Beth, standing beside Anne, blushed. "Thank you, ma'am."

"What a pity Lieutenant Bancroft could not be here tonight. I am persuaded he would be entranced by you."

"I—I—thank you," Beth stammered.

"Beth doesn't lack for admirers." Anne's smile was pleasant, but she met the other woman's eyes with cool steadiness. "But, come, we mustn't keep you, ma'am, there are so many others wishing to speak to you. Will we have the pleasure of hearing you sing tonight?"

Lady Tyngsboro simpered. There was no other word to describe it, Anne thought, incongruous though it was for a woman of her age. "I will do my humble best to entertain you."

"Oh, and I'm sure it will be most humble indeed." Anne smiled and took Beth's arm. "Good evening, ma'am."

"Anne!" Beth hissed as they strolled away. "She knows about Thomas!"

Anne, still basking in the satisfaction of that last Parthian shot, gave her a quick look. "Thomas?"

Beth colored. "Lieutenant Bancroft. She knows about him."

"Why, of course she does. Doubtless others have noticed you with him, as well. But, Beth." Anne stopped, and glanced around to make certain no one was attending to them. "You do yourself no good by reacting as you did. If Lady Tyngsboro suspected something before, now she knows."

"But what was I to do, Anne? I never expected her to say such a thing."

"Smile and say something perfectly above reproach. Never, ever let anyone like her know what you really think or feel."

"Oh. I see." Beth appeared much struck by this. "If she had asked you about Giles, what would you have said?"

"Mrs. Templeton, Lady Elizabeth," a deep voice said, saving Anne from answering. "How lovely you both look."

Anne smiled. "Mr. Campbell. How delightful to see you again."

"And may I say the same." Ian Campbell took Anne's kidgloved hand in his and lingered over it, while his eyes passed over her, pausing for just a moment at her bosom. "You look like the midnight sky in that gown."

"Thank you, sir." Smiling, Anne withdrew her hand. Her evening gown of deep blue sarcenet was simplicity itself, with its unadorned bodice, but, scattered on the skirt were silver spangles. A charming compliment. If only it had come from Giles.

"Good evening, Campbell." A strong hand gripped Anne's arm, and she looked up to see Giles. His smile did not reach his eyes. "A surprise to see you here tonight, sir."

"Oh, Lady T. is bosom bows with my mother," Ian said. "Be sure to get back to her if I didn't show my face here."

"Yes, you do require edifying experiences, do you not? Come, Beth, Anne. Let us find seats."

"Sorry, old man." Ian's smile was as pleasant, and as cold, as Giles's. "Mrs. Templeton is sitting with me."

"Is she? I had not heard of it. If you'll excuse us—"

"Giles!" Julia's voice cut through the hubbub, sounding more animated than it had in many a day. "Do look who is here."

The small group of people turned, distracted. Julia was making her stately progress toward them, a young woman on her arm. She was slender, passably pretty, with brown hair scraped back into a bun, wearing a gown of dull brown stuff, several years out of fashion. Anne started. Jennifer Stafford, of all people.

"You knew she would be here," she hissed to Giles.

"Anne, for God's sake." Giles frowned at her. "Be sensible about this."

"You do remember Mrs. Priestly, do you not, Giles?" Julia said, smiling, with just a hint of malice. "Of course, she was Miss Stafford when you knew her. Anne, I am sure you remember her, too."

"Charming to see you again." Ian sounded bored. "Come, Anne. Shall we take our seats?"

"Thank you, Mr. Campbell." Anne slipped her hand through his arm. "I would be happy to."

"Anne," Giles said behind her, but she ignored him.

Jennifer Stafford! And just when she'd thought that that matter was settled.

"Miss Stafford has worn well," Ian observed, as he led Anne to a spindly chair of gilt and crimson velvet, one of many set out in rows. "A little too brown, perhaps, but rather pretty. I wonder where Reverend Priestly is."

"If you are trying to provoke me, Ian, I assure you it will not work." Anne's smile was tight.

"Tremont has already done so, then?"

"Oh, no. Not Tremont." No. She was annoyed at Giles, even though she knew he had nothing to do with the former Miss Stafford's presence here, but it was Julia that she was most angry with. When would the woman cease to cause trouble?

Oddly enough, she had been able to find it in herself to forgive Julia for her actions of seven years ago. True it was that Julia had meddled; equally true, however, was the fact that she wouldn't have been successful had Anne not allowed her to be. Had she held fast to what she knew was true, had she trusted in Giles and in her own feelings, then Julia's meddling would have come to nought. She was, Anne realized, as much to blame for the past as Julia was. This business of diverting Giles's attention by the presence of a former amour, though, was different. It was deliberate and malicious, and certainly not in anyone's best interests. All it had been designed to do was to anger Anne. In that, the duchess had succeeded admirably. Score another point for her, Anne conceded ruefully. She'd fallen into the trap again.

Across the room, Giles made certain his mother was seated comfortably and then sat down himself, Mrs. Priestly on his other side. Now that he saw her again he did remember her, and his mother's arch attempts at making a match between them. What she had done seven years ago annoyed him; he had just learned of it, and so hadn't yet acquired the perspective of time. Still,

241

he remembered a particular argument he had had with Anne, just before she had married Freddie. If he had pressed her then, if he had bothered to find out what was wrong, instead of retreating behind his own hurt, perhaps the whole matter could have been settled. Instead, they had wasted seven years, and now any chance that they might make up for the past seemed remote. For here he sat with Mrs. Priestly, listening to her prattle on about her work as a missionary and how wonderful her husband was, while across the room Anne was with that damnable Campbell, smiling and flirting. Damn, damn, damn. He would have something to say to her when this evening was over, and his mother, too.

"Good evening," Lady Tyngsboro said from the front of the room, and Giles reluctantly gave her his attention. As the daughter of the house began to play a Mozart sonata, badly, on the pianoforte, Giles leaned back, his arms crossed on his chest. It was going to be a very long evening.

Jamie couldn't sleep. He'd been tucked into bed hours ago, and his mother had come in to kiss him good night, smelling so sweet and looking so pretty. He'd pretended he didn't like the kiss, of course, but in reality, he did. In reality he'd wanted her to stay and tell him a story, like she used to when they were home. Mama didn't seem to have time for that anymore. She was always going to parties, or fighting with Uncle Giles, and Jamie didn't like that one bit.

Arguments were part of Jamie's life. It was what he supposed you did when you grew up. You quarreled. He didn't like it when Mama and Uncle Giles quarreled, though. It made him feel all funny inside, scared and nervous and wanting to cry, even if he was a big boy now. Still, it was different from the fights Mama used to have with Papa. Uncle Giles never raised his voice, and he never looked at you in that cold way that made you feel all small and shriveled up inside. Jamie didn't really remember Papa that much, and he wasn't really sorry he was gone, though he knew he was supposed to be. It was silly. Why should he miss Papa, when he had Uncle Giles and Obadiah and Terence?

At the thought of Terence, Jamie brightened. He hadn't talked to Terence in ever so long, not since that night he had appeared at the drawing-room window. Jamie wished he could have seen that; he'd never seen a ghost, for all Obadiah talked of haunts. He liked Terence. When Mama and Uncle Giles had gone out, when Aunt Julia was feeling too sick to be with him and Nurse was asleep, Terence would talk to him.

Throwing back the covers, Jamie scrambled out of bed and knelt by the grate in the floor, his hair tousled, his nightshirt twisted around him. "Terence," he whispered. When no reply came, he spoke louder, not at all concerned that he would disturb Nurse's snoring. "Terence!"

Silence. Jamie put his ear to the grate and listened very hard, but heard no answer. There was only a faint, hollow sound, like the sea, far, far away. Maybe if he waited awhile Terence would come and talk to him, and teach him more songs. "What do you do with a drunken sailor, what do you do with a drunken sailor," Jamie chanted softly, sitting back with his arms around his knees. Surely Terence would hear, and would come sing with him.

After a time, though, Jamie began to grow impatient. It was cold, and the floor was hard. "Terence," he called out, not bothering to keep his voice down as he pressed his face against the grate. The dim light of the candle that was always kept burning in the nursery was not enough to reveal the mysteries that hid in the depths beyond the grate, though Jamie had looked and looked. It was like a tunnel, just the place for a ghost to live, and it fascinated him. Mama had told him something about it when they'd first come to this house, and then he'd heard Cook talking—

Jamie suddenly shot to his feet and ran from the room, on tiptoe. The answer to the puzzle had been there all along. He knew where the tunnel ended. He knew where to find Terence.

The pianoforte had been played, a soprano had sung, and an amateur, but enthusiastic, group of violinists had scraped their way through a Bach quartet. At last, though, the interval arrived. Lady Tyngsboro's hymns were yet to come, making the exodus to the supper room for refreshment that much more frantic and noisy. The respite would not last very long.

After procuring glasses of champagne and a plate of dainties, Ian rejoined Anne in the supper room. "An interesting evening," he observed. "The things I do for my mama."

"You don't strike me as the sort of man who would be so concerned with his mother's feelings, Mr. Campbell."

"Nevertheless, I am."

"Oh, I meant no harm," she said quickly. "I think it does you credit, sir. 'Tis a side of you no one ever sees."

"Pray do me a favor and tell no one." He smiled at her. "'Twould ruin my reputation."

"Your secret is safe with me. Oh, Giles. Are you enjoying the evening?"

Giles, walking into the room, stopped, giving the other man a look before answering. "Passably," he said. "Should think you'd be bored by now, Campbell."

Ian smiled. "Actually, I'm quite entertained. Interesting, seeing Miss Stafford again after all these years."

"Why, there's Felicity, Giles," Anne said. "I didn't know she was to be here tonight. Shall we go speak with her?"

Giles stared hard at Ian, and then looked down at her. "Of course. If you'll excuse us, Campbell."

Ian inclined his head, a slight, ironic smile on his face. "Yes. I shall speak with you later, Anne."

"Over my dead body," Giles muttered as they walked away.

"Giles." Anne glared at him. "That was rude of you."

"Who was the one who suggested going to Felicity?"

"That was to prevent a quarrel, and well you know it. Really, Giles! Ian is a friend. Must you behave so when I am with him?"

"When he stands there making calf's eyes at you, yes, I must."

"Calf's eyes—oh, for heaven's sake, Giles!"

"He's not for you, Anne."

"And who are you to talk? I noticed you dancing attendance on the simpering Miss Stafford. Exuse me, Mrs. Priestly. I wouldn't have thought married ladies were your style."

"They're not—" he began, and broke off. To Anne's astonishment, a smile spread across his face. "I don't believe it. You're jealous."

"I beg your pardon!"

"You are. You're jealous of Mrs. Priestly."

"Of that little brown mouse? Don't be absurd."

"Hm. Now that she's finally returned maybe I'll—"

"Giles!"

"What?" He gazed down at her, and it dawned on her that he was jesting. He had no interest in the dowdy Mrs. Priestly. Relief warred with fury, and lost. How dare he treat her so?

"It was rude of me to leave Mr. Campbell," she said frostily, and was satisfied to see Giles's eyes flicker.

"Annie. Do you have a *tendre* for Campbell?"

"Why, what a ridiculous question. There, I hear the musicians starting. The interval must be over. Will you escort me back to the music room, Giles?

Giles looked down at her, and nodded. "Oh, very well. But we'll speak more of this at home, Anne."

"We certainly will," she agreed, and turned away.

The entertainment mercifully came to an end an eternity later, and most of the guests left with alacrity. In the Tremont carriage Julia discussed the evening just past, with Beth murmuring agreement. Giles and Anne both were silent. There was tension between them again, but it was different from what it had been earlier. It was a tension born of the evening's events, a tension trembling with words left unsaid and things yet to come. Something had subtly changed between them this evening, something that neither could deny. Though Anne might take refuge in anger and Giles in silence, both were feeling much the same, an odd kind of anticipation. As surely as if they had discussed it, they knew something was going to happen tonight. Something that would affect them profoundly.

The house was lighted from top to bottom when the carriage drew up before it. Giles frowned as he turned from helping the ladies down from the carriage. "It looks as if we're the ones entertaining. What is going on?"

"A shocking waste of candle wax," Julia proclaimed. "I shall speak with Benson on this."

Anne glanced up at the floor where the family slept, and her heart stopped. Her room was ablaze with lights, as was the one adjoining it. Jamie's room. Dear God, had something happened to her son? "Jamie," she said, and dashed up the steps.

The door opened as she reached it, and Benson stood there, looking even more sepulchral than usual. For a moment they stood in tableau, Anne, her throat dry with fear, hardly daring to speak. "Benson," she croaked.

"What is going on?" Giles demanded, striding into the hall, and she turned to him. Thank heavens, here was someone on whom she could rely. "Why is the house all lit up?"

"I am sorry, Your Grace." Benson bowed briefly, his eyes on Anne. "There's, ah, a problem."

"What? Out with it, man. Tell us."

"I'm sorry, ma'am," he said to Anne. "We cannot find Master James anywhere."

Chapter 18

They were words to strike terror into a mother's heart. "What do you mean, you cannot find him?" Anne said, her voice high and tight. "He is in his bed, asleep."

Benson looked uncomfortable. "No, ma'am. I fear—"

"Oh, ma'am!" Nurse shuffled toward her, a copious handkerchief held to her face. "I'm that sorry, but he's gone. My baby is gone. The ghost must have him!"

"Nonsense." Giles laid a steadying hand on Anne's shoulder. "The boy must be here someplace. He cannot have left the house."

"I'm not sure, Your Grace." Benson swallowed hard. "I fear I have been derelict in my duty, sir. I spent some time with Mrs. Justice in her parlor this evening, and he may have got out then."

"The door was unlocked?"

"Yes, Your Grace."

"Then we'll have to notify the watch."

"Yes, sir. I am sorry for this regrettable episode, sir. If you wish to sack me, I shall understand, though my family has served yours for years."

"Don't be ridiculous," Giles said brusquely. "Anne—"

"I've got to find him." Anne broke free of Giles's grasp and ran up the stairs. Jamie, Jamie. He was

248

everything to her, he was her world, the only reason she had kept on. But they were wrong. He was safe, asleep in bed.

She burst into Jamie's room, as brightly lighted as the others, and as empty. The coverlet had been flung back on the bed, revealing that no one hid underneath. Anne got down on her knees and looked, anyway, though she knew he would not go where he thought there were monsters. "Oh, Jamie."

"Annie." Strong hands were at her arms, helping her up. "Come. We'll find him," Giles said.

"No." She pulled away, rushing across the room to the wardrobe and flinging open the doors. "He has to be here. I have to find him, Giles, I have to! He's my baby."

"We'll find him, Annie, I promise. I don't think he got out, but we've notified the watch."

"Oh, God." Anne's face crumpled. "He doesn't know this place. If he's out there, in the fog, lost—Giles, he's only a little boy!"

"He's not out there." Giles gave her a little shake. "This does no good, Anne. You will not help Jamie by becoming hysterical."

Tears blurred her vision as she looked up at him. He was right. She could not let go of hope, not when there was every reason to believe Jamie would be found safe and whole. "I am not hysterical," she said with great dignity, and then spoiled the effect by sniffling.

"Of course you are not. Come down to the drawing room. The staff is searching the house now. He has to be here, Anne. We'll find him."

"Of course we will. I'm sure you'll understand, though, that I would like to search, myself."

Giles nodded. "Will you let me help?"

"I would like it above all things, Giles."

"Good. We'll start up here, then. Your room, first?"

"Yes." Anne looked around the empty nursery. Wherever Jamie spent any time was usually a whirlwind of objects, and this room was no exception. In the last weeks, he had managed to stamp his personality on it firmly. There were his favorite story books, the conch shell found last week on the beach, his toy soldiers, put away on a shelf with military precision. It was the perfect room for a boy. The only thing missing was the child. *Oh, Jamie.* "Jamie!" she called on impulse, and thought, in the second following, that she heard a very small, very distant, mewling sound. "Giles! Did you hear that?"

He shook his head. "Just an echo, dear. Come. Let's start searching."

Anne nodded, though she glanced into the room again. She had heard something. For now, though, there was nothing she could do in here. Searching would at least keep her occupied.

Half an hour later the family sat in the drawing room, Beth looking frightened, Julia very quiet and pale. Giles stood with an elbow on the mantel, his hand to his mouth and his face abstracted, while Anne sat quietly, staring into the depths of the sherry he had insisted on pouring for her. Ordinarily she had no head for spirits, but tonight the drink had no effect on her. Their search had uncovered nothing, though they had looked in every corner of every room and, at Anne's insistence, had lifted the lid of every trunk tucked away in the capacious attic. Though they didn't find Jamie, it was a relief that all the trunks had been empty. One of Anne's worst fears, that he had again become trapped in one, had been eased. But if he weren't above stairs, or in the attics, or even in the kitchens, where was he?

Obadiah came into the room, and, in spite of the silence of his tread, Anne's head jerked up. For a moment they gazed at each other, and then he shook his head. "Nothin', lady," he said, and Anne's head lowered. "Looked everywhere, in all the cellars." His brow wrinkled, and he turned to Giles. "Your Grace, somethin' I want to show you there—"

"Your Grace." Benson appeared in the doorway. "The captain of the watch is here."

"I'll see him." Giles crossed the room, casting a quick, worried glance at Anne. God help them all if the news were bad.

At that moment there was an odd, muffled metallic echo, followed by a wail that filled the room and made everyone's hackles rise. "The ghost!" Beth gasped.

Anne jumped to her feet. "Jamie," she whispered, and then shouted it. "Jamie!"

"Moommmy—"

"Oh, no, he's turned into a ghost, too!" one of the parlor maids, waiting nearby, exclaimed.

Benson rounded on her, his face furious. "Be quiet, you foolish girl!"

"Jamie!" Anne sprinted across the room; the sound seemed to come from everywhere, and nowhere. "Jamie. Where are you?"

"Mommy! Help me, Mommy. I'm stuck."

Giles crossed to Anne's side. "Stuck?"

"Yes, Jamie." Anne kept her voice very calm. "Tell Mommy where you are."

"I don't know. Mommy, I'm scared."

"I know, pet. We'll find you." She turned to Giles, her face bewildered. Thank God, Jamie was in the house, and safe, by the sound of it. But where?

"Mommy," he called again, and Obadiah sprang across the room.

"I know where he is, lady." He dropped to the floor near the cast-iron grate that was set unobtrusively into the corner of the floor, his head lowered. "Jamie," he called, his voice echoing in the same metallic way, "are you in the pipes, boy?"

For a moment, as the people in the room stayed very still, there was no answer. Then there was a sniffle. "Y-yes," a very small voice said, and what before had been a sound that filled the room now came unmistakably from the grate.

251

"The pipes?" Giles said, but Obadiah was already running past him, Anne following.

"The furnace, Giles!" she tossed over her shoulder. "He's got into the pipes that lead away from the furnace."

"Good God!" Giles ran after them, through the green baize door that separated the kitchens from the rest of the house. They clattered down the stairs, bursting into the kitchen together, startling Cook and a scullery maid, both of whom drew back. "Where?" Giles demanded.

"Here." Obadiah led the way through a passage to another set of stairs, descending into deep, deep darkness. Here they paused to light candles, and went carefully down the narrow stairs. Darkness and a faint smell of the sea rose to meet them, and Anne's skin crawled. Jamie was here, someplace. Oh, dear God.

They passed through the wine cellar and the root cellar, and into a room filled with crates, which Giles eyed askance. "Don't tell me there are smugglers around here, Obadiah."

"Don't know, sir." Obadiah was wrestling with a heavy iron door across the room. "Need somethin' to keep the door open, sir. My guess is Jamie came in here, lady."

"But how could he?" Anne protested, watching as Giles thrust a block of wood under the door, to keep it open. "How could he ever have opened that door?"

"Usually it's left open. Be careful, now, lady, very dirty in here."

Giles turned to her. "Anne?"

"I'm all right." Hardly aware of his hand at her elbow, she stepped into the room, dark beyond the glow of their candles. "What is this place?"

"The furnace room, lady." He pointed across the room to a strange-looking device. "They keep coal here to heat it. That's why it's dirty."

"But, Jamie—"

"Is probably in here." Obadiah, candle held high, pointed at a gaping hole in the wall. "These pipes lead the heat into the house when the furnace is going. That plate, there"—he indicated a metal plate leaning against the wall, barely visible in the dim light—"usually covers that hole."

"Jamie couldn't have taken it off."

"He didn't." Obadiah bent and thrust his head into the hole. "Jamie!"

For a heart-stopping moment there was silence. then a very small voice, not so distant, piped up. "Diah?"

"Yes, Jamie," Obadiah said, while Anne shut her eyes in relief. "Where are you, boy?"

"I'm stuck, Diah."

Obadiah exchanged a quick look with the others. With their candles raised they could see that the pipe Jamie had somehow got caught in was square in shape, and large enough across for a small man. Neither Giles nor Obadiah, however would fit into it. "I'll go," Anne said with sudden determination, picking up her skirts.

"Anne, we can get a footman," Giles said.

"No. I can do this." She tossed him a strained smile. "I always bested Freddie at climbing trees, remember?"

"Wait, lady." Obadiah leaned into the opening again. "Jamie, can you move at all?"

"My nightshirt's caught on something, Diah."

"Oh, for God's sake!" Anne exclaimed, pushing Obadiah aside. "Tear it if you have to, Jamie!"

"But you'll get mad, Mommy."

"James Robert Templeton, if you do not do what I say and get out here, I'll come in after you. Do you want that?"

There was a moment's silence. "No, Mommy," Jamie said, sounding subdued. His voice was followed by the sound of fabric ripping.

"There, pet, that's right, let it tear," she encouraged. "Can you see our candles?"

"Yes, Mommy."

"Good. Crawl toward them, now. That's it. Oh, Jamie!" Anne toppled back onto the floor as a very dirty and disheveled little boy hurtled through the opening on top of her. "Jamie."

"Mommy!" Jamie wailed, his fingers digging into her shoulders. "I'm sorry, Mommy."

"Ooh! You should be!" Anne struggled to sit up and grasped his shoulders, holding him away from her. "Don't you ever do such a thing to me again, Jamie, do you hear?"

"No, Mommy. I'm sorry, I really am."

"I know, lovey, I know." Anne squeezed Jamie tightly to her, rocking him back and forth. She was as cold and as dirty as he now, from the coal-dust scattered on the floor, but she didn't care. She had her son back, and that was all that mattered.

"Anne." Giles crouched beside them. "Let me take him."

"No. Let Mommy get up, Jamie. Are you hurt?"

"I bumped my knee, Mommy."

"Did you? Well, we'll look at it upstairs. Come on, now." Bending, she picked Jamie up; his arms clutched about her throat and his legs about her hips. Giles and Obadiah both motioned toward him, but Anne shook her head. Jamie was her son. She was not going to let him go.

It was a disheveled and dusty-looking group that emerged into the front hall to the cries of welcome and relief of the rest of the household. Jamie's once-white nightshirt was now a dingy gray, and everyone's face was streaked with dirt. "You gave us all a scare, boy," Julia growled, though she smiled.

Anne frowned, annoyed. No one scolded her son but her, even if he deserved it. "Nurse, help me give Jamie a bath and get him back into bed."

"Yes, ma'am." Nurse bustled forward. "Oh, ma'am, I'm that glad you found him—"

"So am I." Anne paused on the stairs, looking down.

254

"Thank you, Diah," she said, her voice soft. "You don't know what this means to me."

Obadiah grinned. "Yes I do, lady. You take care of that little rascal, now."

"Of course." Anne turned and made her way up the stairs, Jamie a precious weight in her arms. For now, all was well.

The excitement was over. The lamps had been doused, the candles snuffed, and the household had settled to sleep. All except Anne. Long after everyone had gone to their rooms, she crept down to the drawing room. She couldn't sleep. Though Jamie seemed already to have recovered from his adventure, she hadn't. She wasn't certain she ever completely would. Tonight's events had made her take a long, hard look at herself, and she hadn't liked what she saw.

A noise at the doorway made her look up. "Oh, it's you," Giles said, and walked into the room. He was still in evening dress, though he had discarded his coat, waistcoat, and neckcloth. With his shirt open at his throat, he looked strong, virile, and very masculine. "I was wondering who was in here."

"Now you know." Anne sipped from her glass, filled with an amber brown fluid. "I thought you were abed."

"No, I've been in the book-room. May I join you?"

Anne shrugged. She should, she supposed, feel uncomfortable at this meeting; she was clad only in her nightrail and wrapper, with her hair hanging down her back in a damp profusion of curls. Washing the coal dust off both Jamie and herself had been quite a task, and her midnight-blue evening gown had been ruined. She didn't care. Only Jamie mattered.

Giles sat across from her, his legs stretched out. "Is Jamie well?"

"Oh, he's fine, apart from a scraped knee. He was in high gig, telling me all about how he found the heating

255

pipes and what it was like crawling through them. He seems to think it was a brave thing to do."

"Mm. I think I'll have a brandy. Would you like some more sherry?"

"Yes, actually, I would."

Giles rose. "I've been doing some thinking," he said as he poured the sherry into her glass. "You insist that Jamie is merely high-spirited—"

"Oh, you needn't reproach me, Giles. I've done enough of that this evening to last a lifetime." She took a long sip from her glass. "I quite realize I'm to blame for what happened. Do you know why he did what he did?"

"I was wondering about that, yes."

"He was lonely. Nurse was asleep, Obadiah was busy, and I was gone. He wanted me to read him a story tonight."

"Anne—"

'I couldn't, of course. I was late, as usual, and couldn't stay. Jamie wanted to talk to someone and decided to look for Terence."

"Terence!"

"Yes, Giles. Our ghost. Jamie told me Terence lives in the pipes, and he was looking for him. Everything was fine, apparently, until he got stuck." She set her glass down, hard, on the inlay table beside her. "My son climbed into a maze of pipes and could have been completely lost, because he was lonely and wanted to talk to someone. And where was I? At some god-awful musical evening flirting with a man I do not even like."

"Annie, you cannot blame yourself—"

"Oh, can I not? Who can I trust to take care of my son? Not Nurse. She's too old to control him anymore. And I'll be damned if I'll allow him to be brought up by servants, as I was. He's my son. He needs me. Me."

"Anne, you can't give up your life for him."

"What life? Attending routs with people I don't particularly like, talking idle chatter and the worst gossip and eating indifferent food? And why? All to impress a group of people who among them don't have the brains of a peahen! That's not life, Giles. Raising my child, keeping him safe and watching him grow— that's real. That's life."

"Anne, you coddle the boy."

"You've never been a parent, Giles. What do you know about raising a child?"

Giles eyed her as she downed the rest of her sherry. "Do you know, Anne, I think you are foxed."

"Oh, undoubtedly. So, Your Grace, are you concerned now that Jamie has two drunkards for parents?"

"Two?"

"Didn't you know? Freddie was quite fond of his rum." She gazed reflectively at her glass. "I think I would like some more."

"And I think you've had enough," Giles said, taking the glass from her limp fingers.

"Oh, of course. You always know what is right for everyone, do you not?"

"Anne." He sounded weary. "I don't wish to wrangle with you tonight."

Anne stared up at him. "What would you do? Now, don't cry off, Giles. I know you've ideas on the matter. What are your plans for my son?"

Giles returned her look and then sat, his forearms resting upon his knees as the silence stretched and crackled between them. Damn. This was not the best time to discuss this subject, not after this evening's events, not with Anne in the mood she was in. And rightly so, he thought, looking into the fireplace, not wanting to meet her clear blue gaze. When he had heard that Jamie was missing he had felt the most absolute terror he had ever experienced, as if he were the boy's parent, rather than his guardian. Then his training had taken over and he had, of necessity, taken charge of the situation. If he had felt that way, how much worse must it have been for Anne? No denying,

257

though, that the boy's future had to be discussed, and soon. Matters could not go on as they were. The boy did need more care than he had been receiving.

"Very well," he said, his voice low. "You wish my thoughts on this, I will tell you. Jamie is a bright, appealing child, and I think you've done well with him. However, as I've said, he needs a firm hand."

"He's had that already," she muttered.

"Pardon?"

"Nothing. Do go on."

Giles eyed her a moment before continuing. "He is undisciplined. Tonight's events prove that, if nothing else."

"You never misbehaved as a child, Giles?"

"Of course I did, and I was punished for it. Jamie is not too young to learn that his actions have consequences. He also needs more education than you can provide, Anne. He needs a tutor, and eventually school."

"Giles—"

"I had hoped to leave off discussion of this until we returned to Tremont, but now I see it is necessary. What I decided before still stands. Jamie will stay here, where I can supervise his upbringing, and when he is old enough he will attend Eton."

Anne jumped to her feet, her hand to her throat. "You would take him away from me!"

"No, Anne, of course not." Giles rose, facing her. "I want only what is best for Jamie."

"I am his mother! I know what is best for him. Oh, please, Giles." Her voice cracked. "Please don't do this. Don't take him from me."

"Annie—"

"No, do not touch me!" She backed wildly away from the hand he held out to her. "You can't do this, Giles, you can't. I'd take him back to Jamaica sooner than give him up."

"Annie." He made his voice gentle, quiet, not

258

wanting to startle her. It dismayed him that he was the one who had brought her to such a state. "I have no intention of separating you from him. I know you love him, and he needs you. You're his mother."

"You won't—take him away?"

"Word of a Templeton, Annie."

Anne stared at him, and then her hands flew to her face. "Oh, God." Her voice broke, and she swayed. "Oh, God, I thought I'd lost him."

"Annie." He reached her in an instant, gathering her close against him.

"When Benson said he was missing, and then we couldn't find him—"

"I know," he murmured, rocking her back and forth. "I know."

"You can't know, how can you know—"

"I know, Annie."

His voice was so firm that it penetrated Anne's shock. Slowly she raised her head, crystalline tears clinging to her lashes. "How can you know?"

"Because I love him, too, Annie."

"You . . ." Her voice trailed off. She was caught by his gaze, by the look in his eyes. Never before had anyone looked at her like that, with such tenderness and understanding, and such frightening, frightening knowledge. This man knew her as no other did, yet it was all right. She could trust him. She was safe with him. "Giles," she murmured, reaching up to touch his cheek with gentle, wondering fingertips. "Giles."

He could not bear it. She was in his arms, soft, warm, trusting, and he could not fight it anymore. With a little groan, he brought his mouth down on hers.

No gentle, tentative kiss this, but passionate, wild, as her mouth opened under his; a release from the terrors and tensions of the night, a surrender to the forces that drew them inexorably together. Anne's hands dug into his neck, clutching him closer and closer still, and Giles's arms were like steel bands around her, holding her to him as though he would never let her go. Not releasing her mouth, he bent and caught her around her knees, lifting her high against his chest and then falling back into the chair. He kissed her brows, her eyes, her nose, with ravening, hungry kisses, before his lips came down on hers again, open mouth to open mouth, their tongues dancing in their own kind of waltz. This was right, this was good, their lips moved in perfect unison, their bodies fit together as no others ever had, and Giles could no longer restrain the need to explore her, to know her. It had been so long, so long he had waited for this. Too long.

Her hands pressed at his neck, urging him closer, closer; his roamed over her soft, warm curves of shoulder and back and hips. Her wrapper was an encumbrance; his fingers, clumsy in their haste, fumbled with the sash. Anne murmured something against his lips as he struggled with the knot. The sash came free, and his impatient hand was pushing her wrapper off her shoulder, exposing her prim white cotton nightrail and the delicious secrets it hid. Seven years ago he had held a girl in his arms and exchanged tentative, exploratory kisses with her. Now she was a woman, with a woman's fire and needs, a woman's body. His hand cupped her breast, finding it full and taut for him. This was right, this was good, and though it had been well worth the wait, he knew he could wait no longer.

Anne jerked back. "No," she breathed and then repeated it, louder. "No!"

"Oh, Annie," he groaned, not caring, his mouth at her throat, his hand molding her, shaping her.

"No!" Desperation lent urgency and strength to her hands, pushing him away. He fell back against the chair, and though he would have taken her with him, she was quicker, twisting from his grasp and bolting away. She tripped over her wrapper, stumbling in her haste, and then she was upright, clutching her robe,

260

and her dignity, about her.

"Annie!" Giles jumped up and ran after her into the hall, catching her arm. "Annie."

She looked at his hand and then at his face, her eyes wide. "I—can't, Giles," she choked. "I can't." Jerking her arm free of his grasp, she turned and ran up the stairs.

"Annie," he said again, setting his foot on the bottom step, and then stopping. She was gone. She had been sweet and warm and passionate in his arms, but she was gone. He shouldn't be so surprised, so hurt; Anne was not a wanton, to allow a man to take liberties with her, for all she flirted and teased. He was hurt, though, aching, empty, with a need only she could assuage. No other woman would ever do for him, ever again. It was almost as if he—

Giles stood very still, staring up the stairs, though Anne was long gone. The kisses, his impromptu proposal, tonight's passion—it all came together in one blinding flash of revelation. Good God, why had he not seen it before? It was something he should have known, from the first moment he had set eyes on her again, something he had always known. He was still in love with Anne.

Chapter 19

The wind was whipping off the water and the clouds were thickening when a slight figure cloaked in gray slipped out of the house on the Steyne. A passerby, not paying much heed, might have assumed her to be a maid on an errand, but he would have been wrong. It was Beth who clutched the hood of the cloak closely around her face, Beth who had taken what was, for her, the unprecedented step of going out unescorted. What she had to do was too important to leave off any longer, and was best done without witnesses.

At the point where the Steyne met the Marine Parade, a man stepped forward, the splendor of his uniform in sharp contrast to Beth's mourning-dove gray. "I had your note," Thomas said, clasping her hands. "What is amiss? Are you ill?"

"No, no, nothing like that." Beth stepped back, glancing quickly around to make certain their meeting was unremarked.

"Then what is it? For you to send me a note at camp—"

"I had to see you. Please, can we not walk a bit? Someone will notice us if we continue to stand here."

"Of course." Gallantly Thomas held out his arm, and they began to stroll along the Marine Parade. "What is it, Beth? What has happened to overset you?"

"Is it true you are to be posted soon?"

Thomas glanced down at her, his face growing unreadable. "There are rumors."

"There are always rumors! Thomas, please. I need to know. Have you received your posting?"

He didn't answer right away. "I cannot tell you, Beth," he said finally. "Even if I knew, I could not tell you yet. Now, hush." He turned her toward him, laying his hands on her shoulders and stilling her protest. "When I purchased my commission I committed myself to serving my country. If that means following orders and telling no one about our possible movements, then that is what I must do."

"I wouldn't tell anyone, Thomas."

"I know you wouldn't." His smile was tender. "You've seen the good side of soldiering this summer, the uniforms, the parading, and such. But there's another side to it, Beth. The real side." He paused. "I am a soldier. I go where my country sends me, and I do what my country asks me to do. It means I cannot act as I would wish, but I cannot do otherwise, Beth. If I don't help to subdue Bonaparte and bring peace to the world, I couldn't live with myself."

"I know that, Thomas."

"This damnable war." He gazed out to sea. "If it were just me—but it's my family, too. And now it's you, Beth. I chose the army. You didn't, but if you marry me, you're as bound as I am."

It was Beth's turn to look away. "I cannot marry you, Thomas," she said, her voice little above a whisper.

"What!" Thomas went still as Beth continued to walk, and then caught up with her in two quick strides. "What nonsense is this? Of course you will marry me, Beth. I know it's not the ideal life I'm offering you—"

"It's not that. Oh, Thomas, don't you know I'd live with you in a tent if I had to?"

"The daughter of a Duke of Tremont?"

"Don't say that!" she said fiercely. "You once told

263

me it was an insult to both of us, and I will not allow you to insult me, Thomas Bancroft!"

"I'm sorry," he said, and reached out to touch her cheek. "Beth, I'm sorry. I don't wish to quarrel with you."

"Nor I, you. But, oh, Thomas." She grasped his hand and pressed a kiss into the palm. "This isn't just about us anymore. It's about the country, you've said that yourself. And it's about my mother."

"Dash it." Abruptly Thomas turned back and began to stride along, dragging her with him. "I knew she'd come into it sooner or later. What has the old besom said now?"

"Thomas!"

He caught her shoulders again. "Are you going to let her run your life for you, Beth?" Are you?"

"I'm making my own choice in this." She stood up to him, returning his gaze levelly. "My mother is old, and she is ill. She's hidden it well, but I've seen her in pain. I cannot leave her."

"She won't be alone. She has your brother."

"But she relies on me. I can't leave her, Thomas. She needs me."

"Damn it." He walked a few paces away. "I need you, too, Beth."

"I know. Oh, don't you think I know? I want to be with you, Thomas, I want that more than anything. But I can't be. Not just yet."

"Damn it. I don't understand this, Beth. We love each other."

"I know we do." She smiled at him sadly, feeling infinitely older and wiser than he. "But, just as you cannot turn your back on your country, I cannot turn my back on my mother. I couldn't live with myself if I did." She paused, looking for understanding in his eyes and not finding it. For the first time, she felt annoyed with him. Must men always be so blind to other considerations besides their own? "I can't marry you, Thomas," she said, and, turning, walked away.

"This is what I wanted you to see, sir." Holding his lantern high, Obadiah stepped into the furnace room. Gray daylight filtered in through the cellar windows, and yet it was still a place of darkness. "Somebody's been usin' this room."

"Besides our ghost, you mean?" Giles glanced around the room, and shuddered. Last night Jamie had been here, alone.

"No, sir. I mean the ghost. Can't prove who he is yet, but I know how he did it. The hauntings, I mean."

"He crawled into the ducts, as Jamie did. The sound would carry through the house."

"Yes, sir. Through the pipes. When the furnace is lit, the pipes carry the heat through the house. Think it has to be one of the house servants, sir."

"Maybe. We all knew about the furnace when we came here," Giles said thoughtfully. "It's a novelty."

"Yes, sir. Look. Candle wax."

Giles stuck his head into the opening and looked at the bottom of the duct. There was, indeed, a small puddle of hardened wax there. "How do you know it isn't Jamie's from last night?"

"It's tallow, sir. The family uses beeswax."

"Of course." Giles pulled back. "Any idea who's doing it, Obadiah?"

"No, sir, but I'll keep looking. Thought of setting a trap, but that's no good, now."

"No. Everyone in the house knows about this room." Giles closed the door behind them as they stepped into the main part of the cellar, and fastened a large, solid padlock to it. "That should keep whoever it is out."

"Yes, sir." Obadiah hesitated. "Lady Anne all right this mornin'?"

"I haven't seen her," Giles said shortly.

"I was wonderin' how she took it all. Jamie means a powerful lot to her."

"I know he does." It was Giles's turn to pause. "Obadiah."

Obadiah turned. "Suh?"

"She said something last night that troubles me. Was Mister Templeton a drunkard?"

Obadiah hesitated again. "He did like his rum, sir."

"I see. That must have been hard on Anne."

"I wouldn't know, sir."

"Wouldn't you?" Giles's eyes met his squarely, and though Obadiah was much the taller of the two, there was no question in that moment who had the authority. "I'll wager you knew everything that went on on the plantation. Come, man. I know all was not well with the marriage. Anne pretends it was, but I know her better. Was she happy with Mr. Templeton?"

Obadiah looked at him for a moment, and then shook his head. "No, sir. Not her fault, though. She tried. Mister Templeton, he didn't seem to want to grow up. Wouldn't do what he knew he should, and he'd get mad if someone reminded him."

"Who reminded him, Obadiah? Anne?"

"Yes, sir."

"So they quarreled."

"You ask me, sir, he was no kind of a proper husband!" Obadiah burst out. "None of us liked him, but what he did to Lady Anne—"

"*What* did he do to Anne?"

"Well, sir, many the mornin' she came down to breakfast with her eyes red, so we knew she'd been crying. And—"

"What?"

"Once in a while, sir, she'd have a bruise—"

"He beat her?"

"Yes, sir. She always said she fell, but—"

"Damn his black soul to hell. What the hell right did

266

he have—I'll kill him." Giles strode toward the stairs. "By God, if he weren't already dead, I'd kill him for doing that to her."

"Sir, maybe someone already did it for you."

Giles stopped on the stairs. "What do you mean?"

"Well, sir, that stretch of road where Mister Templeton went over the cliff, he knew it like the back of his hand. The way that man rode, he wouldn't have gone over it himself, not even drunk. No, sir. Everyone thinks some jealous husband did it."

"Good God!" Giles abruptly sat on a stair, staring at Obadiah. "How did Anne take that?"

"With her head high, sir. She's a brave woman."

"I know." A brave, strong woman, who had survived a miserable marriage and yet had lost none of her spirit. And he had thought her desire for independence no more than the whim of a spoiled, flighty widow. No wonder if she wanted to control her own destiny; no wonder if she pushed him away, after what she had endured. The wonder was that she had allowed him close to her at all.

"Thank you for telling me this, Obadiah," he said finally. "It explains much."

"You won't tell her I said anything, sir?"

"No, unless I have to. Come, let's get back upstairs and see what we can devise for our ghost."

The summer was rapidly passing. Events in Brighton had settled into a kind of routine: the fashionable promenade along the Steyne in the morning; shopping and gossiping in the afternoon for the women, while the men paid a visit to Raggett's or the racetrack; balls and routs and soirees in the evening; the daily parade at the barracks of the Tenth Light Dragoons or the other regiments quartered nearby. The most anticipated event of the summer was fast approaching. The Prince of Wales's birthday was in August, and this year its celebration promised to be memorable.

The day for the celebration dawned clear and sunny. Since last week, soldiers from all over the country had been arriving in town, to participate in the mock battle that was to be held at Race Hill, making the town seem like a military camp. Some said there were as many as ten thousand of them. No young lady was safe without an escort, and yet the atmosphere was almost that of a fun fair. The battle was discussed endlessly, with most of the ton pretending a disdain toward it they did not feel. It was not an event anyone planned to miss.

The Tremonts were no exception. Early in the morning the ladies climbed into the landau, all of them dressed in their summer finery, even Julia, who seemed less cranky today. Beside Anne, who was wearing a new walking dress of deep rose with flounces at wrist and hem and a lace jabot, sat Jamie, eager but well behaved. Somehow he had managed to keep his clothes clean and his hair neat. He was a much-chastened little boy since his experience in the heating pipes, at least for the present. Anne didn't expect that to last much longer.

"Mama, when will we get there?" he asked, for what seemed like the thousandth time.

"Soon, pet," Anne said absently, though, judging by the long line of carriages preceeding them it would take a while. They were to meet Felicity and her family there for a picnic before the battle began. She was glad they were going in a group, glad that Giles had elected to ride, rather than to drive in the landau with them. She still did not know how she was going to face him, after that night in the drawing room. Good heavens, she had never been so wanton in her life! The memory of those few, mad moments haunted her continually, filling her with guilt and a curious warmth. What Giles must think of her, she didn't know. He appeared to be avoiding her as assiduously as she did, him. It should have been comforting. It wasn't.

The entire town seemed to be turning out for the

event, the ton in their fine carriages, the townspeople on foot. There were lean, sturdy fishermen; smug, content shopkeepers; shabbily dressed fishwives with unruly groups of children, cheerfully calling back and forth to each other. Adding to the carnival air were hawkers with food, sausages, fish, ale, their cries for their wares echoing and overlapping each other. It was festive, a true summer holiday. A day in which one couldn't help but be happy to be alive, Anne thought, in spite of one's problems, and smiled, as the landau jounced over the grassy track that led to Race Hill and came to a halt.

The carriage door opened, and first Julia, aided by Giles, and then Beth, stepped down. Jamie followed. At last it was Anne's turn, and she looked with some misgivings at the strong hand Giles held out to her. A well-shaped hand, a hand used to working. A man's hand. A sudden chill ran up her spine, but it wasn't unpleasant. Far from it. Nor was the tremor that ran through her as she took his hand and stepped down, though she quickly stepped away. "Oh, look," she exclaimed, and Giles, who had turned to say something to Julia, turned back, to enjoy the scene with her.

The soldiers were in place already, thousands of them, arrayed in precise lines upon the rolling emerald green South Downs. In the bright morning sun their tunics were brilliantly colored, scarlet or blue or green; gold and silver lace and braid sparkled and shone. Light glinted off helmets and bayonets with occasionally blinding flashes. Behind the foot soldiers were the cavalry, regiments of them, mounted on magnificent bays or chestnuts or blacks, war-horses all, superbly trained and beautifully groomed. Offshore hovered several ships, their sails glistening white, ready to play their part in the battle; around them dipped and flew smaller craft, from elegant yachts to ordinary fishing boats, and sea birds. Closer at hand, the spectators had settled themselves, some with opera glasses or spy glasses, others seeming far more intent on gossiping to each other, as if they hadn't just met last evening or earlier this morning. The milling mob, dressed in outfits from the oldest work clothes to the latest in fashion, and the carriages and carts and drays of all description, intensified the feeling of an old-fashioned fair. To her surprise, Anne's eyes prickled with tears. This was home. This was England, and she was very glad she was here.

She looked up, suddenly needing to share her feelings with Giles, to see him watching her. Defenseless in the emotion of the moment, she searched his face, and saw there the same mixture of pride and wonder that she felt, and something else. The light was back in his eyes, but there was something more, something that made her feel warm and breathless. Whatever it was, it held her, bound her to him. When the time came to go, how could she ever leave him behind?

"Your pardon, Your Grace." A liveried footman bowed politely, and Giles turned, breaking the silken thread that had bound them for that eternal moment. "Lady Whitehead has asked me to escort you and Mrs. Templeton to her."

"Thank you." Giles took Anne's arm, smiling. "I might have known Felicity would find a place under a tree. Good view, too, it looks like. Felicity." He held his hand out to her. "I see you've arranged things in your usual exceptional style."

"Of course, Giles. Hello, Anne." Felicity smiled at her. "Why do something if it's not done well? And Your Grace. I have a comfortable chair just over here for you. I am so glad you decided to come, after all.

"Thank you." Julia's smile was wintry, but it was a smile, all the same.

For the remainder of the party, accommodations were provided on rugs thick enough to ward off any dew remaining on the grass. Anne and Beth, along with

270

Susan, settled themselves gracefully across from Felicity and the men, Giles and Lord Whitehead. Footmen handed them dishes loaded with such tidbits as cold sliced chicken, new potatoes in a tangy sauce, and strawberries in cream. The china was almost translucent, the flatware heavy silver, and the champagne was served in crystal flutes. "You have an excellent cook," Anne said, holding up her goblet. "Though I feel quite decadent, drinking champagne at this time of day."

"The occasion seemed to call for it," Felicity said. "I don't know when I've seen anything quite so stirring, and the battle hasn't even begun. I invited Mister Seward and Lieutenant Bancroft to join us afterward."

"Why, how nice," Anne said, not daring to look at Beth. Something was very wrong there. It wasn't just that Julia disapproved of the romance. There was something more. Anne had the awful feeling that Beth and Thomas had quarreled. If that were so, Beth's chance for a normal life was gone.

Cannon booming offshore startled everyone, who turned to see puffs of white smoke coming from one of the ships. "Oh, it's starting!" Susan exclaimed, jumping to her feet, as the drums rattled a tattoo and the band joined in, playing a military air. It was stirring music, and to its beat paraded row upon row, rank upon rank, of soldiers, all in perfect formation, all keeping perfect time. Besides the soldiers rode their officers, their mounts in perfect control. It was so thrilling a moment that, without quite realizing it, Anne held her hand out to share it with someone, and felt a sense of wholeness when her hand was clasped.

The music changed, became more solemn: "God Save the King." "Look," Giles whispered in Anne's ear, pointing toward a small group of men on horseback riding before the troops. On a gray charger, resplendent in the Hussar uniform of the Tenth Light Dragoons, of which he was colonel, rode the Prince of

Wales. Even at this distance Anne could see how fine were his uniform, with its silver lace looped on the cuffs to allude to the Prince of Wales feathers, and his scarlet saddle blanket, so embroidered with gold thread it was blinding in the sunlight. With him were his brothers, the Royal Dukes, all of them also in uniform, except for the Duke of Cumberland. There were also some others, who were unknown to her.

"Who is that with him?" Anne whispered back, as if the Prince could overhear.

"Sir Dundas, the commander-in-chief. You'd think he'd be better off overseeing real battles, rather than mock ones."

"You're sounding more and more like a member of the Opposition every day. I thought the Templetons served the Crown."

Giles shrugged. "I hate to think what this day is costing. The money could certainly be used to better purpose."

"Don't let Prinny hear that, or you'll no longer be one of his favorites." She glanced down and realized for the first time that he was holding her hand. She looked swiftly from their linked hands to his face. "You're holding my hand."

Giles's eyes held hers. "I know. Were we alone, I would kiss it," he said, his voice low.

Her face flaming, Anne snatched her hand away. As if she would let him! But, oh, she wished he would.

With a final flourish of the drums, the ranks of soldiers pulled up to a stop, their lines precise and straight. The Prince rode forward, inspecting his troops, and there was something so majestic about the sight that one could almost believe he would, indeed, lead the men into battle. Anne watched, her hand to her throat, as he rode down the line, and felt again that overwhelming pride in her country. In that moment, she wanted never to leave again.

The troops saluted their Prince, and he saluted back.

For a moment there was a curious silence, in which Anne was certain everyone could hear her heart pounding. She didn't want to return to Jamaica. She wanted to stay here, in England. With Giles.

From somewhere a bugle blew, and suddenly all was chaos, sound and color and movement as the foot soldiers ran forward. With the Prince safely to the side, the mock battle had begun. Cannon boomed from the ships again, and, for the first time, the spectators realized that sailors were storming Brighton's cliffs. Just as if this were a real invasion and those were Napoleon's soldiers, Anne stepped closer to Giles. This time she was aware of taking his arm; this time, she had no desire to pull away.

Another bugle blew and the cavalry charged, the hooves of their mounts sounding like thunder over the Downs, swords flashing. All was dust and noise and heat; if she felt it, just watching, what must the soldiers be feeling? Anne wondered. "Oh, heavens, can you imagine what it is like in a real battle?" Anne said, and at that moment Beth gave a shriek.

"Thomas!" she cried, dropping her opera glasses.

Anne glanced over at her. "What is it?"

"He's fallen." Beth gathered up her skirts. "I must go to him."

"Wait." Anne caught her arm. "You cannot go out there."

"I must! Thomas has fallen. He might be hurt."

"It's not a real battle, Beth," Giles said from her other side, and Anne looked up at him in relief.

"But he fell, Giles."

"Doubtless not for the first time."

"And of course it is all part of the playacting," Anne chattered as they walked back to the others, she and Giles holding Beth's arms. "Though why men enjoy playacting at war, I do not know."

Beth stopped, her eyes stricken. "Someday it may not be playacting."

Giles squeezed her arm, comfortingly. "Bethie—"

"So be it." She lifted her chin, ignoring the comfort. Gone was the sweet, but rather vague, girl Beth had been just a moment before; in her place was a woman, facing the world with courage. The transition was so astonishing that Anne could only stare. "That is something I must accustom myself to."

"Hmph." Julia glared at her as they returned. "Made a spectacle of yourself, Elizabeth, and for what? Some rubbishy soldier."

Beth's eyes widened and her cheeks grew red, sure signs that she was about to burst into tears. Instead, though, she drew a deep breath. "As you say, Mother," she said coolly polite. Over her head, Giles and Anne looked at each other, communicating without words. Beth had changed, and while that was to the good, it was not something Julia would appreciate. There would be trouble ahead.

Another bugle blew, and the troops drew up. The battle was over. Cheers went up from the spectators as those who had pretended to be injured rose up again. Ranks were reformed for the Prince to inspect his troops again. Over the rolling Downs his voice, raised in speech, came to the Tremont party, but they were unable to catch more than a word or two. At last the soldiers dispersed, most to return to their quarters, but others to visit with friends and family. The soldiers of the Tenth Light Dragoons were well-known in Brighton.

Lieutenant Bancroft made unerringly for the Tremonts, and Beth. Julia, still sitting in state under the tree, grumbled something, but Beth, who ordinarily catered to her mother's every whim, today ignored her. Her face shining, she broke away from the group.

"You were splendid," she said to Thomas as she reached him, her voice carrying back to the others.

"Good afternoon, Lady Elizabeth." Perfectly proper, Thomas bowed over her hand. In his uniform with its five rows of buttons and his fur dress cap with its red and white plume, his sword by his side, he looked very much a soldier. "Now how could you have possibly seen me?"

"I had opera glasses. Oh, dear, you've a smudge on your sleeve," Beth said, dusting away the dirt with proprietarial fingers. "Whatever would your captain say to that?"

Thomas looked down at her in surprise. "Told me I was a clumsy horseman, and that I'd better do better in the real thing." Beth looked up at that, and for a moment their eyes held. If something passed between them, only they knew it.

The moment was broken by Giles coming forward. "A good show, Lieutenant," he said, holding out his hand.

"Thomas stepped back from Beth. "Thank you, Your Grace."

"You acquitted yourself well."

"As well, I hope, in the real thing."

"Is that coming soon?" Giles asked sharply, alerted by something in the other man's tone.

"Who can say?" Thomas smiled and shrugged. "Certainly it is not a fit topic for a day like today. Will you be at the birthday ball tonight, Lady Elizabeth?"

Beth gazed up at him. "Oh, yes."

"Then I shall see you there. If you will excuse me, Your Grace, I must be leaving. The captain wants us to return to barracks."

"Of course." Giles nodded. "We shall see you tonight."

"Oh, yes," Beth said again. Her eyes held Thomas's, until, with a quick salute, he turned and marched away.

Anne took Beth's arm. "Do make him do some work for you, dear."

Beth looked up at her. "Why?"

"Because romance means more to men when they have to fight for it."

"Is that so?" Giles asked, from Anne's other side.

"Yes, that is so. I suppose we should be returning,

275

too. We've more ahead of us tonight."

"Elizabeth!" a querulous voice called. "Elizabeth, I need you."

Beth sighed. "Yes, Mother," she said, and turned, but not before giving a distant blue-coated figure one last glance.

Giles turned to watch her go, a little frown on his face. "My mother is not happy about this."

"No." Anne watched as Beth helped Julia to her feet. "But this is natural, don't you think? Lieutenant Bancroft is a handsome young man."

"Yes, but is he the man for Beth?" Absently Giles took her arm, and they began to stroll toward the waiting carriage. "She's quiet and gentle. I can't imagine her with a soldier."

"I think there is more to Beth than there seems." Anne kept her voice light, though she was very aware of his touch. It seemed so natural, so right. All the feelings, all the emotions she had felt in his arms in the drawing room came rushing back, making her feel tinglingly alive and at the same time, curiously weak. She wanted to lean against Giles, but not merely for support. Not at all.

"Do you?"

Anne blinked. "Beg pardon?"

"Well, I suppose you are right. Beth has more spirit than she shows. However, she's been gently raised. A soldier's life isn't for her."

"He's a good man, Giles." Inwardly, she sighed. So much for their own romance, if such there were. Well, what did she expect, that he would take her in his arms, right here on Race Hill? Foolish. She didn't want him to, of course. The way he had made her feel the other night was quite unsettling. "And he cares about Beth."

"I know he does." They had reached the Tremont landau, and Giles handed her in. "Ah, well, it may yet come to nothing. Just another summer folly."

Anne glanced down at him. Was that all she was to

276

him, a folly? "Of course," she said, and turned away.

The day that had started out on such a note of excitement ended quietly. The soldiers had dispersed; the fishermen had gone back to their boats and their nets, while their wives dragged cranky, crying children home, leaving behind them the debris and detritus of celebration. The ton was leaving, too, the only reminder of their presence furrows in the grass fom carriage wheels. Though the sun still shone brightly, though the air was warm and the breeze fresh, a forlorn air hung over the scene. Or was that, Anne thought, climbing into the landau, only the way she saw it? In the space of a few moments, her world had fallen to pieces. She was, after all, just another summer folly.

Chapter 20

"Oh, Mommy, look!" Jamie pointed as another starburst of lights lit up the night sky. "I do like fireworks, Mommy. I wish they could go on forever and ever."

Anne smiled down at her son. It had been a long and exciting day for him. They had seen the Prince drive down the Steyne with his young daughter, Princess Charlotte, looking charming in white muslin and a gypsy hat, and they had marveled at the oxen being roasted for tonight's celebrations by the townspeople. Now there was a wonderful display of fireworks over the sea, ending the day for Jamie. For her, though, the night was just beginning. "I know, pet, but I think that was the last one."

"No, Mommy," Jamie protested as Anne gently, but firmly, took his shoulders and propelled him in from the upstairs balcony where the family had gathered to watch the fireworks. "Maybe there'll be more."

"I don't think so, lad." Giles lifted Jamie into his arms, to Anne's astonishment. "It's bed for you."

"Could we play another game of toy soldiers, Uncle Giles?"

"No. It's past your bedtime." Giles strode along, Anne following, and deposited Jamie on his bed, sitting beside him. "Mind what Nurse says, now. I'll

278

hear about it if you don't."

"Yes, Uncle Giles," Jamie said, sounding subdued, and suddenly threw his arms around Giles's neck in a stranglehold as he tried to rise. "I love you, Uncle Giles."

Over Jamie's shoulder, Giles looked at Anne in blank astonishment. "I love you, too, Jamie," he said, his voice husky, and then lightly tapped him on the bottom. "Bed for you now, lad."

"Yes, Uncle Giles. G'night."

"Good night, Jamie," Giles said from the door, and turned to see Anne regarding him, a slight smile on her face. "What?"

"You'd make a good father, Giles," she said.

"It's as I said. The boy needs a firm hand."

"Humbug. You cannot fool me, you know. Well, never mind. I'll just tuck him in and join you below stairs in a moment."

"Of course." Giles turned, and stopped. "By the way, did I tell you you look lovely tonight?"

"Why, thank you, sir." Anne smiled at him and then whisked herself into the nursery, glad for the moment to escape his searching eyes. Being with Jamie was much, much safer.

The time to leave for the ball at the Castle Inn, being held tonight in honor of the Prince's birthday, came all too soon for Anne. She kissed Jamie, nearly asleep, and then rose, settling the skirts of her gown about her. This was the favorite of all the gowns she had purchased this summer, the turquoise silk shot through with green and golden threads. Cut very simply, with a high, brief bodice and a straight skirt, it draped over her curves in liquid folds and shimmered as she walked. White satin slippers and white kid gloves completed the ensemble, while at her ears and throat she wore pearls. Pearls had also been threaded through her hair, drawn up away from her face and piled atop her head. A simple look, she thought, glancing quickly into the mirror in Jamie's room before leaving, but effective. She would not be the most beautiful woman at the ball, but then, she didn't want to be.

"And remember, Elizabeth, you are not to waltz tonight," Julia was saying as Anne descended the stairs into the hall. "Most especially not with Lieutenant Bancroft."

"No, Mama," Beth said docilely, and looked up. For a moment Anne was certain she saw a spark of deviltry in her eyes. "Oh, Anne, you look lovely."

"Indeed, she does." Giles stepped across to her and bent over her hand, turning it at the last moment so that his kiss fell on her palm. A shiver ran up her arm. "Do you plan to waltz tonight, Anne?"

"Heavens, no!" She was aware her voice sounded breathless, but she couldn't seem to help it. Why did Giles persist in affecting her so? "Not after what happened last time. You would scold me again, Giles."

"Perhaps." Almost absently he took her arm to lead her out, leaving Julia only Beth for support. "I may, though."

"You? You'd never do anything so undignified, Giles."

"No?" Giles's gaze flickered over her, lingering for a moment at her neckline. "I suppose it would depend on my partner."

"And who might that be?"

"I wonder if Mrs. Priestly knows how to waltz."

"What!"

"No, probably not, since she's a missionary." He grinned down at her. "And pray don't tell me you're not jealous."

"I am not." Anne held her head high as she stepped into the Tremont barouche. Giles had been in an odd, capricious mood all day. She would not let him ruffle her, though, no matter how he tried. She might not be able to return home with her heart intact, but she would still have her pride.

280

The ball was already in full progress when at last the Tremonts entered. A country dance was playing, and the room was a blur of color and sound and scent. It seemed as if anyone with any pretensions to fashion was here tonight; the Assembly Rooms, though large, were filled to bursting. It was rumored there were no fewer than eight hundred people present this evening, wearing evening finery of all descriptions. Many ladies were dressed in classical white, in silks and satins embroidered all over with gold or silver or even white silk threads, while the younger ladies wore gowns of muslin that were more demure, but no less elaborate. All wore jewels that were surely worth a king's ransom. Nor were the gentlemen to be put in the shade. Besides the soldiers' scarlet or blue uniforms, there were evening coats and satin breeches in every hue, from the more somber to the outmoded bright colors of an earlier time. Against such a backdrop Beau Brummell and his set, the dandies, impeccably clad in black and white, looked even more distinguished. So, Anne thought, did Giles, in his evening coat of black velvet, worn with white satin breeches. She tried not to be, but she couldn't help being aware of him, of the warm strength of his arm under her fingers, of his solid, yet graceful height, of his burnished golden hair and his compelling warm silver eyes. He was, by far, the most handsome man there, and he was not hers.

"Your Grace. Lady Elizabeth." Lieutenant Bancroft had suddenly appeared by their side, though a few moments before he hadn't been in sight. "A pleasure seeing you again. And may I say, Lady Elizabeth, that you're looking lovely tonight."

"Thank you, sir." Beth blushed prettily, and raised her fan to her face. To Giles and Anne, who had played this game before, the message was clear. Beth, of all people, was flirting. They glanced at each other in quick, shared amusement, before looking away.

"I hope you are not engaged for the next dance."

Beth made an elaborate pretense of studying her dance card. "Why, no, sir, I am not."

"Then I would be honored if you would dance with me."

"Elizabeth," Julia growled.

Beth ignored her. "I'd like that, sir." Smiling up at him, she allowed Thomas to lead her out onto the floor, where the sets for the next dance were forming.

"Hmph. That girl is getting willful."

"You can't expect her not to enjoy herself, Mother," Giles said.

"Hmph. Not with that man."

"It is only one dance." He grinned. "Be glad it's not a waltz."

"She had best not waltz. I will not countenance it. Remember that, Giles. It would only make you look foolish, as well."

"Yes, Mother. Shall we find a chair for you? You won't wish to stand all night. Anne, you won't mind if we leave you for a moment?"

"No, I see Felicity over there. I shall go talk with her." Smiling, she turned away, hoping that Julia hadn't noticed what she had. Beth and Lieutenant Bancroft were not among the couples dancing, and were nowhere to be seen.

"We shouldn't be in here," Beth said breathlessly, as Thomas pulled her along by the hand into a tiny anteroom. "Someone might come in—"

"Let them." He pulled her into his arms and kissed her, hard, so that her protest came out as a muffled squeak. "Do you know how long I've waited for that?"

"Yes." Beth leaned her head against his chest, her fingers clinging to his shoulders. "But I cannot stay here long. Mama already scolded me today about talking with you."

"Beth, Beth. When are you going to stop allowing your mother to run your life?"

282

Beth looked up at him, her eyes huge and clear. "She needs me, Thomas."

"She'll never let you go. Don't you know that?"

"She needs me," Beth repeated sullenly. Oh, couldn't he see the struggle going on within her? Her mother needed her, yes, and yet, since that afternoon, she kept seeing images of Thomas falling in battle, and her not there. It was almost beyond bearing. "Oh, don't let's quarrel, Thomas, not when we so rarely see each other."

"Whose fault is that, Beth?"

She raised her chin, but she was smiling. "That was splendid this morning. Though when I saw you fall." She shuddered. "I thought you were hurt."

Thomas's eyes were serious as he looked down at her. "I'm a soldier, Beth."

"Yes, I know that, silly." She picked invisible specks of lint from his coat. "And a very handsome one, too."

"Beth. Look at me." His eyes were still serious, and she felt her heart fall. "You must promise not to tell what I am going to tell you to a soul."

Dread settled in her stomach like a lump. "You've been posted. Oh, Thomas—"

"Yes. We received our orders today."

Beth's throat felt very dry. "Where?"

"Spain."

"Spain!" She broke free and whirled away, her arms wrapped around herself to keep from shivering. "But— I won't be able to see you."

"You made that choice, Beth."

"Oh, don't be so cruel!" She squeezed her eyes shut. What she had felt that morning was as nothing compared to her feelings now. Then it had been a game. Now it was deadly real. He might never come back. "When?"

"Not for a few weeks." Placing his hands on her shoulders, he turned her toward him. "We have some time, sweetheart. If you'll only admit that what we have is real."

"Giles is planning to return to Tremont soon," she said dully. "He wants to be there for the harvest." She looked up at him, her eyes bright with unshed tears. "Oh, Thomas—"

"Then marry me, Beth," he urged. "Marry me now. We could get a special license, and—"

"I can't." Beth broke away from him. "It would kill my mother."

"Beth, she's never going to let you go! She's had her life. Damn it, when will you have a chance for yours?"

"I have a life, Thomas."

"Oh, do you? Forever at that old lady's beck and call? What will you do when she's not there anymore and no one else needs you?"

"Thomas—"

"What will you do if I don't come back?"

"Oh, that's not fair!"

"I don't have the time to be fair, Beth," he said quietly. "I love you. You mean the world to me. I can't bear the thought of leaving if you are not a part of my life."

"Oh, Thomas, don't make me choose—"

"I have to." He stood still, unyielding. "I want you, Beth, but I want you as my wife. Nothing less will do for me. If you will not marry me, then I will leave, right now, and we won't see each other again."

"Thomas!" It was a cry of pain.

"Which is it to be, Beth? What is your decision?"

"Oh, God." Beth wrapped her arms around herself, and for a long moment there was silence. "All right. All right, I'll talk to my mother. And if she doesn't agree," she swallowed, hard, "I'll marry you, anyway."

Thomas's eyes lit up, and he strode toward her. "Capital!"

"But." She held up her hand. "You must speak to my brother and obtain his approval. I will not break faith with him, too. And you must never, never use such methods against me again, Thomas. Is that clear?"

Thomas stopped still, staring at her. She was no longer a shy young girl, but a woman. "You'd make a good colonel, Beth," he said, grinning, and Beth's face crumpled.

"Don't mock me," she said on a sob, as he took the last step toward her and took her into his arms. "I cannot bear it. Oh, Thomas."

"I'm sorry, sweetheart." He put his hand to her head, pressing it against his shoulder. "Sorry I did what I did. I promise, I'll never do anything like that to you again."

"You had better not, Thomas Bancroft," she said, stepping back, smiling, though her hands were on her hips. "I will make you pay if you do."

"God help me," he groaned, and brought his mouth down on hers.

Giles stood near the wall in the ballroom, watching Anne dance. God, she was lovely. There was a sparkle to her, a vivacity that outshone all others, even the most classic beauties. Yet underneath lay something that he hadn't before realized was there, a sadness and a strength, qualities that hadn't been there when first he'd known her. The strength, he admired, but the sadness hurt.

He understood so much more about her now, since he had learned the truth of her marriage to Freddie. He understood her need for independence, her adamant stand against physically disciplining Jamie, her occasional wariness. He understood why she had run from his arms that night in the drawing room, when the passion and need had risen between them as never before. At least, he thought he did. It was something Obadiah hadn't even hinted at, but he suspected that Freddie had not been a gentle lover. And that meant he had a struggle ahead of him, to prove to Anne that lovemaking didn't have to be that way. Just now that looked like a daunting challenge.

Beth suddenly came into his view, dancing with the others, and his gaze sharpened. Now, where had she been? He thought he had an idea, and he wasn't pleased. In the throes of her first serious romance, Beth was not acting at all discreetly.

"Good evening, sir," a voice said beside him, and Giles turned to see Lieutenant Bancroft.

"Good evening." Giles's voice was cool. "You are not with my sister?"

Thomas hesitated. "I was, sir."

"Were you." Giles kept his gaze impassive, while mentally giving the other man credit for his honesty and courage in admitting such a thing. "Not in this room."

"No, sir." He paused again. "In an anteroom. I asked her to marry me."

"Ah. I see." Giles looked out over the dancers. At all costs, he must make this appear a casual conversation. If the gossip mongers got hold of this, there would be the devil to pay. "Without consulting me first?"

"I needed to know how she would answer. It's not an easy life I'm offering her. At least, not yet."

Something in the other man's tone made Giles look up. "You've heard something."

"Yes, sir. I'm to be posted to Spain."

"When?"

"Soon. This damnable war." Thomas moved restlessly. "We have to beat Bonaparte, and, believe me, sir, I intend to fight with everything that's in me. But, damn it." He ran a hand through his hair. "I didn't have so much to live for before."

"That raises a question. Several questions, actually. What is Beth supposed to do while you're off fighting?"

"I don't intend to bring her with me, sir, if that's what you mean."

"I had wondered about it."

"Beth is stronger than one might think, but following

286

the drum is a hard life for a woman. No, I'd have to leave her behind."

"Mm-hm. And what if something happens to you, Lieutenant? What if you are killed or injured? I wouldn't want to see my sister saddled with a cripple for the rest of her days."

To his credit, Thomas didn't flinch. "No, sir, nor would I. I'm not wealthy, but I do have an inheritance. Beth would be cared for. I may not have a title, but—"

"That is of no moment. You are the first man Beth has been serious about, and it's all happened very fast."

"Yes, sir, I realize that. If things were different I could court her as she deserves. But this is wartime, sir. I haven't much time."

"Then why not wait until you are posted home?"

"I love her. She loves me." He looked directly at Giles. "Will you tell me that counts for nothing?"

Giles looked away. Seven years ago he and Anne had loved each other, and they had let an old lady's maliciousness separate them. That they now had a second chance was entirely fortuitous. What if they had never met again? What if they had lived out their lives, never knowing the love that could flourish between them? Their lives would have been lacking, empty, barren. But they did have another chance, thank God. Lieutenant Bancroft and Beth might not be so lucky. "Beth is of age," he said slowly. "Whatever she decides to do, I cannot stop her."

"But you could make it dashed unpleasant for her, sir. It would hurt her." His eyes grew fierce. "And you would have an enemy in me, sir."

"A dire prospect. No, I do not mock you. I suspect you're deadly as an enemy." He nodded. "Very well. You have my blessing. Beth will stay with us, of course, when you go."

"Of course."

"Good." Giles looked directly at him. "You do realize that my mother is opposed to any match between you."

"Yes, sir, I know that."

"She wants to be certain that Beth will be treated well."

"Of course, sir." Thomas sounded surprised that such a question had to be asked. "I intend to do everything in my power to make her happy."

"Good." The dance had ended, and people were milling about on the floor, chatting and finding new partners. "I'll do what I can to bring my mother around, though God knows it won't be easy. I hope you're up to this fight."

"You can count on me, sir."

"Good." Giles grinned at him. "Now, what are you wasting time with me for? Go to Beth."

"Yes, sir!" Thomas gave him a quick salute and then turned, making his way through the mob to his beloved. Beth, her pretty face screwed up in an anxious pucker, looked up at him as he talked, and suddenly smiled, glowingly. To anyone watching, it must have been obvious what was happening between them. Giles only hoped his mother wasn't aware of it.

"Giles," a soft voice said beside him, and he looked down to see Anne. "Am I imagining things, or did Beth nearly hug Lieutenant Bancroft just now?"

"She did. Thank God she had more decorum or we'd be in the suds for sure."

"Heavens! Whatever in the world could he have said to her to make her behave in such a way?"

"I suspect he was telling her I'd given my blessing to their marriage."

"Giles!" Anne clutched his arm, looking up at him in delight. "Really?"

"Really."

"Oh, how marvelous. I am so happy for Beth. She deserves her own life."

"She does." They stood silent for a moment, watching the crowd. "This is a hard time, with Bancroft

288

going off to war. They may not have a second chance."

Anne looked away from his direct gaze; his meaning was clear in his eyes. "I am so glad you agreed to it, Giles. They're so much in love."

"Indeed, they are." The music started up again. "So they are playing a waltz tonight."

"How scandalous," Anne said lightly.

"You are not dancing?"

"I told you, sir. I intend not to cause any more scenes."

Giles looked out onto the floor. Lieutenant Bancroft, apparently with no such compunction, had caught Beth up in his arms and was already twirling her around the floor. An impetuous young man, and a smart one. If he had the courage to seize the moment, then so did Giles. "Come," he said, taking Anne's arm and pulling her onto the floor. "Let us dance."

"Giles! This is a waltz."

He grinned at her. "All the better."

"Giles," she protested again, but the words died as he slipped his arm about her waist. She was in his arms, close to him again. It was heaven; it was torture. "Giles, what of your consequence?"

"Hang my consequence. You were right, Annie."

"About what?"

"About there being more to life than duty." He swung her in a turn that left her breathless. "I think Lieutenant Bancroft and Beth have the right idea, don't you?"

Anne stopped still. "Giles!"

"Annie, Annie. If you stop, someone is certain to bump into us, and we can't have that, can we?"

"But, Giles!" Helplessly she let herself be whirled around again. "What an outrageous thing to say while we are dancing!"

"What? That they knew enough to enjoy life while they can? That's what I meant." Giles's eyes were innocent. "What did you think I meant, Annie?"

"N-nothing."

"Mm-hm." He glanced around. "Rather warm in here, isn't it?"

"Giles Templeton, now what are you thinking?"

"Nothing." He turned that innocent gaze on her again. "Anne, I am shocked at what you're implying. You really must do something about that suspicious mind of yours."

"I must—suspicious mind," she sputtered, staring at him, and then let out a laugh. "Giles, you are a complete hand!"

His grin was boyish and endearing. "I know. Would you want my hand, Annie?"

"Giles—"

"For dancing," he said, and whirled her around again. This time, she laughed. When had she and Giles last flirted? It was exciting, it was frightening, but the fluttery feeling at the pit of her stomach was not at all unpleasant. She felt young, attractive, alluring. She hadn't felt like this in a very long time.

"For dancing," she agreed, as his hand met hers. Palm touched palm, fingers linked with fingers, and slowly, as their eyes met, their arms slid down. For a moment the laughter, the teasing, were gone, replaced by something more serious, more elemental. Oh, heavens. What was happening between them?

"I've missed you, Annie," he said in a low voice, his eyes still holding hers.

"I've—missed you." She didn't pretend to misunderstand his meaning; she knew he was referring to the distance that had been between them since that night in the drawing room, when he had held her in his arms. But, oh heavens, what was she to do? There was no going back to their former relationship, that she knew. How, though, could they possibly go forward?

"I wonder," she said, her mind veering wildly off at a tangent, "if the ghost is going to make another appearance."

"I doubt it." The look in Giles's eyes told her that he knew quite well what she was doing. "God knows why the prankster did it, but now that we've found out how, I'll be surprised if he tries again."

"Have you any idea who did it?"

"Obadiah's looking into it." He paused. "He's a good man."

"I told you that."

"Don't poker up so, Annie. It doesn't become you."

"Giles—"

"You have to admit, to someone who didn't know the man, it sounded deuced odd. A former slave as overseer."

"I suppose it would. I've grown used to it, of course, and I know what the people on the plantation are like. They're good people."

"I don't doubt it."

"Obadiah really should be reinstated as overseer."

"I agree."

"What?"

"I'm not stupid, Anne. I could see the difference in the ledgers after you took over. It's something I've been considering for a while, since this whole ghost business started."

"Oh, I'm so pleased. Obadiah will be, too. He doesn't like living in England."

"I know." He paused. "Do you, Anne?"

"Why, of course I do. I'm quite enjoying this summer."

"That isn't quite what I mean. I think you know that."

Anne glanced away. The emotion she had felt this afternoon, of never wanting to leave, had faded, leaving in its place reality. "I don't belong here, Giles," she said finally. "Maybe I never did, but I wouldn't have known it if I hadn't gone away. There would always have been this part of me that was unhappy, and I wouldn't know why. Look around us." She gestured

291

about the room. "See how few people are dancing, and all because of public opinion. Good heavens, if I behaved as I do in Jamaica, I'd be beyond the pale. I never wear hats there, Giles, and my skin gets quite brown. I like to run the plantation as I wish. I like running down the beach with my son and not worrying about what people will say, or if I'll be ostracized. I can be myself, there. I can't, here. It's freedom, Giles."

His eyes were intent on hers. "We make our choices, Anne. Choices are made for us, and we're bound by them. I don't believe there really is such a thing as complete freedom."

"No, probably not. But life is richer when you can make your own choices. I can't do that here."

"I understand that, Anne. Perhaps more than you think."

"What do you mean?"

Giles drew to a halt as the waltz ended, and bowed. As he rose, his eyes met hers. "I know about Freddie, Anne."

Chapter 21

Anne stood very still, chilled, though the night was warm. Giles knew about Freddie. He knew, and now what would he think of her? It hadn't been her fault, she knew that now, but she also knew that many others wouldn't agree. Dear God, how was she to handle it, now that he knew—but what, exactly, did he know?

"What a remarkable thing to say," she said, smiling brightly and batting her eyelashes at him. "It sounds so mysterious."

"I think you know what I mean, Anne," Giles said, his eyes never leaving hers.

"Well, there is so little to know about him, really, that you don't already know." She glanced aside. "Heavens, everyone has left the floor and yet here we stand. Everyone must be looking at us."

"And we can't have that, can we. Very well, Anne." He took her arm and they strolled off the floor. "In any event, this is something best discussed in private."

"Heavens, that sounds ominous. Lieutenant Bancroft. How nice to see you tonight. You look very handsome."

Thomas, after casting a quick, uncertain glance at Giles, smiled down at Anne. "Thank you, ma'am. You look lovely, too, but you make me feel most impolite for not saying so first."

"Oh, heavens, as if that matters! Oh, they are playing a cotillion! But if I stand up with Giles again, the tabbies will surely notice."

"I'd be happy to dance with you, ma'am."

"Why, thank you, sir. I'm honored." Anne placed her hand on Thomas's arm and, casting a quick smile back at Giles, allowed herself to be led out onto the floor.

Damn. Giles's mouth set in a thin line. He had bungled that, bringing up her past at a time when they couldn't possibly discuss it. And yet, he was relieved. He had no doubt that what Obadiah had told him was the truth, but he didn't want to know more. Not really.

"Poor Anne," Beth said softly, and he looked down at her.

"Do you not mind that she captured your beau, just like that?" he said. "I've known Anne to be flirtatious, but never to walk off with another woman's fiancé."

Beth's smile was brilliant. "You gave Thomas your approval."

"I did." He smiled. "I must say, I think he's damned lucky. Most young women would be furious at what he did."

"Anne gave him little choice. Poor thing, she must be very unhappy."

"Anne? She looks to be enjoying herself."

"Oh, no. Not really. She only behaves so when she is unhappy. Really, Giles, it was too bad of you to make me think she was so flighty, when really she is one of the most dependable people I know."

"She is flirtatious, Beth."

"Oh, yes, but only, I think, to get attention. How sad."

"What?"

"To feel she has to act so for people to notice her. I wonder if she thinks no one loves her."

"She should know better," he began, and stopped, struck by what Beth had said. No, why should she? Her

294

parents, Freddie, even himself—all had ultimately withheld their love from her. *Good God.* No wonder if, when something hurt her, she ran away, seeking comfort and yet never finding it. He could understand that; had he not done the same thing himself? Perhaps, though, it was time to stop running. Perhaps he could help her face whatever was hurting her.

"Do be gentle with her, Giles," Beth said.

Startled, Giles came out of his reverie. "Pardon?"

"When you speak with her. Be nice to her."

"I will, Beth." He smiled down at her as the dance ended and the sets broke up. "I will."

He had little chance, though, to speak with Anne for the remainder of the night. Popular as she was, she danced every dance. Then, of course, when the Prince of Wales made his appearance, all attention was turned to him, some ladies going so far as to stand on benches to see him. It was just as well, Giles thought, occasionally catching a glimpse of Anne as she laughed and danced, disguising the pain that he knew was in her eyes. This was no place to discuss sensitive subjects.

It was late when the Tremonts at last set off for home, after a festive supper and a truly memorable ball. Beth was still radiant and chatting; Anne, quiet. Giles was tired, from the day's emotions, and more than ready to seek his bed. Damn, what had happened to his nice, quiet life, when his family had behaved in a calm, predictable way? It was all Anne's doing. He didn't know whether to bless her, or blame her.

"Giles. Elizabeth," Julia said as they prepared to go upstairs. "I would see you in the drawing room."

Oh, damn. "Tonight, Mother?" Giles said.

"Yes. Now. Give me your arm, Giles. I am old."

Giles cast a look at Beth, who looked suitably apprehensive. "Very well, Mother. What is this about?" he asked, as they walked into the drawing room.

Julia waited until she was settled in a chair, with a

295

stool under her feet, before she answered. "I believe you know. I want to know, Elizabeth, why you behaved as you did tonight with that man."

Beth threw Giles a quick look and then raised her chin. "He asked me to marry him, Mother. I said I would."

"I beg your pardon?" Julia stared at her daughter, and then, very slowly, gripping the arms of her chair, rose. "*What* did you say you are going to do, miss?"

"I said I am going to marry Lieutenant Bancroft." Beth met Julia's eyes squarely. In the past, such a look from her mother would have made her back down, but not tonight. Though the thought of this confrontation had had her in a quake all evening, now that she had started, she felt surprisingly calm. Never before had she defied her mother. It was rather amazing she hadn't been struck by lightning, simply for contemplating such a thing.

The thought made her smile, and Julia drew herself up to her full height. "You think to mock me, Elizabeth?"

"No. Oh, no, Mother, I would never do such a thing! Please, let us not squabble about this. I love him."

"Bah. Love counts for nothing in our world. Giles can tell you that, can you not?"

Giles, who until now had been leaning against the drawing room wall, uttered a silent sigh and stepped forward. At this moment, this was the last thing in the world he wished to discuss. When would he be able to turn his attention from his duties to be with Anne? "Actually, Mother, I believe love does count, no matter one's station," he said.

"What?" Julia peered at him from under lowered eyebrows. "You can say that after what Anne did to you?"

"Yes, and we both know why she did it, don't we?"

Under his steady regard Julia's eyes dropped, but

only for a moment. "Nonsense. It was her choice to leave. She chose another man, Giles. So much for love."

"Mother!" Beth exclaimed.

"We made a mistake." Giles refused to rise to the bait, though inside he was quivering with anger. "I don't intend to let the same thing happen to Beth."

"What? What are you saying?"

"I'm saying that I've given my consent to the match."

Julia sat down abruptly, her face pale. "Good God. Have you run mad, Giles? He couldn't be less suitable for Beth."

"To the contrary. Do you think I agreed to this without thinking it through first? No, Mother, I know my duty." Julia flinched at the word she had thrown in his face so many times, but he continued inexorably on. "Lieutenant Bancroft is a good man. He comes of good family, has an unblemished record in the army, and owns a small estate. Not, perhaps, what Beth is used to, but with her portion, they'll manage fine."

"Her portion! Oh, no. She'll get nothing from me, do you hear? Nothing!"

"He doesn't want money," Beth put in, her face pale.

"It's not your money to give," Giles said at the same time.

Julia stared at them both. "Are you going over my authority, boy?"

"No, Mother. Simply exercising my own."

"My God." She glared at him. "This is a betrayal, boy, do you understand that? After all I've done for you."

"I'm sorry." Giles sounded not in the least penitent. "I've made my decision. Beth has my blessing to marry Thomas Bancroft."

"Well, she hasn't mine," Julia said bitterly. "And you should be ashamed of yourself. Have you thought of what her life will be like, married to a half-pay officer?"

"He isn't," Beth protested.

"What is she supposed to do? Follow him all around the continent? Good God, Giles, use your sense!"

"I have, Mother. Beth will stay with us while he's away."

"I will not!" Beth exclaimed.

"She will not. I won't have her in my house, do you hear me?"

The silence rang with her last words. "Yes, Mother, we heard you," Giles said finally, crossing the room and putting his arm about Beth's shoulders. "I think perhaps it's time you listened to us. No, you've had your say." He raised his hand. "I am the head of this family. I have deferred decisions to you, but no longer, If that means I have to make some hard choices, then so be it." He looked at her, and his gaze softened. "Come, Mother. Can you not simply make peace with the idea? We're not children anymore. We can make our own decisions."

"Foolish decisions." Julia rose, her face twisted. "Oh, go on, go on to ruin, both of you! If you won't listen to me, I can do nothing to force you." She paused at the door, and though her gaze was as fierce as ever, something had gone out of her. She looked smaller, frailer. Old. "But you'll regret it. Mark my words. You'll regret it."

Silence echoed in the wake of Julia's departure, broken only by the thump of her cane as she made her way upstairs. Brother and sister stared at each other in speechless silence for a moment, and then Giles held out his arms. "It will be all right, Bethie," he murmured, as she ran to him and his arm closed about her. "She'll come around."

"I don't think so, Giles." Beth's voice was steady. Where, he wondered, was the shy, quaking girl she had been? "She doesn't like Thomas."

"It's of no matter. You'll always have a home with us."

298

"My place is with Thomas, now."

"Good God." He pulled back. "Do you really mean you'd follow the drum?"

"Of course."

"Beth, that's no kind of life for a woman."

"It's the life I want." Beth's voice was firm. "I love him, Giles. And, do you know, I think I'm stronger than anyone ever thought. Even myself."

"Good." Giles pulled away. What had happened to the women of his family? They had all changed this summer. "If it's what you want to do, I can't stop you. You'll have a hard time convincing your lieutenant, though."

"Oh, I'll manage Thomas." Beth's smile was brilliant, and quite unlike her usual one. "He won't want to be separated from me, either. Just as Anne doesn't want to leave you for Jamaica."

Giles looked sharply at her at that. "That's another matter."

"Oh, I'm so happy, Giles!" She threw her arms around his neck. "I want you to be happy, too. You will speak to Anne, won't you?"

Under Beth's bright, expectant gaze, he couldn't bring himself to say that he doubted it would do any good. "If I can." He hugged her. "I wish you happy, Beth. I love you, you know."

"Yes, I know." Beth pulled back. "Now, please, find Anne and tell her the same thing."

"Yes, ma'am!" Giles saluted, grinning. Damned if he wouldn't, now that Beth's future was settled. Damned if he wouldn't.

The night was hot and close. A thunderstorm was brewing, Obadiah had said earlier. The cool linen sheets of Anne's bed were twisted and hot around her, and beads of perspiration trickled down between her breasts. Dear heavens, why could she not sleep?

Certainly she had been busy enough this past week, attending balls and such and paying assiduous attention to Jamie. Anything to avoid Giles, anything not to think about the things he had made her remember. She should be tired. She certainly was during the day. Sometimes at routs she had to press her lips together to stifle her yawns. She needed sleep, but the more she courted it, the farther away it seemed.

Damn, it was hot! She sat abruptly up in bed, pushing her heavy hair away from her face. She could not face another moment of this, or she would go mad. She knew one method of finding sleep. Swinging her legs out of bed, she rose, smoothing her crumpled nightrail. It was late, and the entire household slept. No one was about to see her. She would not bother to wear her wrapper. It was far too hot.

The house was silent, as still as the night, making her tiptoe down the stairs and catch her breath each time a board creaked beneath her bare feet. No one stirred, and so she made it downstairs in safety. Unerringly she turned toward the drawing room; unerringly she found the flint and struck it, lighting a candle by its brief spark. There, she could see her destination. The table of decanters, behind the camel-back sofa.

The sherry glowed a rich amber in the dim light as she poured it into her glass. A fine wine, she thought, curling up on the sofa and holding the glass to the light. She should know. It had helped her find oblivion more than once this past week, and would do so again. Thank heavens for it. What would she do without it?

Yes, and what had she done without it? a niggling voice inside her asked. Usually she ignored the voice, but tonight she must have been more tired, more on edge. Tonight, the voice was loud. About to take a sip, Anne stopped and pulled back, looking at the glass. Dear lord, what was she doing? She should know better than to travel this road. Down such a path had gone Freddie.

Slowly and deliberately, she poured the sherry back into the decanter. She might not sleep tonight, but somehow that didn't matter. There was a peace inside her that she had not felt in a long time. Freddie had not been evil, just weak. He had allowed the liquor to take over his life, and everyone had paid the price. It wasn't her fault he'd behaved as he had. She had done her best to be a good wife to him, even after she'd realized she didn't love him. Liquor, and Freddie's own demons, had destroyed him.

She had just set the stopper on the decanter when there was a footfall at the doorway. Hastily she spun around, her arms protectively crossing her breasts. She could not see past the glow of the candle to the figure who held it, but then the person moved. Giles. Only Giles. She felt weak with relief, and something else, something she didn't want to acknowledge. "Giles?"

"I heard a noise and thought perhaps it was our ghost," he said, placing his candle on a table.

"No, 'tis only me. Sorry. We haven't heard from him lately, have we?"

"No. Is aught wrong, Anne?"

"Heavens, no. I simply cannot sleep, 'tis so hot."

"Surely you're used to worse than this in Jamaica."

"Yes, but we have breezes to keep things comfortable. Obadiah said we'll be having a storm."

"Hm. I wonder what kind of storm he meant."

"Beg pardon? I would think a thunderstorm."

"I think it just as likely there'll be a storm inside. Or haven't you noticed that things have been tense lately?"

"Oh, yes. With Beth planning to marry—"

"I'm not talking about Beth," he said, and Anne fell quiet. "Anne, you can't run away from me forever."

"Heavens, whoever said I'm doing that?"

"Annie." He walked across to her and tilted her chin up with his fingers. "You can't fool me, you know. You've been avoiding me." His voice was quiet. "I

301

know your marriage was unhappy. I also have a fair idea why."

Anne looked up at him and drew a deep, shaky breath. "It's past, Giles."

"Is it? No, don't turn away from me, Annie. If it is in the past, why are you so adamant about never being in a man's power again? Your own words, I'll remind you."

"Heavens, I was just being dramatic."

"Annie."

She closed her eyes. He knew. "How much do you know?"

"Enough. Too much." Giles's hand curled into fists. "If I had Freddie here—"

"It's past, Giles. Really. I survived it."

"Did you?"

"Yes."

"Then why did you not tell me?"

Anne looked down at her toes, now curled over each other, and muttered something. "Excuse me?" Giles said.

"I said it is none of your business," she said, looking up at him defiantly.

"No." He caught her chin in his hand. "That's not what you said."

Anne squeezed her eyes shut. "Giles, please."

"You're afraid I'll think less of you. Why?"

"Oh, for heaven's sake, Giles!" She jerked away from his hand and glared at him. "Think of how it looks, that my husband beat me. I must have deserved it, mustn't I? Why else would he have done such a thing? Giles, how could you not think less of me?"

Giles didn't answer right away. What *did* he think of this situation? His initial reaction had been an angry protectiveness, followed by indignation that she had chosen a man who would mistreat her, over him. And hadn't a part of him wondered what she had done to

302

provoke such mistreatment? But, damn, he'd been angry with women, with her, and never once had he felt the urge to raise his hand. The fault hadn't been in Anne. It had been in Freddie. "No, Annie," he said. "To the contrary. I think you must be very brave and strong to have come through it as you have."

Tears pooled in Anne's eyes, blurring her vision. He meant it. Of all the reactions her past could have received, this was the most unexpected, and it made her feel absurdly grateful to him. Grateful, and something else. Cherished. Cared for. "Oh, Giles—"

"Annie." He was by her side in a moment, wrapping his arms around her and drawing her close, feeling the warmth of her through the slight barrier of their clothing. She wore only a nightgown. Of that he had been acutely aware since stopping at the door and seeing her figure outlined by the candle's glow. He wore only his dressing gown. Dangerous, this, but he didn't want to let her go. He needed this closeness as much as she did. "It's all right."

"What you must be thinking, Giles, that I chose someone like that over you."

"No." He shook his head. "I always thought Freddie was too weak for you, but I didn't think he'd behave as he did."

"He was weak. That was one of the reasons he did it, I know that now."

"Why didn't you tell anyone, Anne?"

"Who could I have told? No one would have helped me in Jamaica, and nor would my parents."

"You could have told me."

"Could I? Remember, I thought you were marrying someone else. And, in any event"—she swallowed, hard—"I was ashamed."

Giles had to bend low to catch her last words; the impact of them brought his head up sharply. "Ashamed! Good God, why?"

"I thought it had to be my fault." Her fingers opened and closed on his shoulders, opened and closed. "I thought I had to be doing something wrong. First, my father—well, I know why he didn't love me, I wasn't a boy! Then you, marrying someone else, as I thought, and that hurt. Oh, it hurt. So, when I provoked Freddie and he reacted, I—well, I assumed it was my fault."

"Annie." His voice was as gentle as his fingers, brushing away her tears. "You know that's not true."

She nodded quickly. "Yes. Oh, yes, I know that now, I've known it for a long time. Because." She stopped, closing her eyes for a moment. "Because maybe I provoked him, but Jamie was only a baby."

It took Giles a moment to realize what she meant. "Good God! He hit Jamie?"

"Once. Only once." Her eyes were calm now, and resolute. The eyes of a survivor. "I don't think Jamie remembers, he was so young, but I do. It made me realize that Freddie was the one to blame, not Jamie, and not me. And I never let him touch me again."

"Good God," he said again, running his hand through his hair. "Anne, you could have come home."

"To what? To scandal? Who would have been on my side, Giles? You know as well as I that no one would think Freddie's behavior unusual. Not when women are considered a man's property." Her voice was bitter. "It's almost as bad as slavery, but at least he gave the slaves their freedom."

"I can't imagine any man thinking he could own you."

"No, I thought it best to stay where I was. At least there I had some control over my life, and the servants were with me."

"Including Obadiah?"

Anne smiled for the first time. "Especially Obadiah."

"Good." Giles's voice was grim. "Freddie always was a bit of a coward."

"Yes. Obadiah didn't even have to use force. All it would take was a voodoo chant." Giles burst out laughing. "Nothing harmful, of course, but Freddie didn't know that. After a time, you know, he was glad to avoid me. He had his rum, and his other women." She stopped abruptly. "It's past, thank God. It's over. And I learned a lot from it." She drew a deep breath. "I learned I never again wish to be in a position where I am dependent on a man."

"I can understand that, Anne, except that not everyone is like him."

"Oh? Then will you allow me to run the plantation? To educate Jamie as I see fit? No, don't answer, I can see it in your eyes." She turned away. "Poor Giles."

"What? Why?"

"You cannot change, can you? Even if you want to."

"That's not fair," he protested. "I was brought up to believe that it is a man's duty to protect his woman."

"I'm not just any woman, Giles, and I'm not certain I need protection."

Lightly, he trailed his fingers down her cheek, making her jerk back. "No, not in the ordinary way."

"What is that supposed to mean?"

"It means that you are far more sensitive than you would have people think. You need someone who'd understand that."

Anne gazed up at him. His eyes were soft and warm in the candlelight. Someone who understood her. Had anyone ever had? Only Giles, when they had been children playing together, when they had first been engaged. That understanding was still there. He knew her, and he loved her anyway. Had loved her. What they had had was as past as her life with Freddie, and there was no going back. There was no future between them.

"Giles, even if I found someone like that, I'm not sure . . ." Her voice trailed off, and she shrugged. "I

305

don't know. Perhaps I'm just tired."

"No wonder if you are, carrying that burden."

Anne opened her mouth, and then closed it again. "Yes."

"Annie." Giles held her shoulders lightly, his eyes intent on hers. "You're not alone anymore. You do know that?"

"Yes, I do." Anne returned the gaze, seeing in his eyes depths she had never noticed before. In that moment she fell finally, completely and irrevocably, in love with him. He wanted her. She could tell, not just from the heat of his body, but from the way he looked at her. Why not? Had she not sometimes wondered, when she was with Freddie, what that part of marriage would have been like with Giles? She was free, now, with no one to answer to but herself, and a great need to be held, to be loved. And then?

She pulled away, pushing her hair back over her shoulders. "I can't, Giles."

Giles didn't pretend to misunderstand. "I'm not asking you for anything you can't give, Annie."

"It's something I may never be able to give you, Giles." She faced him squarely. "I know you're not Freddie, but neither am I the girl you once knew. I used to take chances, Giles. Not anymore.

"I understand," he said softly, after a moment, making Anne blink back tears. Anger, unreasoning and irrational, rose with her. He shouldn't be so understanding, not in this! He should fight for her, press her, and then—

And then she could claim, in self-righteous indignation, that it hadn't been by her choice, thus putting all the responsibility on him. How despicable she was, she thought, dispassionately. When—if—she ever made love with Giles, she would not do so as she once had with Freddie, unthinkingly, trying to escape a pain that would not go away. She was a mature woman now, and

306

that was how she would give her love. If she ever could.

"You deserve better than me, Giles," she whispered, and jumped to her feet, running from the drawing room to the sanctuary of her room.

"Annie," Giles said, and stopped. All he could do for her was to let her go. To chase her, to persuade her to stay with him would be wrong, after what she had just revealed. It would be forcing her into something for which she was not ready, making him as bad, in his own way, as Freddie had been. Anne deserved better.

He twisted on the sofa, pouring out the same sherry that Anne had earlier refused. A fine dry sherry, this, but he drank it down without noticing its taste. Tonight the gap between him and Anne seemed very wide, indeed.

Setting down the glass on the sofa table, he lifted his candle and turned away. He had time to bridge that gap, now that he knew what had caused it. At least, he hoped he had. Something had happened to him a few moments ago, when he had looked into Anne's eyes and seen there only candor and vulnerability. He had thought he loved her before; now he knew that what he'd felt was only an infinitely tiny measure of what his love for her could be. He was totally, irrevocably in love with her. The thought of living the remainder of his life without her was insupportable. Somehow, he would win out over her memories, and the pain of the past. He had to. His very survival depended upon it.

"Now where is that bonnet?" Anne muttered, rummaging among the boxes in her dressing room. "I know I put it here. Are you sure you didn't move it, Jenny?"

"Yes, miss, I'm certain." Jenny lifted the lid off one box, peered inside, and shook her head. "It's not here, ma'am, but I'd swear I put it away right there."

"Yes." Anne looked up at the shelf. She'd seen the box there, too. Now what was she to do? She had an appointment to go driving with Ian Campbell, and she was already late. Worse, that bonnet was the only one that matched the walking dress she was wearing, of an unusual shade somewhere between lavender and blue. Nothing else would quite do. "Oh, bother. I hate wearing hats. I suppose I'll have to change."

"Maybe Terence has it," Jamie, sitting on the chaise longue, piped up.

Anne exchanged a glance with Jenny. "Why would Terence have it, pet?"

"To play a joke, of course." Jamie's eyes sparkled. "He said he'd put it on Prinny's statue—"

"When did he say this, Jamie?"

"This morning, Mama." He jumped off the chaise. "Shall I go ask him for you, Mama?"

"Just a moment." Anne held out her hand. "You know where to find him?"

"Of course." Jamie looked surprised, as if he were trying to fathom the ways of adults. "He's just downstairs, Mama."

"Just—I'm coming with you, Jamie."

"Oh, ma'am." Jenny wrung her hands. "Shouldn't you tell His Grace first? To face a ghost alone—"

"Oh, he's not a ghost," Jamie said cheerfully. "He said that was a joke, too. Come on, Mommy!" He tugged at Anne's hand. "Let's hurry before he gets busy with something."

"Jamie," Anne gasped as he pulled her along the hall to the stairs. "Who is it?"

"I can't tell you, Mommy. I promised. Look! There's your bonnet."

Anne stopped at the foot of the stairs. Her bonnet was, indeed, gracing the bust of the Prince, which stood on a table in the front hall. Anne's lips twitched. "Rather fetching. I'd like to meet Terence, Jamie. Will

308

you find him for me?"

"But he's right here, Mommy. Terence!" Jamie called, and ran across the hall, throwing his arms around the legs of the man who stood there. Benson, their very proper butler.

Chapter 22

Anne stared for a moment and then, her legs going weak, collapsed on the stairs in gales of laughter. "B-Benson? Are you telling me, Jamie, that our ghost is B-B-Benson?"

"Yes, Mommy." Jamie beamed at her.

Benson's face had gone red. "I thought that was to be our secret, lad," he said. In spite of his discomfiture and the small boy clinging to him, he somehow managed to hold onto his dignity.

"But Mommy needed her bonnet," Jamie said, torn, for the first time in his memory by conflicting loyalties. "Did I do something bad?"

"N-no, Jamie." Anne had herself under control now, and was wiping her eyes. "You did exactly right. But you, sir. Are you really the ghost?"

Benson bowed his head. "Alas, madam, I fear I am."

"But your name's not Terence," she said, knowing it sounded absurd. What did one say to a self-confessed ghost?

"William Terence O'Neill Benson," he said, rather proudly. "My mother was Irish. And my brother is in the navy."

"Oh. That explains the choice of songs."

Benson reddened again. "Well, yes," he said, and Anne again went off into peals of laughter. Benson, stiff, dignified and proper, singing bawdy songs and leading everyone on a wild chase? But who else was better suited to the part? As butler, he knew everything about this house, and the people in it. The only question was, why?

"What is going on?" a voice said crisply from down the hall.

"Uncle Giles!" Jamie released Benson and ran to Giles. "I found Terence."

"You what?" Giles looked at Anne for confirmation, but she had her head down and was laughing helplessly. "Anne, what in the world?"

"Ahem." Benson stepped forward. "I fear I have a confession to make, sir. I have been pretending to be a ghost."

Giles looked from him to Anne. "Has everyone in this house run mad?"

"Oh, it's quite true," Anne said, wiping her eyes. "His middle name is—T-Terence!"

"For God's sake." Giles dropped down beside Anne, who was off again. "Whatever possessed you to do such a thing, Benson?"

"Yes, Benson." Anne's voice quivered with laughter. "Why did you do it?"

"Because Her Grace asked me to, of course. Oh, dear." The two people on the stairs were staring at him, the mirth slowly fading from their faces. "Oh, dear, I've put my foot in it this time, haven't I?"

"Quite," Giles said, his voice grim. "Are you saying the duchess asked you to impersonate a ghost?"

"Yes, Your Grace." Benson bowed his head. "I'll quite understand, sir, if you wish to sack me. I see now I quite deserve it. Although I might remind you, my family—"

"Has served mine for years. I'll take that into consideration, but—"

"Uncle Giles, don't!" Jamie wailed.

"Hush, Jamie!" Anne said sharply. "Go upstairs to

311

Nurse, now. I'll be up to talk with you later."

"Good God." Giles was shaking his head. "Why would the duchess ask you to do such a thing, Benson?"

"You'll have to ask Her Grace, sir. Although—"

"Yes?"

"She doesn't like Brighton. She hasn't felt at all well since we arrived here."

"Hasn't she?" Giles said in surprise.

"No, Your Grace. But if she knows I told you that, she'll sack me herself."

Giles and Anne exchanged glances, and then rose. "Thank you, Benson, that will be all. Will you please go to your quarters until I call for you?"

Benson bowed his head. "Yes, Your Grace."

"Oh, and Benson."

Benson turned, just as he was about to go through the green baize door at the end of the hall. "Yes, Your Grace?"

"Whom did Mr. Freebody and I chase the night we thought there was a ghost at the window? You were here all along."

"No one, sir. At least, no one I know."

"So we let ourselves be fooled," Giles said ruefully. "No wonder we didn't catch anyone."

"No, Your Grace." Benson's voice was wistful. "It was rather fun while it lasted."

Again Giles and Anne exchanged glances. "You may go, Benson," Giles said.

"Yes, Your Grace. I'm sorry, Your Grace," Benson said, and at last left the hall.

"Benson. Good God." Giles rubbed at his chin. "No wonder we couldn't find out who the ghost was."

"I know." Anne shook her head as they began to ascend the stairs, toward the drawing room. "He seems so unlikely."

"Yes, but he's loyal to my mother."

"Giles." Anne stopped on the landing. "Why in the world would she do such a thing, when someone could

312

have been hurt—Giles!" She gripped his arm. "Jamie. When I think of what could have happened to Jamie—"

"Anne. Listen to me." Giles put his hands on her shoulders, turning her to face him. "I'm angry, too. But let us hear what she has to say—"

"That's flummery, Giles! My child could have been hurt, or I could have lost him altogether. If you had a child, you'd understand, but how can you—"

"I care about Jamie," he said sharply. "Don't you think I was worried about him, too, the night he was missing? But, be fair, Anne. No one meant any harm to come to him."

"No, but it happened, anyway, and all because of some silly, stupid scheme. God knows why."

Giles was afraid he knew quite well what the reason behind the scheme had been. To separate him from Anne. If so, it had backfired. "I'll talk with her."

"Of course we will. I want to know what she thought she was doing."

"No. I'll talk to her alone."

"But—"

"It's my problem, Anne."

"After what she did?"

"It's my problem. My mother, my problem." His gaze softened. "Don't worry. I've no intention of letting you or Jamie come to any harm."

"I didn't think that."

"No, but you don't quite believe it yet, do you?" With the back of his fingers, he stroked her cheek. "Trust me to take care of this, Anne. I promise I'll do my best."

"I know you will." She gazed up at him, mesmerized by his touch, his eyes, and then broke away. What was she doing? Now was not the time to be acting like some silly moonling. "I'll be with Jamie," she said, and then, to both their surprise, reached up on tiptoe to kiss his cheek. "For luck," she said, and quickly ran up the stairs.

Giles followed more slowly, heading toward his

mother's room. He did not relish the prospect of the next hour or so.

Sometime later, Giles knocked at Anne's door. He looked tired, she thought, older, with lines around his eyes she'd never noticed before. She'd thought that he enjoyed being duke, and that he liked his duties, but now she could see it was a burden to him, too. Anything that happened in the family was his responsibility. He had to be the one in charge, the one who took care of things. Who, though, took care of him?

Impulsively she reached out and took his arm. "Come in and sit down, Giles."

"No." He shook his head. "It wouldn't be proper. I just wanted to tell you—"

"Oh, bother proper! Very well, if you won't, then let us at least go down to the drawing room."

"Anne, let's deal with this with as little fuss as possible," he said, but his tone of voice belied his words. He made no further protest as Anne steered him toward the stairs, nor did he appear to mind when they went into the drawing room and she closed the door behind them. Wordlessly she crossed the room and poured out a measure of brandy. Equally wordlessly he took it from her, drinking it down in one long draught.

"Ah." He set the glass down hard on the table next to him. "That was good. Not a good way to drink a fine brandy, though." Wearily he rubbed at his forehead. "I have had better days."

"Your mother?"

His hand dropped. "Oh, she did it. She admitted it."

"Good lord! But why, Giles?"

"I don't really know. Not much of what she said made sense." He got up and paced over to a window. "She's not well, Anne. She hasn't been since we got here, though she didn't say anything. Apparently the sea air has bothered her rheumatism."

"Yes, but Giles, the hauntings started right away."

314

"No, they didn't." He turned. "When we arrived, Benson told her the rumors. That gave her the idea. As you recall, she never wanted to come here." He paused. "She didn't mean any harm to come to anyone, Anne. She was horrified when Jamie went missing. All she wanted was to go home."

"She must be very unhappy."

Giles turned and stared at her in surprise. "You're taking this better than I'd expected."

"Yes, well, I've been thinking about it." What, she had wondered, could have made Julia do such an outrageous thing? What could mean so much to her? The answer to that question had come quickly, out of Anne's own experience. Her children. Out of the desire to protect her children had come the scheme to make the house appear haunted, and bring them back to the safety of Tremont Castle. It didn't matter that Giles and Beth were grown, or that Anne herself believed that Julia was wrong about what was best for them. Julia had done what she thought she had to for her children, and for that Anne felt a reluctant sympathy. She wouldn't tell Giles any of this, though. It would only add to his burden.

"She's old, Giles," she said, her voice gentle. "It's the first time she's left Tremont since losing your father, and it must have been hard on her. I'm not saying what she did was right, but except for Jamie, no harm was done. And who could have predicted what he would do?"

"She cares about Jamie, you know."

"Yes, I know she does. And I know she wouldn't have hurt him deliberately." She got up and poured him another brandy. "What are you going to do?"

"What can I do? We'll go back to Tremont, of course. We were going to soon, in any event. Summer's over."

Anne glanced away. Summer was, indeed, over, and with it the hopes that had been slowly growing inside

315

her. Foolish of her. After all this time, all that she'd been through, she really should have known better. "We have yet to decide Jamie's future."

"I know. We'll discuss that at Tremont. Somehow, this—" he glanced around the room—"doesn't seem the proper place."

Anne's smile was tinged with sadness and nostalgia. "It was great fun, Giles. Most of it."

"Yes. Fun, and folly." The look he gave her was quizzical. "If you'd had any idea when you came here what would happen, would you have come?"

Anne rose. He wasn't referring to the hauntings, or his mother, or Jamie's future. He was talking about what had happened between them. "I had no choice, did I, Your Grace?"

"Anne—"

"Never mind. As you said, it was folly." She smiled at him, and left the room.

Folly? Giles reconsidered the word as he stood there alone, breathing in the memory of her perfume. Had it really been folly? Yes, that was his word, and perhaps several months ago he would have meant it. So much had happened this summer, turning his neat, predictable world upside down, that he had been in a constant state of confusion. His mind had cleared now, though. He knew, at last, what he wanted. He wanted to live at Tremont and enjoy the life he'd built these past years, but he wanted to do so on his own terms. He wanted to be his own man, not simply following his duty as it had been outlined for him. Most of all, he wanted Anne.

Folly? No. To the contrary, it was the wisest decision he'd ever made. He wanted Anne. If she really thought he was going to let her go, she was in for a surprise. This time, he was going to fight for her.

With her plot discovered, Julia gave up all opposition to Beth's wedding; Giles gave her little choice.

316

Plans were quickly put into train, before Thomas was sent to take up his post in Spain. A special license was procured, arrangements made at the church, and invitations were sent out for the wedding breakfast. Giles had suggested returning to Tremont, where Beth could be married from her home by the Reverend Goodfellow, but she had refused the suggestion. There wasn't the time to travel there. She wanted to be with Thomas for as long as possible, before he had to go.

Since Julia genuinely was not well, much of the work of the wedding fell on Anne's shoulders. She was glad of it. The distractions of choosing floral arrangements and deciding on a menu, of organizing a wedding party and helping Beth find just the right gown, were welcome. They kept her from thinking about things that were best forgotten.

On the morning of the wedding Anne stood with Beth, ethereally lovely in ivory satin and orange blossoms, in the vestibule of St. Nicholas's, arranging her veil of creamy white lace about her. "Beth, you look beautiful," she said, standing back to admire her handiwork. "Lieutenant Bancroft is a lucky man."

"Thank you." Beth flashed her a smile. "I intend to see to it he knows it, too."

Anne laughed. Beth had changed since coming to Brighton. Gone was the shy, plain girl who had allowed others to rule her life; in her place was a vibrant, confident, serene woman. "Good for you."

"Oh, I can't thank you enough, for all you've done." Beth grasped her hands. "And I'm so glad you agreed to be my matron of honor. I want this to be a special day. I want Thomas to have happy memories."

Anne tweaked the veil again, and then stepped back, picking up her own bouquet. "Why shouldn't he? You and he are going to have a happy life together."

Beth's smile dimmed, and her serenity momentarily faltered. "He's leaving next week. Oh, Anne, I don't know if I can bear it."

"Beth." Ane grasped her hand. "You'll find you can bear whatever you have to."

"I know. And I shan't cry. Thomas deserves better." She smiled again, and it was as if the dark moment had never been. "But, oh, Anne, stand by me! I shall need you so."

"Of course I will." Anne patted her hand, impressed and a little surprised. There were depths of strength in Beth she had never suspected were there. Thomas Bancroft would leave for his post next week, never realizing how unhappy his bride was. She would make the leave-taking easy for him, and that took courage. Anne only hoped she would be as strong when the time came for her to leave, too.

"Giles." Beth held out her hand as he slipped into the vestibule from the church. "Is Mother all settled?"

"Yes." He smiled down at her as he tucked her hand through his arm. "It's time, Bethie. Your lieutenant is waiting for you."

Beth's smile was brilliant. "Wish me happy, Giles?"

"You know I do." He bent to kiss her cheek, catching Anne's eyes as he straightened. Her own eyes faltered, and she went to stand before them, waiting for the processional music to begin. She could feel his gaze on her back. Why was he looking at her so? It was an intent gaze, a burning gaze, quite inappropriate for a wedding. For someone else's wedding, she thought, and felt suddenly very warm.

To Anne's eternal gratitude the music began, and she stepped down the aisle. People smiled at her, and then past her, at Beth. At last she was at the altar, taking Beth's bouquet, helping her with her veil. Then there was nothing for her to do but to step back and watch the wedding.

And to see Giles, who had returned to his seat in the first pew, next to Julia, staring at her.

Anne's throat went dry. It wasn't that he was so handsome, although in his gray morning coat, immac-

318

ulate and impeccable, he was. It wasn't just that he was looking at her as no other man ever had, with a barely disguised hunger that both scared and elated her, and a tenderness that was vastly reassuring. It was also where they were and what they were doing, and what might have been between them, had fate not intervened. She felt, not like a bridesmaid, but like the bride.

> *I, Giles . . .*
> *I, Anne . . .*
> *Take thee to be my lawful wedded wife . . .*
> *. . . My lawful wedded husband . . .*
> *To have and to hold, Anne . . .*
> *In richer and poorer . . .*
> *For better, for worse . . .*
> *From this day forward . . .*
> *Forever, Anne.*
> *Forever, Giles.*

"You may now kiss the bride," the minister said, and Anne jumped, coming back to reality. Not her wedding at all, though Giles was still looking at her, his lips slightly puckered. Flustered, Anne stepped forward, to help Beth fold her veil back from her face, and then watched, smiling, as Lieutenant Bancroft and his bride exchanged their first kiss as man and wife. Instinctively her eyes sought Giles's, to share the moment, and again his lips moved. She quickly glanced away, feeling her cheeks go pink and her own lips tingle, just as if he had kissed her. Heavens! What was wrong with her? She hadn't felt this way even at her own wedding.

Beth and Thomas left the church among a hail of congratulations and a shower of rice. Anne, escorted by Lieutenant Seward, the best man, smiled and smiled, but her mind was far away. She felt as married now as she ever had, as if she had indeed gone through the ceremony. Something had happened to her when she had looked at Giles. Without her realizing it, the last of her fears had slipped away, leaving her free. She was whole again, herself again. The scars from her marriage had healed, leaving her stronger. She could do anything she wanted to do, including marry again, if she so desired. This time, though she knew more. This time she would be more careful in her choice.

Her eyes sought Giles's. He was standing at the bottom of the church steps, his hand at Julia's elbow, supporting her. As if he felt Anne's gaze, he looked up. He smiled at her, a smile of complicity and shared secrets, a smile meant for her alone. Giles wasn't Freddie. For the first time she felt the truth of that deep within herself. Nor was she the same as she once had been. Giles had his faults, but brutishness was not among them. Even had it been, she needn't fear that she would lose all she had worked so hard for, her precious self-confidence and independence. Those would always be a part of her, no matter what she chose to do with her life. No man could ever take them away from her again.

And so she returned the smile, adding to it her own message, an unspoken promise, knowing Giles would understand. Weddings affected Anne, made her feel romantic, but there was more than that at work here. At last she had overcome the past, and the future lay before her. A future with Giles.

The wedding breakfast was joyful and noisy, with all their friends crowding into the drawing room and drinking toast after toast to the newly married couple. In the midst of the celebration Anne had little chance to talk with Giles, but occasionally their eyes would meet across the room, his sending her a message too potent to be ignored. Soon, she thought. Soon.

At length it was time for the newlyweds to start on their brief wedding journey. Beth began up the stairs to change into her traveling ensemble, and the guests crowded into the hall to watch her go. Halfway up she stopped, ready to toss her bouquet to the small group of unmarried girls who had gathered under the stairs. Then, scanning the crowd, she hesitated.

"Go!" Felicity hissed in Anne's ear, pushing her toward the stairs.

Anne stumbled, off-balance, and caught at the wall to save herself. "But I've been married!"

"You're a widow. Go! Beth wants you to catch the bouquet."

"What?" Anne said, but Felicity's hands were at her back, pushing her through the girls to the very front of the group. People murmured around her, some in resentment, and she looked up to see Beth, smiling with satisfaction. *No,* Anne mouthed at her, but the same mischief that sometimes appeared in Giles's eyes gleamed in Beth's. With a pitch that would have done a cricket player proud, she hauled her arm back and threw the bouquet straight at Anne. Other hands grabbed out at it, other girls surged forward for it. Instinct made Anne throw up her arms, to protect her face. Instinct made her catch the flowers when they touched her hands, instinct, and something else. Suddenly she very badly wanted this bouquet, and what it symbolized. Her fingers caught at the trailing silk ribbons before the bouquet could fall to the floor, caught and held. She hauled it up, until she was holding it close, like a bride. Someone in the crowd laughed, and someone near her muttered in disappointment. She didn't care. Looking up, she smiled at Beth. There was a certain inevitability about this. It was another step in the long journey that would, at last, bring her back to Giles.

Beth turned to continue up the stairs, and the small moment of drama was over. The guests broke up into smaller groups, talking and chatting. Anne stood, smiling down at the flowers. Her own hurried wedding hadn't been like this at all. There had been no guests, no music, no flowers, only the minister and his wife, to stand as witness. If she married again—when she married again—she would do things properly.

"So," a voice said beside her, cold and stern, and Anne looked down to see Julia. "I suppose you think now you are going to marry my son."

Chapter 23

Anne caught her breath. In the midst of all the gaiety and happiness, Julia sounded as malicious and venomous as ever. Looking down at her, though, Anne saw something in Julia's eyes she'd never noticed there before: bewilderment, bravado, unhappiness. Above all else was fear. Fear of what, Anne didn't know, but she could guess. It made her voice soften with compassion when she spoke.

"You and I need to talk," she said, taking Julia's arm.

"Indeed we do, madam." Julia didn't budge. "However, you know what I think of you."

Anne glanced quickly past her. Several people were gazing at them with interest. This was not a conversation she wanted to have before witnesses, for both their sakes. "I'll speak with you in private later. I don't wish to ruin Beth's day."

Julia's eyes narrowed, but she nodded. "Very well, madam. We'll talk when Elizabeth is gone."

The newlyweds left a little while later in another shower of rice, Beth looking radiant in a traveling dress of sky blue, Thomas handsome in a well-cut coat of dark blue superfine. Guests and well-wishers ran after their carriage, and then they were gone. The wedding was over. Slowly the guests began to drift away, until only the family and a few friends were left.

323

The people sitting in the drawing room were quiet, pleasantly tired and lost in thought. "A fine wedding," Felicity said finally. "Beth looked so beautiful. Though doesn't it feel funny without her here?"

Giles, standing at the mantel, smiled. "We'll have her back soon," he said, his eyes meeting Anne's with such warmth that she had to look away. Everything had changed: Beth would return, of course, while her husband went off to fight, but she would be different. There was also the little matter of what was between her and Giles. The thought made Anne tingle with excitement and anticipation.

"I am tired," Julia declared, rising with some difficulty. "Weddings can be difficult affairs. Help me upstairs, Anne."

Giles moved away from the mantel. "Mother, let me—"

"I want Anne." Julia's chin was raised.

"It's no trouble, Giles," Anne murmured, crossing the room. She was aware that Giles was regarding her with surprise, but she ignored him. For now.

"You have a good, strong arm," Julia said as the two moved off, out of the room and toward the stairs.

"Thank you, ma'am," Anne murmured, amused. It was the first time Julia had ever said anything the least complimentary to her.

"It comes of working on a farm, I suppose."

"Probably. Here, mind that step, we don't want you falling." Slowly they took the stairs, Julia leaning heavily on the younger woman, and at last reaching her sitting room. Julia was old, Anne realized again. Old, and the world was changing all around her.

"There, ma'am." Anne bent to place a stool under Julia's feet as she sat. "Shall I ring for your maid?"

Julia glared at her. "I don't need your pity, madam."

"I wouldn't dare pity you, ma'am." Anne crossed the room to close the door, and then sat facing the duchess. For a moment they eyed each other, taking their measure. Julia was old, yes, Anne thought, but still well in control of her faculties. Underestimating her would be a mistake. She was still a formidable enemy. Except, Anne thought, she no longer wanted to fight with this woman. "Well, ma'am?"

"I owe you an apology," Julia said abruptly. "I never meant your son to be hurt."

Impulsively Anne reached over and laid her hand on Julia's cool, wrinkled one. "I know. I know you care about Jamie."

"Hmph." Julia glared down at Anne's hand, making Anne feel as if she had been inordinately impertinent. "If your son behaved as he should, nothing would have happened to him."

"Jamie is only a boy."

"Hmph. And you are much too indulgent a mother."

"I—!" Anne stared at her. "You dare to criticize the way *I* raise my child?"

"My son would never have done the things your son has."

"Your son did," Anne said, recovering her sense of humor. "Or have you forgotten?"

"Giles is a good boy."

"Giles is a man." Anne's voice was gentle. "Just as Beth is a woman. It's time to let them go, don't you think?"

Julia looked away. "I had three sons," she said finally. "Three sons, and two daughters. Losing my two babies was hard enough, but when Edward died . . ." Her voice trailed off.

Anne's fingers tightened together. "I can't imagine it, ma'am. I don't know what I would do if anything happened to Jamie. When I realized he was missing that night—" Her voice cracked. "I think you must be very brave, to carry on as you have."

"One does what one has to." She looked at Anne then, no longer a disagreeable old woman, but a mother. "My children mean everything to me. I would do anything I had to to keep them from harm. Anything, d'you hear?"

"I understand. But they're grown now."

"Hmph. They still need my guidance."

"They need to make their own mistakes, and learn from them." Anne paused. "As I did."

Julia raised her quizzing glass. It was, Anne supposed, meant to intimidate her, but she would not give in. She looked right back, and Julia was the first to look away.

"You always were a flighty girl. Not the kind to make a good duchess."

"Giles is a man. He needs more than a duchess. And pray don't tell me, ma'am, that people in our station don't require love. I lived in a loveless marriage. I know what it's like."

"I suppose you expect me to apologize for that, too."

"Oh, no," Anne said, making Julia look at her in surprise. "I will admit I was angry when I learned what you'd done, but it wasn't all your fault. If I'd stayed and confronted Giles, instead of running away, I never would have married Freddie. But I would not give up my years in Jamaica, and I certainly would not give up Jamie."

There was a gleam in Julia's eyes that Anne couldn't quite identify. "You've got spirit, girl. I'll give you that. So you're not scared of me, eh?"

"No. At least, not anymore."

Julia cackled and, to her own surprise, Anne smiled. "You'll do, girl, you'll do. I still don't think you're right for Giles," she said, very direct.

"Why not?" Anne asked, equally direct.

"You're still flighty. You'll distract him, girl. Giles has duties and responsibilities."

"He also has a life, ma'am. He'd never ignore what he sees as his duty, but there's more to life than that." Anne leaned forward. "Surely you haven't forgotten that, have you? Don't you remember what it's like to be young? To want to enjoy life, and to live every day to its fullest? Giles needs that, ma'am. He is the duke, yes, but he is also a man."

"I'm sure I never neglected my duty, miss."

"No, and I'm sure that you never allowed anyone to tell you what to do, either."

Julia stared at her, and then let out another cackle. "You're in the right. Went my own way, as much as I could. These milk-and-water misses today—bah. At least you're not like them, I'll give you that."

"Thank you. I think."

"Oh, it's a compliment, girl. I've always rather liked you, you know."

"You're bamming me!"

"Oh, no. I like a girl with spirit."

"Good heavens." Anne stared at her. "If you feel that way about me, why were you so opposed to my marrying Giles?"

Julia looked away, and her voice when she spoke was barely a whisper. "Because you would have taken him away from me."

Anne sat back, stunned. Julia feared her. All these years Anne had thought her a monstrous old woman, and now she knew the truth. Julia had fought as hard as she had, because she was afraid. "I suppose I would have," she said finally.

"And you still would."

"No." Anne shook her head. "No. Seven years ago I was young and foolish and probably selfish. I'm not the same girl I was, then. I've learned a lot. I would never come between a mother and her child." She paused. "So long as that mother didn't come between my husband and me."

"You're telling me not to interfere, missy?"

"Yes, I suppose I am telling you exactly that."

"Hmph. You'd have me believe, I suppose, that you wouldn't do all you could to protect your son."

"Of course I would, but—"

"But me no buts. You don't show it, missy, but you're as protective a mother as I am."

"I'm not!"

"Aren't you? Oh, yes, I know you've opposed every plan Giles has made for James. Well, it's high time you faced the truth. James will need an education, and he'll need to be acquainted with his peers. He can't get either in some colony."

"But that is where he will live—"

"Hmph. You don't want to give him up, that's what it is. And you tell me I should let go."

"I—" Anne began, and stopped, staring at her. "I'm doing what's best for him."

Julia smiled grimly. "Precisely. And you won't admit that someone else might have better ideas."

Anne jumped up and paced to the window, her hands balled into fists at her side. "He's my son."

"So he is. And someday he'll be a man who'll need more than you can give him. As my son needs more than I can give." Her voice softened. "Easy to tell someone else how to raise her children, isn't it?"

Anne turned from the window, her eyes looking blind. "I—my God. I never thought I'd be saying this, but you're right."

"Of course I'm right. I usually am." Julia put her hands on the arms of her chair and, with much creaking of her stays, pushed herself to her feet. "I am tired. Ring for my maid, girl."

"Yes, of course," Anne murmured, crossing to the bell cord. "I—you've given me a great deal to think about."

"Good. You don't know everything, do you, missy?"

"No." Anne laughed. "You are a terrible old woman."

"I know. And don't you forget it."

"Oh, I won't." The smile Anne gave her, though, was warmer than any she'd exchanged with Julia in the past. For the first time, she understood the other woman. The knowledge she had received about herself was harder to assimilate. "Have a good rest, ma'am," she said, and, curtsying, left the room.

The house was quiet. Without Anne's even realizing it, evening had fallen. No longer were the days so long as they had been, a sure sign that autumn was coming. In the dusk, Anne looked into Jamie's room, to see him sprawled atop the covers of his bed, fast asleep. Poor lamb, he must be worn out from the excitements of the day. She brushed his tangled curls back from his face and bent to kiss him. Her son. Julia was right. She would do anything she had to, to protect him. In most cases, that was as it should be, but not all. Not when her protectiveness turned into overprotectiveness.

Blinking, Anne resisted the temptation to haul Jamie into her arms and rock him back and forth. He wouldn't welcome it. He was her son, but he was also a person, and that was what she had forgotten. Strange, she thought, at last going to her own room, that it was Julia, of all people, who'd made her see it. Sinking down in her chair, she shuddered. She had so nearly made the same mistakes as Julia had. She would have held her son fast, doing everything for him in her need to provide him with the happy family life she had never had, and what would have happened? She would have lost him. Already Jamie was independent-minded enough to care when she interfered; how much more so would he be when he was grown? She would, someday, have to let him go, and she had to start now.

Leaning her head back against her chair, she smiled. Lord, what a day it had been. First the wedding, emotional as that had been, followed by that mysterious, wordless exchange with Giles. Now, this. Nothing she had held true seemed quite right anymore. If Giles had changed this summer, becoming more open and lighthearted, then so had she. She had learned some truths about herself, and about others, that weren't always pleasant. Giles had not betrayed her; Julia was not wicked; and she, herself, had made her life what it was. She had no one else to blame now, or in the future, for how she lived.

Someone, probably her maid, had brought in the bridal bouquet and laid it on the dressing table. Spying it, Anne rose and crossed to pick it up, burying her face in the fragrant blossoms. So she was to be the next bride. Amazing. Not so astounding as it once might have seemed, though. She loved Giles, with her whole heart and soul and body; she always had. The thought of leaving him was intolerable. The only question was, did he love her? He wanted her; that she knew. But love, that was a very different matter. She would not willingly enter into a loveless relationship again.

There was more noise in the house as Anne descended the stairs. Though the guests had gone, she could hear the servants in the hall below, chattering as they cleaned. Anne glanced quickly into the drawing room, already neat and tidy, and turned away, disappointed. Not a sign of Giles, when she wanted so badly to see him. She would simply have to look someplace else, and that might be difficult, with the servants about. She spun on her heel, and came up against Giles.

For a moment, she couldn't move. Had her life depended on it, she couldn't have moved. She was caught there, held, by the burnished silver glow in his eyes, gazing down at her. It was quite improper, really, for them to stand like this, her breasts pressed against his chest, her thighs against his, feeling their hard-muscled strength. Quite improper, with the servants just downstairs, but she didn't want to move. Then Giles stepped back, a little smile on his face.

"Anne, the servants," he said in an exaggerated whisper, and she spun around, deeply and unaccountably hurt. Why must he mock her, after all that had happened between them today? What, though, had happened? Nothing, really. An exchange of glances. Deep, soul-searing glances, true, but only glances. A brief touch. Something that was almost, but not quite, an embrace. And a bouquet tossed, and caught. Nothing but dreams and fancies. Nothing had changed. She had been foolish to think it had.

"Annie." Giles's hand rested on her shoulder, and she stilled. "Don't go."

"I—came down for a book."

"The book-room is downstairs."

"Then I'll go—"

"No. Keep me company for a moment." His hand slipped down to her elbow, the caress sending shivers through her. Dazed, she allowed him to escort her into the drawing room and close the door behind them.

"I really should see how Jamie is," she managed to protest as he steered her over to the sofa.

"Jamie is asleep." Giles turned from the table, where he was pouring each of them a drink. "Sherry, my dear?"

"Yes. How do you know that about Jamie?"

"I looked in on him."

"He's my son, Giles."

"I never said otherwise."

"You—oh." She put the back of her hand to her forehead. "Forgive me, but I just had the most extraordinary interview with your mother."

Giles paused, and then handed her a crystal goblet of sherry. "Is that where you were?"

"Yes, for part of the time. Were you looking for me?"

"I was wondering where you'd disappeared to." He sat beside her, so close that she would have shifted away from him, except that she was already sitting in the corner. "What did you speak of?"

"This and that." She looked down at her glass. "I

understand her a great deal more, now."

Giles covered her hand with his free one. "Do you? I'm glad. Not that it would matter."

Anne looked up at him, startled. "What do you mean?"

"We've let enough come between us, Annie. And we've both taken care of other peoples' needs long enough. Isn't it time we saw to our own?"

There was no pretense in Anne's eyes, huge and deep blue, no evasion. Inside her was a growing sense of elation, overtaking her hard-won caution. "What does that mean, Giles?" she whispered, turning her hand to twine her fingers with his.

Giles twisted and set his glass down on the sofa table. "This morning, Annie, when Beth and Thomas were married, I felt like I was the one saying the vows."

"Yes."

"I felt—I don't know. A connection between us that's never been there before."

"No, never."

His fingers caressed her cheek. "Not even seven years ago."

"Not even yesterday."

"I've been blind, Annie. Blind, and stupid. When I first saw you again—but I thought it was a passing fancy. A summer folly."

"I thought it was folly, too. But then I realized . . ."

"What?"

"We have a second chance."

Giles gazed at her a moment, and then reached to take her glass from her, setting it down. "I know you had a rough time with Freddie, Anne," he said softly, still stroking her cheek. "I can understand how you feel about marriage. But we have time, sweetheart, now that we've found each other again."

Anne turned and pressed a swift kiss on his palm, making his hand jerk. "I think it wasn't meant to be."

332

"What?"

"Our being together seven years ago. Oh, poor Giles, did you think I meant now?"

"You did give me rather a scare."

"I am sorry." Again she kissed his hand, imprisoning it in both of hers. "We're different people from who we were then. Better people, I think. I know I am." She smiled brilliantly at him. "I would have led you a merry dance, Giles."

"As if you didn't, this summer," he said, but he was smiling. "You turned my life upside down."

"And mine."

"Yes, I know. I meant what I said, Annie. We've time."

Slowly, Anne lowered their linked hands. "But I don't need time, Giles."

"Annie—"

"Are you going to make me say it first?"

"What?"

"You know quite well, what."

Giles leaned back, his arm stretched out across the back of the sofa. "Do you know, I think I just might? I've waited a long time to hear those words."

"What words?"

"I love you."

"Oh, Giles, I love you, too!" Anne said, and threw herself at him, laughing. "You did say it first."

"You tricked me into it." He grinned down at her, now in his arms, her face raised to him. Slowly, his smile faded. His Annie, in his arms again. "I do love you, Anne," he said, his voice low. "I never stopped loving you. I tried, but I couldn't."

"I know." She reached up and slipped her arm around his neck. "I tried to forget you, I really did, but then something would happen to remind me of you. I'd hear a jest I thought you'd enjoy, or Jamie would turn his head a certain way and look so like you, or I'd

333

dream about you."

"Oh?" His smile was teasing. "What kind of dreams?"

"Good dreams. Sad ones. I'd have to forget you all over again."

Giles's face was very close. "And all the time I was here, waiting."

"For me?" she whispered, feathering her fingers through his hair.

"For you," Giles said, and at last lowered his mouth to hers.

It was a long, slow kiss, a kiss of promise. Now that they had found each other again, there was no need to rush. They had been separated, true, but now they were together, and the future was theirs. Anne lazily ran her fingers through Giles's hair, her lips parting as his came down on hers, again and again. His arms held her in a close, but not confining, embrace. Here was a man who would hold to her forever, but who, at last, understood how important it was to her that she remain herself and not become a part of him. And because of that giving, she very much wanted to be part of him.

It was Anne who surged up against Giles, pressing her breasts against his chest and wrapping her arms tightly around his neck. It was Anne who twisted her head, urgently seeking for ways to deepen the kiss, to prolong the intimacy. Giles grunted low in his throat, in passion or surprise, and caught her to him, his hands on her hips holding her fast. This was good, this was right. There was no fear of what might happen. Giles wouldn't hurt her. Giles would love her, for herself.

"Annie." Giles pulled back, and she followed, pressing kisses on his cheeks, his chin, his throat. "Annie, this has to stop."

"Why?" she murmured, stretching to catch his lips with hers. He let himself be caught for just a moment, and then pulled away again.

"This isn't the place, Anne." Putting his hands on her

334

waist, he lifted her and set her firmly away from him. "Not with servants just downstairs."

"We could lock the door," she suggested, smiling impishly.

"Annie."

"Don't you want me, Giles?"

He looked at her lower lip, thrust outward in a mock pout, and then down, to the low neckline of her gown. "Oh, yes. Very much. Too much. But when we make love, Annie, we'll do it right. Not hurriedly on a sofa, afraid someone might come in at any moment, but properly—"

"Giles, Giles. Must everything be proper?"

"—in a bed, with candles lit all around and nothing between us, Annie. No nightgown, no nightshirt. And all the time in the world for me to love you." Very slowly, giving her a secret smile, he trailed his fingertips along the neckline of her gown, making her shiver. "That's properly, love."

"Oh," she said inadequately.

"And it will be soon."

Anne looped her arms around his neck; she very badly wanted to feel his hands on her again. "Why not now?" she murmured, her voice low.

"Annie." He shook his head at her, smiling. "What of your reputation?"

"There are times, sir, when I consider a reputation to be a vastly overrated commodity."

"I don't agree. I won't have people talking about my duchess."

Anne went very still. "Your duchess?"

"Of course. You will marry me, Anne."

"I will?" Delight tingled through her. "Have I any say in the matter?"

"Have—oh. Of course you do." Suddenly he looked endearingly uncertain. "Annie, you do want to marry me, don't you? I know you were unhappy with Freddie, but—"

"But he's gone." She placed a finger on his lips, stilling him. "Oh, Giles, of course I'll marry you. How could you doubt it?"

A slow smile spread across Giles's face. Anne expected him to take her into his arms; instead, to her surprise, he jumped to his feet and began pacing back and forth. "Capital. Capital. I should have known this was coming from the first moment I saw you again, but I didn't. But now we can make plans." He bent to plant a kiss full on her lips, and then resumed pacing again. "There's much we have to do."

"Giles." Anne laughed a little. "We have time."

"Yes, yes, but we want to do this right. I've a duty, you know."

"Duty?"

"Yes, to my title. A duke cannot just plan some hole-and-corner affair for a marriage."

"No, of course not. I want a nice wedding, too, Giles, but—"

"It will be at Tremont, of course. Mother will probably want us to wait and marry at Saint George's in London, but—"

"But it's not her wedding, Giles."

"The chapel at Tremont is small," he went on, as if he hadn't heard her. "We won't be able to invite many to the wedding itself. We'll ask the Prince of Wales, though, and hope he'll honor us by his presence."

"Yes, and my family."

"Of course. Damn, being a duke, there are others I must ask, too. We'll work that out with my mother."

"Giles, not now." Anne held out her hand as he wheeled to the door. "Surely there are other matters we can discuss between ourselves." She smiled. "The honeymoon trip, for example. Oh, Giles, we should both go back to Jamaica. It would be perfect. You could see the plantation and help me decide how it should be run—"

"You don't have to worry about the plantation," he

336

interrupted. "Obadiah will be the overseer, just as you wished."

"But who is to manage it, if not me?"

"We'll find someone."

"Giles, it's my son's property—"

"And I'm Jamie's guardian. Do you think he'll mind, having me as a father?" He grinned at her. "He'll be glad to stay in England—"

"He dislikes England."

"—where he belongs. I'll write to the headmaster at Eton. In the meantime I'll arrange for a tutor for him."

"Giles." Anne was standing, all traces of a smile gone. "Am I to have no say in any of this?"

"Of course you will." He grinned at her. "You'll be my duchess."

"Do you want a duchess, Giles, or a wife?"

"Both. Definitely, a wife." He gave her what could only be called a leer, and she relaxed a very little bit. "It'll be a different life for you, Anne, from what you're used to, but I know you'll cope. You'll make a magnificent duchess. You'll have duties, of course—"

"No! No, Giles."

He stopped and looked at her in surprise. "No? What do you mean, no?"

"Duties, Giles. Life is not all duty."

"Annie." His smile was at its most winning. "All the time you managed Hampshire Hall, was that not out of duty?"

"No. It was out of love, and choice."

"Oh, well." He dismissed that with a wave of his hand. "It amounts to the same thing."

"No, it doesn't, Giles." She stared at him, frustrated. Giles hadn't changed. He was a man raised to do his duty, and he could not see that there was a difference between doing that duty willingly, out of love, and being coerced into it. He didn't want a wife so much as he wanted a duchess, one that would do whatever he expected of her. Giles would be as much of a jailer,

337

albeit a gentle one, as Freddie ever had been.

"Never mind." He walked toward her, his hands outstretched. "We'll be happy, Anne. I'll make you happy."

Anne eluded his grasp, slipping behind the sofa and leaving him staring at her in surprise. "Oh, Giles. Don't you see? You can't make me happy, as if it's part of your duty. You have to let me *be* happy."

"What?" He frowned at her. "Anne, what is this?"

She stared at him in dismay. "You really don't understand, do you?"

"I understand only that you are coming up with some nonsensical objections, my love."

"They're not nonsense! Oh, Giles. I cannot do this. I cannot live the rest of my life allowing a man to order my life. I need more freedom than that."

"Freedom!" Giles stared up at the ceiling, as if searching for control, and then looked back at her. "What the hell is freedom, Anne, but loneliness?"

"Self-respect, Giles." She faced him calmly. Inside her was an aching, empty void, and yet she knew she could not give in to him. Not on his terms. "Peace of mind. Independence. I've fought very hard for all of those things. I'm not about to give them up now."

"For God's sake, Anne! What do you need with those? You're only a woman."

Anne froze. "Who should be grateful for a man's guidance? Is that what you're saying, Giles?"

"Yes. No! Annie, for God's sake, what is all this? I love you. You love me. Why isn't that enough for you?"

"Because you don't love me, Giles. Me." She came around the sofa, pointing at her chest. "You love some idea of me that you have, of what you think I should be. You'd try to make me into that woman, Giles, you'd try very hard. And little by little, I'd turn into her, until you wouldn't know who I was anymore. I wouldn't know who I was. And anything I feel for you would die. Oh,

338

Giles, please try to understand! I don't want that to happen."

"I'm trying to, Annie." His brow wrinkled in a frown. "I'm trying to understand. I don't want to coerce you into anything. I only want you to be happy."

"I know that, Giles."

"What more can I do, Annie? I'm offering you everything you could possibly want."

"At a very high price, Giles. I'd have to stop being me. I won't do that. Not for you, not for anyone."

"Are you saying you won't marry me?"

Anne briefly closed her eyes. "Yes, Giles. I'm afraid that is what I'm saying."

Chapter 24

Giles took a step toward her. "My God, Anne—"

"No!" Anne held out her hands to ward him off, and he stopped. "No, please, don't come near me!"

"My God." He stopped. "Are you afraid of me?"

"No, Giles." It was herself she feared. If he came close, if he touched her, she would melt. She would dissolve in the nearness of him, and then she would truly be lost. And so would he.

Giles paced away. "You think I'm like Freddie, don't you?" he accused.

"In some ways, yes."

"By God, Anne, I am not like him! I would never lay a finger on you."

"I know that." Anne's smile was sad. "But you would hurt me anyway, Giles. You wouldn't mean to, you wouldn't know you were, but you would. And I'd hurt you in return. I can't do that to you, Giles." She swallowed, hard. "I love you too much."

"You won't marry me because you love me?"

"I know it sounds strange, but, yes."

"Women!" He thrust his hand into his hair again. "I will never understand women. I'm giving you my heart, Annie, my soul. What more do you want from me?"

"Your respect." Giles opened his mouth to speak, and then closed it. "I cannot marry you, Giles. I cannot

340

lose myself again."

"I see." He straightened, suddenly very much the duke. Helplessly Anne watched as the light left his eyes, leaving them dark and opaque. She had thought he understood her, her desires, her needs. Now she knew he didn't. There was no mending this situation. "What will you do, then?"

Anne lifted her chin. "Return to Jamaica, before the winter storms set in."

"I see."

"Jamie belongs there, with his people. However, I do agree with you that he needs an education. Do you think we could find a tutor to come back with us?"

Giles inclined his head. "We shall advertise for one."

"Good. Then, when Jamie is old enough, he can return to attend university here."

"As you wish, madam." Giles turned away, and paused at the door. "You won't change your mind?"

She almost gave in, then. She almost ran to him, almost threw her arms around him, begging him not to go, promising that she would be anything, everything, he wanted her to be, if he would only love her. Only pride held her still. "No, Giles."

"So be it." He opened the door. "I'll make arrangements for your passage," he said, and went out.

"Thank you," Anne said, but he was already gone. She was alone and, as she sank down onto the sofa, she thought about what had just transpired. She had won. She had got what she wanted, had done the right thing. Why, then, did it hurt so much?

Anne put her face in her hands, and stayed there for a very long time.

Summer was over. The Prince of Wales reluctantly made arrangements to leave Brighton, where he was well liked, for London, where he was not. Many would be returning with him, for the Little Season, but most people were returning to their estates. There was the harvest to be got in, and after that was Christmas, when no right-thinking man would be from home. It was time to move onto other amusements, and duties.

A ship waited in Portsmouth harbor, ready to sail with the tide for Jamaica. On the shore Giles stood, watching as a long boat rowed out from the quay, carrying everything he held dear. Anne. He'd lost her, After finally finding her again he had lost her, and he didn't really know why. Seven years ago, perhaps he hadn't been as understanding as he should have been, as attentive, but surely he had made up for that now. Good God, he'd said he'd give her all the time she needed, and all she could do was spout some nonsense about respect and independence. Of course he respected her. If he didn't, he wouldn't want to marry her. His feeling for her aside, he needed someone wise and intelligent to be his duchess. A man had his duties, after all. And she had dared to say he reminded her of Freddie? The memory still rankled. He was nothing like Freddie, damn it! If she couldn't see that, then perhaps he was better off without her. But he didn't really believe it. God, how could he ever let her go?

The long boat bumped against the ship's hull, and a rope ladder was lowered down. Carefully Anne began to climb, blinking back the salt spray that threatened to blind her. It had to be spray; what else could it be? She would not cry for that man, not anymore. She had spent enough tears on him, and they had done her little good.

Safely on deck, she turned to help Jamie, who scrambled aboard like a little monkey. Standing sturdily on legs already braced against the sway of the ship, he glared at Anne. "I don't want to go," he declared.

"I know." Anne put her hand on his shoulder, and he jerked away. "But, really, Jamie, once we're back in

342

Jamaica, you'll be happy. It's much better there than here."

"No, it isn't." His lower lip thrust forward mutinously. "My pony's not there."

"Jamie, we'll get you another pony."

"Don't want another pony. I want to stay here with Uncle Giles and Aunt Julia."

"Oh, Jamie."

"I'll take him below, ma'am." Their new nurse, a young, no-nonsense woman with the saving grace of humor, came forward and took Jamie's hand. "He's overt-i-r-e-d," she said, resorting to spelling so Jamie wouldn't understand.

"I'm not tired, Mommy!"

"Of course not, pet." Anne smiled at him. "Why don't you take Nurse below and show her where everything is?" She went down on one knee. "She's never been to sea before, you know. You'll have to help her get used to everything."

Jamie gave her a look that said clearly that he saw through that nonsense, but he didn't protest when Nurse took his hand. "All right. I'll go. But I don't want to, and you can't make me!"

"Oh, dear." Anne rose to her feet as Jamie walked away. "He's terribly angry with me, Obadiah."

Obadiah glanced at Jamie, and then turned back to her. "Are you sure you're doin' the right thing, lady?"

"Oh, Diah, not you, too?"

"The duke doesn't want you to go. Could see it in his eyes, lady."

"Diah—"

"I said I saw hauntings, a dragon, and a fair knight, lady, when we arrived."

"You were jesting."

"Yes, lady. But we did have the hauntings and the dragon."

Anne looked away. "I don't want a fair knight,

343

Diah," she said finally. "I want a man. But he wants a duchess."

"He wants *you* for his duchess. There's a difference, lady."

"Not much." Anne looked up at the sails, and sighed. "Well, we're here, Diah. There's no turning back."

"Not if you don't want to, lady." He bowed. "Best I go see everything's settled below."

Anne smiled. "Thank you, Diah," she said, and moved away.

The wind was fresh, offshore. The tide was just coming to the full and soon would turn, rushing out to sea again. With it would go the ship, to meet the convoy with which it would travel across the Atlantic, protected from Napoleon's navy. The crew scurried about the deck, raising the anchor, readying lines, unfurling sail. Careful to keep out of everyone's way, Anne made her way aft, to the stern of the ship. With the captain's compliments, she had been invited to stand on the quarterdeck as they cast off. From there she would have the best vantage point to see their departure.

At the taffrail in the stern of the ship, she stopped. Before her lay a forest of mast and spars, and, farther away, the waterfront of Portsmouth. All was hustle and bustle there, except for one still figure at the end of the quay near the steps, a man dressed in gray. Anne caught her breath. Giles. Even at this distance she recognized him. Giles, watching her. Oh, if she had wings to fly to him, to tell him she didn't want to leave, if he would only take her back.

The figure on shore raised his hand in salute, and then turned, striding away. Anne's shoulders slumped. He was gone, and with him went every chance of happiness. It was what she had wanted, what she had asked for. Her self-respect was intact. Her precious, bloody, lonely self-respect.

Anne raised her head. She'd made her choice. Once again she was leaving, rather than face a fight she couldn't win. The time for looking back was past. She would look forward to the future, no matter how bleak it seemed, and bare. It was all she had.

Giles strode into the private parlor he had taken at the inn, slapping his gloves down on the table and striding across to the window. "They're gone," he said.

Beth, sitting over her embroidery, looked up. "The ship has sailed?"

"No. But the tide was about to turn. By now, they're gone." Beth murmured something, and he turned to look at her. "What was that you said?"

Beth secured her needle in her work before answering. "I said, 'tis a pity."

"I don't need pity, Beth. Yours or anyone else's."

"Oh, I don't pity you. Men who behave stupidly are hardly deserving of pity."

Giles stared at her. "What did you say?"

"You let her go, Giles. I find that remarkably stupid."

"She wanted to go."

"You should have made her want to stay."

"How?" he shouted. "She didn't want to. My God, I told her we'd marry, I told her she'd be my duchess, and all she could do was prate on about respect and independence. My God, what does she expect from a man?"

"You told her that?" Beth stared at him, her embroidery bunched in her lap. "Oh, Giles. Even you couldn't be so stupid!"

"I am not stupid, damn it! I offered her everything, Beth. Everything I could give her."

"Except the one thing she really wants."

"What is that?"

"She told you. Respect."

"Respect. Damn it, what does that mean?"

Beth rose and crossed to him, laying her hand on his

345

arm. "Oh, Giles. Don't you know Anne by now? Order her to do something, and she'll do the exact opposite. But talk to her reasonably, and she'll do anything, if she thinks it's right. You can't browbeat Anne into things, Giles."

"I didn't browbeat her." He paused. "At least, I didn't mean to."

"No, I'm sure you didn't. You do have a tendency to tell people what they should do. I know it's your duty. But Anne needs more from you than duty. She needs love." Beth shook her head. "Frederick must have been very cruel to her."

Giles stared at her and closed his mouth with a snap. How did she know that about Anne? Even he hadn't known it, until she had told him. "She seemed to trust me," he said, more to himself than to her, crossing the room and sitting down. "Everything was fine, and then—damn it, then I did start telling her what to do." He raised dazed eyes to her. "I didn't mean to. Surely she knows it's just my way."

"But you changed this summer, Giles. Do you really want to go back to the way you were?"

Giles paused in the middle of answering. Had he changed? Anne seemed to think so, and yet in the middle of the most important moment of his life he had reverted to his old behavior. He had to admit it. In his pride and happiness he had become, not a man in love with a woman, but a duke, arrogant and self-important. It must have sounded to Anne as if it didn't matter to him whether she were his bride, or someone else. This, to a woman who had seen her husband go off with other women. This, to Anne, who had learned, painfully, that she had to control her own destiny, because she could not rely on anyone else. No wonder she had left him.

"My God," he said. "My God, I've been every kind of a fool."

"It's not too late, Giles."

"Yes it is, damn it. She's gone."

"Then go after her. Giles." She leaned forward. "You have a choice. I didn't. I had to let Thomas go. Don't let Anne go."

"She's on a ship! You know me and boats, Beth. It's folly—"

"Sometimes 'tis folly to be wise! If you don't go after her, Giles, you'll never forgive yourself."

"Damn it." Giles stared at her. "Damn it, you're right," he said, and ran from the room.

The tide had turned. Serene and majestic, the great ship sailed out of the harbor, past schooners and frigates and men of war, straining at their anchors, equally anxious to be gone. Above canvas was being spread from every yardarm; below, the ship's wake bubbled in a white froth. They were under way.

Anne stood on the quarterdeck, her hand on her son's shoulder, resolutely facing forward. England was, again, part of her past. She had a plantation to run and her son to raise. Eventually she would find contentment again. Happiness? No, that she couldn't imagine. But contentment, yes.

"Ahoy, the ship!" a man's voice called, strong and determined, audible even over the creaking of the timbers. It sounded like—good heavens, it sounded like Giles!

Anne ran to the rail, Jamie a scant step ahead of her. "Mommy! It's Uncle Giles!" he said, jumping up and down in such excitement that she put her hands on his shoulders, for fear he'd go overboard. "Look, in that little boat."

"My heavens." The words flew involuntarily from Anne's lips. There, bobbing in their wake, was a small boat, occupied by one man. Though their ship was large and fast, by necessity she was proceeding slowly in such a crowded harbor. A small boat could maneuver better among the other ships, which explained why it was able to catch up with them. What was astonishing was the identity of the man in the boat. The sun, coming out from behind a cloud, glinted off his golden hair and touched upon muscles that rippled as he rowed toward them. Giles. What in the world? "Giles?"

He turned in the boat. "Ahoy, Anne," he yelled, half rising, and sat abruptly as the boat rocked. Anne gasped; even from here she could see that his face had turned green.

"Oh, what is he doing, when he hates boats—we must stop!" Wheeling away, she fled across to the deckhouse, where the captain was conferring with the pilot. "Captain! Please, we have to stop."

The captain looked up from his chart. "Are ye daft, ma'am? We can't stop now."

"We have to. There's someone who wants to come aboard."

"Now, ma'am." The captain exchanged a look with the pilot and came forward, taking her arm and speaking in what were evidently meant to be soothing tones. "No one can come aboard. We're under way now, see? Now, I know leaving is powerful hard on ladies, so if ye'll just go below to your cabin—"

"Captain, the Duke of Tremont wishes to come aboard."

"Madam, I wouldn't stop now if it was the king himself."

"Ahoy!" The voice floated up to them, and the captain blinked. "Ahoy the ship! Annie?"

"Cap'n!" A sailor ran up, looking amazed. "Someone's trying to board us from a boat. What should we do?"

"By Neptune, no one comes aboard my ship without permission," the captain growled, and strode to the railing. "Get ye away—Yer Grace!"

Anne leaned over the railing. "Oh, Giles. What do

you think you are doing?" she called.

Giles shipped the oars as he came alongside. Though he hadn't been in a boat for years, clearly he hadn't forgotten how to row. "Good morning, Captain," he said, making a smart salute. "Permission to come aboard, sir?"

"Per—toss down the ladder!" the captain bawled, and stepped back as two of his crew went to work. "By Neptune, I've never seen anything like it. The man must be daft."

Mirth was rising in Anne, like the bubbles of their wake. "Oh, I hope so," she said, earning herself a look from the captain. "I do hope so."

"Uncle Giles!" Jamie, dancing with excitement, threw himself at Giles as he climbed over the side of the ship. Giles tottered a bit, his arms going out automatically around the boy, his eyes searching out Anne. Clad only in pantaloons and a shirt, he looked very masculine, very compelling, and more than a little seasick. "Are you coming with us?"

Giles ruffled Jamie's hair. "If your mother lets me."

"Mommy! Uncle Giles is coming with us!"

Anne sat abruptly on a hatch cover. "You can't—you can't be serious, Giles."

"Why can't I?" Giles stumbled as he crossed the moving deck toward her, and then recovered. "Good morning, Captain."

"Because you hate the sea. Where in the world did you get a boat?"

"I bought it."

"Bought it!"

Giles caught her hands and pulled her to her feet. "It was the only way I could get to you. Annie, don't go." His eyes searched hers. "Don't leave me."

"Oh, Giles—"

"I'll do anything you want. We'll live in Jamaica, we'll never go back to London, anything you want Anne. If you'll only stay with me."

"By Neptune," the captain muttered. By now most of the crew, well disciplined though they were, had left their posts and were staring at the couple on deck, who seemed to have eyes only for each other.

Anne searched his face. "Is it me you want, Giles? Truly? Because I'm not certain I'd make a very good duchess."

"I don't want a duchess. I want a wife," he said, and, hauling her into his arms, kissed her soundly. The crew sent up a ragged cheer, making the captain turn to shout at them, giving orders to heave to. Within a few moments most were back at their posts, and the ship was losing speed.

Anne pushed ineffectually at Giles's chest. "Giles, you are making a spectacle of yourself!"

"I don't care. Marry me, Annie. Please?" His eyes bored into hers, intent and pleading. "I love you. I need you. I don't like what I become without you. You see, I'm not telling you what to do. I'm asking you."

"Oh, Giles." Anne laid her hand on his cheek. "Of course I'll marry you."

Giles's face lit up, and he swung her around, making the crew cheer again. "You won't regret it, Annie," he said into her hair. "I swear to you you won't regret it."

Anne clung tightly to his neck. "I know I won't. But, oh, Giles!" She pulled away. "You've no clothes, and you'd hate an ocean voyage—"

"Of course we'll go on. The captain can marry us, and we'll have our honeymoon in Jamaica." He caught her eye. "That is, if you want to."

"No, I do not want to, Giles Templeton," she scolded, but she was smiling. "I'll not be cheated out of a fine wedding again. We'll return to Tremont and marry with all due pomp and ceremony. After all, you are a duke."

Giles grinned. "So I am. And," he said in a low voice, leaning forward, "I am also a man who loves you very much."

"Mommy?" Jamie tugged at Anne's skirt just as she gave herself to Giles's embrace again. "Mommy, are we staying with Uncle Giles?"

Anne looked up from Giles's kiss, just a little dazed. "Yes. But he won't be your Uncle Giles anymore."

"But I want him to be."

Giles crouched down. "What if I'm your father, lad? Would that do?"

Jamie appeared to consider that. "Yes, sir. It'll do."

"I'm glad you approve." He exchanged a grin with Anne as he rose. "Do you approve, Obadiah?"

Obadiah's face was split in a grin. "Yes, mon. You take care of her now, hear?"

"Oh, Diah!" Anne ran to him and threw her arms around his neck. "I shall miss you so."

"Yes, lady, and I you. But you're where you belong." He pulled back and looked past her to Giles. "Your fair knight has come to rescue you."

She looked up at him and smiled mistily; that was more true than she would have thought when Obadiah had made his prediction. "Take care of Hampshire Hall for Jamie."

"Yes, lady. And you, mon," he said as Giles came up to them, "you got a fine lady here. You take care of her."

"I plan to." Giles shook Obadiah's hand, and then turned to the captain. "We'll need to have Mrs. Templeton's trunks brought up, sir. My apologies if this is an inconvenience to you. You may keep the passage money, of course."

"By Neptune, I should think so," the captain muttered, and turned away, to give the necessary orders. "Folly, by Neptune. Pure folly."

Giles grinned at Anne and caught her up in his arms, swinging her around. "Giles!" she protested, laughing. The light was back in his eyes again. She intended to see that it stayed there forever. "Put me down!"

"Is it folly, Anne?" he demanded. "Is it?"

351

"No, Giles." Smiling, she looped her arms around his neck as he set her down. Folly? No, not when his arms felt so right about her, when she felt so complete. What had once seemed only to be folly had become love. And that, Anne thought, as Giles's lips descended on hers, was very wise indeed.